CONFIRMING JUSTICE

A NOVEL

CONFIRMING JUSTICE

DIANE / DAVID
MUNSON

FaithWalk
PUBLISHING
Grand Haven, Michigan

Printed in the United States of America
11 10 09 08 07 06   7 6 5 4 3 2 1

Library of Congress Cataloging-in-Publication Data

Munson, Diane.
 Confirming justice / Diane and David Munson.
 p. cm.
 ISBN-13: 978-1-932902-59-4 (pbk. : alk. paper)
 ISBN-10: 1-932902-59-7 (pbk. : alk. paper)
 1. Indians of North America—Crimes against—Fiction. 2. Trials (Bribery)—Fiction. 3. United States. Federal Bureau of Investigation—Officials and employees—Fiction. 4. Judges—Fiction. I. Munson, David. II. Title.
 PS3613.U693C66 2006
 813'.6—dc22
 2006009644

DEDICATION

This book is dedicated to MaryBeth, Patti, and the many others who have donated a kidney, and continue to live out Christ's command:

Love your neighbor as yourself.

Mark 12:31 (NIV)

ACKNOWLEDGMENTS

The years we spent in the Justice system have contributed to the many experiences that now overflow into our writing. While our work is fiction, we want to recognize the many federal agents, police officers, prosecuting attorneys, and judges from whom we have learned in Washington D.C., and elsewhere. We salute the men and women who spent long hours beyond those they were paid for, in the pursuit of justice. Though you remain nameless, you know who you are. David thanks those who protected his back, as he did theirs. Thanks also to the DEA pilots who flew undercover missions and those who helped maintain David's cover, especially Bill Atkins, who provided technical support for this book.

Because we've handled many adoptions, and assisted in the search for biological families, we understand the deeply felt emotions that are involved. None of the events or characters described in *Confirming Justice* resulted from those cases and any similarity is a coincidence.

To M.D. Van De Mae, M.D., who gave us valuable medical insights and so much more; you have our enduring gratitude. Your tireless efforts to heal the sick inspire us. Special thanks to Lee Titus, Canine Enforcement Director, U.S. Customs and Border Protection, for your input to make this novel technically correct regarding the diligent canines and the men and women officers who are their partners.

We appreciate the entire staff of FaithWalk Publishing and are grateful to Dirk Wierenga, Louann Werksma, and Ginny McFadden for your continual encouragement. To our family, who graciously understand our time away to research and write, we love you.

ONE

Something was about to happen in the courtroom. Judge Dwight Pendergast sensed it as surely as he knew Owen Jones was guilty. No one watching could know that Dwight longed for the trial to end and the jury foreman to announce, "On the count of conspiracy to bribe the Secretary of the Interior, we find the defendant, Owen Jones III guilty." A federal judge wasn't supposed to think like that. The jury would decide the verdict. Still, looking at the defendant sitting at counsel table in his thrift-store suit, a wily smile on his face, Dwight felt his stomach churn.

Jones may not be on trial for mass murder or terrorism, but he had the aura of someone that bad. Dwight's dark eyes, which saw nearly everything in his courtroom before it occurred, searched out the defendant's. They were light brown, big-cat eyes that made Jones look like a hungry tiger on the prowl. Early on in the trial, Dwight was caught off guard when he saw Jones signal to a man in the gallery. Dwight immediately halted the testimony of an FBI agent, called the lawyers to the bench, and ordered Constance Ingles to keep her client in line. Since then, Jones sneered at Dwight whenever their eyes locked.

Oh, he was savvy enough to mask his arrogance for the jury, but this morning the fourteen good men and women had been sent to the jury room, thanks to the maneuverings of Ms. Ingles, who now was thumping the podium in support of her motion to dismiss. His head splitting, Dwight renewed his vow not to be caught again. He gripped his wooden gavel and his fingers itched to pound it, silencing the defense attorney. As soon as she drew a breath, he would.

Outside, a summer storm raged, but in the courtroom, Dwight couldn't hear thunder, or see flashes of lightning. All the same, he felt static buzz on the back of his neck, pricking the little hairs that had grown there since his last haircut. The recent warning from his friend and fellow judge Louis Sumner, tormented Dwight: *Jones is a political fireball. Touch his case and you'll be burned.*

An expert fisherman since he was a boy, Dwight was familiar with sudden squalls that swept water into your boat and swamped you, but he'd never been caught in any political storms. That was luck, he guessed. But, Louis was right about one thing: This case had all the signs of a relentless storm, one that tore from its moorings the kind of justice Dwight had spent a lifetime working for.

At last Dwight shifted in his chair, bought for his six-foot-one-inch frame, and interrupted the longest-practicing attorney in Alexandria right in the middle of a sentence. "Ms. Ingles, it's the government's turn to rebut."

As if he were co-counsel, rather than a defendant facing criminal charges in U.S. District Court, Owen Jones leapt from his seat. He hurried around the table and tugged on his lawyer's jacket, almost pulling her over. A Deputy U.S. Marshal rose to his feet, while Constance caught herself on the podium with both hands.

Dwight slammed down the gavel. "Mr. Jones, take your seat immediately, or I will have the Marshal remove you!"

Before sauntering back to his chair, Jones whispered something to his attorney, all the while glowering up at Dwight as if daring the judge to toss him out. After thirty years in the legal profession, Dwight saw through Jones's subterfuge—playing a poor dupe for the jury, but causing trouble whenever they were out of sight. A woman reporter in the back row got up and hurried out, as if she were about to call her editor and release a scoop. Like every other courtroom regular, she had to be aware that Constance Ingles never surrendered a microphone easily.

Dwight's smile turned to a scowl as Constance persisted. "Your Honor, the government needs Agent Williams to prove my client conspired to bribe the Secretary of Interior. And—" she whirled around and faced her opponent, "the prosecutor's key witness is AWOL."

Dwight barely heard Constance drone on. He was transfixed by Jones, who grabbed his water bottle and was slowly twisting the neck with both hands. Dwight was about to call over the Marshal and have the bottle removed when the doors burst open.

Four men wearing suits and earpieces entered the room, fanning out against the perimeter like secret service agents protecting the President. The court-watchers' gasps magnified Dwight's own surprise. Blood throbbing in his ears, he wondered if Louis's warning was somehow coming true.

Dwight motioned forward Deputy U.S. Marshal Hal Leitsma. As Hal hastened to the bench, Dwight noted no trace of the injury that had sidelined the seasoned marshal for almost nine months. Hal sustained a gunshot wound to his leg in a Washington, D.C. courtroom shooting the year before.

Dwight cupped a hand over the microphone. "Is this show of force related to the missing FBI agent?"

Hal leaned so close, Dwight saw the jagged scar that ran from his lip to his chin. "There's a gun in the building. A security guard let it pass without seeing it, but another guard glimpsed the imprint still on the monitor. Judge Sumner has a civil trial, and we sent deputies up there."

Dwight decided instantly. "I'll order a break. Can we set up magnetometers outside my courtroom before we let anyone back in?"

Hal nodded gravely, then stood in front of the bench, arms folded across his chest like a human shield ready to safeguard Dwight from any threats.

Oblivious to the marshals, Constance held her ground. "Judge, because you prevented me from cross-examining the government's prime witness, you must dismiss the case!"

Laughter rippled through the courtroom. Dwight pounded his gavel for quiet, his black eyes becoming darker still as he narrowed them in disapproval at the defense attorney. The trial had been delayed the week before because of the defendant's antics. Yesterday, in the middle of the defense cross-examination of FBI Agent Frank Williams, Dwight called a recess for his own personal reasons. When Williams failed to reappear for cross this morning, the jury was sequestered to let the lawyers argue, so at least *they* were out of range of the missing gun.

Dwight was losing patience fast. If Williams was avoiding being cross-examined, he'd throw him in jail, FBI agent or not. Constance smiled at her client, who nodded his mop of brown hair back at her, then narrowed those tiger eyes at Dwight as if to say, if you don't dismiss my case, you're part of the conspiracy.

Dwight announced, "We'll take a ten-minute recess."

Just then, a tall man in the middle of the second row stood up, his long, flowing hair an odd contrast to the tailored gray suit he wore, and reached inside his suit coat. Dwight watched Hal bolt toward the man, giving Dwight a kernel of hope that Hal would not let violence erupt in the courtroom.

Still, his mind raced. It might be the gun! Dwight's left hand hit the silent alarm button under the bench. Hal jumped over the rail that separated the well from the gallery. The tall man unfurled something. The white blur didn't look like a gun. He spun around, holding up a banner for all to read: JUSTICE DENIED, TWICE DENIED. Hal reached the assailant, grabbed his hand, and wrested the banner away.

Dwight blew out his breath, took in another sharply. Two more marshals joined Hal and pinned the man in a bear hug. The man shouted, "The tribes have rights!" Then, as the deputies wrenched him by the arms and hauled him out the doors, he began to chant, "Justice denied, twice denied." Like a radio being turned down, the strange words echoed behind him.

Was the man a victim or a troublemaker trying to get on the nightly news? Several journalists scurried out. Dwight ground his teeth as he pictured the *Washington Star* headline, "Pendergast denies free speech to Native Americans."

A court security officer spoke into a walkie-talkie, while another deputy marshal assumed his post to protect Judge Pendergast. Dwight slammed down his gavel and shouted, "Order in the courtroom!"

Nothing happened. He yanked off his reading glasses and looked across the courtroom at FBI Special Agent Griff Topping, who had taken over the investigation of the defendant when Agent Frank Williams was transferred to Arizona a month before. Topping stood tall, both hands by his waistband. His chiseled features and thick moustache reminded Dwight of the carving of Theodore Roosevelt at Mount Rushmore. Next to Topping, Assistant U.S. Attorney Patrick O'Rourke sat in a wheelchair. A car accident at sixteen had left O'Rourke paralyzed from the waist down.

The judge's gavel came down again. "Anyone who interrupts this trial will be held in contempt of court. Clear the courtroom, and I want both attorneys in my chambers. Now!"

He left the bench, black robe swirling behind him like a western dust storm. A U.S. District Judge in the Eastern District of Virginia for five years, he usually relished the challenge of applying the law from his bench. But not this morning. These events made him feel as if a prankster had ripped the blindfold from Lady Justice. Today was different all right, but Dwight had no idea how it would stick to his future like glue.

In seconds, he cleared the reception area and told his secretary, that he was meeting the attorneys in chambers. "Keep the doors locked, Gladys. There's a gun in the building. Have Hal get a female deputy in here.

I want the attorneys checked before they come in." Constance Ingles would not like being searched, but he wasn't taking any chances.

Dwight strode into his private office, closed the door and tried to calm himself. Trophy fish hanging on one wall were vivid reminders that his love of fishing had nearly killed him, once. Ever since, life seemed more precious. He yanked a bottle of water from a compact refrigerator under his credenza and gulped the cool liquid. It soothed him as he reviewed the chaotic state of the case before him.

Owen Jones III held the fancy title of Special Assistant at the Department of Agriculture. Daddy's boy was accused of being overzealous in helping Native Americans to become a federally recognized tribe. AUSA Patrick O'Rourke had not finished his case, and that was Dwight's fault.

Yesterday, Dwight had interrupted Constance Ingles's cross-examination of Agent Williams so that he could make his dialysis appointment. Now, he wondered, would the fallout from that awful day torment not only his body, but his judicial career?

Despite what happened to him, Dwight still went after bass whenever he could. Rain, shine, dawn or dusk. That is, whenever he was not presiding in court, where he ruled much like he fished. Any catch too small or caught by illegal means, he released. The keepers were confined, as in the live well, trophies of the prosecutor. At this moment, locked in his chambers, he felt like the bass he pursued, hiding in a weed bed to avoid being snared. In his gut, Dwight knew Louis was right to warn him. Still, the Jones case was his to get right or have reversed on appeal, which had occurred only once since he rose to the federal bench.

Gladys called on his private line. "Judge, a reporter came in with the attorneys. She wants to interview you about the agent who disappeared."

"Who had the cheek to waltz into my chambers?"

"Mary Katherine Kowicki, goes by Kat. Before you get upset, Hal Leitsma ushered her out. She left a card."

"Call the Kat woman, tell her I don't give interviews. You can send in the lawyers."

He finished the water. All he needed was a nosy reporter to make this case even stickier. Agent Williams was undercover when Jones bragged to him that he took money from the White Pine Indian Tribe to grease the Secretary of the Interior's decision. The troubling part was that Secretary Jones was the defendant's father.

One media outlet had intimated that the younger Jones was sure to get a fair trial from Judge Pendergast, who had been appointed by the same President who appointed the elder Jones to the Interior post. That charge did not bother Dwight. This close to the nation's capital, he was used to hearing claims of political favors, but such things had no bearing on how he dispensed justice. He would be fair and follow the law, no matter who was President.

His real problem was that he wanted to give the prosecution more time to prove its case. It went against Dwight's code to give defendants more than they were entitled to by law, even though he had once sat on that side of the courtroom. But he drew the line when a jury was involved. And this jury had been kept in the jury room for an hour. Without men and women who were willing to decide if a defendant was guilty, the entire American system of justice could collapse.

His door swung open, and in came the lawyers. With two pairs of eyes staring at him, Dwight shifted the burden back on Patrick O'Rourke. "Was Williams called back to Arizona to testify in another case? Since Agent Topping wasn't in the undercover meeting, he can't testify to what Jones said. That's hearsay."

Patrick's usually sanguine expression was vexed, his complexion mottled red. "Williams has vanished. He called his supervisor yesterday to say he was staying over to testify today."

Dwight ran a hand through his thick brown hair. That meant the agent had planned to be in court today. "You called his hotel?"

"This morning. Agent Topping tried to find him, but so far, nothing."

"Call another witness while we wait for Williams."

Patrick spoke slowly. "Your Honor, *he* is my last witness."

If the prosecutor knew where Williams was, he'd admit it. This was getting nowhere. Constance sliced in her opinion, like a knife through a ripe peach. "Williams is vying for attention from his wife. She came back to Virginia shortly after they moved to Phoenix."

Dwight could not fathom how she learned that. It proved she was more of a celebrity than a lawyer. He forced his mind back to the riddle of the missing agent.

O'Rourke was heated. "We need more time. Topping is trying to reach Frank's wife."

Her almost-white hair curling around the collar of her purple suit, Constance took the fountain pen off Dwight's desk and wrung it in her hands. Those bony hands, knuckles large as if laden with arthritis, made Dwight realize he knew little of the attorneys who argued cases in his court. Christine gave him that pen; it was his favorite. If Constance didn't put it down, he'd grab it.

A soft knock, and Gladys peered around the door. "Sorry to interrupt, but I thought you'd want to know. Hal said to tell you they found the gun. A police officer testifying in Judge Sumner's civil trial brought a gun in his briefcase. Oh, and the man with the banner is from the Indian tribe."

Well, that was good news about the gun. Gladys closed the door behind her. There was nothing Dwight could do for the tribes, except to ensure justice was done in this case. Dwight looked at Patrick. "If I give you more time to find Williams, Ms. Ingles may have a chance to finish questioning him."

Patrick spoke with feeling, "Exactly, Your Honor."

Dwight frowned. He did not like funny business when he had a jury waiting. "The missing agent's report mentioned another man was in the undercover meeting. This mystery man is not on your witness list and Williams failed to record the conversation."

With his broad hand, the judge massaged his temple. Either O'Rourke or Williams must have promised the man he would not have to testify. Dwight knew how the game was played, but that was no excuse for lack of evidence. "Mr. O'Rourke, in this 'he said, he said' situation, you can't produce your 'he said.'"

Patrick leaned from the edge of his wheelchair. His voice was forged steel. "I wasn't assigned to the case then, but Jones picked the location and insisted on meeting Williams at the spur of the moment. Recording was impossible."

Ms. Ingles interjected, "My client's rights are being jeopardized."

This time, Patrick's reaction was swift. "Judge, give me one more day. If Williams fails to appear, the government will dismiss the charges without prejudice."

Dwight reached across the desk and held out his left hand. Anything to wipe the pleased expression off the defense attorney's face. Constance returned a blank stare. "My pen," he said firmly. She looked startled, then handed it to him with a lopsided grin.

Dwight made up his mind. "I grant a continuance until next Monday. No harm to the defendant, who is out on bond."

When Constance objected, Dwight's blood grew hot. Patrick, or whoever, better find Frank Williams. This case had to go forward. The whole nation was watching the outcome. "Ms. Ingles, there is no jury to impress in here. The charges against your client are serious."

"But, Your Honor—"

A southpaw, Dwight held up his left hand. "We'll put it on the record." He hoped there was enough time to track Williams down. Constance Ingles picked up her leather briefcase and marched out. Patrick's hands were on the wheels of his chair and he was heading out the door. He looked back at Dwight as if to assure him. "Griff is one of the best agents in the FBI. He'll leave no stone unturned to find him."

Dwight quelled an urge to find the missing agent himself. Of course, that was foolish. But, there was something he *could* do, and once he discharged the jury, he would waste no time doing it.

TWO

Senator Zorn's handsome features masked the malice in his heart. Even the television cameras, which filmed him regularly, did not reveal the darkness that lurked beneath the dazzling smile. If asked, he would claim that his plans to bring down the President and his party were for the good of the country. But, make no mistake, it was malice all the same.

Lars Zorn, the junior Senator from California, drummed his fingers on the desk. Where was Arnie, who was supposed to bring the ammunition Lars needed to sink the nominee to the Supreme Court? His chief of staff was late, and that was unacceptable. Arnie better show his face soon; Lars had to catch a flight to San Diego for a fundraiser. He needed the info that Arnie had to assure his supporters that Nolan Cuttering would not be confirmed.

With the precise attention a CEO paid to the earnings of his company, Lars spent years crafting his career, from films to the California Governor's mansion to the United States Senate. His office in the Dirksen building, across from the Capitol, was as elegant as he was. One entire wall boasted smile after smile—all photos of him—including his favorite: In a racing suit, he leaned on a race car, with a helmet under one arm and a quart of milk in his hand, as though he'd won the Indy 500.

His success in the movies, where Lars won two Oscars and could have won more, skyrocketed his political career. The adjacent wall displayed pictures of him with other politicians, including Presidents from both parties. Standing before a mirror, Lars bent his knees and, blue eyes staring intently at his reflection, he smoothed his reddish-blonde hair and straightened his tie. As he did often, he smiled at the man in the mirror, congratulating himself on how far the son of a Swedish immigrant had come. In a blue suit, white shirt starched at the collar, and honey-colored tie, Lars was ready—as always—for the cameras.

His father, Karl Zorn, knew the ethic of hard work, eventually becoming the Lieutenant Governor of Texas. Lars wasn't as enamored
of hard work as his old man was. After he graduated from law school,
he flunked the California bar exam. With his Dad's help, however, he
waltzed into a position on the Senate Judiciary Committee to work
on the Watergate Hearings. More political connections helped Lars get
hired next by the FBI. Promoted quickly, Lars nonetheless cut short his
tour at FBI headquarters when he was presented with the ultimate ego
builder, a role in a movie.

While Lars loved acting, one thing tempted him to give it up, and
that was a chance to become Lieutenant Governor of California. His
mentors told him then, "The only barrier between you and the White
House is a stint in the Congress."

Eleven years ago, he'd run for Governor of California and won.
Served two terms. Three years ago, he breezed into the U.S. Senate
with the highest margin ever for a Senator from that state. His political
success came despite several deferments that kept him out of Vietnam.
Lars did not intend to stop at the Senate long; he wanted to be more
than one of a hundred committee members. He had his eye on the top
prize. President of the United States. That election he intended to win,
no matter what it cost.

The American people wanted experienced leaders, and Lars was
keenly aware he had something that other ambitious Senators did not:
a resume that included governorship of one of the largest states. Lars
checked his watch again. Where was Arnie? He dialed Arnie's office
number and listened to it ring. Even though the next election was a
few years away, Lars was already running for President, and he could
not afford any missteps.

Besides making himself look good, Lars had another goal, and that
was to make the President look weak. Force him to put up a different
Supreme Court nominee. Special interest groups were finally seeing
Lars in a new light, a presidential one. A recent photo of him with Harry Briggs, the Senate Judiciary Chair overseeing the nomination hearings, proved Lars could reach across the aisle to the majority party. Lars
did not intend to languish long in the minority. The only non-lawyer
on the Committee, Lars made sure he got along with all of them.

His party chairman called him a natural. It didn't hurt that Lars was
a dead ringer for the actor who played the lead in *The Natural*. Hollywood groups backed his Agenda for America, poured money into his

campaign. It also helped that his wife, a beauty queen from Georgia, bore him two equally photogenic children, who loved having their pictures taken with their dad in his racing cars.

At last, with no knock, Arnie Berglund walked in, sufficiently out of breath to satisfy Lars that he had been busy on Lars's behalf. To Lars's delight, the other Swede on his staff carried no files. Best no record was made of what they said.

"It's about time you got here," he barked at Arnie, but with a smile that reassured, he sat down behind his antique desk and rubbed his hands together. "So … how do we make sure Nolan Cuttering is not confirmed?"

Arnie perched on an armchair opposite the desk. "He's on a glide path to victory."

"And the vote?"

Hands on the edge of the desk, Arnie looked stressed. "Seventy for, thirty against."

Lars studied a gold-edged pen, given to him by a thankful constituent. How to get Arnie to do his bidding, without telling him to do anything illegal? "What opposition is there? The hearing is next week. We have to move fast."

Arnie leaned in. "Animal rights people and environmental activists want Cuttering out. Their six-million-dollar ad blitz started yesterday. Two new blogs came on line today. I urged them to use their imagination and told them that, if they unearth anything, you wanted to see it. I have someone else helping us."

Then Arnie simply looked at him coolly, as if waiting for a reply. When Lars had none, he added, "But you don't want to know who."

"Of course not. That's why I pay you all that money. And don't forget what is at stake."

Inwardly, Lars smiled. When he occupied the White House one day, his chief of staff could hit the West Wing running.

On the other side of the Potomac, back at his bench, Dwight put the continuance on the record. Ignorant of Senator Zorn's plans to wreck the nomination of his friend, Judge Nolan Cuttering, Dwight dismissed the jury and and made for his office. As he swept by Gladys she held out a handful of message slips for him. Other judges let their secretaries log messages on the computer, but Dwight liked his written on slips, so he could call them in order of importance. These he stored in his wallet or ran through the shredder. A man who valued his privacy, he was never sure who could access the computer memory.

Messages in his hand, Dwight realized he left his reading glasses in the courtroom. "Anything urgent?"

His secretary for sixteen years, Gladys had moved with him from the Ebbott and Longstreet law firm, to the Supreme Court of Virginia, to his present position. She patted the bun twisted behind her head, then shadowed him to his private office. "The White House called. So did Mandy. I put hers on top."

As he often did when thinking, Dwight yanked on his ear lobe. It was Dwight's most distinctive feature, coming to a point at the bottom like half of a diamond. "I see. Mandy is more important than the White House. Did you tell the President I was too busy to have lunch with him?"

She pursed her lips, which bore no lipstick, ever. "Of course not. Had the President called, his would be on top. No, it was Veronica who called from the White House. Try Mandy first, she called twice."

Dwight's oldest daughter, Veronica, was a liaison officer in the White House office for intergovernmental affairs. Her job was to convince the nation's governors and legislators that the President's policies deserved support. She worked in the Eisenhower Executive Office Building, next to the White House, and her boss had regular access to the President.

Veronica's husband, Stuart, commanded her first attention, so Dwight and Christine did not see much of them lately. Christine didn't seem to mind, remarking when he mentioned it, "After all, she is married."

"Did Veronica say what she wanted?"

Gladys just shook her head and walked out.

He closed the door behind her, set the messages by the phone. The next thing to go was his black robe, which today made him sweat, especially when that tall man stood up in his courtroom and Dwight thought he had a gun. The robe went onto a hanger, which he put on the back of his door, leaving him much more comfortable in just his short-sleeved white shirt, tan slacks, and precisely knotted red tie. He rummaged in his desk drawer for his old reading glasses.

They must be somewhere. He found them somewhat squashed, under last year's court rules. From his small refrigerator, he took out a cold orange juice to tide him over until lunch. Dwight picked up the phone and punched in Veronica's office number.

"Dad!" she squealed. "Guess what? We wanted you to be the first to know."

She sounded happy. His 34-year-old daughter was his shining light. Veronica had inherited her dark hair and complexion from him. In addition to her demanding career, she was working on a doctorate in Revolutionary War studies.

Dwight settled in his chair. Stuart was an adequate son-in-law. Dwight might have helped him get his position at Ebbott and Longstreet, but he had to admit that Stuart worked hard to keep it. And, he plainly adored Veronica. "Was Stuart promoted to partner already? He's only been there four years."

"*No*, Daddy. We're *pregnant!*"

His spirits soared. "That's wonderful, Honey!" He imagined his daughter's amber skin glowing even more than usual.

"I think you'll like being called Grandpa, Grandpa."

That gave Dwight a start. Husband of Christine. Father of Veronica and Amanda. Lawyer, Virginia Supreme Court Judge, then federal judge. Now, the grandest title of all, grandfather. Unbelievable.

"To say it twice, you must like the sound as much as I do."

Her laughter bubbled up, "You're going to *be* a Grandpa twice. I'm having twins!"

Dwight squinted at his watch. In three minutes, he should leave for lunch with Bernie Spitzer, his former law partner. Punctuality was a hallmark of both men. The next subject could take a while. Should he even mention it? He did.

"Veronica, I'm speechless! Does your mother know?"

"I thought you could tell her tonight. She and I—" Veronica stopped.

Oh, oh. Christine and Veronica were on the outs, again. This time, Dwight did not ask the reason. Ever since Veronica was about two years old, Christine had had a difficult relationship with their oldest child. He tried to understand their competition, but that sort of wrangling was not in his blood. When he last asked Christine, she said there was nothing wrong with her love for Veronica. For the rest of that day, he was rewarded by a cold shoulder. Since then, he'd kept his mouth shut.

"Your mother might enjoy hearing it from you."

"She does not enjoy much about me."

This was partly true. Dwight wished he knew why. "You and Stuart come to the lake this weekend. Mandy will be there." He hoped so, anyway. No time to call his other daughter now. "I'll grill steaks. You make up with your mother."

Veronica sighed deeply. "Dad—"

"Bring your research. We'll discuss General Washington's victory at Trenton."

Her "Okay" was drawn out. Then she changed the subject. "I'd like your advice. The White House has a new staffer, Barbara Jo Houston. She's Special Assistant to the President and reports to him through Jasper Collins, his Chief of Staff. I called her today to confirm the Michigan Attorney General's meeting with the President tomorrow. Last week, she sent an e-mail assuring me tomorrow was fine. Now she says she never did, and there is no meeting."

Dwight hesitated. White House politics belonged in a universe of its own. Did he dare tread in that sphere? "If you saved your e-mail and her reply, you could forward it to her."

"Dad, I sent that to Ms. Houston. She claims I made it up."

He had a short-term fix for the tension he heard in his daughter's voice. "The President expects you to reach out to the attorneys general. If you are sure you did not make a mistake, tell your boss and let him tangle with Ms. Houston's boss."

Veronica was silent as she contemplated her father's suggestion. "That's good advice, Dad. Jasper is fair-minded."

After congratulating Veronica again and urging her to spend the weekend with them at the lake, Dwight hung up. He surrendered the cares of a father as he scanned his other messages. Before he could call anyone, Gladys walked in and closed the door, her back against it, eyes huge. "Mr. Owen Jones, the father, is on the phone."

Dwight was flabbergasted. The Secretary of the Interior must know it was out of line to call the judge who was trying his son for bribery. He stood up, shoved his chair under his desk, and said, "Tell Mr. Jones I am late for an appointment and cannot take his call."

Gladys slipped out without a sound. Never before had Dwight been so thankful for a lunch date with Bernie Spitzer, his oldest friend and the managing partner of Dwight's old firm. Stuart was on the partner track there. Maybe that was why Bernie asked him to lunch—he wanted to know if Stuart had the stuff. If so, Dwight would have to walk a fine line between telling the truth and helping Veronica and his future grandchildren.

The fact that Secretary Jones had called stuck in Dwight's mind like barbed wire. The more he thought it over, the more the sharp edges cut his principles. He removed his glasses, held them in one hand, stared into space. Try as he might, there were no words written on the ceiling or walls to tell him what to do. So this was how the game was played. Federal judges were supposed to be immune from politics.

Why Jones called was a mystery. Maybe to force some kind of mistrial. Dwight buzzed Gladys. She was not at her desk. He then rang Louis Sumner to ask his opinion about the missing agent. Louis answered his private line.

"Your case caused quite a ruckus today, Louis!"

Sumner chuckled. "Sorry to intrude on your high profile case. Will I read about you tonight in the *Washington Star?*"

Dwight managed a short grunt. "That's what I'm calling about, but I have to leave for a lunch appointment."

With no trial tomorrow, Dwight planned to take Christine to the lake tonight. But, talking with Louis was more important. "Can you stop by the house on your way home? Christine will give you some of her strawberry lemonade you like so much."

Louis accepted. "Perfect timing. I have something to ask you, too, and Naomi is away."

"Come for dinner then."

They agreed on six o'clock. Dwight shuffled his remaining messages. One from his doctor caught his eye. He probably wanted him to play in the charity golf tournament. Dwight had no interest in golf. When not on the bench, he fished. Ever since he began fishing for bass with his dad at age five, Dwight loved the smell of fresh water, the constant breeze. These helped relax him like nothing else.

Before he left for lunch with Bernie, he called Christine, who was working from home today. No answer. He left a message that Louis was joining them for dinner and that they'd go to their cabin at Smith Mountain Lake in the morning. She always checked her messages, so Dwight did not feel awkward inviting Louis at the last moment. For her, five hours was plenty of time to whip up a superb meal. A fabulous chef, she could make a soufflé from eggs and stale crackers.

Besides being a gourmet cook, Christine played a classical violin. While Dwight enjoyed her music, he listened to tunes from the sixties and seventies on his car radio. Their different tastes in music only deepened their interest in each other.

He walked through his door into the reception area. Gladys was back at her desk, eating what smelled like tuna fish. "The storm's over, but it's blistering hot, Judge. Wherever you're going, I hope you drive."

"I'll be at the seafood restaurant that Mr. Spitzer has been raving about for weeks."

She sipped soda from a can. "I reached Secretary Jones's assistant. It seems you both graduated from Georgetown Law School and, as the event chair, he wants you as speaker for the annual fall dinner."

Gladys peered at him above her glasses, no doubt wondering if he saw the dangers in such a request. "My fall schedule is booked. Please tell that to his assistant."

He didn't mention that he hoped his lunch was more appealing than hers. As he walked out the main office door, which could not be entered without an electronic buzz, she called, "You have a bond hearing at three."

Dwight waved a hand, barely thinking of the drug defendant on the afternoon docket. It was an appeal of the magistrate judge's denial of bond. Instead, Dwight was still caught up in his strange morning. Veronica's call thrilled him, but thoughts of bouncing grandchildren on his knee in the future were squeezed out by the much more immediate prospect of Native Americans upset by a possible dismissal of the Jones case. What did the man mean, "Justice denied, twice denied"? He had a hunch the missing FBI agent would change the outcome of the case. What he didn't know was that it would change his own life.

THREE

Summers in Virginia were brutal, and today was a prime example of why he hated that polyester robe. En route to the restaurant, even in his cotton shirt, sweat pooled under his arms. No antiperspirant could stand up to this heat and humidity. Dwight wished he had taken Gladys's advice to drive rather than walk. It had to be ninety already. As soon as he got back to the office, he'd ask Gladys to order a new robe, a cotton one.

One summer he considered wearing khaki shorts under the robe, but such a liberty was risky. In an emergency, if he was found wearing shorts and a tee shirt under his robe, it would never do. For the next hour, he would leave behind his judicial robe, in more ways than one. Bernie liked to steer clear of Dwight's cases and talk about his own.

By the time he grabbed the carved sailfish door handle, he had a monster thirst. The bubbling saltwater tank with its yellow and orange tropical fish made him thirstier. At the hostess stand, a petite woman with enormous hair smiled in greeting. "Do you have a reservation?"

Her accent sounded like she lived much of her life in Greece. He and Christine spent two weeks on the Isle of Corfu, where azure water and white stucco houses painted striking memories. Dwight loved Greek food, and broiled fish would be a nice change from the chicken sandwich he usually ate at his desk.

"Bernie Spitzer is waiting for me."

The woman's eyes narrowed and she stepped backward. "Judge Pendergast?"

Had Bernie given his name, or had she served on one of his juries? He wondered if perhaps he had sentenced her husband to prison. There had been that case in which a Greek financier was convicted and sentenced to many years for insurance fraud.

"Yes." Dwight squinted in the darkness, trying to recognize her. Let her take her best shot. He was ready.

"Your friend is waiting. This way, please. "

Relieved, Dwight followed her past other patrons to a section by the windows. He spotted Bernie first. Hands around a glass, probably sweet tea over ice, his oldest friend stared out at a park. The years had been unkind to Bernie. He combed sparse blond hair off his forehead, kept it long in the back. Deep grooves etched the sides of his lips.

The hostess plunked down a menu, startling Bernie to reality. Dwight pulled out his chair. Their server, a young man built solid and square like a high school football player, appeared immediately and asked Dwight if he wanted a drink.

"Iced coffee, with extra cream." Dwight settled his frame on the wooden captain's chair. "Sorry to be late. My trial imploded."

Bernie sipped his iced tea. "I've been here two minutes."

With Bernie's glass almost empty, Dwight wondered if that was so. He'd buy lunch to make up for being tardy. The server returned with Dwight's iced coffee, then left them to study the menus. Dwight put on his glasses, stirred in two containers of cream and sampled the concoction. He licked his lips.

"Nothing tastes better on such a blistering day. You're wearing a suit jacket. How do you stand the heat, man?"

Bernie laughed. "I remember, when we roomed together at Georgetown, your mother sent you a window fan to keep you cool. The heat never bothers me. Even in Vietnam. Course, I wasn't there too long before I got shot up and came home to find you and Christine married."

Pity and guilt collided in the pit of Dwight's stomach. Within the first month after he was drafted, Bernie took shrapnel above his left eye. It became infected and had to be removed. Bernie now had a prosthetic left eye.

Dwight removed his glasses, stuck them in his pocket without thinking. "Did you ask me to lunch to talk about Vietnam? You know I was proud of you, still am. Unlike some with a low draft number, you didn't run to Canada. I would have gone if I'd been called, but I had a high number, and it never was."

Bernie finished his drink, set down the glass. "That's what you always say. But then, your life has turned out better than mine."

"How can you say that? You're the managing partner of one of the most prestigious law firms in Washington."

"But, I will never be a federal judge."

Dwight saw the skin vibrate beneath Bernie's prosthetic eye. "Is that what you want?"

Bernie waved over the server, said they were ready to order. "Grilled salmon in bourbon sauce. Salad with blue cheese. Lots of it. More iced tea."

The server turned his massive shoulders toward Dwight. "And you, Judge?"

What was with everyone in this place? Did he have a sign on his forehead that read, "I'm a judge?" He'd ask Bernie not to do that again.

"I'd better eat light." He turned to Bernie. "You know how Christine likes to cook when we're at the lake. You and Rita should drive down on Saturday."

"Sir, if you're not ready, I'll give you more time."

Dwight could not remember if trout was on the menu. With his glasses in his shirt pocket, he ordered a cold lunch of blackened chicken salad, lemon wedges for dressing, even though it was not what he wanted. "Skip the croutons, and no onion."

The fullback snapped up the menus and strode away, leaving the two men in a moment of silence. What was on Bernie's mind? The Vietnam War was fought over thirty years ago. This was the first time Bernie had talked about it since they became partners at Ebbott and Longstreet.

Bernie gazed at Dwight. "Forget what I said. They weren't taking married guys with kids anyway. You served in your own way, on summer breaks, working for the defense contractor."

His friend of nearly thirty-five years sounded bitter. Dwight knew him well enough to know something was bothering him. He would ignore the bait and not delve into old wounds. Maybe Bernie was about to let Stuart go.

Dwight sipped his iced coffee. "Is this about my son-in-law?"

"No, he's doing fine in the real estate section. Brought in a new client yesterday. A developer named Jenkins from Jefferson County."

Bernie's eyes, including the glass one, bored into Dwight's. Dwight tried to guess where this was leading. "Maxwell Jenkins was a friend of my dad's when he worked on rocketry at Jenkins and Richter Space Industries. Any relation?"

Bernie pursed his thick lips. "I forgot about that old man. I'll have to ask."

"I bought my place at Smith Mountain Lake from him."

"What about property there? Rita and I are thinking about buying a place on your lake."

Dwight's iced coffee was gone. "Values are up sharply since we bought there."

Bernie looked around for the server, who had not brought him any more tea. "As I recall, you got it dirt cheap from Max."

Finally, the server brought their food, replenished their drinks. Dwight stabbed a lemon wedge with his fork and squirted it on his salad. A few drops flew to his cheek. He wiped them off. "How are you and Rita these days? We haven't seen you much."

Bernie looked at him with a troubled eye. "I don't know how to tell you this."

Concern gnawed at Dwight's stomach. No wonder Bernie looked terrible. Something happened to Rita. "Please say it, Bernie. We've been friends, best friends, forever. Our wives are friends. I know something is bothering you."

Bernie had not touched his salmon. "You have a drug case coming up for trial. Multiple defendants are charged with dealing cocaine."

Dwight's lemon slipped from his fingers. He looked at his old friend. "You never bring up my cases."

"One defendant, Tyler Cooper, contacted the firm. Our top criminal guy is leading defense, but Cooper wants me as co-counsel because of the money laundering counts and my financial acumen. Will my appearance cause a recusal?"

Dwight drew in a quick breath. "Does your firm want to remove me as judge?"

"It does not."

Dwight eased out his breath. They should not talk about a pending case. He told Bernie so. "You defend, and I'll try the case with fairness and equality. In the trial before me, without naming names, a key witness is missing. I gave them until Monday to pull it together."

Bernie seemed to know all about the Jones case. "I know you won't let a cabinet member's reputation be ruined because of his son's misdeeds. Not without a compelling case. Besides, the President issued a statement today, expressing complete confidence in Secretary Jones."

As Dwight read between those words, the salad felt like a concrete block in his stomach. When they practiced together, Bernie competed with Dwight for clients and a share in the firm's profits. Now, it appeared Bernie was not only invading his courtroom in a drug case, he was lecturing him not to make a political mistake in Jones.

Dwight switched to his iced coffee and a safer topic. "Anything new on Nolan Cuttering's nomination to the U.S. Supreme Court? His hearing is next week."

Bernie said he was glad Dwight mentioned it, and asked if Christine was planning a party for Nolan after his confirmation. Dwight didn't think so, but he offered to ask her. No, Bernie would tell Rita to plan one. Unaware that Bernie and Rita knew Nolan, Dwight pushed away his salad. Nothing about D.C. politics surprised him. He joked about what it would be like to know a sitting justice on the Supreme Court, but Bernie seemed miles away.

Dwight shared Veronica's good news, then warned, "But don't say anything to anyone. Christine doesn't know, yet."

"Oh?" Bernie suddenly seemed interested.

Not wanting to reveal Christine and Veronica's seesaw relationship, he backtracked. "Veronica called me just before I left the office."

Bernie ate the last of his salmon. "Your wife is a marvelous advocate for the family."

"She will appreciate the compliment." The server brought the check, which Dwight grabbed. "My treat, to make up for being late." He put his credit card on a black tray. "Come down to the lake tomorrow with Rita. We'll catch our supper."

The server took his card, and Bernie slid back his chair. Dwight wagged a finger. "Remember, say nothing about our being grandparents."

When Bernie laughed, which was not often, his face looked lighter. "Scout's honor, Judge. I wouldn't want to be thrown in jail for contempt of court."

Dwight checked his watch. "Better head back."

Bernie touched his arm. "One more thing."

Did he want to bring up that drug case again?

"Our daughter, Linda, just got engaged. Thought you'd like to know."

Bernie's one child was a year older than Mandy. Dwight shook Bernie's hand as the server returned the credit card slip. Dwight added a tip, and folded the receipt in his wallet. "Who's the lucky fellow, the President's nephew?"

Bernie got mysterious again. "Rita can surprise you about our future son-in-law. How about if we all come to the lake Saturday afternoon?"

"Okay." Dwight smiled and played along, slapped him on the back. "Let us know how many and what time. You've got my cell number, right?"

Bernie tapped his temple. "Memorized it. Did you walk or drive?"

"Thought the exercise would do me good. In this heat, I was wrong."

"I'll drive you back."

Outside, Dwight was greeted by a blast of humid air. Thankful for his friend's offer, he let Bernie drop him on Elizabeth Lane, next to the courthouse. As Dwight got out of the car, Bernie said, "See you at three o'clock."

In the bright sun, Dwight squinted his eyes. "You and Rita are coming tomorrow at three?"

"No. My drug client I told you about, Tyler Cooper, has a bond hearing today at three. You're the judge."

So that was what lunch was about. The whole thing seemed a little sneaky. Dwight's reply was heartfelt. "You will do an admirable job, but we should not discuss it again." He slammed the door to the sounds of Bernie's laughter and watched him roar away.

Barbara Jo Houston, newly appointed Special Assistant to the President, walked into her office in the West Wing, her spiky heels making depressions in the plush carpet. They were small reminders of where she'd been. That distasteful call from Veronica Fife could not erase the pride she felt in achieving her goal to work in the White House. At her desk, she unlocked her private drawer and drew out a photograph of a smiling woman, with black, curly hair, her arms around a young girl in a lavender lace dress. The little girl held a baby rabbit, one she and the woman had just found under a leaf in the back yard.

Barbara Jo softly kissed the face of the woman who had named her. It was the closest she could come to her mother now. She should have left the picture in the drawer. The horrors of the summer's day ten years ago jolted her all over again. Barbara Jo covered her ears, but it was no use. Her own screams were as real today as on her twelfth birthday. She yanked out a box of tissues, but she could not stop her mind from cartwheeling back to her birthday party.

Her mother had baked a bunny cake and invited Barbara Jo's friends. They played dressup, in fancy hats and scarves. Barbara Jo blew out her candles, laughing. Mother's face turned an ugly red, got pinched. She grabbed her chest and fell off the chair. Her whole body crashed into a pot of flowers. Barbara Jo ran to her mother, screaming. She felt her face, shook her, but there was no life left in her.

Now Barbara Jo's face fell into her hands, but no tears came. From that awful moment, her heart changed. A once happy little girl turned into a sour teenager. Her father ignored her, poured himself into his work, left her to the care of nannies. Planted in a small corner of Barbara Jo's mind was a seed that she owed this position to her father, longtime friend and major contributor to the President. Her heart snapped off such thinking at the root.

Once her paperwork for this political job was approved and she was sworn in, she'd called her father in Russia. Busy putting final touches on an oil and gas lease for an American company, he spoke with her for two minutes, then claimed he had to go to dinner with the Russian ambassador.

Barbara Jo slid the photo of Mother into her drawer, alongside another photo of a man, then locked it. In their last session, the therapist asked if her penchant for locking things symbolized how she treated her father since he remarried. Total nonsense. Dad replaced her and she would replace him. Didn't she now work for the President?

She raked fingernails through black hair as dark as Mother's, which she wore in a sleek bob. Cut below her chin, she enjoyed its swinging when she walked. Pink nail polish matched the blouse she wore over a white linen skirt. Beige shoes completed her outfit, one of many new ones hanging in her closet.

The assistant to the President must fit in at the White House, and she was fastidious about her appearance. Thanks to Mother's trust fund, Barbara Jo spent unlimited amounts on her wardrobe. She punched in the telephone number of the man in the other photo locked in her drawer.

A secretary connected her. When he answered, the sound of his voice soothed her. He was one man who would not leave her for another woman. A voice whispered, *Like your father.* She stamped her foot, the voice disappeared, as she trained it to, and she said brightly, "Guess where I am?"

When he replied, "The White House," she giggled.

His voice grew stern, "Did you tell my secretary who you were?"

"Of course not. You asked me not to let anyone in the White House know we're dating. We've been so careful, not even the FBI found out when they did my background check."

His laugh was slightly sinister. "Keep it that way."

Barbara Jo plopped in her chair. "I'm here now, so it should *not* matter. Lots of couples in Washington, some on television, work both sides of the political spectrum. When we're married, we'll make oodles of money advising the opposites."

"Listen," he whispered, "even Senator Zorn doesn't know we're an item. And, it will stay that way until after the Cuttering hearings."

"Arnie—"

He cut her off. "Either that, or we don't call or see each other until it's over. You decide."

Arnie was being silly, but she decided not to press him. Her job kept her busy most nights, so she had few chances to go out. "All right. How about dinner tomorrow night? Dad and his wife are in Moscow. I'll ask the cook to whip up your favorite, four-cheese ravioli."

"Just a minute." He muffled the phone, then came back. "Senator Zorn is having a press conference to show how radical Nolan Cuttering is. Don't forget what I asked."

Barbara Jo eyed the locked drawer. "I'll bring it home tonight."

"Good girl, Barbara Jo. I'll come for dinner tomorrow."

Like a song written for her, his words of approval swelled in her mind. Arnie Berglund was terrific, a rising star on the Hill. The best part was, he was all hers. His advice on how to handle that upstart, Veronica Fife, was perfect. Just because her father was a federal judge did not give that politico the right to push around Barbara Jo.

So far, everything Arnie told her had worked according to plan. She chose to ignore that her boss, Jasper Collins, asked why she refused to allow the Michigan Attorney General to see the President. "He had no appointment," she'd said, and the Chief of Staff dropped the matter. The one irritating thing about Arnie was that, so far, he hadn't mentioned marriage. He might ask her tomorrow night, once she gave him the file, now locked in her drawer.

FOUR

FBI agent Griff Topping skipped lunch entirely. In the squad bay at the FBI field office, he was no closer to finding Agent Frank Williams, the key witness in the Jones case. If Frank failed to show, Judge Pendergast would suppress his testimony or, worse, dismiss the case. Griff reached another answering machine, and before the voice asked him to leave a message, a high-pitched squeal let loose in his ear. He hung up in disgust.

In his part of Virginia, Griff built major cases and worked them to indictment, then to conviction. On the verge of nabbing a contractor for fraud, he handed it over to the agent across the aisle when his boss asked him to fill in on the Jones case. Salcedo Domingo would do a decent job, but Griff took pride in honing his techniques to an art form. His track record proved it. The first day he read the Jones file, Griff wanted to throw it in a drawer.

Owen Jones III was a two-bit hack who made money the easy way, by conning victims. Now, fellow agent Frank Williams had up and disappeared. The Frank whom Griff knew worked ferocious hours, and you could trust him with your wallet, or your bucar, the "bureau" car that the FBI assigned to each agent. The last case they had worked together was four years ago, and a lot could happen to an agent in forty-eight months. Rumors flew around the office that, after Frank got transferred to Phoenix, his wife stayed three weeks then returned to Virginia. Said she missed her dogs. That could seriously mess up a guy.

Griff had never met Frank's wife, Marilyn. All he knew was that she insisted on being called Norma Jean, and one word described what Griff thought of that. Weird. Under his breath, he said, "Any woman named Marilyn who wants to be called Norma Jean must be nuts."

A voice called out, "Topping, you talking to me, or yourself again? You gotta cut that out, or the Bureau will set you up to be evaluated."

Griff wheeled his chair back three feet. Sal grinned at him with large white teeth, which seemed even brighter against his dark hair and eyes. An agent for ten years, Sal was a few years younger than Griff, who was in his late thirties. He was also a bigger jokester than Griff, which was one of the things Griff liked about his office mate.

Another was that Sal cooked authentic Latino dishes. Sal's folks hailed from the Dominican Republic, near Puerto Rico where Griff's maternal grandparents were born. Griff's Latin blood was cooled by his paternal side of the family, who lived on another island—Great Britain, at the remote southwestern end. Griff made a mental note to call his Gram, who had written him last week asking him to come visit her in Cornwall.

"You'd talk to yourself, too, if you inherited the Jones case. Have you heard from Frank since he moved to Arizona? I'm pulling my hair out trying to find him. All I came up with was a flat tire this morning after court."

Sal came over and moved his index finger over his thumb. "Know what this is?"

Griff frowned. "The world's smallest violin. That's old, Sal, really old. You need time off to get new material."

Sal laughed. Griff leaned in his wooden chair, and it squeaked. "Seriously, what's the deal with his wife? I need something to go on. I called his cell, left a dozen messages."

"Met her once when I dropped Frank off at home. Just a minute, my cell is vibrating." Sal yanked the phone from his hip, looked at the number on the screen. "No problem. Where was I? Oh yeah, Frank asked me in. Must have been six mutts, with black and white faces, jumping all over me. Norma Jean gave them names from Marilyn Monroe's old movies."

Griff swept his moustache with the palm of his hand. "I called her this morning. She said Frank stormed out last night at eight. Thinks he's on a drinking binge."

Sal leaned his wiry body against the half-wall. "I thought he gave up beer after his gall bladder came out."

Griff nodded. Norma Jean probably exaggerated her husband's faults for reasons of her own. When he heard lines like, "he never cared about me," and "he always put the bureau first," Griff grew wary. There was more to it. She told Griff that Frank left in their white Honda Civic, took his own set of keys. Norma Jean gave Griff the Arizona license plate number. She thought Frank was coming back because their only other car was still in Arizona.

"After we talked," Griff toyed with a magnet base and chrome nuts that formed a tower on his desk, "I drove by Frank's house, and his car was not in the drive. One thing struck me funny. It's the middle of the day and all the blinds were drawn."

"In this heat, women keep the sun off their furniture."

"Good thinking, Sal. Norma Jean was leaving for the animal shelter in a car borrowed from her neighbor. During lunch I stopped at the shelter and waited for her to leave, then talked with a clerk, who wanted me to adopt a dog."

"Tell me you didn't, Topping."

Griff's cell phone rang and he looked at the screen. It read "private." He answered, in case it was Frank. Nope, it was Eva Montanna, a Special Agent with Immigrations and Customs Enforcement. Griff had worked with Eva on a joint ICE/FBI anti-terrorism task force. She asked him to have dinner with her and her husband, Scott, at their favorite Chinese restaurant, that night. After he'd agreed, she mentioned she had also invited a lady friend from their church who was a doctor. When would he learn?

His magnet tower toppled all over his desk. "Eva, can I call back in five minutes?"

"Sure. On my cell." She hung up.

He picked up the nuts. "Sal, I'm off to Front Royal. Want to come nose around?"

"Can't. Taking my son to the dentist. I'm on vacation tomorrow. What's in Front Royal?"

"I told the clerk at the animal shelter that I had my heart set on a Boston terrier, the same kind Frank and his wife have." Griff had not flashed his badge. He'd tried to find out what he could on a pretext. Many times the badge had the opposite effect. People clammed up if they thought a friend was in trouble.

A chrome nut had flown under his chair. Griff reached over and snagged it. "I was told Norma Jean breeds Boston terriers. Zoning rules prevented her from having so many dogs at home, so she and her partners bought a kennel in—"

"Front Royal," Sal interjected. "Maybe Frank took a ride out to clear his head."

As soon as the clerk had said it, Griff thought the same thing. If Norma Jean knew he was hiding there, that would explain Griff's misgivings about her story. "The clerk gave me the phone number and address. I called a few minutes ago and got an answering machine. It sounds like a mom-and-pop operation."

"Gotta run. I've nothing pressing over the weekend besides helping my wife with a garage sale. I'd much rather haul down to Front Royal with you." Sal saluted and left.

Griff hadn't been to Front Royal since his wife Sue died from ovarian cancer. Every fall, they drove out I-66, meandering through the mountains along the Blue Ridge Parkway. The last plane trip they took was over those mountains. The sunset filled them with light, which too quickly faded into sickness, doctors, and chemo.

He knew one thing, he did not want to have dinner with a doctor. Not tonight. He dialed Eva's cell. "I can't make dinner." Eva's sigh in his ear forced him to explain, "I'm leaving now to run down a lead in Front Royal. Instead of six, could we make it six-thirty or seven?"

"Scott's in a meeting with the Secretary at an undisclosed location. He'll go straight to the restaurant. I could leave him a message and hope he gets it." Eva's husband worked for the Secretary of Defense.

Griff worked with Eva for years, and he knew by her tone that the time change was a problem. He guessed correctly. She said, "There's another glitch in switching."

"Oh?"

"Surely you remember my friend, June Livingston, is joining us."

The pediatrician. Of course he remembered. Griff tried again to get out of it. "I know I won't be back in time. The three of you meet at six as planned. I'll come another time."

He almost folded his phone shut when Eva said, "You can make it if you want to."

It was the same blunt tone she used when she wanted him to mentor a young task force member, Trenton Nash, which hadn't worked out at all. He'd put that behind him, but was glad he no longer had to work with a junior partner. Once, he casually mentioned to Eva he had a hard time getting over his wife's death. Ever since, Eva had tried to fix him up with her friends. They never amounted to more than one date until Griff met Eva's twin sister, Jillie.

Griff and Jillie had really hit it off. For the first time since Sue's death, he felt ready to live again. Then Jillie was killed in the attacks on the Pentagon on September 11. After going through that kind of gut-wrenching grief twice, Griff decided he was not meant to have a mate. He'd live alone. So, he worked, ran, and occasionally flew his Cessna Skyhawk.

After their last case together, Eva took maternity leave and Griff didn't see the Montannas as often. But, after her third child was born, Eva got back to work and back to her mission to find Griff a mate. Now, she couldn't say enough good things about June. Maybe that meant Eva finally was getting over Jillie's death.

"Don't expect me before six. And Eva, no promises. You know me. I'm content. I'm going to see a breeder of Boston terriers in Front Royal. It's business, but you never know."

"Be careful. Dogs are too much work. That's why we have a cat."

Griff checked his watch. "See you in four hours."

The bond hearing for Bernie's drug client took so long, Dwight did not leave the courtroom until five. Against his better judgment, he set bond at three hundred thousand dollars and ordered the defendant to surrender his passport. Bernie argued that Tyler Cooper was a certified public accountant with ties to Columbia City, Virginia, for twenty-three years, and dismissed the claim that the drug case extended from Florida to the Bahamas, saying "the government is overreaching."

An accident on Route 495, a major artery Dwight drove to get home, snarled traffic, so he didn't get home for another hour. Before he left the office, he called Christine again, but there was no answer. He left another message, thinking she had dashed to the store. When he pulled in the driveway at one minute to six, Dwight was relieved. Louis had not arrived ahead of him.

He pressed the door-opener to raise the third stall of the garage and carefully parked his cream-colored 1971 GTO convertible, known by car enthusiasts as "The Judge." Seeing the other two stalls empty, he grabbed his briefcase and hurried inside to see if Christine left him a note.

There wasn't any, and the house was eerily quiet. Dwight looked at the answering machine. No lights blinked, so she must have wiped off his earlier message. His brow furrowed. It wasn't like her not to call back. He checked the refrigerator for signs of dinner. His eyes rested on a crystal pitcher filled with strawberry lemonade. Next to it was a dish of sliced berries and lemons to float on top. That was so Christine.

She gave wonderful dinner parties and loved to play the hostess. He did forget that her last formal party was well over a year ago. Some notions about spouses are hard to dispel. That his wife was perfect was one Dwight clung to. Where was Christine? Louis would drive up any second.

Then, he remembered. With the late bond hearing, he'd forgotten to check his cell phone. Dwight pulled the phone out of his shirt pocket and retrieved two messages. One from Mandy. Then he heard Christine's businesslike voice, as if he was a copier salesman and she was ordering the toner. Fox News wanted her to comment on a youth gang from El Salvador that was threatening D.C. and she would be home when she could. A chicken enchilada casserole was in the freezer. He should cook it in the microwave for fifty minutes. She was sure Louis would understand.

Dwight was thankful she was all right, but there was no sugar coating it: Christine let him down. So what if Louis was the most compassionate person Dwight knew? He was their invited dinner guest. Her job as director of Career Moms for Kids, which she had for three years, demanded more and more of her time. When she wasn't a regular fixture on the cable channels, she was fund-raising or working on whatever book she was writing.

Dwight deleted her message. When they first met, he would have saved any recording of her voice. Those carefree days when they dated at Georgetown were relegated to a scrapbook in some cabinet. More pressing things filled their lives these days. Christine was passionate about strengthening families. She also wrote a column that appeared in more than twenty newspapers across the country and frequently testified before Congress.

He pulled on the freezer door. Inside, stacks of plastic containers were coated with ice. How long had that stuff been in there? He shut the door. Dwight paid no attention to how Christine put their meals on the table. His days were long, coddling juries, keeping lawyers in line, and reading mounds of legal briefs. Most nights, he read every book written about the Revolutionary War. Dwight had begun drafting a treatise on what modern commanders could learn from George Washington.

Until this moment, Dwight had ignored why Christine was gone so often. Now, he saw that she lived apart from him. Not from Mandy, though. They were like schoolgirls, laughing over Mandy's latest guy in a whole string she had dated. Was Dwight imagining a loss that wasn't real? The missing FBI agent and the whole situation with Bernie and the bond hearing must be to blame for this melancholy mood.

A car door slammed. No time to cook a frozen casserole in the microwave. The door bell rang. A man of resources, Dwight's mind traveled through the local eateries that specialized in take-out. For the first time in years, he had to fend for himself.

At Lo's Chinese Restaurant, Griff poured soy sauce on his cashew chicken. As he predicted, he arrived late, and Eva, Scott, and June Livingston were into a second pot of tea. The evening shifted for the better right after their food came. That's when the doctor was paged and left her food uneaten to set a boy's leg at the hospital.

Eva stuck out her bottom lip. "I feel bad a little boy broke his leg."

With chopsticks, Scott plunked a green bean in his mouth. He swallowed, then poised another bean near his lips. "Relax, Eva. At least Griff made a clever entrance."

Along with Scott, Griff roared with laughter. "Before I could stop my mouth, the words escaped, 'Doctor Livingston, I presume.' Maybe that'll teach Eva to quit fixing me up. I don't think I made a good impression on June."

Eva didn't laugh. She sipped her tea. "She flashed you a big smile."

Griff's bushy eyebrows shot up. Eva meant well, and he did not want to hurt her feelings, especially in front of Scott. So, he took the high road. "Thanks, both of you."

Scott sat next to Griff, an arrangement he appreciated so that he didn't have to sit next to June. Eva was across from Scott. "I'm reluctant to admit it, but I'm glad June had to leave."

Scott glanced at Griff and shrugged. Griff guessed that Eva's husband knew what she meant. Griff and Sue used to finish each other's sentences. As much as Eva wanted him to date, Griff had no desire for that kind of love with another woman. "You got me. What's up?"

Just then, the owner Mrs. Chang, stopped by. "How is everything?"

Scott tapped the pot. "More tea would be nice."

She dipped her head. Griff hated tea, but before he could request more decaf, she hurried away, her silk jacket rustling.

Griff arched an eyebrow at Eva. "Well?"

Eva folded and unfolded her napkin. She looked unusually nervous. "After more tea."

Okay, Griff decided, Eva realized June was not for him and wanted him to meet someone else. If so, he'd make sure she drank plenty of tea and never raised that subject. Mrs. Chang brought clean cups and a large pot of tea.

Griff needed no more caffeine and asked for ice water. Before any more was said about blind dates, he took charge. "I need advice about something I've been unable to solve."

Eva and Scott traded a look Griff could not decipher. Scott nudged him to get out. "I'll call home, check on the kids."

Griff lowered his voice. "No, stay. This morning, FBI agent Frank Williams failed to show up to testify at the Jones trial. That's why I went to Front Royal today."

Eva twisted her napkin. "You told me you had a lead. What happened?"

Griff explained Norma Jean's dog operation, and that he talked to her partners, who claimed they never met Frank, didn't know he was with the FBI. "I'm suspicious of Norma Jean, because she is so, ah—" Griff stopped a moment, turned the sugar packet over, "—unfeeling. She doesn't seem concerned about her husband's disappearance."

Eva was full of questions. "I assume you've combed the obvious hotels around the airport. Has the Phoenix FBI office scoured their end? Have you checked hospitals?"

"Checked the jails, too, although that was a stretch. Talked to Frank's new supervisor, and every commercial airline."

Mrs. Chang removed their plates, leaving them to talk in private. The fortune cookies sat on the plate, uneaten.

Eva picked up where they left off. "Has Frank's cell phone been used?"

Before Griff replied, Scott added, "If global positioning is on, it could help track him."

Griff rattled the sugar packet. He wasn't nervous, he just wanted to get back to trying to find Frank. "When I called his cell signal provider, his phone hadn't been used since last night."

He managed to tear a hole in the package, and sugar sprinkled around his hands. Eva pushed a strand of her wheat-blond hair from her forehead, and Griff thought she looked tired. Why mention his troubles? The owner returned with the check, Griff snagged it. Scott's larger hand landed on his. "No way, buddy. We asked you to dinner."

Griff shook his head. "Nope. My treat for you listening to my woes." When Scott did not move his hand, Griff insisted, "You buy next time."

Scott laughed. "Did you hear, Eva? Maybe your career as a matchmaker is not over yet."

"Ah, I didn't mean—"

Eva touched Griff's hand. "He's kidding. Will the company tell you if his phone is on?"

Griff put his credit card on top of the bill. "I thought the security director told me it was not on, but I should check again. It's been a crazy day."

Her next question caught Griff off guard. "Did you search in any woods for Williams?"

"Do you know something?"

Her eyes searched Scott's, and Griff grew restless. "Eva, what is it?"

She puffed out her cheeks and blew out the air. "Scott took me and the kids to Great Falls Park last weekend. We hiked to the falls. This was before I knew about Williams, okay?"

Griff nodded. "So?"

Scott interrupted, "Griff, has Eva told you that what she dreams sometimes comes true?"

"Not that I remember." As Griff suspected, Scott was in on whatever Eva couldn't spit out. Griff and Eva had worked together on and off for years, and Eva never mentioned anything remotely wacky. She was as straight an agent and person as he'd ever known. And she and Scott had three great kids. This must be a joke. Although, Eva never remembered a punch line.

Eva sipped some tea. "Griff, I've never told anyone but Scott. Remember when Lou, our former boss, fell at his beach house? That morning, I had a vision of him lying on the ground, yelling for help. When I got to work, you told me he'd fallen and was in surgery. It nearly knocked me over!"

Scott placed a hand over Eva's. "It's not the first time, Griff; you need to know that."

"I don't understand it, but I believe you. How is dreaming of Lou's accident related to me? Did you dream I got sick on Chinese food?"

At least, Eva laughed, and he was glad that her mood had lightened.

Seconds later, she had on her serious face again. "This wasn't a dream. It was more like a vision. We just passed the ruins on Matildaville Trail. It was late afternoon and I had Martin in the baby carrier. Scott ran ahead because Kaley and Andy were climbing on a big rock and he wanted their picture. I heard a spine-tingling scream. It's hard to describe."

She closed her blue eyes. When they opened, she said, "I think it was a barred owl. Still, it really shook me. The rest was like a preview to a movie. It blew past my mind, then quit. I don't know the ending." She stopped talking, her breath came in spurts.

Griff sipped his water while Eva gulped her tea. Maybe having a third child recently had wound her up.

Scott poured her more tea. "Eva Marie, tell Griff what you saw. He's a big boy and can decide what, if anything, to do with it."

She peered into her cup as if there were tea leaves in it. "You were held hostage in some thick woods. Your arms and legs were bound. You thrashed on the ground, turned on your stomach to crawl to your cell phone." She gripped his arm, just above his wrist. "Griff, I heard a shot. Martin started to cry. I didn't see or hear anything else."

Griff smiled at their worried faces, pulled out his cell. "See, I don't go anywhere without it. Eva knows mine has GPS positioning. If I'm lost in the woods, the satellite can track me."

She pulled back her hand. "I'd feel better if I was on this case with you."

Scott was quick to object. "Eva, don't go there. With the baby, you promised no more rough stuff." He patted her arm. "Griff, I've got her where I want her. Safely doing paperwork."

"Chained to the desk," Eva grumbled. "Griff, if they offer you a promotion to group supervisor, turn it down. You and I were meant to be field agents."

Griff had no intention of moving up the career ladder. He had things just how he wanted them. Well, except for the Jones case and the missing agent.

"Promise me, Griff," he heard her say.

"Promise you what?"

"That you'll be extra careful and call for backup sooner than later."

"You don't get this creepy when I fly the Cessna by myself."

Griff's cell phone whirred against his belt. He removed it from the leather holder and checked the number displayed on the front. It showed a restricted call. Griff went to his received-call list and recognized the number as Frank Williams's unlisted home number. He replaced the phone. "This has been great, but I have to take this one."

They said a good-bye, then Griff climbed into his personal car, or as the agents called them, his P-car. It was a Dodge Ram truck. Before turning onto the road, he rang Norma Jean. She had no new information on Frank's whereabouts, but gave him the name of a local pub where Frank might have gone. Griff pulled the shifter in drive and headed for the pub, which was a long way from home.

FIVE

While Griff sped down to Springfield to pull Frank from some Irish pub, Dwight and Louis relaxed on wicker chairs on Dwight's screened porch. The scene fit, because Louis was a Virginia gentleman down to his cropped hair and bow tie, with a lineage he could trace back to Patrick Henry. The sun would set in an hour. Christine called to say she was leaving the Washington television studio. But, instead of enjoying his Greek salad, Dwight grew angry all over again at the thought of Secretary Jones's telephone call.

Louis mopped up olive oil and oregano with a slice of pita bread. Their glasses empty, Dwight retrieved the pitcher of lemonade from the fridge. When he returned to the porch, Louis had found the remote and was watching cable news. A reporter was saying that Native Americans were upset at being taken advantage of by Owen Jones III. Dwight picked up the remote, then pressed the mute button.

Louis held out his glass and Dwight poured. His friend took a long sip. "Fabulous." Then he changed the subject from his appreciation of Christine's lemonade. "That reporter, Kat Kowicki, said she tried to get a statement from you, but you refused. My Pappy used to sit for hours on a porch like this one, teaching me to play checkers. It took me a long time to learn the power behind a crowned king. Our media is a little like that."

Dwight kept his voice low. "Louis, I feel the same way. Washington led us to victory against King George, but the press sees itself like royalty. With few checks and balances, justice is what they say it is."

Judge Sumner was not done talking checkers. "Pappy and I played for hours, and I learned some real gems, like 'one who seizes a dog by the ears is no better than a passerby who meddles in a quarrel not his own.'"

Dwight appreciated the powerful imagery, the truth of which was played out weekly in his courtroom. "Your Pappy was a wise man."

Louis laughed spontaneously. "When I got older, I found out where he got his wisdom."

"From life's experiences?"

"No, from the Bible. Listen, Kat will continue to ride hard on your case."

Dwight's reply was out of character, but he felt it all the same. "No doubt, to boost her career. Reporters are all alike. They look for someone in authority to get on video, to get their theory of the case on the air."

Dwight's mind traveled to a far field. The missing agent, then the outburst. His courtroom was becoming a circus. Well, he'd maintain order and not let it become a thing of ridicule.

Louis was talking. "There are seven other judges and a couple seasoned lawyers from Maryland and Virginia. We're all from different churches. You brought up the very person I came to see you about. Will you speak to my Bible study group about George Washington and his faith?"

Dwight shifted his gaze from Louis to a sketch of Washington that Christine bought him at Middleburg, their favorite getaway from Washington. Should a judge meet with a group of Christians? It mattered not if they were judges and attorneys. Word could get around. He thought of Constance Ingles telling her clients before sentencing, "Judge Pendergast is religious. Tell him that you are, too, and he'll cut you a break."

He popped a kalamata olive in his mouth, chewed it slowly and spit the pit on his fork. In studying the nation's first President, Dwight's focus was on Washington's leadership, not any spiritual side. Still, Judge Sumner rarely asked him for a favor. "All right, but I'll need time for research. I know zero about his faith."

Louis's smile was genuine. "No doubt, you will enlighten us with what you learn."

Dwight took a sip of lemonade. "I may as well tell you, several problems have crept in. You did warn me."

"If it makes you feel better, Naomi and I pray for you, that you will have strength and wisdom."

Louis often talked of bringing matters of concern to his god. It meant nothing to Dwight, but he appreciated the effort. He continued explaining. "For health reasons, the first federal prosecutor was taken off the case three weeks before trial. The new AUSA is Patrick O'Rourke. He tried one other case before me. He's tenacious, and his briefs are on point. You can believe what he says. "

Louis didn't know O'Rourke.

"Patrick filed a motion asking for more time to prepare. Wanted a week. Constance Ingles objected. I allowed a few days. Then, after the first day of testimony, the defendant, who is out on bond, has a car accident."

"Was he drinking and driving?"

The thought of Jones's arrogance made Dwight bolt from the chair. Holding his empty glass, he paced across the porch floor. "Jones was a passenger. So the report said, anyway. He had a broken jaw and broken nose, which produced another delay. I expected to see him coming into court with his head bandaged, so Constance could offset the sympathy for a prosecutor in a wheelchair. Now, there's a new wrinkle. The FBI agent—"

"Is missing," Louis filled in. "The reporter said so. What are you going to do if the FBI agent fails to show on Monday?"

Dwight tapped a finger on his crystal glass. Christine insisted on Waterford. Nothing but the best for her family. A huge leap from green plastic cups they drank from during their first year of marriage. Those cups were thrown in the garbage long ago. Thinking of Christine, Dwight hoped she was not stuck in traffic on the Beltway.

Louis interrupted Dwight's thoughts with a question. "What about his Grand Jury testimony? A prior statement given by a witness under oath may be used if the government proves he or she is unavailable."

"Williams testified on direct and I interrupted cross-examination. It was to resume this morning." Dwight wiped his brow.

"If the case stands without the agent, exclude his testimony, and instruct the jury to disregard everything they heard."

Dwight walked over to Louis. "Williams is essentially the whole case."

Louis stood. "I should be going. My civil trial resumes in the morning."

They picked up plates, walked into the kitchen, when Louis asked the bombshell question. "How does the Secretary of the Interior figure in?"

Dwight paused, then, "I wish I knew. If the government is still investigating his involvement in the bribery conspiracy, I wouldn't know it. But, he called me today."

Louis's lined face grew grave. "Did you speak with him?"

"Not one word. Gladys said he wanted me for Georgetown's fall dinner. I don't believe it."

Judge Sumner frowned. "He's playing a dangerous game. When he was practicing law, he arranged a large contribution from the Russians to the groups who are opposing oil and gas exploration at the Artic National Wildlife Refuge. I thought it would be an issue during his Senate confirmation hearings, but it seemed to fly beneath their radar." Louis was silent for a moment. "No doubt the President would be relieved if the case is dismissed."

Dwight stared at Louis. Did he think that Dwight's judgment in this case was biased? No, of course not. "Some allege I'm in favor of the defendant for political reasons, but I would never decide a case other than based on the facts and the law. Besides, the jury will decide if Jones is guilty or innocent."

"I know that. The President's opponents are whispering it. Your only solution is to put everything on the record. What was done to find the agent, why he is critical to the case. You cannot be faulted for this."

Dwight was no closer to a solution when Louis picked up his sporty cap, which he always wore when he drove or walked anywhere. Almost in parting, he said, "We didn't get a chance to talk about Nolan Cuttering. Briggs asked me to testify for Nolan." Senator Harry Briggs was the Senate Judiciary Chair in charge of the confirmation hearings.

Dwight wasn't sure it was proper for Louis to appear. "Will you, as a sitting Judge, I mean?"

"Yes. Cuttering clerked for me and Briggs agreed to keep the questioning to that."

"And I suppose you trust a politician?"

Louis grinned. "I have an in, with a higher power."

"The President?"

Louis clapped Dwight on the shoulder. "Think higher, like the creator of the universe. I'll keep praying for you. This Jones case will turn out how it is supposed to."

Dwight ushered Louis out to the drive, his friend's sentiments providing no answers to the twists and turns of *United States v Owen Jones III*.

Eight hundred miles away in Florida, two men put final touches on a plan to make them money, lots of money. Their scheme would reverberate all the way to Virginia. A huge man called Moose was behind the wheel of a late-seventies Cadillac. On the radio, loud rock blasted out the open windows of the Caddie, which had no air conditioning.

All the better for the passenger, Skeeter, who was staring out his window. Whip thin, his weight was all muscle earned the hard way, by pumping iron. Skeeter tried to block out the blaring music. He had more important things to do, like look for heat. Even when the police thought they were being cool, he could spot the man. In prison, he learned to use an alias when making deals, like tonight. So, Moose knew him as Grady. No last name. Skeeter's former cellmate, Crazy Ken, arranged their meeting and chose the name Grady. He and Moose knew each other only by first names. It was safer that way.

If the law got wise, Moose could not point a finger to Skeeter. Careful not to let Moose know his identity, Skeeter wore a blue bandana over gray-streaked hair that fell halfway to his shoulders. Tonight, his thin face was camouflaged by a moustache and beard that had grown in red.

When he got out a few months back, Skeeter told himself he'd go straight. That was before his probation officer pressured him to find a job or give her proof that his shrimp boat made enough to pay his bills. That was before the hurricanes that tore up the Gulf. First the Chinese imports almost destroyed his business, now Mother Nature.

It seemed he never won. So, Skeeter fell back on what he knew. An hour north of Tampa, Homosassa Springs was hot. Humidity clung to his shirt, his palms, even to the woods along the river. Not quite dark, he could see next to the road, where canals connected homes on stilts to the Gulf. Big city money hadn't moved this far north. Inside the tiny homes were people struggling to make it. Like him.

On the way from his coastal haunt in the Florida panhandle, Skeeter told himself he had no choice but to be a middleman in this drug deal. Moose couldn't afford cocaine but knew people who could. That's why Crazy Ken arranged for them to meet. Skeeter didn't have cocaine, but knew people who could get it in large amounts. Both would help the sale and get a big commission. Skeeter would make enough money to pay off the loans on the truck and shrimp boat. Then, he was off crime forever.

A little while ago, he had parked his truck at a fast food restaurant and walked to the Homosassa Springs State Park pavilion, where Moose picked him up. In the large man's gravel drive, Skeeter saw no other cars. That was good. The porch sinking to the ground, Moose's house looked like a shack. The place Skeeter lived in was better than this. Sounds of barking dogs reached his ears.

Skeeter tensed. He hated dogs. "How many dogs you got?"

The Cadillac's tires skidded on gravel. "Enough to keep my customers in line." He pointed at the plastic grocery bag Skeeter carried. "I don't see the stuff yer gonna sell."

Skeeter got out, slammed the car door. "Nah. It's nearby. These are burgers."

His partner in this deal heaved himself out of the driver's seat. "It better be close." He took Skeeter to the front door. In a pen next to the house, Skeeter saw at least two jumping dogs. Their wild barking put his whole body on edge, like he was walking on glass in his bare feet. Pit bulls, dogs of choice for criminals he'd known. Though Skeeter spent time in and out of prison, he didn't think of himself as a criminal. Just unlucky.

Inside, Moose shut the door behind them, then locked the deadbolt with a key, which he stowed in his pants pocket. That move surprised even Skeeter, who thought he was ready for anything. Wound up, he walked on the balls of his feet, telling Moose the plan.

The big man erupted. "Grady, you're crazy! My buyers expect the product to be here when they arrive. Yer gonna mess with them, get yerself killed!"

As Moose slammed his massive fist on the crooked table next to him, sounds of violence rocketed against streaked, dirty walls. Skeeter stood aloof from the man, twice his size, head completely bald. His beard was black and covered most of his face. Skeeter took a drag on a cigarette, knocked the ashes on the floor. "Relax, man. I've done deals like this before. They'll do it my way, or not at all."

Moose's customers would show up soon with a quarter of a million dollars in cash, and Skeeter's people would bring cocaine worth that much. It made his head spin. How did he get himself into this? It was his PO's fault, wanting him to show he could pay his bills. Without this deal, or one like it, he couldn't.

Skeeter was amazed at how fast Moose bounded out of his chair. His eyes burned red, like the end of a live cigarette. He ran straight for Skeeter. With speed he learned in the ring, Skeeter ducked behind a table in the kitchen and escaped Moose, who looked like he wanted to snap his neck like a dry twig. Forty years in and out of juvenile hall and prison taught him more than how to throw a punch. Skeeter knew how to survive.

Moose stopped an inch before ramming into the table, and thick rolls of fat shook under his chin. "Grady, I'll kill you myself."

Skeeter snubbed the cigarette out on the filthy table. The man was on the verge of blowing out of control. If he did, Skeeter needed a way out. His hazel eyes scanned the dim room. From the corner, he couldn't tell how far it was to the back way out. He didn't even see a rear door. Skeeter was sure he could outrun Moose, who weighed a good three hundred pounds. But, what if he had a gun hidden somewhere? Skeeter's truck was parked way down the road.

With more bravado than he felt in the steamy room, Skeeter improvised, "Moose, quit whinin'. We agreed. When your buyers get here, they show me the money. I take one of them in your car to see the kilos."

Skeeter took a pack of smokes from his shirt pocket and lit another one. He inhaled and held it in his lungs for a few seconds. His urine was randomly tested for drugs, but nicotine was not forbidden by his PO. Besides, he had to keep his mind sharp if he wanted to stay alive.

"No way, man. These people will think we're trying to rob them. I told you to bring the coke here." He hit the table so hard with his fist that Skeeter's lighter bounced to the floor. Skeeter bent to pick it up and, as he straightened up, he spotted the back door. Was it locked?

"Wrong. They'll expect it to go down my way. It's the only way to protect them and us from gettin' ripped off."

Moose unrolled his fist, moved back. Skeeter sauntered to the window, took a final puff on his cigarette. With the heel of his scuffed cowboy boot, he crushed the butt. Skeeter acted sure of himself, but he didn't know much about Moose or his customers. Most likely, his life was in danger and there was not a whole lot he could do to save it, locked in this dump.

As Louis's red taillights disappeared down the street, Dwight walked toward the house. The two-story home was large for three, especially with Mandy away at school or with her friends. At a happy thought, Dwight smiled. The backyard was a perfect size for two grandchildren to play in. Maybe they could build a big play area.

His smile quickly faded. He doubted Christine would give up her flower garden, but it might not hurt to ask. When she got home, he planned to tell her that they were going to be grandparents. Dwight stopped long enough to gaze at the darkening sky. He spotted faint, emerging stars. Louis spoke of a creator, as if he knew him personally. When he was young, Dwight's parents took him to the local Episcopal parish twice a year, on Christmas and Easter.

With his busy career, he hadn't continued the tradition with his children. Spiritual matters didn't factor into Dwight's life, but Louis knew what he believed and why. In a simple way, he challenged Dwight's beliefs. Even gave Dwight a Bible and suggested he read the gospel of John. He had made it through the second chapter when a twelve-week antitrust case began. That was a year ago.

Maybe tonight, he'd start the third chapter of John. Dwight roamed to his study and searched the shelves for the leather book. He found it, then settled into a chair. A member of the Jewish ruling council named Nicodemus knew Jesus was a teacher from God because of the miracles he performed. They met one night and Jesus told him he must be born again. Nicodemus asked how that was possible. Before Dwight could read Jesus's reply, the phone rang.

It could be Christine, in trouble. He walked over to the extension phone. "Hello."

A rush of breath. He asked, "Christine, are you all right?"

This time a giggle. "Dad?"

It was Mandy! She was laughing. Or was she crying? He could not tell.

"Honey, what's wrong? You called me so many times today, but you never left a number."

She drew in her breath, then gushed, "I know. We're down at Kitty Hawk. Chad asked me to marry him."

He was stunned. Mandy first mentioned Chad a month ago. Dwight had heard of his father, the head of the largest brokerage firm in New York. At twenty-two, Mandy was as impetuous as her sister was focused. A week ago, or so it seemed, she said she was going to get a Master's degree in English at George Mason University, but instead she got a job teaching English to juniors at a private high school.

He picked his words carefully. "Mother and I would love to talk with you about it."

"Put Mom on. I can't wait to tell her."

Dwight stalled. "What are you doing at Kitty Hawk? It's getting late."

"Chad drove me to where the Wright brothers flew the first airplane."

"You'll be driving home in the dark."

Another giggle. "Nope. We're staying at his Aunt's house on the beach."

"The two of you?"

"Silly, his Aunt and Uncle live there. My ring is almost two carats."

Dwight was concerned for Mandy. "What about your master's degree?"

He heard his daughter whisper, "Just a minute," then, "Be sure to tell Mom."

She had hung up on him. Dwight slowly set down the phone. Today, both daughters called him with important news, and Christine knew none of it.

SIX

Skeeter heard the crunch of tires on the gravel drive. Moose balled a fist and shook it at Skeeter, but his threat was drowned by fierce barking. Skeeter stiffened. Those pit bulls scared him almost more than the thought of going back to prison. He stared past the grime on the window and, in the glow of a mercury vapor light on the detached garage, he saw them—Moose's buyers. Two men Skeeter had never seen before got out of a dark SUV. With their shaved heads and tattooed forearms, they looked like rejects from a wrestling show. His arm muscles twitched. One jab to their puffy faces, they'd drop. He was sure of it.

Then, a third man got out of the back seat. He looked different. His black hair was caught up in a short pony tail. With the edge of his sleeve, Skeeter rubbed dirt away from the window. The third man shut the SUV door but still didn't turn. *Come on, show your face.* Skeeter pressed his eyes closer. The man turned and it was like his cold steely eyes pierced right through the dirty window. Skeeter knew those eyes. They were in the face of the man who had arrested him before. Federal Drug Agent Nick Tascoda.

"The feds!"

Skeeter ran across the room and dove head first out the single pane window, landing right on his shoulder. Glass wedged in his hair, his clothes. Pain pulsed in his shoulder, over his eye. He scrambled off the palmetto bush. On his feet, he took off running. Skeeter ran fast, as he'd trained in federal prison at Danbury, ran away from the DEA agent who arrested him four years ago. How could he have been so stupid? Moose was probably wearing a wire. Skeeter never checked.

He jumped a three-foot fence. That's when he tasted blood. Glass must have cut his face, but he wouldn't stop. Beyond Moose's yard flowed a creek. Voices sounded behind him. Not waiting another second, Skeeter launched himself into the water. It was risky, but if he ran in yards, he'd meet up with barking dogs or, worse, a homeowner with a gun. If he ran in the streets, lights would give him away. The feds and local police would track him until he was caught like a mouse in a trap.

In the water, Skeeter half-ran, half-swam. He slipped on a rock and went down in black murky water. It flowed over his face. He swam as well as he fought, so it was nothing to float to the surface. Skeeter eased down the tributary of the Homosassa River, hoping he hadn't stirred up the creatures that feed at night.

Still, going back to prison was a thousand times worse than facing a poisonous snake or an alligator. Skeeter could wrestle a gator. He had before. Well, a four-foot one. If an eight or ten-footer got him, no need to worry about being slammed behind bars. In the dark, he picked his way slowly. The night was loud all around him. Like magnified sounds of a jungle trip he'd heard on television, night birds croaked and cackled. They made so much noise, it was hard to hear if anyone was after him. It was hard to hear his own thoughts. Maybe that was a good thing.

Quok-quok sounds of black-crowned night herons feeding on the river bank would attract gators. He tried to avoid them and snakes, which he should have done with Moose. What was he telling the feds? Skeeter's supplier also knew him as Skeeter. But, since Skeeter failed to call him on his cell phone, he'd leave the area with the cocaine. If not, he was the one link back to Skeeter. He wanted to warn him, but couldn't risk it. Better stay in the water where dogs couldn't track his scent.

He heard voices. Did they come from the creek's edge or from Moose's yard? Skeeter tried not to panic. He lived by rivers and the Gulf his entire life, when he wasn't locked up, and knew sounds echoed over water for quite a distance. He quit moving, remained low in the water. Only his nose, eyes, and ears stuck out in the air. Then he felt an enormous jolt against his left side. Fear coursed through him. Skeeter felt cold like ice. A gator!

He stifled a scream, bolted from the water, and scrambled up the bank. It was slippery. He fell back into the water again, landed on a large mound. If it was a gator, in seconds he'd be turtle food. Skeeter pushed off with his bare hands. He felt skin, not scales. Skin that was rough like an elephant's. Relief washed over him. This was no flesh-eating animal.

It was a manatee, gentle giant of the sea. They ate plants, not people. Sailors called them mermaids of the ocean. Skeeter was in no danger. He'd swum with these endangered creatures since he was five years old.

Skeeter continued up the creek. The manatee came along, but Skeeter pushed her away. Each time she returned, it made him think. He thought she was a gator and she wasn't. Maybe Moose wasn't Moose. Who in the world was he? Was he the snitch that almost got him caught, again?

Dwight's dinner and talk with Louis were over an hour ago. Christine should have been home by now. He picked up the phone and hit the speed dial button for her cell number. She answered, said she was on the George Washington Parkway. "After the taping, I went to the office, to get caught up. We should have a wonderful weekend."

He pictured her toothy smile and hardly noticed her Austrian accent. "I have lots to tell."

"Sorry not to be there for Louis. Of course, you managed without me. You always do."

"Bernie and Rita are driving down Saturday. Their daughter is engaged." Dwight thought he would see how Christine reacted to that news.

Christine sounded hurt. "When I spoke to Rita this morning, she mentioned nothing."

"Drive carefully."

Dwight slumped in the chair, forgetting Jesus and Nicodemus. Their daughter was engaged to a man whom Dwight met twice. Both times were rushed affairs. Chad picked up Mandy, driving a red sports car, too fast. He did not care how rich Chad was, Dwight did not like the kid.

His own past smacked his mind like a bat against a baseball. Six weeks after he and Christine started dating, he asked her to marry him. His parents were alarmed. Filled his head with stories of a ruined life. He and Christine turned out all right. Louis raised two daughters and a son and Dwight knew what he'd say. Pray about it. But, one had to have an idea to whom one was praying.

He opened his Bible and finished reading the third chapter of John about the Jewish leader who had faith in Jesus. Dwight decided to bring the Bible to the lake and see if he could find the evidence Louis claimed was there if he just looked for it.

Skeeter approached the restaurant through a field. The night was still dark. He crouched behind a dumpster for thirty minutes. Stayed in the shadows, watched his truck. At two in the morning, headlights swept the parking lot. A car pulled up in front of the dumpster, and Skeeter was ready to run for his life. Heavy steps came closer. Was it a police officer with a badge and a gun?

Skeeter held his breath, not wanting even that sound to give him away. He ducked lower, expecting a flashlight to shine in his face. His body coiled. Overhead, he heard the thud of garbage bags being thrown into the dumpster. The steps crunched away. He breathed. His head ached, his stomach growled. Who knew when he last ate? Those burgers he bought were left behind when he dove out the window.

At three in the morning, a metal door clanged shut. He peered around the dumpster and saw a man, probably the manager, drive away in the only car in the lot. It was almost safe to go. Sure there were no feds or police nearby, Skeeter climbed into his Ford F150 monster truck, which rode high above its large tires, and headed home.

Apalachicola, the locals called it Apalach, was hours away. Could he survive the in-between towns without being caught? Skeeter drove slowly through Homosassa Springs, then turned north on Route 19, the stretch of highway that would take him up the coast. When he sailed through Crystal River, he checked his rearview mirror and sighed. No lights shone. He was safe. For now.

Skeeter left behind gas stations and peanut stands. Behind the dumpster, he had poured water from his boots, but his socks were still wet. His jeans and western shirt were damp. The lashes of his right eye were stuck together. With a finger, he wiped his eyelid. Blood!

His mind raced faster than his truck, which he drove one mile below the speed limit. No way he'd stop for stitches. The police might check the hospitals for him. Of course, the cops might not know he was cut. What if he left blood on some glass? His past crimes were drug crimes and petty theft, so he'd never been forced to give up a DNA sample. His foot hit the brakes and his stomach lurched with the truck. He had donated blood in prison!

It was a good thing he slowed. In Chiefland, the speed limit was thirty and the police nabbed you for going one mile over. At a truck stop, he pulled in and parked between two semi trucks. Skeeter angled his bandana over his eyebrows, then went straight to the bathroom, where he washed the blood from his forehead and eye. A burly man walked in, looked Skeeter in the face. "What did you do to the other guy?"

Skeeter shook his head, then lied. "I should have known not to spill beer on a biker. He drove a Harley, too. "

The truck driver laughed. Left alone at the sink, he pressed a paper towel on his wound. In the chipped mirror, Skeeter checked the gash. It stopped bleeding. In the station, he poured a cup of hot coffee, grabbed a sandwich from the case, then paid the cashier a damp five-dollar bill. Before leaving, he scanned the parking lot for suspicious people. Just the trucker climbing into his cab. Skeeter drove off in his truck, anxious to have Chiefland in his rearview mirror.

It was too late. A white Chiefland police car idled in a grocery store parking lot. Skeeter checked his speedometer, thirty-five. As if his foot was burned on the bottom, he let off the gas. He passed the cruiser, looked in his mirrors with his eyes, making sure his head was still. Furtive moves were the number one reason cops stopped your car.

His empty stomach rolled. The sandwich was on the seat, but he was not about to reach for it. Sure enough, the cop pulled in behind him. *Don't panic.* Blood rushed to Skeeter's head, he had to go to the bathroom. He passed two pizza joints, a pancake house. Still, the cop followed. The speed limit went up to forty-five. Skeeter picked up speed. The good thing was, the cop hadn't blasted on any red and blue lights.

A lighted sign at a furniture store on his right proclaimed, "Lean on Jesus." Why should God help him now? He hadn't gotten him out of his earlier scrapes. The Chiefland Police car was still back there. Skeeter passed by a motel.

A church sign was lit. "Give the devil an inch and he'll think he's the ruler." If it wasn't for the cop behind him, Skeeter would think that was funny. He remembered as a little boy being taken to a church. He didn't know where or by whom. Those innocent days were long past. If only the copper was as far gone.

If Moose described Skeeter or gave his cell number to the DEA, they couldn't trace his cell phone. It was a prepaid kind. But, what if he kept using it? Maybe they could trace the cell tower, then his location. When he crossed the Suwannee River, he'd pitch the thing out the window and buy a new one. Moose had not seen his truck. It was easy to spot, with oversized tires and confederate flag on the antenna. He'd ditch the flag, too. It might be a magnet for cops.

In his rearview mirror, darkness greeted him. No cop car lights. Where had the policeman gone, home to bed? Maybe the officer radioed ahead to the next town. There was no peace for Skeeter this night.

He could take the back roads, drive through the lower Suwannee National Wildlife Refuge. That part of the Gulf coast was mostly woods, scrub oaks, and wilderness. Swamps were a perfect place for him to hide. Except for the alligators.

Skeeter shivered, but kept going, the only vehicle on Route 19. He had some things to figure out. If Moose knew Nick Tascoda, the same DEA agent who trapped Skeeter before, then maybe Moose was a snitch. Or, was it Crazy Ken from Danbury, the one who introduced him to Moose?

At the outskirts of Perry, Skeeter stopped at a rundown gas station for fuel and more coffee. The cashier looked at him funny. Was his photo already on the news? Wanted: Fifty-something relic with a bloody eye and criminal record as long as your leg. Skeeter pocketed his change.

Finally, he reached the road that would take him along the Gulf coast, through the Florida panhandle, to Apalach. His home was not much, but he owned it. That was one reason he never sold drugs out of the house. No way the feds could seize it. No lights reappeared in his rearview mirror. Had he gotten away with it tonight?

If Agent Tascoda recognized him and suspected Skeeter was a middleman on tonight's failed drug deal, he'd notify Skeeter's PO. Grateful that the blue rag he'd worn had hidden some of the gray hair at his temples and the beard and moustache covered his face, Skeeter knew Moose could only give a vague description.

At dawn, he crested the tall curving bridge entering Apalachicola. Below, he saw the lights on the Dora Ruth, looking forlorn where she was tied up at the dock. The one good thing in his life was being used by another fisherman. Over fifty and never married, if Skeeter kept putting together risky deals, next time he'd go to prison and stay there until he died. No one would care. And he'd never take the Dora Ruth out to sea again.

The last time he went in, Skeeter leased his boat to a shrimper even older than he. Homer was strong, though his nephew worked with the nets. When released, Skeeter discovered a sad truth. Florida shrimping business had been gutted by the Chinese, who raised shrimp on farms and flooded the U.S. markets with cheap shrimp. Apalach shrimpers now supplied Skeeter's customers with live bait. Skeeter had to find some other way to live.

Before turning in his driveway, he drove around the block, and

parked outside the one-stall garage behind his house. Nothing looked
suspicious. Skeeter left a long blade of grass above the top hinge of his
backdoor when he left. It was right where he put it.

When he opened the door, warm air hit him in the face. The sun
was just coming up, and it was hot already. Before turning on the light,
Skeeter listened but heard nothing except the sound of his own breath.
At least, he hoped it was his breath. He flipped on the lights, his eyes
sweeping the scantily furnished living room.

A thirteen-inch television sat on an orange crate next to a chair
with stuffing trailing out thanks to a kitten he rescued when he first
got home. Papers were stacked on a card table and on four metal chairs.
He dropped into the no-longer-overstuffed chair, pulled off his boots.
Never should have gotten mixed up with drugs. Shrimping was his
business, even if profits were down.

"You're a loser, Skeeter. Always have been. When you gonna wise
up?" It was his voice, but it sounded so like his foster father's had when
he sent him to his room lots of years ago. And for what? Not feeding
the dog! Why should he have fed it? The mongrel taunted him every
day after school when he was home alone. Skeeter finally ran away. Not
only from the dog, but from the foster parents and their son. Two years
older and twenty pounds heavier than Skeeter, every inch of that kid
was a bully.

He'd punch Skeeter in the back or trip him on the road on the way
to school. He laughed when he gave Skeeter a black eye. No one did
anything. In the three years they had him, they never bought Skeeter a
new pair of pants. He wore nothing but his foster brother's hand-me-
downs.

Skeeter jumped up from the chair. It was too quiet for memories
that searched, some forty years later, for a foothold. So what if they
once bought him a pair of Keds? A month later, the shoes disappeared.
Skeeter never asked what happened to them. Back then, because he
was a scrawny kid, the law never found him. Not until he got caught
breaking into an old man's garage looking for a place to sleep.

When the law sent him back, and the foster family learned he had
taken money from them, they sent him to detention. No one cared
that all he wanted was to buy a new pair of shoes. The old ones crushed
his toes. When he got out of detention, back he went to the same fosters, and lasted a week. Their dog savaged Skeeter's leg, and he ran away.
This time for good. Bloody leg and all.

In the bathroom, a tiny stall of a room, he lathered his face with shaving cream. It took a while to scrape off the beard and moustache. At the sink, his elbows touched the wall on both sides. He put a bandage over his cut. His face stinging, Skeeter plodded to the kitchen in bare feet and opened a cupboard that held only two plastic plates, some foam cups, and a salt shaker. On the second shelf, behind the plates, was his folder where he kept his release papers, boat title, and a special letter.

From the folder, he smoothed a crumpled paper, and read it again. What a fluke he ever found his sister. His caseworker asked the fosters to give her letter to him, but the foster dad threw it in the trash. Skeeter saw it all from the crack in the kitchen door. He awoke that night and searched in the can till he found the letter, written just for him.

Her writing was beautiful, not stubby like his. She loved him, wanted to see him, she said. Made him think being born wasn't so bad. It had taken weeks to find her street. He bagged groceries, collected scrap steel, which he sold to the junk man to get money for a bus ticket. Finally, Skeeter bought a ticket, and meeting his sister was worth every penny. They lost touch, a long time ago, when he went to prison the first time.

He saw the answering machine light was flashing. Few people had this number. As the kind female voice spoke his name, his heart thumped. "It's Dawn Ahern, your probation officer. On Monday, bring your sales receipts and check register. Don't forget."

Eleanor's letter went back into the folder. When he met his PO, he needed a clear head and heart. But, first, he had a woman to see, and Skeeter hoped Mona Lisa would do him a favor, just this once.

SEVEN

By Friday afternoon, Griff's frantic search for Williams bottomed out. The bartender at the pub remembered serving Frank a couple of beers, but did not know when he left. Griff called Norma Jean at the animal shelter where she worked to see if she heard from him. She was not in. All he got when he called her place in Front Royal was another high-pitched squeal.

Eva's suggestion over cold Chinese food prompted Griff to check if Williams's phone was turned on. He called Bob Rice, security director for the cellular phone company in Phoenix, and left three messages for the guy. Not one had been returned. Because he was searching for a missing agent, instead of using the FBI liaison agent in Phoenix, he made the calls himself. The tricky part was that Griff had to keep secret the reason he was searching for Frank's phone. When he talked to Rice yesterday, he hinted the agent's cell was stolen and Griff was trying to recover it.

He faxed the company a subpoena for records, so legally they were covered. Not expecting to get an answer, Griff punched in the extension. Surprise, surprise. Rice answered. "This is Griff Topping, the FBI agent you spoke with yesterday about the missing cell phone issued to our agent in Phoenix. I left a few messages today."

"Sorry. With the extreme heat here, we have rolling blackouts. I've been in meetings all day. Has it been recovered?"

Griff doodled on a note pad. "No. I thought your office would notify me if the phone was found or used. Since I've not heard anything, I'm checking on the status."

He heard Bob's fingers negotiating a key board. "Wow, this is incredible."

"What?" Griff sat straight up, pen ready.

"Someone has this phone. They placed a call at three o'clock this afternoon, your time. It was routed from one of our towers in Front Royal, Virginia. Is that somewhere near you?"

He knew it! Griff's pulse pounded. Williams was in Front Royal. But, yesterday he'd seen no sign of him at the dog kennel. Mr. and Mrs. McBride told him they had never met Norma Jean's husband. At the time, he found that odd, but dismissed it because Mrs. Williams was strange, preferring dogs to her husband. She probably never went anywhere with him.

Griff kept to the facts. "Can you tell me anything more?" He made notes while, in his ear, Bob's keyboard clattered.

"Whoa, this is interesting. Guess what?"

"Is the phone on right now?"

"Hold on. Yesterday, at roughly the same time, a call routed from that same tower. It lasted for fifteen minutes."

Griff wrote fast, his mind calculating even faster. "Do your records show what phone number was called?"

The key strokes continued. "Each went to an international number."

Griff interrupted with the obvious, "Where?"

"Russia." He paused. "This is embarrassing. We should have notified you when the first call was made. I thought I set the system to alert me."

Before Griff could shout, "Yeah, you fouled me up. I wasted my time there yesterday," Rice continued, "Here's what I'll do. Give me your e-mail address. I'll send the data. You'll have better luck identifying the called number in Russia. I'll establish a clone in my system for the missing Phoenix cell phone. Every time it makes an outgoing call, I will be alerted and call you, tell you what tower it's on."

Ready to jet back to Front Royal, Griff needed to know where to look. "If we activate it, will the missing phone tell the tower of its exact location?"

"It's possible only if the phone is in your possession, and it isn't."

That was a problem Griff could not overcome. He gave Bob his e-mail address and, in seconds, Bob told him he could go online and retrieve the data. Griff hung up, checked his watch. Two minutes to five. With Frank's past work with the Soviets, he could know anyone in Russia. By Monday morning, Griff had to track it down. In Russia, it was Friday night. But, even if he found the person in Russia, could they or would they lead him to Frank?

He called a buddy in the counterintelligence section, hoping he had not left for the weekend. Was a miracle too much to ask? Yup, it was. Griff was on his own, once again.

Unlike Griff, Dwight managed to put the missing agent from his mind. Out for a spin in his eighteen-foot bow rider, named Arbiter, he was showing Bernie and Rita some of Smith Mountain Lake. Nestled in the Blue Ridge Mountains in southwest Virginia, it boasted 500 miles of shoreline. At their retreat, Dwight felt far enough away to put his courtroom and Washington politics behind him for a couple of days.

For a Friday afternoon, the twenty-thousand-acre body of water was calm, except for an occasional wake from a pontoon or ski boat. Tomorrow would begin the rush of folks coming for next week. Tall trees reflected along the lakefront, and idling boats caught relief from the heat of the sun in the deepest shadows. To avoid the heat, Christine stayed at the chalet, marinating swordfish kabobs for the grill. She urged *him* to take their guests for a ride without her.

Dwight wished he hadn't complied. In shorts and white tee shirt, he felt clammy. He pointed out newer homes for sale. Because they liked to golf, Bernie and Rita had bought a cottage at Myrtle Beach. So, he wondered, why did they want to move here, now?

Dressed in a peach sleeveless top and white shorts, Rita fanned herself with a magazine, a bored look on her face. With large hazel eyes and reddish hair, she was a smart-looking woman. Not as pretty as Christine. Her hair had no gray, and Dwight wondered if she colored it. Bernie gaped at a large, three-story brick home for sale.

Dwight slowed the Arbiter, christened by his daughters when he bought it. "You are looking at one million, at least. The owner is German."

The cost didn't faze Bernie. "Rita, the deck is fabulous. We could really entertain there." He reached across the seat, patted her hand. "Should we contact the realtor and see it?"

Dwight motored in twenty feet. With little rain, the water was shallow here, so he was careful not to get too close. Because the lake generated electric power, it rose and fell a few feet every day.

Rita lifted up designer sunglasses. "We do not need such a big place for the two of us."

"Honey, it's perfect. I want to see it. Once she's married, Linda will come."

Rita slid her glasses back down over her eyes. Her tone was caustic, "No. I like Myrtle Beach."

To break the tension, Dwight motioned Bernie to sit. "I'm going to kick it up a notch."

He throttled the inboard engine and the nose rose in the air. Rita gasped. Within a minute, Dwight leveled out his boat and planed at twenty-five miles an hour. Bernie took a seat in the bow, and wind whipped strands of his blond hair. As the swift air moved across Dwight's face, he felt cooler, more calm. His parents raised him to avoid public disagreements. He passed this credo to Christine, and they spoke of sensitive matters away from friends and family.

Minutes later, Dwight snuggled the Arbiter next to the floating dock. Rita scrambled out and hurried across it, leaving Bernie to help Dwight secure the boat with nylon ropes. "Later, you and I will catch some bass. This lake holds the state record for striped bass, a fifty-three pounder."

"I don't like to fish, but I like your idea. Since Linda got engaged, Rita is frazzled."

Dwight clapped Bernie on the back. "Buddy, I hear you loud and clear. In my sweet spot, last time I caught and released ten good-sized fish."

On the way back to the chalet, he talked of the graphite rod and special lure he'd let Bernie use. Inside, Rita was nowhere to be seen. Taking a shower, he supposed, when he heard the water running. Bernie went upstairs without a word.

In the remodeled kitchen, Christine was washing celery. It had been Christine's idea to replace the chalet's rough-hewn pine cupboards with white designer cabinets. His wife's blond hair hung loose, framing her face. She looked up at him and smiled. "I got tickets for the tour."

Dwight rubbed her neck. "Christy, I promised to take Bernie fishing."

Christine turned to face him. Her blue eyes, a shade darker than chipped ice, were pleading. "Using my pet name won't help. When I told her about the charity, Rita wanted to go."

Each year, families in the larger homes on the lake hosted a tour. Dwight gave a little shrug. So much for putting the Jones case out of his mind with a little bass fishing. He was going to spend the rest of his afternoon looking at other people's homes.

Dinner was hectic. Veronica arrived without Stuart, who stayed in town to work. Mandy was dropped off by Chad, who drove back to his folks' summer place by the dam. Then Bernie's daughter Linda arrived with her new fiancé, Winston Ebbott, the grandson of the founding partner of Ebbott and Longstreet. Good thing Christine had prepared enough food for an army.

Dwight put the swordfish on the table, and Stuart called from the office, where he was preparing for depositions on Monday. He'd join Veronica in the morning. She ate quietly and went upstairs to lie down. Dwight hoped she was all right, but had no chance to ask.

Chad returned to take Mandy back to his folks' house to show off her glittering diamond ring. Linda and her boyfriend tagged along. When they drove off in Chad's red Mazda, way too fast, Dwight brooded. With the stir over Mandy's wedding plans, Christine simply pecked Veronica on the cheek when she'd arrived, said nothing about the expected twins, and pored over pictures of wedding dresses with Mandy, Rita and Linda. Veronica sat quietly, looking on with a wan smile.

As it turned out, once the charity home tour and dinner were over, Christine had more plans. She was not one to sit and do nothing. Tall glasses of strawberry lemonade by their sides, the four of them played Scrabble. When Veronica and Mandy were young, they had played it as a family. Too many years had passed; Dwight's strategy was rusty. But, he gamely went along, silver reading glasses on the edge of his nose. Seven wooden letters spread in front of him, Dwight made a mental note to talk to Christine about her ignoring Veronica.

His wife started the game with BRIDE, for a double word score and sixteen points. He never let Bernie know his personal problems. The only person he felt comfortable sharing personal things with was Louis Sumner. Louis said only the best about people, and Dwight enjoyed that about him. Bernie was loose-lipped.

Bernie picked up a tile. "Christine, you were a beautiful bride."

"I was thinking of Mandy. Play your word."

Her clipped Austrian accent was more pronounced than usual, which happened when she got nervous. Dwight was used to her accent, but when she appeared on television news programs to talk about issues facing families around the country, she got e-mails asking where she was from. Was she worrying about Mandy's wedding or something else?

Bernie played off Christine's word to make BEAUTY, the A on a triple letter score. "How lucky was it that we got to tour the red brick home, the same one Dwight showed us from the boat? Rita, I liked the view. Did you?"

Rita shrugged, then zoomed into the lead with JUG.

"Way to go, Rita." Dwight scrutinized his options, repeatedly moved his letters.

In another minute, Bernie interrupted the quiet. "Do you want to declare a recess, so you can consult a dictionary?"

Dwight squinted at the board and rearranged his letters. "Bear with me. Your wife has presented me with a gift and I don't want to waste it." He picked up his first letter and smiled slyly at his friend. "It's not too late to quit, rather than suffer defeat."

Dwight then used all seven letters to tag onto Rita's word with JUGGERNAUT. "Thirty-eight points. Plus a 50-point bonus for using all my letters."

Rita's mouth popped open. "Wow!"

Bernie drank some lemonade. "Juggernaut—anything that elicits destructive devotion. What did you have in mind, the law or religion?"

Christine studied the board. "What do you have against religion? Judge Sumner is a Christian and is wonderful to be around."

Bernie focused his good eye on Christine. "Most are hypocrites, like my neighbor. He's always asking us to give money for their church, isn't he, Rita?"

Bernie's wife simply nodded, a bored look on her face. Christine always told Dwight, if she ever cut her hair, she'd style it like Rita's, in a wedge cut. He asked her not to; he loved her hair the way it was.

Bernie drew his chair away from the table, stretched his legs. "My neighbor borrowed my lawnmower because his was broken. The next time I started it, it rocked back and forth like it was doing the hula-hoop. I shut it off, looked underneath. It had half a blade. He must have hit a rock and broke it off. Why didn't he tell me?"

Without waiting, Bernie answered his own question. "He's a hypocrite, that's why."

Dwight had no interest in unearthing Bernie's prejudices. His friend had been on a crank since Thursday lunch. Probably still thought Dwight showed him up in front of his client at that bond hearing. Dwight put Bernie through his paces, made him answer why a man accused of dealing drugs should be out on bond, but no more zealously than he would any other lawyer who appeared before him.

Christine looked cute studying the game board. Before she played her word, Veronica came into the room, a cell phone in hand.

"It's long distance." Veronica scrunched up her thin face, causing freckles to dance on her cheeks and nose.

Dwight hadn't heard it ring because he left the cell upstairs on his dresser. When Christine didn't look up, Dwight took the phone. "Sorry it woke you."

"I wasn't sleeping. I was online on your computer upstairs."

He walked outside for some fresh air and was surprised the call came from Austria. It was not good news, but there was not much he or Christine could do about it right now. When he rejoined the group, Veronica was in his chair, watching the game. He spoke in her ear, "Better go off line, in case someone else tries to call."

She mouthed, "Oops," then slipped out of the room.

Some new words were on the board. Christine informed him, "I got five points for NOD and Bernie twenty-four for VANITY."

He was thankful no one asked who called. The news he received would put a damper on the festivities. Rita drew four letters, built the word DECEIVES. "Triple word. I get forty-five points, plus I used all my letters, too, Dwight!" She squealed, then sat back, a pensive look on her face.

Dwight did some quick math. He needed thirty points to jump ahead, but Rita acted like she needed to win. He put one letter on the board for only three points. In the next round, Christine took the hint, played off his AD to form ADD, using a blank tile.

With no chance of winning, Bernie built the word ENSNARE. Rita drew her tiles from the dwindling stack. When she did not play her word right away, Christine drank the rest of her lemonade. "After this round, we'll have dessert. Black Forest Cake. My grandmother in Austria handed down the recipe."

Bernie scowled at his wife. "Rita, we're waiting." Then, turning a smile on his hostess, he asked, "How are your folks, Christine?"

"Getting older. We hope to fly there once Dwight's trial schedule eases."

Dwight's eyes swept over Christine's face, adoring it even with pinched mouth and sad blue eyes. He vowed to take her to see her parents soon. It had been two years, and they weren't getting any younger—as the phone call minutes before had revealed.

Rita snapped down four tiles. "FALSE is my word." She looked up triumphantly. "Double word score for sixteen points."

By this point, Dwight just wanted to end the game. He spelled out TOT, and declared, "Rita Spitzer is the winner."

Christine smiled at him. "That has a nice ring. Fun game."

He supposed so. As Dwight moved to follow Christine to the kitchen, so did his thoughts leap from the game to the Jones case, to what Monday would bring. At summer's end, he would remember this day and wonder how he missed such a big clue. It was staring him in the face, and he never saw it.

EIGHT

Saturday morning, Dwight awoke at six. For some seconds, he lay motionless. When he heard no voices, he folded back the sheet. Christine's even breathing meant she was asleep. No doubt, their guests were, too. He escaped from bed feeling alive.

For the next hour, Judge Pendergast would be free from the usual suspects who demanded his attention. In the bathroom, he changed into a torn tee shirt and faded shorts—Christine would object to the unworthy clothes if she saw them—and slipped into deck shoes he had owned since they bought the home at Smith Mountain Lake. Dwight crept downstairs, ready to match wits against an elusive opponent.

He turned on the coffee maker to brew a pot for whoever woke up. A man with nothing on his mind but to catch fish before breakfast, he collected the gear from the screened porch and stretched his legs on the forty-foot dock. Yellow light bathed the water in front of his retreat.

Time held no moment for Dwight. Before going to sleep last night, he told Christine about the phone call from her parents' housekeeper. They had been visiting relatives in Argentina and, on their way to the plane for the return trip, Christine's mother sprained her ankle. So, they would not stop and see them in Virginia. Christine was totally surprised that they had planned to visit. She and her parents often failed to communicate. Dwight was glad that he'd given his father-in-law their cell number; at least the housekeeper got through.

One small bass after another struck his bait. Unfazed, he simply released them into the lake. His hopes of beating the state record came to an abrupt end when Veronica called out from the chalet, "Daddy, I made pancakes. Get 'em while they're hot."

After indulging in the outdoors, with a mallard pair for company, he supposed it was time to mix with his family and friends. Dwight reeled in the line, his lips stretched across his face in a smile. He never tired of fishing, no matter how many times he tossed the line in the water and

drew it back empty. Out here, pressures of sorting out winners and los-
ers in civil cases and sending defendants to prison melted away.

As Dwight removed his lure, doubts about the Jones case came roar-
ing back. After the Scrabble game had ended, Louis called to encourage
him, said he prayed for him. Dwight brought the Bible, but with all
Christine's plans, he did not even open it.

"Daddy," Veronica called again.

Dwight picked up his tackle box and saw her on shore waving, her
hair flowing past her shoulders. She held out a mug, which he took.
"Has Stuart arrived?"

"About lunch time."

"Sometimes I feel I'm in a bubble and the whole world is watching.
Waiting for it to burst," Dwight grumbled, "But not when I fish."

Veronica smiled a knowing smile. "Come on Dad, admit it. You
would be lost without the law. What tales of monster fish might we
hear over breakfast?"

If only he could forget the intrigue of trying a Cabinet member's
son. Dwight took a swig of the coffee. The bitter taste nearly made him
choke. "Nothing as exotic as this brew. What happened to the coffee
I made?"

A breeze picked up Veronica's brown hair, blew it off her shoulders.
"Mandy strikes again. A concoction of cinnamon, vanilla, and chai tea
she learned at college. I dumped my cup. But, "she grinned, "knowing
you live on the edge I thought you'd want to try it."

"Good idea." He emptied the cup in the bushes.

Dwight's easy laugh erased the worry line, a deep furrow that spread
from one side of his forehead to the other. He and Veronica were close,
had been ever since she was three and she raced to greet him each
night when he came home from his law practice. She would hug his
legs and squeal, "Love Daddy!" He understood her in ways Christine
didn't want to.

They walked up to the cedar log home, a copy of a chalet Christine
lived in as a small child in the Alps. "After breakfast, want to water-ski
with me and your little sister?"

Veronica shook her head. "At twenty-two, Mandy is not so little.
She's taller than Mom. No skiing for me. I promised Stuart."

Dwight glanced at her out of the corner of his black eyes, well
trained to watch the constant parade of criminal defendants and their
attorneys, as well as federal prosecutors and juries, and keep them all

in line. He silenced internal anxiety over the Native American protestor and saw his daughter's lips were drawn into a little pout. Better not to ask why she had made such a promise. Probably related to her pregnancy.

She sighed. "Stuart wants to look for Civil War antiques."

"I see," was all Dwight said.

He opened the screen door and let her walk past him onto the front porch. Powerful smells of fried bacon greeted him. Dwight set rod and tackle in their usual spot on the porch, then hurried to the breakfast nook, where he found Christine dressed in a white top and yellow capri pants. Her blond hair was swept back by a gold band. She looked wonderful.

He planted a kiss on her cheek, then snatched some bacon from the plate she carried. Dwight savored the sweet-salty meat, cooked how he liked it. His wife did not share his pleasure. She put the bacon on the dining room table. "Your pancakes are cold."

"We're in trouble now, Daddy," Veronica whispered.

Last night, Dwight had forgotten to say anything about Christine's icy attitude to Veronica. "The bass fishing contest is two months away. I was practicing, but no records this morning. Where is everybody?"

Christine set a steaming platter of scrambled eggs and sausage on the antique shaker table. "Start. I don't want these getting cold, too. Bernie took Rita for a drive."

She disappeared once more into the kitchen. It sounded like she did not want to wait for them. He sat, and served up the tempting fare on three plates. Then he thought better of it. "Where is Mandy?"

Veronica squirted catsup on her eggs. "She left with Chad. Early tennis doubles."

Dwight stopped himself from commenting that Chad drove recklessly. He had to find a way to get along with him. He and Mandy were to be married in less than nine weeks. Christine brought three glasses of fresh squeezed orange juice. She sat across from Dwight and handed him his juice. "Chad is perfect for Mandy. He keeps her interest."

His wife had a doctorate in psychology. Dwight ventured on shaky ground when he said, "Wouldn't it be better to finish her Master's degree before she gets married?"

Over the top of her juice glass, Christine favored him with a look from her vivid blue eyes. "You and I didn't finish college before we got married. Let's have a nice breakfast before I leave."

Veronica lifted her head a smidgen, her eyes stayed fixed on her food. "If you're going shopping, I'd like to go, Mom. I need maternity clothes."

Christine smiled. "Not this time. I'm heading to Washington. Another taping at Fox News for a special on school bullies."

Dwight stopped chewing. Christine seemed to always have some new scheme, and she didn't mention this one last night. What was he supposed to fix Bernie and Rita for lunch—his specialty, toast with peanut butter?

She put her hand over his. "The producer called while you were casting for the big one. I tried to postpone, but it airs Sunday night. They want me in the studio, not over the phone."

It sounded reasonable. "Veronica and I will do our best to entertain." Dwight smiled at her. "She's becoming a great cook, like you."

The phone interrupted his praise. Christine answered it. "Hello."

Dwight noticed the singsong melody of her voice. He felt lucky Christine was his wife, even if she did devote too much time to work.

"It's you, Bernie." Her voice deflated like a tire without air. "You did? That's great."

Dwight tried to imagine what he was saying, because his wife's voice held no enthusiasm. "Yes, Dwight is here. I'll put him on."

He took the portable. "What's up?"

Bernie laughed. "Rita and I are putting in an offer on that house we went through last night. We're at the sales agent's office now. I wanted you and Christine to be the first to know."

A piece of bacon stuck in Dwight's throat. He started to cough, gulped some orange juice, which only irritated it more. "Hold on." He fled to the kitchen. From the faucet, he filled a glass with water. After guzzling it, his tickle subsided. He picked up the phone. "Will you sell your place at Myrtle Beach?"

"Called our agent in South Carolina to draw up the paperwork. Just think, we'll be able to do things together. With our daughters both getting married, you can teach me to fish!"

That was what Dwight was afraid of. His retreat, his home away from home, would be a distant memory. Maybe he should call Louis, ask him to pray that the deal would fall through. As soon as he birthed it, he regretted such a selfish thought. Bernie and Rita were their best friends, and they deserved happiness.

"Want to try some casting today?" Dwight held his breath.

"Thanks anyway. We'll wrap up things here and drive home. Rita has a meeting."

Dwight let out his breath. Lobbyists weren't so bad after all. In January, Rita registered as one, after working twelve years as Communications Director, then Chief of Staff, to the Senator from Virginia who was retiring this year. With his wife's new job, Bernie must think they could afford an extravagant home.

Dwight wished him well, then hung up. Veronica and Christine stared. He wagged a finger at his wife. "To coin a phrase I heard minutes ago, your pancakes are getting cold."

He sat and plunged his fork into the scrambled eggs. With Bernie and Rita not coming back, and Christine driving to do her television special, he could get in hours more of fishing before Stuart arrived. Then, there was Sunday morning when he'd go for a really big bass. For the first time in days, maybe weeks, Judge Dwight David Pendergast was happy.

Sunday was Griff's day to sleep in, then run a few miles. Not this time. Instead, he entered I-66 from the Washington Beltway and headed west to Front Royal, again. Yesterday, he went there and returned home, but not with Williams. Strong coffee burned his stomach. He left mostly uneaten his usual eggs and toast. Unanswered questions did not sit any better than the food.

Dressed in jeans, Washington Nationals jersey and shades, Griff pushed the accelerator on the bucar, a Pontiac Grand Prix, to seventy and set the cruise control. I-66 was not crowded, so his mind wandered. He got stuck behind a string of tow vehicles with unusual cargo, dozens of wrecked cars. Fenders banged in, crumpled windshields taped with plastic, all headed for a salvage yard, fate unknown. Like Frank Williams? he wondered.

He passed them easily, put them out of his mind. Another five miles, his cell phone rang. Griff pulled it off his belt—he never used earplugs—and looked at the screen. A 703 number, the local area code for Columbia City. Griff answered.

It was FBI agent Sal Domingo. "Anything new on Williams?"

Griff tapped his brakes to release the cruise control. "You're supposed to be selling junk at Maria's garage sale. She's not going to like you shirking."

Sal lowered his voice. "I'm calling to see if you need me. Get my drift?"

Griff briefly explained about the calls from Front Royal, the dead-end yesterday, and that he was on his way back there. "I called AUSA O'Rourke and brought him up to speed. He thinks that Frank's wife bears watching."

"You need help all right, the kind that can't wait." Sal lowered his voice even more. "Call me back in two minutes."

The line went dead. Griff could not believe Sal was up to something so sneaky, but he called him back anyway.

"Sal here!"

A semi-truck zoomed by at hurricane speed, and pushed Griff's car to edge of the highway. "What are you up to?"

"Hello, Griff. Maria and I are selling stuff in the garage. There are some ladies here now, but I have a feeling it's going to be a prosperous day."

Griff tested his suspicions. "Why did you want me to call you back?"

"Can't you find someone else?"

"Sal, this isn't a good idea. I don't need help."

It was like Sal was not listening to Griff, but was talking for Maria's benefit. "Okay, if you put it that way, Griff. If I was missing, the entire bureau would turn out. It's just that I was looking forward to being with my wife today."

Griff shook his head. "Sal, you shouldn't do this. Maria will hate me because you don't like garage sales."

"You're right. I would be a real slug if I didn't join you and the others. No, Maria understands the importance of finding a missing agent. She'd want everyone to find me."

Since he had not yet passed where Sal lived, Griff reluctantly agreed to pick him up in fifteen minutes. At the Manassas exit, he parked in the commuter lot and waited for Sal. With the windows down, Griff replayed in his mind every lead he had so far.

Someone was using Frank's cell to call Russia from Front Royal, the same place where Frank's wife had a dog breeding operation. That was no coincidence. Even if the agent didn't like dogs and was not at the kennel, Frank had to sleep and eat somewhere. Griff was certain of one thing, until he found out what Frank was up to, he wouldn't ask the local police for help, or put out a bulletin for Frank's white Civic. If the agent was intentionally AWOL, it would cause embarrassment and unwanted publicity for the Bureau.

A loud noise caused Griff to jerk his head. Sal shut off his P-car, a late-eighties Camaro, which sounded like thunder. The FBI agent eased out of the car, shut the door gently. That gesture seemed out of place with the yards of duct tape and bondo that covered Sal's car. No problem leaving that junker at the lot, no one would steal it. Sal locked the door with his key.

In the passenger seat, he held up a sack, then shot Griff a wide smile. With his dark, curly hair and black sunglasses, he looked like he stepped from a TV commercial for fast food. "Maria sent brownies. Thanks, I had to get out. A guy can only stand so many fights over videos and toys."

Griff raised the windows and punched on the air. His foot hit the gas. In seconds, they were back on I-66. "Never been to a garage sale. I give away my old stuff or throw it out."

"Yeah. Frank sure put a wrench in your trial. Whaddaya figure he's up to?"

Griff held out a hand for a brownie. "No breakfast."

Sal pulled out two, gave one to Griff, whose brownie was history in seconds. "When I get my hands on Frank—" Griff shook his head. "I don't know what he's up to. The only thing I can figure is, he got in touch with a former Russian snitch and is working a new case in Phoenix. He used to work a counterintelligence squad on the Soviets."

Should he mention the rumor of Frank and a Russian spy going deep undercover? No one knew whatever happened to the spy. Once Griff got to know Frank, he dismissed it as bureau legend. Today, he let the legend rest.

Sal put the bag of brownies in the back seat. "The Russian mob out west has carved a market in auto theft rings, running dope and white slave trade. Who's Frank calling in Russia?"

Griff looked in the rearview mirror, for the sack. Funny how his mind wanted what it couldn't have. All morning, he was content to work without food, didn't want any, but that brownie set off a chain reaction like the bell did for Pavlov's dog.

He forced his mind back to finding Frank. "Yesterday, I was checking motels in Front Royal, when the cell phone security director called. For the third day in a row, Frank's phone was on again, calling Russia. If we knew to whom, we'd have a better chance of finding him. I drove all over town during the call." He banged the wheel with his hand. "Found no trace."

Sal snapped his fingers. "You were that close and he vanishes. What else?"

Griff wove in and out of traffic, and told Sal most of what he knew. "Norma Jean's partners seemed normal, not fidgety like they're hiding something." He paused, "Or someone."

"Did you look around the place, without a warrant?"

Griff mimicked how eager the couple was to show him around. "They showed me a batch of puppies."

"They're called a litter."

"Since when are you a walking dictionary? The pups had tiny black and white faces." Griff skipped over telling Sal what happened went he went to the far kennel. "All calls to Russia are made around three o'clock. Today, we'll be in Front Royal before then."

"When did Williams quit the Soviet desk?"

Griff was not sure. "After the collapse of the Iron Curtain, the Bureau revamped and Frank no longer worked the Russians."

Sal looked at him. "Want another brownie?"

"Boy, do I."

Sal reached in the back seat, got one for each. "I feel empty inside. Look for a restaurant."

"I drove this route twice since Friday. There's nothing. When we get to town."

Sal wiped his mouth with his hand. "Coffee would taste good. I hate to say it, maybe Frank's old spy got him."

Griff's head snapped to Sal. He had heard the same rumor. "I don't believe it."

"Since Frank quit drinking, he was like a regular guy. Coached his son's soccer team. Who knows what it was like working against the Soviets."

Frank and Norma Jean had issues, but would she purposely try to hurt him or his career? Griff tried to picture what it was like for Frank, alone in Phoenix, and Norma Jean back with her dogs. He was still perplexed by what kind of woman, whose legal name was Marilyn, would insist on being called Norma Jean.

Griff devoured the brownie. "Frank's supervisor said he's working on some case involving Mexican narco-traffickers."

The two agents looked at each other. Griff didn't have to mention Sal's family friend, the DEA agent who was kidnapped and killed in Mexico by a drug cartel. It was years ago, but it was obvious the pain lingered.

Sal shrugged, looked away. "Drug lords are all ruthless killers. They'll do anything to protect their profit. If they're behind Frank's disappearance—"

"This is where we get off. I'll find you coffee, Sal."

Sal was right. Griff should find out more from Frank's supervisor in Phoenix. Drug cartels had long tentacles that reached anywhere in the world, even Virginia. Like terrorism cases, such as the one Griff worked on last year with Eva, drug trafficking led agents to treacherous people. The danger kept Griff from dating. It was too risky to get attached. People you loved died. Then, you were alone.

Griff heard Sal talking. "They have no tail." It was nice to have someone to bounce things off of, but Sal talked like he drove, fast. His call sign on the radio was Speedy.

"How could I put a tail on Frank when I didn't know he would disappear?"

Sal rolled down the window. "I hate air conditioning. Give me a convertible any day. Topping, I said nothing about Frank. I said, Maria's sister took my place at the garage sale. She and her sister are tight," Sal crossed his fingers, "like this. She raises cats with no tails."

"Sal, no dogs, no cats." Everyone was trying to fix him up with a date or an animal. His life was not that pathetic.

"No one said so." Sal reached in the backseat for another brownie and polished it off.

NINE

In Front Royal, the gateway to the Blue Ridge Parkway, the mountains loomed in the distance, a hazy blue. The famous skyline caverns were nearby, but Griff would make Sal check them out while he waited in the car. He refused to don a hardhat with a flashlight and squeeze into some narrow cave looking for Frank.

On his last case with Eva, he learned the hard way that a man his age did not outgrow claustrophobia. When he flew, the Cessna's cabin rarely bothered him. Maybe it was the vast sky around him or the fact that he controlled the plane's movements. A loathing of small spaces was why Griff never pursued an instrument rating. He couldn't stand to be under the hood while learning, or blanketed in by clouds while flying.

Take yesterday. Shirley McBride took him to a far kennel to see a Boston terrier. When he was forced to duck under a walkway with a low hanging ceiling, he broke out in a sweat. He nudged his mind into another gear. "We'll drive around, look for Frank."

Sal leaned out the window, caught the breeze in his hand. "It's odd he got transferred in the middle of the Jones case. The Bureau could have waited until it was over."

That had bothered Griff, mostly because he was stuck with Jones until the jury reached its verdict. "You check the right side of the street for his car."

On Main Street, they passed pedestrians and cars parked along the narrow street, which reminded Griff of the center of London. He ran a yellow light. No police in his mirror. Not yet, anyway. At thirty miles per hour he wound past the gazebo and the visitor's center, scrutinizing every white Honda Civic and any man similar to Frank.

The problem was that Frank wouldn't stand out in a crowd. He wasn't tall. His frame was slight. He combed his hair from the left side over his forehead. One feature popped out at you, one not seen from a distance. Up close, Frank's deepset black eyes were a stark contrast to his sandy-colored hair and brows.

Maybe the Russian spy had got to him. Maybe a drug dealer. But, then again, maybe it was someone whom Griff never met—Frank's informant in the Jones case. He said this to Sal, who agreed. "Some agents get too close to their informant, then run into trouble. It hurts to say it, but the wise guys can be smarter than an FBI agent with a law degree."

By the car wash, Griff slowed. Thought he saw a white car. It was another foreign breed, not a Honda. "Especially an informant who entices a desperate person to go along. Their cunning ways corrupt the sharpest among us, if we're not careful."

"Look!" Sal pointed.

In front of them, a white Honda made a sudden right turn. Griff swerved to the right lane. He accelerated to the intersection, turned the car sharp and fast. A block ahead, they saw it. The Honda turned left. Instantly, Griff copied the turn. Their prey parked in front of a bungalow. Griff eased off the gas, got a good look at the occupant without giving away their presence.

It was a teen-aged boy, holding an athletic bag. He looked innocent enough. Griff was the first to notice the plate didn't match Frank's. It had a Virginia plate, not Arizona. Undeterred, Griff went around the block and got back onto Main Street.

Sal hung his arm out, like they were on a Sunday drive. "Is Jones a good case?"

Griff drove and talked, while keeping an eye out for Williams or his car. "I would not have developed it. A typical sting, some casino operator got in trouble. Claimed he could help the government catch Mr. Big, if his own case went away, which it did. He's been kept out of the reports and the trial."

"Did you meet him?"

"No. Since he's not testifying, I won't. The Native American operator defrauded the casino of millions of dollars. When Frank confronted him, the man claimed to be involved with a syndicate that was using the Interior Secretary's son to get federal approvals for the tribes from his old man. All to build more casinos. The Indians are protesting in Pendergast's courtroom, but they'll never know that the man behind Jones is an Indian himself."

Sal peered at Griff. "Can we get some coffee? I'm parched."

This part of Virginia, with the mountains nearby, attracted scores of tourists, and the mild summer days tempted visitors as far away as

Wisconsin. It seemed every fourth automobile was a white sedan but, so far, they spotted none with Arizona plates.

Sal pointed to a restaurant shaped like a giant chicken. "We could get wings."

"Nah. I need something filling."

They passed a low-slung silver car. Sal whistled. "You don't see many of those."

"We seized a DeLorean once. It's a casket on wheels."

Sal rubbed his cheek. "I forgot to shave. Hope your Jones case is not another DeLorean."

Griff thumped Sal's shoulder. "I don't like you saying it's mine. But, I guess if it sinks, so do I. The Bureau got such flack after DeLorean was acquitted."

It had been years since the automobile genius, John DeLorean, found himself in dire financial straights. Griff thought the jurors voted to acquit DeLorean because they believed the government enticed a man with no prior criminal experience. Now, the FBI had stricter guidelines for "sting operations."

Griff told Sal more about what Frank told him when he inherited the Jones case. "The informant alleged the Secretary of Interior was involved in other criminal activity, just was never caught, so Frank convinced our boss that Secretary Jones accepted money for tribal designations in the past. Only, before Frank got proof on the father, the son put his car and house up for sale. Concerned he was spooked, the agents arrested him before he fled the country."

Sal's face wore a grimace. "Sounds like the arrest went down too soon."

Griff turned the corner. "That's what I think."

Sal shouted and pointed, "There!"

Griff whipped his head to the right. "Where? I don't see a white Honda."

Sal showed a lot of white teeth when he grinned. "Not Frank. Coffee shop."

They were on the Queen's Highway, near Rt. 522. A sign in front, designed like a fish, proclaimed "HeBrews." It boasted an internet cafe, fresh-ground coffee and wireless connections.

They got out of the bucar, and Griff locked it with the remote. Inside, Sal found the washroom, while Griff scoured the menu, written in white chalk on a board with the words above it, "Beat the daily grind with our brew."

The types of coffees and sizes were endless. Espresso, cappuccino, grande latte. A young man with a buzz cut and a navy blue shirt with the fish logo stepped to the counter. "Decided, sir?"

Griff was impressed by his efficient demeanor, one of a college student about to go back to school. "Large coffee, two creams. Got any sandwiches made up to go?"

Sal returned. "How about a Philly cheese steak?"

"We have tuna on whole wheat pita, or turkey and mozzarella on foccacia bread."

Foccacia sounded more like a foreign car than something to eat. Griff asked what it was.

The young man put one hand on top of the other, palms together. "Like a flat pancake, but thicker. It's packed with sun-dried tomatoes and oregano. If you want my opinion, I'd get that."

This wasn't Griff's kind of place, but his stomach demanded satisfaction. "Ham and cheese?"

"We don't carry that, sir."

"Give me the turkey on the French bread."

Sal chimed, "I'll have the same as him."

"Foccacia," the clerk corrected.

Griff slid a credit card from between the fold in his wallet. "Are you in college?"

The kid pulled two sandwiches from the refrigerated case. "I am starting as a cadet at Virginia Military Institute."

Griff thought that fit. "Want a career in the military?"

He handed them two large foam cups with raised lids, and their sandwiches. "That or a Secret Service Agent, like my brother."

Griff paid with his credit card, then stirred two creams into the steaming liquid. He snapped on a lid. Sal drank his black. Griff caught the young man's eye. "Both choices would be good careers."

"I prayed about which direction to take. So far I've not received an answer."

Did the kid think someone was going to answer his prayers? As a child, Griff watched the Wizard of Oz movie and was horrified to discover the wizard was an old man behind a curtain blasting thunder and lightning on a control panel.

He balanced his sandwich on top of his coffee. "Good luck in school."

Sal popped off his lid, threw it away. "Kid, you keep praying. God is listening."

Griff raised an eyebrow. He and Sal never talked religion. The door locks deactivated, he slid behind the wheel, then secured his coffee in the cup holder and sandwich on his lap. Before Sal closed his door, Griff looked up and saw a white Honda Civic in the mirror.

"Get in," he hissed. "It's too far away to see the driver."

Sal slammed the door. Griff started the car. The Honda passed. It wasn't Frank. A young woman was driving, her hair drawn into a thick ponytail. Another car was close behind the Honda, too close for him to see the license plates. Murphy's Law, again.

Griff pulled onto Queen's Highway without buckling his seat belt. Could this be the break he had spent days looking for? He'd have to wait for the answer. Two cars now separated him from the Honda.

Sal strained forward against his seat belt. "I see her." He pointed ahead. "Don't get stopped at the light. It's turning yellow."

"Right." Griff edged the nose of the Grand Prix behind an old man in a luxury sedan, and tailgated his bumper through the light. Small towns had an advantage when it came to surveillance. There was less opportunity for Griff to get lost. But, Front Royal had plenty of twisting and turning roads. Griff tried to keep up without getting caught speeding. Half a mile later, the Civic turned into a supermarket parking lot.

Griff turned down the side street, when the woman made a surprise move. She pulled forward, then backed the car against a wooden fence that surrounded a dumpster.

Sal snickered. "Clever. Hides the only plate from view. If that car was from Virginia, it would have a plate on the front. But, there isn't one, so I guess it's an out-of-state plate."

Griff swung into the lot. "Until we see the back plate, we won't know if it's from Arizona." He slowed, which allowed the female driver to walk in front of him. She was slim, about thirty, wore jeans and a Georgetown sweatshirt, which seemed heavy for a warm day. A purse was slung over her shoulder.

Griff could not see if she had a cell phone clipped to her waist. "If we get out, she'll see us. Let's see what she's going to do. We can always split up and follow her."

When she walked to the stall, and pulled out a grocery cart, Griff decided this was a good time to eat. He backed into the spot across from the Civic. Close to the main street, he and Sal could see passing traffic, as well as any coming into the entrance.

The windows down, motor off, Griff got comfortable. He took two bites of the sandwich, then set it on the wrapper. "I thought so."

Sal looked at him. A piece of cheese hung from the corner of his mouth. "What?" The cheese fell onto his leg. Sal threw it out the window.

Griff took another bite, followed it with coffee. "A fancy name and higher price doesn't make the sandwich. It's still a high-priced turkey sandwich."

"Yeah, a stale turkey sandwich. Coffee's good, though."

They finished their meal in silence, while Griff figured how to see that license plate. "Watch for Ms. Ponytail. I'll be back." He strolled outside, as if heading into the store. By the Civic, he pulled out his cell phone to talk to an imaginary caller, but gaped behind the car. The plate was not visible. Griff walked around the car, looked it over. Then in plain sight, he saw it!

He rushed back to tell Sal, who had unfastened his seat belt. "Two white sedans passed. None looked like a Honda Civic."

Griff crouched by Sal's window. "That's because Franks' car is parked right there, driven by the woman inside."

"You saw the plate?"

Griff shook his head. "Nope. Remember the black holsters we were issued for our Glock, the ones like fanny packs? There's one in the back seat. That car has to be Frank's."

Back in Apalachicola, Skeeter was on a mission to help himself. He pulled off his shades, looped them over the shirt neck, and strolled into the Outrigger Grill after the Sunday brunch. Dark inside, it took a minute for his eyes to adjust. Smells of potatoes frying, meat grilling met his nose. The musty aroma and getting closer to Mona Lisa were things he thought of when he lived behind bars. That and being out on the Gulf on the Dora Ruth.

Today, after he talked to Mona Lisa, he was going to find Homer. White Christmas lights glittered around the bar, the mirror. Where was his friend? Strange to think of Christmas—it was almost the end of July. He missed last Christmas in the joint.

Because Skeeter had given the feds info about a big-time drug dealer, DEA Agent Nick Tascoda went back to the judge under a special rule and got his time slashed. Not his "on paper" time, though. He still had two years of being watched by his PO. Elbows on the bar, he sighed. Twenty-three months to go. At his age that not only seemed like a lifetime, it was.

If Tascoda saw him run away from Moose's the other night, he'd try to get him sent back to prison. Skeeter would do anything to stay out. Anything. Mona Lisa scurried out of the kitchen. He touched her arm, but she shrugged him off. He tried again. "I hafta talk."

She nodded, pointed to a table in the corner. "Family reunion from all over Florida."

Skeeter watched her drain beer into tall glasses and take them to the table. They were attacking a pile of peel-n-eat shrimp. That was good, but he still had to get her attention. He liked the food here, so did a lot of other people—and not just locals. Since he came back home, he saw more tourists eating at his favorite spot.

A man with long sideburns, who Skeeter recognized as the owner of a used car lot, sat nursing a beer. Skeeter felt a tap-tap on his forearm. He jolted, ready to run if he saw Moose's ugly face staring at him. He turned slightly. It was the town councilman, a friend of Mona Lisa's. In his fingers, he held a ten-dollar bill. Why was he giving Skeeter money? Had he forgotten a bet on football? He'd use it for a soda and Buffalo wings. Skeeter loved them hot and spicy.

As usual, the money wasn't for him. "Put the money in the jar for me. I can't reach it."

Skeeter took the ten—it felt good in his hands—and forced himself to drop it in a half-gallon mayonnaise jar sitting on the bar. "What's it for?"

The councilman pointed. "See her picture?" A photo of a pretty young girl, sitting on a pony. "Read the note." The girl, whose name was Becky, needed a heart transplant. Skeeter gazed at the written plea for donations.

Another tap. Mona Lisa glared at him. "It's about time. You've been scarce."

It was easy to lie to her. "I was lookin' for work." This was true, but he didn't mention it was the kind of work that could send him away again. "Honest, Mona Lisa."

She slapped him on the chest. "Quit calling me that. My name is Lisa."

"Okay, okay. I see my PO on Monday. She's gonna call you to verify the paintin' I did at your house." Skeeter treated her with a wink, like the one that got her to cover for him before. "I think you paid me five hundred dollars."

Although Lisa threatened, she was done lying for him, he knew she always would. Skeeter nodded at the mayonnaise jar. "How about we put a jar out for ol' Skeeter? He's got lots of needs."

Lisa leaned both elbows on the counter, blond hair swirled over rounded shoulders. Her face got so close to Skeeter's, he felt the warmth of her breath. "How about we take care of Becky and Skeeter gets out there and starts busting his hump? Becky will die if she doesn't get help."

Skeeter looked at the girl's face. She seemed too young to die. "You're kiddin'. Where's she gonna get a heart anyway?"

Lisa's hands moved to hips, covered with an orange apron. "Her mother works at the drug store and eats lunch here. They're hoping someone who dies unexpectedly is a registered organ donor. The money is for Becky's heart transplant. The expenses are huge."

Skeeter jumped off the stool. "Don't forget when my PO calls." He winked at her again. "What time ya off tonight?"

Lisa wiped the bar. "Midnight. But, I'm free tomorrow."

"Pick you up after I go to Panama City, take you for a burger and a shake. Sound okay?" Lisa packed away the fries and her frame showed it. She was a good gal though, didn't stiff him.

A phone rang behind the bar. Lisa flicked her blond curls at him and answered it. Skeeter left the Outrigger with old plans in place and a new one hatching in his brain.

TEN

Barbara Jo Houston had given their cook the weekend off. Though she invited Arnie for dinner on Friday, he called at the last minute to cancel. Said the Senator gave him an urgent assignment. She had not heard from him since, so on Saturday she shopped for a new suit and matching shoes. Today, she had her nails done, got her hair trimmed, and felt ready to face another day at the White House.

In an oversized jersey and spandex shorts, Barbara Jo made a light snack before spending an hour on the stair-stepper. She was mashing an avocado on toast when someone knocked at the door. Not expecting anyone—her father and his wife would not return for weeks—she trotted in tennis shoes to the front entryway and peeked through the curtain on the narrow window by the door frame. Barbara Jo yanked open the door.

Arnie held out flowers. "My peace offering. Senator Zorn has me running circles."

Barbara Jo put the rosebuds to her nose, but there was no fragrance. "Thanks." She set them on the hall table. "You could have called."

Arnie closed the door. "I'm here now. Don't worry, you look great."

She stared down at her gray outfit. Her hair was not brushed and she wore no lipstick. "I was going to work out."

"All right, I won't stay long. Where is it?"

Barbara Jo's mind rewound to their conversation on Friday. She sighed. He came to look at the file. No joy in her step, she walked through the dining room, to the living room where Ming vases rested on teak tables, and a stained glass window from an old church in Italy hung above a sofa from England. Her father's famous collections meant nothing to her.

She moved a picture, which actually hid a safe, and dialed in the combination. A little gray door opened, and she slid out the private file of Judge Nolan Cuttering. She gave it to Arnie, who rifled through it.

Barbara Jo sat on the sofa. "Aren't you worried you'll get finger-prints on it?"

Arnie jerked back his hand as if hot steam rose from the file. "You turn the pages."

She took it back, and he sat alongside her, looking at every page as she revealed it. At the end, Arnie stood up nervously. "There's nothing in there we don't already know. There must be another file where the White House secrets the private stuff."

"Not that I know of."

Arnie strode purposefully to the door. "I'm on my way to Capitol Hill. The hearings start Tuesday. I've got to be on the top of my game." At the door, his voice softened. "Barbara Jo, do you think you could look around for another file? This is most important for my career."

He reached out and held her close, her face against his strong chest. In his arms, troubles melted away. She looked up into his brilliant green eyes, which danced with happiness. He smiled at her. She had so hoped this weekend he would ask her to marry him. Maybe once this dreadful confirmation hearing was over, he could be himself again. Of course, she would help him.

Sunday afternoon, Dwight was dropped off at home in Great Falls by Veronica. He threw his keys on the kitchen counter. "Hon, I'm home." Christine did not answer. He took the stairs two at a time, found her asleep on the bed, hair spread out like a beautiful sunflower. His wife's steady breathing meant she had not heard him come in. Flushed cheeks explained why she failed to pick up the phone when he called on the way.

The joy he felt being near Christine was different from the thrill of catching a striped bass. He had missed her. It was warm in their bed-room. About to leave to turn up the air conditioning, Dwight noticed a sheet of light blue paper in her hand. With bridal magazines spread over the bed, it might be wedding invitations. Yet, the way she gripped it made him look twice. It was impossible to pull it from her hand without waking her.

Dwight tiptoed from the room, closed the French door behind him, hoping it wasn't more bad news about her mother's ankle. On the way downstairs to make supper, he passed Mandy's bedroom and heard crying. He knocked on the door softly. "Mandy, it's Dad. Are you all right?"

Mandy opened the door a crack. Red eyes and blotchy face were telltale signs she'd been sobbing for a while. His youngest daughter, who looked like Christine, with the same blue eyes and blond hair, had her maternal grandmother's temperament. She never owned up to feelings, bottled them up for years. If he asked her outright, Mandy would say nothing was wrong.

"Mom's resting. I'm rustling up burgers for the grill. Keep me company?" He purposely did not ask her to help him. She didn't share her mother's or sister's love of cooking.

Mandy swiped a tissue across her nose. "I guess so."

She closed the bedroom door and followed him to the kitchen, where she plopped on a stool. He searched the fridge for hamburger. Instead, he found a package of loin steaks that Christine must have bought for dinner. He could handle steaks. "Know where Mom keeps the potatoes?"

Without a word, Mandy went to a bottom cupboard and pointed. "Mom pokes them with a fork, zaps 'em in the microwave."

"Would you do that while I season the steaks?"

Mandy grabbed a handful and washed them under the faucet. She was about to stab them with a fork, when she choked back a sob. Dwight hated to see his daughter suffer. Even if she told him to mind his own business, he had to ask.

He set down the pepper mill. "What's wrong? The last I saw, you and Chad were headed over to see his parents at the lake."

She held up the fork. "See this? That's how Chad's folks treated me."

Dwight didn't see the connection. He remained quiet.

"I thought they liked me." Her voice grew hard. "Instead, they stabbed me in the back."

"They did what?"

Mandy poked a potato with a fury. "The whole time they made snotty remarks."

"Be careful with that fork. You'll get your hand. What did they say?"

"Dad, it was humiliating. I can't remember their exact words, but it was like, Chad and I should wait to get married."

She blinked and tears cascaded down her face. Dwight took the fork from her hands, set it on the counter, and wrapped an arm around her shoulder. "Would that be so bad?"

Mandy's head slumped on his shoulder. "You and Mom didn't wait to graduate."

"Things were different then. There was the war." That sounded lame even to his ears. Dwight sighed. "Did Chad agree with his parents? Is that why you're upset?"

His daughter lifted her head and gave him a look that betrayed how hurt she felt. "Chad said I should grow up and stop thinking of myself all the time. Other people count, too."

Maybe Chad's taking his parents' side was the real reason behind his daughter's misery. Like finding a firm spot to stand on in a trout stream, he chose his words carefully, "Have you asked Chad what he wants?"

Mandy picked up the fork, punctured a new potato. "He wouldn't listen. Chad is—"

Dwight wanted to blurt out, "Immature!" but held his thoughts. He peppered the steaks, and waited to hear Mandy's impression of her husband-to-be. Instead of words pouring from her lips, they quivered. Tears flooded her eyes and ran down her cheeks.

At a time like this, what should a father do, tell her to wake up her mother? That was not fair to Christine. Dwight washed his hands. Chad was too young to be responsible for a wife. If he said that out loud, Mandy would dig in her heels, insist on marrying him.

There was only one thing to say. "You and Chad need to talk about it. In over thirty years of marriage, your mother and I learned we have to confide our concerns as well as dreams."

His daughter pulled away, went back to stabbing a potato with the fork. Dwight wondered if this had anything to do with the letter in Christine's hand "Why not call Chad, ask him if he wants to wait?"

Mandy's strong look startled him. It was so like Christine's when she had made up her mind. She shook her head. "Give him a chance to back out? No way. I already bought my dress."

Dwight opened the patio door to start the grill, gripped with a sense that Mandy was making a huge mistake. If only he and Christine could talk about it, but that might violate Mandy's privacy. He'd see if Christine mentioned it, or the letter clutched in her hand.

Back in Front Royal, Griff and Sal were in Griff's car waiting for the woman to come out of the grocery store. Sal gripped the door handle. "Mind if I look in the store?" Then, he drew back. "Don't look. Williams' friend is beating it to her car, pushing a cart of groceries."

Griff watched her transfer some prepared food containers and three twelve-packs of beer into the rear seat of the white Honda. He raised his eyebrows. "She's having a party."

Sal put his empty coffee cup in the holder. "Or has a major sub-stance problem."

The woman got behind the wheel. Griff was impatient to see the license plate, but hope quickly faded. Rather than start her engine, she unfolded her cell phone and placed a call. He and Sal watched her talk on the phone. Neither could read her lips. She was too far away.

Two minutes later, Griff's cell rang, a private caller. Was it Williams? He answered warily. "Hello."

"Agent Topping, it's Bob Rice. If you want your lost cell phone, it's active right now."

"From where?" Griff turned to Sal and whispered, "Frank's phone is on again."

Could they get there in time? If the Honda Civic across from them was a goose-hunt, he'd be angry. Rice said something, which sounded like static. Griff yelled, "Say again, Bob."

This time, Bob's voice boomed. "The same as before. Front Royal."

A jolt of excitement shot through Griff. "We're in Front Royal now!"

Bob Rice told him he would monitor the signal. "If it moves to another tower, I'll call you immediately so you can detect which direc-tion the person is moving. Previously, the signal never left the Front Royal tower. I'll call back if the call ends."

Griff didn't want to lose contact with Rice, but the security director would need his phone line open. Besides, Griff might need to make a call. To be safe, he gave Bob Rice the number to Sal's cell.

Rice's signal was stronger now. "I'll keep you posted."

Griff's eyes swept the parking lot, then the street. Even if he left the white Civic, he had no clear evidence of where the call was coming from or going to. Then it hit him. He should have asked Rice where the call was going. Rice hadn't mentioned it was Russia. As fast as fire-works, a thought burst into his mind—that beer-loving woman was using Frank's phone.

Maybe he'd sent her to buy the beer. Marilyn Williams, or Norma Jean, or whatever her name was, said her husband was on a drinking binge. Griff blew out his breath and stroked his moustache.

Sal pointed to Ms. Ponytail. "Look at her laugh. If Frank's hiding in Front Royal, and trashing your case, I'll nail him."

Griff's mind ran through the options. He willed his eyes to find something he could go on. "We've got to see that tag. Frank probably told her to back in, obscure the plate. Where else would she get that idea?" Griff started the car, buckled his belt. "Yours, too, Sal." He wanted to be ready when she drove away. "I say she's on her cell, talking to Williams, who is at their hideaway, talking on his cell to her."

While he and Sal downed dry sandwiches, Williams was planning a party. It was too much. But, he had a lot invested to give up now. The Civic jerked from its spot, veered to the side street. One thing went their way. She had to wait for traffic to clear.

Griff angled his head, peered out the open window. "Can you see the plate?"

Sal turned his head. "No." Griff whipped the car, did a ninety-degree turn and pulled in behind her. The license number leapt off the plate. His blood pressure soared. Ms. Ponytail was driving Frank's car.

"Okay, Sal. We'll find Williams, give him a piece of our minds."

Inwardly, Griff went ballistic. For an FBI agent, Frank had a lot of nerve not showing up at court. Blowing off a federal judge took guts. So what if he got transferred to Arizona? Agents did all the time, and dealt with it. Griff was angry. Frank risked Jones being acquitted, all because he wanted to party and get revenge on his wife for choosing dogs over him.

The Honda turned west out of the lot. Griff got caught waiting for an oncoming car, which put a buffer between him and the woman. That was okay, it kept her from seeing him in her rearview mirror. Let Frank be surprised. Through the car in front of him, Griff saw the Civic wheel south onto route 522. The buffer car shot through the light.

Sal jammed his foot to the floor, like that would make the car go faster. "We're losing her. Why hasn't the cell guy called? She's off the phone."

Traffic cleared. Griff made the south turn. "Act normal, okay?" His mind was tracking that car, and had no time to answer Sal's million questions. He fell in about a block behind their prey. To avoid detection, he hoped another car might pull in between them.

Sal slugged Griff's right arm. "If you don't back off, she's gonna spot us."

Griff never knew Sal was such a backseat driver. He slowed, which gave the sedan behind them a reason to pass, and Griff once again had a buffer between him and the Honda.

They left Front Royal proper, passed the light industrial area. According to a highway sign, she was headed toward Chester Gap. She increased her speed to match the limit. The car running interference for them turned on Queens Highway. Griff laid back about half a mile.

Sal peppered him with questions. "Where did Frank meet her? On his Russia gig?"

Griff shrugged. "We're going to have to report this. He's in a load of hurt from the Bureau for all kinds of ethical violations."

Sal opened the glove box and tore through the papers. "I wish we'd left some brownies. I'm starved."

"You just ate. My car is not a rolling canteen, like yours." Griff's right hand itched to punch Frank's nose for being on a lark. But, what if the woman was a former source from within the Russian Embassy, or the wife of a source?

Sal banged the glove box shut. "His career's over. No doubt the Director will transfer him again. This time to Butte, Montana."

Griff drew his lips into a tight line. "They closed the office in Butte."

"Well, to some other remote place. Nome, Alaska."

"Does the Bureau have an office in Nome?"

Sal's laugh sounded like a bad car muffler. "How do I know? Frank can send us a postcard."

Griff didn't even grin. He was sick of the whole case. But, he could not lose Frank's car. Out of the city now, they passed open fields, then paralleled a creek. Ahead, the Honda's stop lights lit up, then disappeared west. Griff sped up until they reached the spot where she turned. Down the gravel road, which was so narrow Griff could see the road didn't go through. It went up over a swollen creek. As the compact car drove up into the foothills, Griff passed the road.

Sal snapped his head. "What's up with that move?"

Griff tapped the brakes, waited a few moments. "In case she's watching from her mirror."

He turned the bucar around, drove slowly west on the gravel road. Years of working undercover taught him to minimize attention to his car and the swirling dust that rose from dirt roads. Griff put up the windows, turned on the air. They meandered on by fields, and Sal talked nonstop. "No sign of her. Think she turned off?"

Griff sighed. The last few months, he'd gotten used to working alone. With no partner, he drove with talk radio on. In a way, Sal was no different from the host behind the golden microphone. Griff tried to tune him out and think what to do if the white car did not appear. How far did this road go? It was getting more desolate, and he wasn't sure where the Civic had gone.

They passed a couple mailboxes, for homes built far off the road, so far that Griff could not see them. Two-tracks, not asphalt drives, snaked their way into pine trees, that overlapped with wide oak trees, that converged with maples. The bottom line? He could not see the car for the trees.

The road ascended over deep ruts. Griff felt the bottom of the bucar lurch. With the Shenandoah National Park all around them, it better not die on him. There were no service stations or wreckers up here. Good thing they had cell phones. He had an idea.

"Sal, check your phone. See if you have a tower."

He snapped it open. "Nope. Let me see yours."

Griff handed it to him. As they climbed higher, Griff hoped the darkening clouds did not mean more rain. A sudden downpour like last night would wash out the road, which was becoming more like a wide path. Now, the road curved.

"Got it! Yours has a cell tower."

Sal's outburst startled Griff and he nearly missed it, nearly drove by a patch of white that snagged the edge of his eyesight. He twisted his head, gazed more closely. There it was, a beautiful white Honda Civic, parked diagonally near a house made entirely of cedar logs.

He let out a low whistle, pointed through the trees. "We got it all right."

Sal ducked to see under heavy branches. "Pretty fancy place Frank is holed up in."

Griff had seen a brochure advertising chalet homes, which were out of his price range, by about four hundred thousand dollars. "Oh, oh." Griff gripped the wheel.

A muscular man with sandy-colored hair stepped off the porch.

Sal's head bobbed. "Definitely not Frank. That guy's got tattoos up both arms."

"I see that, Sal. The question is, who is he?"

Muscle man, seemingly oblivious to Griff's car as it barely crawled past, unloaded beer from the Civic. Griff figured the guy wouldn't ignore them for long and was about to step on it, when a sign in front of the house saved them. With a faded number it advertised, "For Rent."

Griff motored on by, continued up the road where there were no more houses, no open spaces. Just dense woods. It would be hard to turn around.

Sal tapped on the windshield. "Just ahead, on the right. It's like a maintenance road."

A metal chain hung across it. Griff backed into the spot, but couldn't stop what happened next. Eva's warning seared his mind like a flare from his flare gun. What had she said? Dark forest, handcuffs, a gun shot!

He forced her vision or dream or whatever from his mind. He'd seen no gun on the guy. And Griff Topping, FBI agent who tracked terrorists and mobsters, whose grandfather was a decorated Admiral for the British in World War II, had a suspicious nature, but there was no room for mysteries. Eva said she'd pray for his safety. At a time like this, that couldn't hurt.

After several tries, he got the car turned. On the gravel road again, he glanced at Sal. No wonder Eva kept her vision thing to herself. Out here, with his quasi-partner tapping the dashboard with two fingers like he was playing the drums, humming a tune that Griff did not recognize, it seemed surreal. He was glad Eva was like him in one respect. She was a pure professional. She never pushed her faith on him. After their last big case together, she did mention she finally got things straight with God. Good for her.

They came to the cedar home again. White car in place. No one in the yard. Window curtains closed.

Sal's fingers beat on the dash. "We gonna stop, go in? I'm ready to bust his chops."

Sal seemed as eager as Griff to get it over with, but a tension in Griff's gut told him to hang back. He blew out his breath. "Let's try something else first. I don't like Ms. Ponytail's male friend. Do we have a cell tower now?"

Sal picked up the phones from the tray in the middle. "Mine does."

"Punch in the number on the for rent sign."

Back on Route 522, Griff stopped the car by the side of the road and called the number using Sal's cell phone. No answer. Three minutes went by on his watch. Griff tried again and this time a man said, "Hello."

It wasn't that simple word that caused Griff to shudder. It was the way he said it. Before he could think, Griff hung up. He handed the phone back to Sal. "The man who answered the number on the for rent sign has a Russian accent."

In that instant, Griff knew this was more than a drunken binge. Things smelled funny. Griff had honed his techniques in sniffing rats as much as he had his technical know-how. He and Sal needed a plan that would lead them to Frank. One without bloodshed.

ELEVEN

I gnorant of the danger Griff faced while trying to find Frank Williams, Dwight was in his study preparing for Monday. There was really nothing more he could do for the Jones case, so he read a brief Bernie wrote to suppress a statement his drug client, Tyler Cooper, made to a DEA agent. Cooper claimed the agent did not read him his Miranda rights when they came to question him at his accounting office. The government argued the rights weren't necessary because Cooper was not in custody.

The motion was a waste of time, but defense attorneys filed them anyway. If they failed to, they risked malpractice or ineffective-assistance-of-counsel claims. He made a note to his law clerk to schedule a hearing for next week. Let the government put the agent under oath and testify if Cooper was free to order agents out of his office or, at a minimum, not answer their questions. Case law was long settled. Miranda warnings were required only when a person was under arrest and not free to leave.

Dwight promised Louis he would speak to his Bible study next week, but he wasn't ready. On the way home from the lake, Veronica took him to a bookstore, where he picked up a couple new tomes on George Washington. It was funny how he was named after President Eisenhower, but had yet to delve into his life. Maybe when he satisfied himself with the first President, he'd tackle the thirty-fourth.

He selected a thin volume about Washington's picks for the Supreme Court. The early Supreme Court did not render many decisions and lacked the breadth of power it wielded today. He found it fascinating that, while John Jay was still Chief Justice, Washington sent him to negotiate with the British to avoid another war. Once Jay left the Court, Washington picked John Rutledge, who spoke out against Jay's treaty. This upset the Federalists, who controlled the Senate. Rutledge was never confirmed. Political motives, which influenced selection of Supreme Court Justices in Washington's day, had magnified in importance since 1795, the year that Rutledge left the bench.

Dwight read a few more chapters, then put down his pen. Washington's vision for the federal judiciary was that it was like blood vessels connecting the states to form a perfect body. Did his vision hold true today? One decision, *Brown v. Board of Education*, which struck down separate but equal education, brought the body closer to the Constitutional ideal, that all are created equal. Another one, *Roe v. Wade*, which made legal the abortion of babies, had ruptured a main artery. Dwight wondered if Washington would approve.

In another volume, he learned Washington added the words, "So help me God," to his inaugural oath. Before he became President, he said in a speech to Delaware Indian Chiefs, who wanted their young to learn in American schools, the Chiefs would do well to learn the American ways of life and, above all, the religion of Jesus Christ. Dwight noted this direct statement of faith and was interested in reading more. In a 1787 farewell address, Washington cautioned the nation not to believe in morality without religion.

Dwight fired up his computer, clicked onto the website for Mount Vernon. Only two of George's letters to his wife survived. In 1775, he wrote Martha, whom he called Patcy, that he trusted his future in the Revolutionary War to that Providence who was more bountiful to him than he deserved.

Louis was right. Historical evidence, including a letter from Washington's granddaughter, showed he was a man of faith. Why hadn't Dwight seen these materials before? He studied Washington for years, his military strengths and weaknesses, how he rallied his troops to win the battle of Trenton, how he led the nation. Dwight firmly believed the assessment of historians that, without Washington, America might not exist.

Why had so little emphasis been placed by historians on Washington's faith? Perhaps those who wrote about Washington were not interested in religion. Perhaps it was fashionable to turn the past on its head and rewrite history. He was about to pick up the telephone, and ask Louis if he knew anything about the Truro parish where Washington attended church, when the phone rang. He answered, wondering if Mandy had more trouble with Chad.

"Dwight, it sounds like you. This is Nolan Cuttering."

Dwight leaned back in his chair. This was a treat. Besides being the President's next pick for the Supreme Court, Nolan was Dwight's friend. "It's good to hear your voice. Christine and I are cheering for your upcoming confirmation hearing. It can't be easy bearing the scrutiny."

A long sigh on the other end. "Questions about my judicial philosophy are one thing. I don't know how much you've seen on the news, but every day this past week, activists littered my front yard with animal carcasses. Racoon, squirrels, and rabbits."

Dwight was appalled. "Who would do such a thing? I hope it's road kill and they're not killing the animals."

"The Marshals thinks it's a fringe group trying to end all hunting of game in this country. Media warfare against me is heating up, too." Nolan stopped. He sounded tense. "A law professor called for me to withdraw because of an opinion I wrote."

"About what?"

"I ruled that creationism should be allowed to be taught alongside the theory of evolution, which is not science, because it has never been tested and proven."

Dwight felt compassion for Nolan. Strange he should call while he was studying Washington's vision for the federal courts. He mentioned that to Nolan, then added, "He wanted our federal courts to hold the country together. The way confirmation hearings are today, they divide us. I wish there was something I could do for you."

"Ah, a perfect lead to why I am calling. With my Senate hearing now starting on Tuesday, I cannot keep my commitment to speak to law students at Georgetown on arguing appeals. You are a Georgetown graduate, and served on the Virginia Supreme Court. Would you be able to take my place?"

Well versed in the art of appellate practice, Dwight had heard more than three hundred oral arguments. "I'm sure they will be disappointed not to hear from you, the prospective justice for the Supreme Court, but I will do my best to be a fill-in."

Nolan promised to fax Dwight the syllabus after they hung up. Dwight was happy for Nolan, despite his difficulties. "In another week, you will be a justice on the U.S. Supreme Court, and I want to be the first to congratulate you when you are confirmed."

It was two hours since Griff requested agents from the Bureau's Kidnap Squad be dispatched to Front Royal. While waiting for them to arrive, Griff raised the hood on the bucar to feign motor trouble. At the side of the road, he and Sal went over the plan twice and in his mind, Griff replayed it a third time. Not once did Eva's vision intrude, which was good, because this type of operation required him to keep his wits fully engaged. Any slip meant lives could be in danger.

A black car drove up behind them and Griff recognized Roger Gant, the supervisor of the Kidnap Squad. He got in and left with Roger, while Sal pretended to wait for a tow truck. What he was really doing was eyeballing the road while the others met in town to develop the Ops Plan. That way, if the white Honda left, Sal could follow it and alert the others.

Griff and the squad met at a schoolyard in Front Royal where he briefed them on his plan, drew a diagram of the road and the house, and provided descriptions of Ms. Ponytail and her muscle man. Back to the chalet, Griff drove the Jeep that was assigned to the female agent in the passenger seat. She was meant to look like she could be his wife. Griff stopped by Sal, who lowered the hood of the Pontiac. "We're moving in."

Sal jumped in the backseat and ducked down. A bucar with other agents turned down the gravel road ahead of Griff. They stopped short of the chalet and drove down a two-track, into the woods. Out of sight from the house, they would sneak up to the rear. Griff passed by their turnoff and, moments later, heard via their encrypted police radio, that they were in position, ready to assault the house from behind.

Close to eight o'clock on Sunday night, Griff rolled the Jeep into the driveway of the log house. As the sun dipped behind the backside of the mountains, menacing shadows converged, reminding him of a meth lab he raided in West Virginia. The DEA agent was shot as she served an arrest warrant, and the bullet shattered her femur. He had to forget Eva's vision!

He angled the blue SUV in behind the White Honda Civic, and gave final instructions to his "wife" to stay put for the time being. Griff eased out and quietly closed the door. He ignored Sal, crouched on the rear floor with a shotgun. This had to work, they had to get to the bottom of Frank's disappearance. Griff only hoped he was alive.

Dressed in a lightweight jacket and jeans, Griff was the typical Sunday driver who stumbled on the seasonal hideaway he might rent. That's how he appeared from the front as he approached the railed porch. His backside revealed something more ominous. The 9-millimeter Glock protruded from his rear pocket, ready when needed. For added protection, his personal .38 caliber rested in his ankle holster.

The Civic hadn't moved, so Griff was confident the couple was still inside the chalet. He knocked on the door, leaned on a porch post. He acted casual but, like an animal ready to pounce, every fiber, every nerve flexed. Alert to each new sound, he heard a crow caw in the distance. Nothing unusual there.

Twenty seconds went by. No one came to the door. Griff listened, heard no footsteps or voices from inside. He rapped on the wooden door. The curtain at the window rustled, as though someone was checking on him and the Jeep. A lock disengaged. Then, the door opened forty-five degrees, and the man he had seen carrying beer from the car appeared, looking like he had awakened from a nap. Dressed in a long-sleeved shirt, the man grasped the door edge with his right hand. When Griff saw his left thumb tucked in the top of his jeans, relief flooded his mind. He saw no gun.

In a friendly attitude, Griff nodded toward the for rent sign by the road. "My wife and I were out for a ride, noticed this place is for rent. Is it available for weekly rental?"

The man smiled. "I rent, too. Owner's number on sign."

At his reply, Griff tensed. The accent was Russian, a thick one that dropped unnecessary English words. Pleased the Russian didn't seem suspicious, Griff kept talking. "You leased it for long?"

"One week." The man pronounced the "w" like a "v."

Ms. Ponytail hovered behind the door, in the same sweatshirt. No sign of Williams or anyone else. Griff stepped toward the door. The Russian moved back as though to close it. In a flash, Griff shoved his foot against the bottom of the door.

Glock in hand, he extended his arms, locked them in a firing position. He announced loudly enough to be heard throughout the house, "FBI. Hands up, where I can see them. Freeze."

The Russian moved to the side, but then did exactly as he was told. The woman fled to the back, when Griff heard a violent crash. FBI agents rushed in through the rear door and came face to face with her. In an instant, Sal was beside Griff, carrying his shotgun and ordering the Russian to the floor.

Griff's pretend wife stood over the man, moved his arms to a position where she could secure his wrists with handcuffs. Other agents moved quickly through the large great room and into one of two bedrooms. An agent came right back out and flashed a thumbs up to Griff. Unsure if that meant the woman was secured, he hurried to find out if Frank was in the house. Several agents guarded the Russian, who was spread out on the floor. In the back bedroom, what Griff saw sickened him. On a bed made of cedar logs, FBI Special Agent Frank Williams was dressed in a pair of slacks and chained, shackled, and muzzled. As Griff gently peeled off duct tape covering his mouth, his wild eyes followed Griff's every move.

The female FBI agent came in, gave Griff a handcuff key. "Found it in the woman's sock when I searched her. She's Russian, too."

Griff unshackled Frank. His tongue spun over lips cracked and speckled with adhesive. He tried to talk. All that came out was "Ugh." Tears streamed down his filthy cheeks. Over his shoulder, Griff asked an agent behind him to get some water. He turned to Frank, "Hey, buddy, we're here now. It's over. What did they do to you, man?"

Someone handed Frank a mug, and Griff recognized Sal's watch. Frank drank the water eagerly, then found his voice. "Norma Jean and I had a fight. I stormed out, took the Honda to Kelley's bar."

That was the pub Griff went to. Frank broke down sobbing. "Had a couple of pints of good Irish beer. Should'na. Met them." His head jerked around the room.

Griff thought Frank looked like he would pass out. "Have you eaten anything?"

"Nah. Cheese once. I don't know."

Griff removed his jacket, had Frank put it on. "Who are they? Why kidnap you?"

Frank wiped his face and eyes on the jacket sleeve. "Had too much beer. They seemed nice, spoke to me in Russian. You know I worked with Russians. One was my best friend. They offered to drive me to my motel. They were in town on business, staying there, too, they said."

Sal took Frank's hand, tried to get him to stand. No bones were broken. On the way out, he identified the woman and man as the people he met at the bar. Griff and Sal got Frank into the passenger side of the Jeep.

Frank's head was bowed. "I must have fallen asleep in my car. The next thing I knew, I was being hustled into this place by the big man. I fought him, but he was strong, forced me to this room, where they tied me—" His voice faltered. "You saw what happened."

Griff asked an agent to take Frank to a hospital. The female FBI agent debriefed the woman in the kitchen, while Griff and Sal interrogated the man, whose name was Lev. Griff learned enough to unravel part of the terrible plot. Not once did Lev ask to speak to a lawyer. In fact, Lev seemed downright sorry for what he'd done and was willing to cooperate.

TWELVE

Lev Federov told Griff and Sal he was the son of a former military attaché to the U.S. Embassy. After being co-opted by FBI counterintelligence agents, his father passed information to the U.S. government for years. When told the Soviet military was transferring Dmitri Federov back to what was then the Soviet Union, just prior to the fall of the empire, Lev chose to remain in the U.S., against his father's wishes.

Sal stood with his back to the wall, arms folded, and glowered at Lev as if he was already convicted of heinous crimes. Griff made notes of Lev's halting answers. "So, you believe when your father signed on to cooperate, the U. S. government gave him a stipend. You got used to prosperity and the comforts of American life. Your father went back to Russia with the rest of your family, and was angry at you for remaining in the U.S."

Lev's hair drooped over his eyes. He didn't look at Griff, his voice was monotone. "When recruited by FBI, our family live worry free. Now, I am gardener. It is difficult."

Lev told an incredible story, which someone would have to check out. He claimed his father never knew or worked with Agent Williams. Griff suspected Lev's father might be the Russian spy that had gone missing while working with Williams. Apparently, this was an entirely different family, but Griff felt certain there must be some connection.

One day, Lev got in his battered pickup truck, which was parked in front of the home where he was cutting the grass. On the ripped leather seat, he found a large envelope. Inside the envelope, there was a thousand dollars in one-hundred-dollar bills. Besides the money, there was a cell phone and cell phone charger. A note was written in English. Lev had no idea who left the envelope. He was running the lawnmower and saw no one.

He showed the money and letter to his girlfriend, who was also Russian. Ulanova, a.k.a. Ms. Ponytail, was being interrogated in the kitchen by other FBI agents. The note said a call would come that same night at nine o'clock from the man who left the money. Lev hid the money between the pages of a telephone book. As it was supposed to, the call came that night on the cell phone. For one thousand dollars, Lev could not refuse what the man asked him to do.

Griff stopped writing. "What did he want you to do?"

Lev squeezed a thumb with his other hand. Sweat glistened on his forehead. Griff debated whether Lev was being totally honest. Yet, Lev did not seem capable of engineering this crime.

Griff moved his chair closer to where Lev sat on the sofa. "The only way we can help you is if you tell us everything. How did the man identify himself? Was he young, old or what? Did he offer money to kidnap a federal agent?"

The Russian's English suddenly got more broken. "Phone only got calls."

Griff strained to understand. "So, you could not call out?"

Lev nodded.

"Who called and when?"

Lev's words became slurred, as if he had drunk all the beer that Ulanova bought. It took a long time for Griff to discover that the same man called each night at nine o'clock with instructions. He didn't sound young or old, never gave his name, and ordered Lev to use his Russian girlfriend to approach Williams. Lev never knew how the man found out about Ulanova.

Griff figured the mastermind of the kidnapping conspiracy planned it for some time. He must have followed Lev, and seen him with Ulanova, before ever making contact. Somehow, the man stumbled onto Lev's dire financial condition. After much back and forth, Lev admitted the caller left other items on the seat. A photo, key, map and handcuffs. Sal found the chalet key in Lev's pocket and cell phone on the kitchen counter.

Now, Sal plopped next to Lev on the couch, shoved his face into the Russian's. "Was the photo of Agent Williams?"

Lev rubbed his face and nodded.

Griff had to get Lev to finish talking before Sal's aggressive nature caused him to clam up. "Sal, could you get him some more water?"

Without a word, Sal slapped his knee and got up. Griff worked fast. "Where are the picture and the map?"

Lev pointed to the fireplace. Griff walked across the room, moved

the black screen and several unburned logs. Sure enough, he pulled a
plastic bag from underneath the bottom log. Careful not to compromise fingerprints that might be on it, he used a cotton hankie from
his back pocket to open the bag. Inside, he drew out a photo taken of
Frank walking out of court.

Griff could not figure out why Lev would hide the photo and map,
when he kept Williams in plain sight in the chalet. It was all pretty
strange. "What happened next?"

Sal came back with soda. "Thought Lev might like some cola to
wet his tongue."

He handed it to the Russian, who took a long drink. Griff called Sal
over. In a low voice, he asked what Ulanova was doing. Sal shook his
head. "Sitting there, doing nothing."

Griff returned to Lev, who wiped his mouth on the back of his
hand. "Ah, good. The man tell me, keep the other man here." He held
up two fingers.

Griff clarified, "He wanted you to keep the agent here, locked up
for two weeks?"

"I say he pay more, for so long."

Griff's stomach growled, but he ignored the gnawing feeling. It was
not like they could call pizza delivery. "How much money did you
want?"

Lev held up three more fingers. So an extra three thousand dollars
helped convince the poor Russian to kidnap Frank. A question nagged
at Griff. Why? Was Norma Jean that anxious to get rid of her husband?
From everything Griff learned, she was one weird woman. Frank was
better off without her. But, why resort to a kidnapping plot and keep
Frank hidden for two weeks? To scare him, or give her a generous
property settlement, or could it be related to the trial?

Maybe it was more than that. Norma Jean might be after Frank's life
insurance. Agents with families had big policies.

As Lev spilled more of what happened, the mystery deepened. The
man at the end of the one-way phone promised Lev another twenty-
thousand dollars after the end of the two weeks. Lev did not know
what the extra money was for. He had yet to see it.

Griff checked his watch. It was nearly nine o'clock, the purported
time the man called. He had to convince Lev it was in his best interest
to help the FBI capture the unknown man. Griff used a well known
technique: If Lev cooperated, he would try to convince the prosecutor

not to charge his girlfriend, Ulanova. Truth is, she might be the brain behind the whole thing, so Griff was going out on a limb. But, time was of the essence, and he had to do it.

Sal jumped on the idea. "Picture her being sent back to Russia. She's illegal, right? She was not in on the deal the FBI made with your father, was she?"

Lev looked stricken. What Sal blustered must be true. It took another minute for Lev to break completely. If Griff and Sal kept Ulanova out of it, and gave him a favorable recommendation at sentencing, Lev even agreed to testify. On the way to the kitchen to get the cell phone, Griff planned what to do when it rang.

Roger Gant quickly equipped Lev's one-way cell phone with a recording device, then Griff coached Lev on how to pitch his new idea. When the mystery man called, Lev was to tell him nothing about Williams being found. He was to demand not twenty-thousand dollars, but fifty-thousand. If he did not get the cash immediately, he would take Frank to the Washington Monument and release him.

Griff lobbied, and Roger agreed, that Sal and the kidnap squad would be responsible for the case from here on. This meant Griff would not be the lead investigator. He did have to be in court tomorrow morning, with Frank, on the Jones case. Griff would stay long enough to help arrest the mastermind.

On the sofa, Lev sat between Sal and Griff. He'd not been allowed to talk with Ulanova. She was taken by agents to a car outside so that she could not interfere with the expected phone call. Griff held Lev's cell phone and checked his watch. Seven minutes past nine o'clock. No one had called on the prepaid cell.

Griff began to believe Ulanova planned the whole thing. Maybe she was the daughter of the Soviet snitch that Williams had burned, and this was for revenge. That must be who Ulanova called every day in Russia, for instructions.

He was about to draw Sal aside, tell him his theory, when his own cell phone vibrated against his waist. The LED screen said it was another private caller. The other phone was supposed to ring, not his. Who could be calling? He soon found out.

When he answered, the woman sounded relieved. "Good, you're all right. I debated whether to call. Can you talk?"

He handed Lev's phone to Sal and mouthed, "I have to take this."

Griff stepped out onto the porch. "Eva, I can't say more, but I found my package."

Agent Eva Montanna was not easily put off. "After dinner the other night, I dug around. Did you know a Soviet spy went missing, one your package worked on years ago?"

Griff's eyes swept to the window. It was getting darker outside and he could see Lev in the light of the room. "I'll talk with you about it another time."

What could Eva tell him now that would make a difference? If she had inside intel on Lev, that would be one thing, but he figured she was just missing "the hunt." He didn't have time to fulfill her need for vicarious snooping. The bottom line was that Lev's supposed boss man had not called.

"I'm fine, but not alone." Let her think he had company. That would get her to hang up and quit worrying. It was also true and would throw off anyone listening to their conversation that shouldn't be.

"Sorry. Let us know how it all works out. We're praying for you."

"Thanks." Griff closed his phone, put it back in its leather sling. Back inside, Sal's glare needed no interpretation. Why hadn't the guy called? It was nearly fifteen minutes past the hour. Lev leaned his head on the sofa. His eyes were open, glued to the ceiling.

Just then, Lev's cell phone rang and Sal warned, "Like we said, or you're toast."

Lev put the phone to his ear, and started to twist the wire that extended from the ear piece. Griff quietly eased Lev's hand away, to ensure the recording device was not disabled. Lev said everything according to their drill. The Russian shrugged, held the phone up in the air. The connecting wire was stretched to the limit.

Sal grabbed the phone. "What did he say?"

"Cursed, hung up."

Griff's mind reeled in a circle. What he did not know bothered him. Maybe he should have heard Eva out. His eyes darted to the front window, and he walked back behind the stone fireplace, out of range of flying bullets. Earlier, when he called Bob Rice to report Frank's phone was found, he asked if Bob knew how to trace a prepaid phone. He did not. Before Griff redialed Eva to see what else she learned, the prepaid cell phone rang again.

Lev answered, then said, "Da."

Griff knew little Russian, but understood that meant yes. He and

Sal listened to the conversation, which was being recorded. The man agreed to drop the money at Great Falls Park. Lev could pick it up at 7:20 a.m. He gave the exact location for the money, then ended the call.

They got with Gant, and the three concocted a new plan to flush out the man behind Lev. For the time being, they would stay at the chalet with Lev and Ulanova, while the rest of the squad removed to a hotel. Griff believed, and Gant agreed, that until they had the brains behind the kidnapping in custody, Frank should remain incognito. Because an emergency room doctor proclaimed the only thing injured was Frank's ego, Griff suggested he rest at the same hotel, along with the agent who took him to the hospital.

Not only for his safety, but because they did not know the depth of the conspiracy, Frank would remain there until Griff came for him. If the Russians were behind it, CIA and State Department would have to be notified. At this moment, it was a criminal investigation and Griff had yet to make those calls. He warned Williams not to contact anyone.

As Sal prepared to get some shut-eye on the couch, he called Griff aside. "Guess who Ulanova called in Russia?"

Griff shrugged.

Sal grinned. "She used Frank's free-FBI phone to call her mother. Nice of us and nice of her, because that's how we got Frank."

Griff was not sure that her calls to Russia were so innocent. He assumed watch on Lev, handcuffed and slumped on a chair. It was four in the morning and in a man-sized chair next to the fireplace, Griff stretched his legs to the edge of a low table. The arrangement was uncomfortable and did not keep him from massaging tomorrow's plan in his mind.

Soon, like unknown animal tracks in the snow, other things wandered through it. His wife, Sue, loved to paint. Her watercolor of a Lake Michigan lighthouse still hung in the bedroom. Eva's phone call had started him thinking. She and Scott supported one another in their tough careers, loved their kids. Griff had no kids. Sue died before they had a chance.

One summer, he'd flown her to a small airport in Holland, Michigan, near where Eva's grandfather was raised. They rented a car and drove along Lake Michigan, stopping at the beach to make sandcastles in the sugar-white sand. It was the best week the two of them ever had.

He now lived alone, but wasn't that the way he wanted it? Griff mostly worked, except for baseball and flying, which was rare for him these days. He'd lost his love for it.

Sal's loud snoring invaded his mental sleepwalk, which was okay. Melancholy thoughts weren't his style, and he had important things to decide. Such as, could he prove Frank was a victim or had he done something during the Cold War to bring about his kidnapping? Frank claimed to know nothing, and Griff had no evidence to doubt him.

Soon, they would all find out. Then, he and Frank could wrap up the Jones case. Griff arranged for a surveillance post at Great Falls Park. In less than three hours, Lev would go to the desolate park near the Potomac River, and find an envelope with fifty-thousand dollars. The man on the phone must want Frank to be held captive pretty badly.

Griff was nodding off to sleep when he remembered that Great Falls Park was where Eva had the vision of him being shot. He nudged Sal awake. But, as Griff lay on a sofa in the rolling hills of Front Royal, agents were assembling in Great Falls to capture the man who seriously messed with not just one FBI agent, but a whole squad. Adrenaline rushed through him. Justice was close at hand. He only wished he could take down the criminal, whoever he was, right now.

THIRTEEN

Griff was staked out in a construction trailer early Monday morning at Great Falls Park. Before dawn, he and Sal were dropped off, then walked into the park. They joined two other FBI agents from the kidnap squad who had been in place since 3:00 a.m. The night in the park was quiet, except one agent thought he saw a lone figure enter on a bicycle. Surveillance outside the park saw no one.

A blue Jeep, the same one Griff drove yesterday, pulled into the lot. A man and a woman got out. Their running clothes camouflaged their true intent—to hit the trails and give Griff and his team additional coverage. After some quick stretching exercises, they jogged off to the trail.

With the four of them in the trailer, and the two agents who would circle back behind the restrooms, Griff felt the area was covered. From years of dealing with the criminal mind, Griff knew that whoever hired Lev to kidnap and hold Frank would not permit Lev to blackmail him. Now, Griff had to keep that person from killing the bait, Lev Federov.

In a few minutes, Lev would pick up the package, then drive out of the park. The surveillance that remained on the perimeter would clean his tail before pulling him over in a safe area. Griff looked out the cube of a window. No other cars had driven in.

At this moment, two agents in a single bucar were following Lev, who was driving Frank's Civic. Ulanova was taken to the FBI field office. Griff's radio squelched. He answered with his code name for the plane he flew. "Skyhawk, here."

It was from the agent tailing Lev. "It's Neptune. We have a problem. Our package is three miles from the entrance, pulled to the side of the road. Out of gas."

Griff began to sweat. He had a true dilemma. No way this thing could be done before court started at eight thirty. Judge Pendergast expected Frank to testify. But, if he told the prosecutor Frank was on ice, he'd have to tell the Judge, who would have to tell the defense attorney. Constance Ingles could blow the whole deal, and endanger catching the mastermind.

"Can you help him? He needs to get here ASAP."

The agent's tone was casual. "We're driving him to a gas station to get a can. We'll get the biggest one they've got, so we won't have to stop again until we get to your location."

"10-4. Quick as you can. All is quiet here."

Griff hoped it wasn't too far to a gas station.

Forty-nine minutes later, Griff watched out of a streaked window with binoculars. At last, Lev drove the Civic into the parking area, the second car in the lot. The Russian swung his legs from the car, then banged the door shut. Arms stretched over his head, he walked toward the public restrooms, checking several times over his shoulder. Orange cones and fluorescent paint marked off a square on the sidewalk, which was being repaired.

With an unsteady gait, Lev headed, not for the men's, but the ladies' restroom. Griff knew with all the agents surveilling him, there was no way Lev had been drinking. He hoped the Russian could pull this off. He must have it in him. If Lev kidnapped a federal agent for a few lousy thousand, why seem reluctant now? What was Griff missing?

Binoculars pressed to his eyes, he asked Sal, "Can you see him?"

Sal was at the window by the door, his own binoculars to his eyes. "Yeah. Looks fishy."

Griff made an adjustment to his right eye. That was a little clearer. "Ulanova's being held. He better play straight."

Sal shuffled his feet on the dusty floor. "Watch out. Maybe Lev's gonna take the envelope inside the restroom, hide some of the cash so he can return later to retrieve it. Thinks we're stooges."

Another possibility haunted Griff. When Lev picked up the money, if it was there, the package could be rigged to explode. There was no way Griff could get to it first without compromising the investigation. The kidnap squad should have brought bomb-sniffing dogs, like Griff wanted.

"We'll see," was all Griff could say.

Precisely at 8:30, Monday morning, Dwight took his seat behind the bench, and called his court to order. With the jury reassembled, he would not waste another second.

"Mr. Prosecutor, call Agent Williams."

At counsel table, Patrick O'Rourke spoke in the microphone. "He is not here, Your Honor. I did mention that fact to your clerk."

Dwight looked at Mickey, the clerk who had been with him since he ascended to the federal bench. His head barely rose above the edge of the desk. Right now, the clerk fiddled with something, refused to look his way. Dwight expected Constance Ingles to leap up and make a motion.

Instead, she remained seated, a purple scarf looped over both shoulders. Her face was grim, as if she detested being in his courtroom. If Constance was unhappy, perhaps the day would not be bad. Dwight glanced to his right. Oh, that's why she looked gloomy. Her client, Owen Jones III, was not in his seat.

Dwight felt his blood pressure climb, not a good thing on a day when he'd go for dialysis. "Ms. Ingles, where is your client?"

She rose slowly. "He was to meet me here at 8:15. I am sure he can't find a parking spot. The ramp is closed for repairs."

Other reasons leapt to Dwight's mind, as they must have for the Native Americans in the gallery, because whispers grew loud, like a swarm of angry hornets. He noticed O'Rourke had no agent next to him. "Where is Agent Topping?"

Patrick spoke for the record. "I last heard from Agent Topping on Saturday, when he was pursuing several leads on the whereabouts of Agent Williams."

Dwight surveyed his jury. One man with white sideburns and beard looked confused, while another juror, a nuclear physicist, sat with arms folded, staring at the judge. During voir dire, that juror asked to be excused, claimed he was working on a top-secret program for the government. The attorneys did not exercise a challenge, and Dwight did not think it was an adequate reason to be let out of jury duty. If he allowed this one, others would make the same plea. He imagined they all had had about as much of the delays as they could take.

"While I sort this out, the jury may have a five-minute break."

The fourteen men and women filed out. When they were safely behind the door, Dwight banged his gavel. "Attorneys, in my chambers, now."

Seconds later, he blew through the outer office. A tornado had taken up residence somewhere between his stomach and diaphragm. Gladys spoke, but he had no idea what she said. His hand found his doorknob, and a growl escaped his lips. "Let the lawyers in."

It was all he could do to quell the urge to slam the door. A federal judge must show restraint, and Dwight did, as a badge of honor. It was not easy, especially when his jury was made to wait, once again, while he made sense of this case. Constance stalked in. Patrick wheeled in through the doorway, and spoke first, "Your Honor, I told Mickey neither the defendant nor Agent Topping arrived. I assumed he told you."

Dwight motioned to Constance Ingles to sit. She waved back. "No need. Your Honor, I want—"

The judge interrupted, "Your client is absent from my court. I may issue a bench warrant. I suggest you sit."

Dwight's eyes snapped to Patrick. "If you can't call Williams, is your case done?"

Constance lowered herself in the chair, picked up a silver card case from the judge's desk.

Patrick massaged the back of his neck. "I have no other witnesses to call."

Dwight tented his hands. "Either of you have information not for the record?"

Patrick dropped his hands and wheeled closer. "Your Honor, I left a message on Agent Topping's cell phone that it was urgent he call me. I phoned his office. No one answered."

The AUSA's sincerity poured out of him, which made it harder for Dwight to do what he must do. "We've a few minutes before the jury is brought in. I will take that time to decide." Through his reading glasses, he checked his watch. "Reconvene in three minutes."

The attorneys left. Out of his fridge, Dwight drank a can of tomato juice, careful not to get any on the robe. All he had thought of at breakfast was the government finishing their evidence, the defense putting on theirs, and the jury returning a guilty verdict by this afternoon or tomorrow morning.

Out the window, he gazed at monster cumulus clouds. As a boy, he'd stare at those clouds and dream about the rockets his dad built. Watching a Snark rocket lift off at Cape Canaveral was an experience of a lifetime. Well, it was a lifetime ago. He wasn't building rockets or involved with space travel. His father had wanted him to follow in his footsteps, but Dwight chose the law. He tossed the empty can in the wastebasket. A hollow sound echoed against his ears.

FOURTEEN

Judge Pendergast reconvened his courtroom. In their assigned seats, jurors waited for him to speak. Constance Ingles was not in hers. She plunged through the gate to the well, her carefully coifed hair blown into white tufts, like clouds in a wind storm.

Dwight had made his decision. "Mr. O'Rourke, I see no agents present. Do you have other witnesses?"

Patrick cleared his throat. "No, sir. The government's case is completed."

At this, the spectators started to rumble. Dwight pushed his glasses to the end of his nose, glared at the crowd. "Quiet in the courtroom. Ms. Ingles, I see your client is not here. Before I issue a bench warrant for his arrest for failure to appear, do you have a motion to make?"

Constance leapt to her feet. "In the interests of justice, I ask the Court to grant my motion for judgment of acquittal. The government has not proved the case. Its main witness failed to appear, so I could not complete my cross-examination."

Ah, the interests of justice. By that, Constance meant if Dwight dismissed the case with prejudice, the government could not retry Owen Jones III on the same charges. Dwight's hand rested on his gavel. A reporter dashed from the courtroom, no doubt to call his paper or news station to herald the latest developments in *U.S. v Jones*. Well, Dwight was about to declare another twist, one sure to be unpopular with the victims. He banged his gavel once, hard and loud. Murmurs ceased.

"I take no pleasure telling the jury that I must dismiss the case against Mr. Jones. And in the interests of justice, I do so with prejudice. The government failed to prove that Mr. Jones conspired to bribe a federal official. Agent Williams was the only witness to testify to the alleged conspiracy."

Everyone started talking at once. He pounded his gavel again. Things quieted, for a moment. "It is not a conspiracy when the only other person meeting with the defendant is a government agent who is doing

his job. Agent Williams has not returned to be cross-examined. The
Court casts no blame on the federal prosecutor for this failure, but the
Court cannot allow the defendant to be tried again for this crime on
these facts. That would violate his rights against double jeopardy."

Dwight gulped in a large breath, exhaled slowly. "The case is dismissed. The Court thanks the jury for its service."

A woman reporter, who by now he recognized as Kat Kowicki, hurried from the courtroom, the doors swinging as she left. No doubt her
station would cover the dismissal as headline news. He left the bench
and walked behind it, then shook each juror's hand, as was his custom
when a trial finished. This one turned out far differently from what he
imagined.

On the way back to his office, Gladys handed Dwight a pink message slip. Her thin lips were pressed together. "You won't like it," she
warned.

Puzzled, Dwight slipped on his glasses and saw the unmistakable
name and number for the Secretary of the Interior. "I thought you
called and told him I could not speak at that dinner."

"Judge, I did as soon as you told me to. What should I do?"

Dwight crushed the pink slip in his hand. "I've just dismissed the
case and am not calling the Secretary back. You won't be, either."

Dwight tossed the message in the wastebasket, with no idea what
trouble his decisions of today would bring to him personally.

At the park, Griff's radio crackled and one of the FBI agents posing as
a jogger said, "Smitty has moved up behind the restroom. No sign of
anyone in the woods nearby."

"10-4. Our guy is approaching the garbage can by the woman's entrance."

Griff strained his eyes to see. The trailer was stifling, and they could
not open the window until they were sure Lev had the money. Outside
the ladies' restroom, Lev lifted up the gray garbage top, peered inside.
The Russian reached in, dug around, then pulled his arm back out

"Oh, oh." Griff adjusted his binoculars to get a better view.

Lev replaced the lid, then looked around, confused.

"The other one," Sal whispered.

As if Lev also heard, he swiveled his head to look at the construction trailer. He wiped his hands on his jeans, then went to the men's
entrance, where another trash container had been dragged. He lifted
the hinged lid and reached inside. His hands came out empty.

Griff was impatient. He'd played the tape of the mastermind telling Lev where to come and what time. Was Lev's running out of gas connected to his finding no money in the trashcan?

Lev walked into the men's room. Sal was all over that move. "What did I tell you? We've got no agent in there. By now, Lev's stuffing the dough under a brick."

"Sal, settle down. We can search the place if it's not all there. Let's see what happens."

Five minutes later, Lev walked out, clutching a large manila envelope close to his chest. From Griff's binoculars, it looked bulky, like it held bundles of cash. Lev stood there, as if he forgot what he was to do next.

Griff coached him from inside the trailer, but of course Lev couldn't hear. "Get in your car, Lev. Drive out of the parking lot."

Sal started angling to the door. "He's not the brightest, is he?"

Griff was grateful no bomb had detonated. "Then, he probably didn't hide any money." In an instant, relief turned to disappointment. Where was the mastermind to challenge Lev? Griff was about to leave the trailer when a figure emerged from the women's restroom. He had not seen anyone go in there. In a ski mask, blue jacket and pants, she hurried toward Lev, who was walking away.

She was the same size and height as Norma Jean. The shock of seeing her come out of the ladies' room dulled Griff's reaction for a second. Frank's wife must be behind the kidnapping, must have hired a man to leave the money in Lev's truck, make the phone calls. Griff saw something dangling by her leg. As he thought of it later, he would wonder why he didn't move out the door faster. Griff heard Sal yell in the trailer and in his ear at the same time.

"Subject behind him with a ball bat. Go! Go!"

Sal and Griff, and the other two agents, flew to the door, then struggled to get out of the construction trailer at the same time. Sal was the first, and Griff was right behind him. The woods came alive with screams, "Freeze, FBI!"

Lev turned to look behind him. The ball bat was meant for Lev's head, but when he turned, the woman hit him on the shoulder. Lev screamed. His assailant threw the bat at Griff. He stumbled on it. Sal was next to her, but the woman was fast. She tore off down the jogging trail.

Griff yelled in the microphone, "Subject on the trail, running for her life." He stopped to check on Lev, on the ground writhing in pain.

One of the two agents came up and asked, "Should we radio for an ambulance?"

"No. It doesn't look fatal. One of you see to him."

He ran after Sal, who chased the woman. Hopefully, the one FBI jogger still on the trail would have heard his radio message and come back on the trail. In good shape from running every week, Griff passed Sal in a few seconds. "See her?"

"She's straight ahead."

"Watch my back," Griff puffed, "I'll watch your front."

Thick rhododendron and scrub hid the edges of the trail. He supposed she could have veered into the brush. As he passed an enormous oak tree, he saw the woman running ahead. Griff called, "Stop, FBI!"

She kept running. Griff urged his body to go faster. His heart was pumping. He had to stop her before she disappeared in the thicket. Then, they'd have to call in the dogs. He lost sight of her around a curve. Dirt flew under his feet. Sal was still behind him.

A noise in the distance. Griff raced ahead, in time to see a jogger make a flying tackle on the stalker. In an instant, Lev's assailant was face down in the dirt, her slacks wet with morning dew. Griff ran up, pulled her hands behind her and into cuffs.

With his foot, Griff turned over the woman on the ground, pulled off the ski mask. What he saw shocked him more than seeing the woman spring from the restroom. It was a man. One he'd seen before.

This must be the mastermind. His face was scraped, but beneath the blood and dirt, Griff saw a man filled with such hate, Griff recoiled. At least they caught him, without any more agents getting hurt. Sal arrived as Griff read him his rights.

"You're under arrest for kidnapping a federal agent and attempted murder. You have a right to remain silent, the right to an attorney and if you can't afford one, an attorney will be appointed to represent you. Anything you say can and will be used against you."

The man rolled over, got to his knees. He glared at Griff, and the evil in his heart, showed in his eyes. "I know my rights."

FIFTEEN

D awn Ahern was at work in her Panama City office, navigating the computer that helped her track all of her releasees, the men and women who were out of prison and on supervised release. A federal probation officer, it was her job to ensure that her charges followed the conditions of release to the letter. If not, the judge could find they violated the conditions of their release and send them back to prison. With her guidance, some tried to put their lives back together.

She was trying to finish her monthly report before her next appointment arrived. On the shelf above her computer, Brian smiled at her from the cockpit of a bi-wing aerobatic plane. Her fourteen-year-old son sat in the front seat, while her husband, Bert, waved from the back. The photo was taken two years before at an air show.

Her mind caressed the memory of that day, fresh as a just-picked orange. With tanned fingers, nails bitten to the quick, she picked up the gold frame. Brian's brown eyes, replicas of his father's, beamed at her. He wanted to fly, just like both parents. Dawn got her pilot's license in Hawaii, when she was a teen. Bert was a U.S. Air Force pilot for twelve years.

A queasy sensation burned in her stomach. She slid open a drawer, plopped the photo on top of a box of tissues, and closed it. Brian and Bert could come back out after the last releasee left her office. It was protocol for probation officers to *never* give a felon clues to their personal habits or family.

Dawn was fine with keeping her life private, but she did wear on her wrist a starfish bracelet that Brian gave her for her birthday. Since Bert's death to a heart attack a month to the day after that photo was taken, she found it hard to make friends. Their friends were couples and, when Bert died, she and they knew things were different. Dawn's new friend Renae from church was a lifeline. Her husband traveled for his job, so she and her fifteen-year-old son, Justin, went with Dawn and Brian to the beach and for pizza.

Tears stung her eyes, and she forced herself to think of Brian. They spent a lot of free time together, which made her feel guilty. He needed to fish and swim with guys his own age. But, he'd rather fly with her. This summer, he got a job at the local hardware store. The owner also went to their church—Redeemer Community Church. It helped to know Brian was busy while she was at work.

A few clicks on the keyboard, and her monthly report was done. She printed a hard copy, then routed it on the network to the chief. The receptionist buzzed. Her eleven o'clock was there, and Dawn went out to meet him. Five inches taller than she, graying hair was tucked behind his ears.

This time, Skeeter was clean shaven and businesslike in gray slacks, woven shirt and polished shoes. She knew better. His record was spattered with felony convictions, although none was violent. His last was for introducing a drug dealer to a buyer, who turned out to be a federal agent. Before that, he defrauded the government by filing a false claim for relief from Hurricane Earl, which slammed into the Florida panhandle, for a destroyed house which he did not own. To his credit, he paid back all the relief money. If only this time she could make a difference.

She shook his right hand. Rough and calloused, it was a shrimper's hand. If his business thrived, he could get on his feet. He leased out his boat now, but the income was meager. "Come on back, Skeeter."

Dawn would try to get him to see reality. If only she could share with him how another offender got help from the church. It changed that man's life. Dawn's own life was reborn with the right kind of support and the true inner light.

Her eyes glanced at the clipboard and envelope in his left hand. "You got my message."

He handed Dawn the clipboard. "I filled it out before I came."

In her office, she sat in the swivel chair behind her desk. Skeeter settled in one opposite. "I got everything you asked me to bring. Homer's not meetin' his end of the lease."

Dawn held up her hand. "Let me check this."

Her eyes searched the form. Skeeter dragged his chair closer to her desk. Instinctively, she drew his file closer to herself. Dawn had discovered that inmates learned to read files upside down and backwards.

"You're avoiding other felons. Is this true for the last thirty days?"

"Yes, Ms. Ahern."

Experienced eyes swept his face. He seemed to be telling the truth, but you never knew. After all these years, he was practiced in the art of deception. "You are looking for gainful employment, while trying to get your shrimping business back on its feet."

"I am." Hazel eyes met her black ones. A slight smile hovered on his lips, just like her son's when he finished painting the fence and sought her approval.

"You own your house." Dawn folded her arms across her abdomen and looked Skeeter straight in the eye. "How do you pay for your utilities, loans, and food?"

Skeeter straightened in his chair, and put on what Dawn considered his law-abiding face. "Homer's sellin' live bait to my customers, but he's barely makin' it. He missed the last two payments. Says he's gonna pay soon."

He actually folded his hands in his lap. Dawn decided to see where Skeeter was going with this. "I can't just take the boat back. He made his other payments, and my bait shop customers seem satisfied."

She had an idea, but pointed to a section on the form. "You made five hundred dollars doing odd jobs. You'll need to give me the name, address, and phone number of who employed you."

Skeeter bent toward her slightly, his voice greased like butter. "Of course, I should have wrote that down. I scraped and painted for Mona Lisa Tubbs, manager of the Outrigger Grill."

Her pen poised, Dawn stared at Skeeter. Was this a joke? He did painting for Mona Lisa? "Her address and phone number, please."

Skeeter gestured with his hands. "Ms. Ahern, it's across the street from the shrimp docks, but the exact address, I'll have to get from her. I should know the phone number, but we always talk in person, when I stop to eat. Never at night. You know, I don't drink or take drugs."

Dawn lifted her chin. She made a mental note to drive to Apalach next week and check on Skeeter. She was not buying his story. Of course, she would not tell him when. "You tested negative for drugs on your drop. That is good to see."

"I promise to call you with the address and phone number. What's a good time?"

"As soon as you get there, Skeeter. Now, let me see your checkbook register."

He handed her the envelope. Inside was a thin notebook, with entries written in pencil. Checks written for the power company, telephone, and the local grocery store. "I see the deposit for five hundred dollars. What's this three-hundred-dollar deposit?"

Skeeter rubbed his forehead, creased with lines from having spent too many years in prison or the sun. Dawn was unsure which aged you more.

"That's from Homer for leasin' the Dora Ruth."

"You told me he missed the last two payments."

Skeeter's tongue flicked over his lips. "He still owes me another three hundred for the month of July and didn't pay me for August, yet." He held up two fingers. "That's two and he'd better pay up soon, 'cause I need to pay on my truck."

Dawn asked Skeeter how much he owed on his truck. He bought it on some kind of contract from a friend and still owed a thousand dollars. "Have you received money that you didn't deposit in this account?"

"Nope."

She made notes in his file. "What do you do when you're not painting for Mona Lisa?"

"I got no social life, just fishin'. I wish I could make money on that."

Her very idea. "Turn the Dora Ruth into a charter fishing boat."

Skeeter scratched his head. "She's expensive to operate and geared for nets. She'd have to bring in a lot from charters. I don't know."

"That's your assignment. Report back to me at our next session."

She stood, put out her hand. Dawn encouraged offenders she worked with to try their best. She gave them respect, until they proved her wrong. Skeeter had yet to do that. But then, he had been under her charge for a little over a month.

He shook her hand. "Thanks, Ms. Ahern. I'll call you as soon as I get home, and I mean the very minute, with Mona Lisa's address and number. She will vouch for me. Don't worry."

"Skeeter, one more thing. I notice you have a cut above your eye. How did you get it?"

He touched the scab. "It was dumb, but I walked into a cable on the Dora Ruth."

Dawn nodded, then signed him out. It was lunch time. She usually ate a cheese sandwich at her desk, and paid bills, sent e-mails, or read her Bible. She took a thirty-minute lunch so that she could leave work early to pick up Brian at the hardware store. They shopped for dinner, cooked it together. A nice ritual, she was sure it was helping Brian to heal from his father's sudden death.

Dawn went to the kitchen area, opened the refrigerator, and took out her lunch bag. Paula, the receptionist, stuck her head around the door. Much younger than Dawn, she was friendly. "Want company? I notice you eat alone."

It was the last thing Dawn wanted, but she said yes. She listened to Paula bemoan her boyfriend, who lost his roofing job, and now worked in Alabama. Dawn finished her sandwich and was about to tell Paula she was not really alone when another probation officer came in and told Dawn that DEA agent Nick Tascoda was on the phone for her.

Brows drawn together, she zipped up the cooler. "I'll be right there." Her colleague nodded, then walked out. Dawn did not want to disappoint Paula, who seemed eager for a friend. "We'll talk later. I am interested."

On the way to her office, Dawn wondered why a DEA agent was calling, or if it was an offender pretending to be someone else.

Deep in the night, the same night Dwight dismissed the Jones case, he could not sleep. He got up for his favorite snack, a glass of milk and toast with peanut butter. But tonight, nothing consoled him. How was he supposed to know that right as he was dismissing the case, Owen Jones III was being arrested for kidnapping and assaulting Agent Williams?

Jones paid off an impoverished Russian immigrant to hold Frank Williams until he could be sure of a mistrial or acquittal. Two questions nagged him awake after he'd slept for all of ninety minutes. Could he preside over the kidnapping case with fairness and honesty, and why had Secretary Jones called him again?

A novel by Charles Dickens, *Bleak House*, lay open on his lap. The story of uncertain justice suited his mood tonight. He touched the pages of the old volume, a first edition. As justice eluded the main character in Dickens's story, so it escaped the White Pine Indian Nation. Must be that Constance Ingles had hinted to Jones that, without Williams, his case would fall apart, which is exactly what happened.

Dwight restored Dickens to his proper space in the cabinet behind the glass door, and went to the kitchen for another glass of milk. If the defense attorney had any inkling of the plot, he'd have her law license. He felt like throttling Jones for pulling a stunt like that. Still, his hard feelings might pass in a day. If they didn't, and he was assigned the new case, he'd recuse himself. It was the ethical thing to do.

In the morning, Dwight was to address Louis's Bible group on how Washington relied on his faith. The purpose of prayer eluded him. If he had prayed to God about his case, would it have turned out like this? Louis said *he* prayed—and look at the results.

Dwight drank the cold milk and turned off the lights, adrenaline pumping through his veins like gasoline. The Michigan tribe was holding a press conference tomorrow. Tonight, several stations ran it on the news as a teaser. The reporter, Kat, bombarded his office with calls. Deputy U.S. Marshal Hal Leitsma, followed him home, just in case there were protestors. There weren't. After he made sure Dwight's security system was operating, the Marshal left him home alone.

That was when Dwight discovered Christine's note attached to a magnet on the fridge. She and Mandy were shopping, he should heat a frozen burrito in the microwave. Dwight followed her suggestion. When they came home with Mandy's wedding dress, he put out of his mind this terrible Monday. Not having heard the news, Christine had no idea of his angst. He chose not to enlighten her. Mandy patched things up with Chad, so the wedding loomed seven weeks away.

As Dwight slipped back into bed, he changed his mind. Before drifting to sleep, he decided the new charges against Jones—kidnapping an FBI agent and attempted murder of his Russian hatchet man—were far more serious than persuading a federal official to recognize an Indian tribe. No matter that his father was a heavy-hitter in the President's cabinet, Jones deserved to spend the rest of his life behind bars. Dwight hoped he was the Judge to make sure he did.

SIXTEEN

The next day, Dwight enjoyed his time at the Bible study. The group, composed of several men and one woman, seemed genuinely interested in the tidbits he shared about George Washington. Louis invited him to be part of the group. Back in his office later, he never turned on the small television to watch the Michigan tribe's press conference. He read briefs instead. Let them say what they will; he stayed in his chambers. Kat Kowicki tried to get him on camera. He refused to comment on either case.

About to return a call to Louis, his intercom chirped. It was Gladys. "Agent Topping is here. Says he has an appointment."

Gladys's irritated tone hinted that Dwight had failed to mention the agent was coming. "I'm sorry. Since we've nothing on the calendar, you should go home early."

He heard a smile in her voice, "My granddaughter turns ten today. I baked her cookies."

"That's nice, Gladys. Better send in the agent."

Griff's finding Agent Williams against tremendous odds spawned Dwight's idea. Besides his heroic work on the Jones case, Dwight tried two other complex cases where Griff was the lead investigator. The Washington legal community courted rumors that Griff and Eva Montanna had arrested a top terrorist. Judge Pendergast knew it was true. He'd signed the arrest warrant.

Thankful he had not drawn that terrorist's case for trial, which was twenty times more politically charged than the Jones case, Dwight walked from behind his mahogany desk, a relic from the basement of the old federal building. No one knew the original owner, but he must have been someone important. It was hand carved.

He and the agent stood eye-to-eye and shook hands. At fifty-two, Dwight's hair was still almost as dark and full as Griff's, who was years younger. He never admitted, even to Christine, that the lack of gray gave him a confident feeling. Dwight closed his door, so softly that his black robe hanging on it barely moved. Griff took a seat across from him in the leather chair.

Dwight smoothed a blue tie dotted with gold eagles. "Let's get a couple things straight. O'Rourke told me that he was unaware you found Williams before I dismissed the Jones case."

With a large hand, Griff swiped his moustache. "Your Honor, the way things went down, if it leaked we found Williams, we wouldn't have caught Jones. He'd be in another country by now, like Gordon Fare."

Dwight removed his glasses, tapped them on his hand. What the agent said made sense. "That's one case I try to forget. Fare embarrassed his attorney and me by fleeing a one hundred thousand dollars-secured bond."

Griff crossed his leg and began to look a little more relaxed in the judge's chambers. Dwight might have sounded a little gruff. He softened his tone. "I don't blame you."

Griff flashed a grin. "I thought I had good instincts about people. Even I was surprised that Fare didn't stick around for trial. Nothing about Owen Jones surprises me."

They were on better footing. Dwight leaned back in the leather chair. "You are not the lead investigator on the new case, correct?"

"Agent Sal Domingo is handling it."

Problem one out of the way. Dwight wanted no conflict of interest, but he had forgotten about Fare. Perhaps, he couldn't ask Griff for help after all. Dwight tugged on his left ear lobe. "Mickey said Fare was arrested last week. I guess we'll see you for his trial."

Griff's answer brought a new twist. "Apparently you didn't hear the whole story."

Dwight snapped forward, his hands folded. "No."

"Fare applied for a sizable loan at a branch of the same bank he had defrauded. They called the FBI, and agents from the Atlanta office called me. I verified Fare was a fugitive who jumped bond on our case. I called the U.S. Marshal's office. They faxed a copy of the arrest warrant to Atlanta. That's probably how you heard of it."

Dwight searched the recesses of his memory. He shrugged.

Griff continued, "Fare was arrested, transported to the Atlanta FBI office. Here's where the story gets odd. He wasn't our Gordon Fare, but a thief who stole Fare's identity, and tried to get a loan based on the real Fare's credit record."

"So, the case will not be tried before me?"

"Right, it stays in Atlanta."

"Good. I have a personal favor to ask you, unrelated to any case."

Griff took out a small notebook from his rear pocket, turned to the middle. He removed a pen from the inside pocket of his gray blazer. "How can I help, Your Honor?"

Dwight thought about what to say. "I am an only child. My parents, still living, are close to eighty. You may know I am an avid sports fisherman."

"Yes, Your Honor."

Dwight laughed. "Let's get another thing straight. In the courtroom, it's fine to refer to me as Your Honor. If we meet in the hall, call me Judge. Back here in chambers, or at my home, where no one else is around, please call me Dwight. I'll call you Griff."

The agent's eyebrows darted up a fraction. "Yes, Your Honor, I mean, Dwight."

"Last year, my name was passed over for U.S. Court of Appeals. I soothed my flagging ego by entering a bass fishing contest, deep in the Appalachian Mountains, and landed a striped bass I was certain would set a record."

He saw Griff taking notes. "This is extremely confidential."

Griff quit writing. "You can trust me to keep it to myself."

"That is exactly why I ask for your help. In my haste to reach the shore, when I stepped from the boat, I slipped and gashed my arm on the dock." Dwight's stomach contracted at the thought of his stupidity. "Landed in the water, where I floundered and bled. Sucked in a lot of water. Long story short, the catch got away. I ended up sick. Really sick."

Dwight checked his watch. He had six minutes. He might be late for his next appointment, but could not rush this. "I couldn't keep anything in. I was sick for weeks, and was so dehydrated and weak, that I finally called my doctor. Maybe you heard something about it?"

Griff had not. Good, Topping would say if it had gotten around. "They never tested for what I had. I now know it was from some bacteria, called Aeromonus. Toxins built up in my system, which led to acute renal failure."

Griff looked up from his note pad. "Now you want to sue. Maybe you need a private investigator."

The judge gestured with his hand. "No lawsuit. My doctor said most labs don't initially test for the bacteria, because it's everywhere.

My request for help lies in a different area. Will you help me find my brother?"

"I thought you said you're an only child."

"I am adopted."

"But you have a brother?"

Dwight nodded. "Fern and Ambrose Pendergast adopted me as their son before I was two years old. They are Mom and Dad to me. My father, whom I never knew, was in the Air Force. Dad was a rocket scientist at the same base and that's how he found out about me."

Griff let out a long whistle.

Talking of his dad, Dwight felt tension ease. "Dad is the smartest man I have ever known. My biological father, Joseph Bailey, died in Korea, but after the war. My mother, her name was Maureen, tried to raise us two boys and my sister on her own. Then, she and my sister were in a car accident. Both were killed."

Griff sat forward, his face troubled. "I am sorry."

Dwight pulled papers from his desk drawer, slid them to Griff. "I was still a baby and don't remember any of them. For a while, my brother Arthur and I stayed with my mother's sister. She was the only family left."

"Do you have any idea where they are today?"

"Start with Florida. Based on what Mom and Dad told me, I contacted a Florida judge, got an order for my original birth certificate and my adoption file. Mom and Dad kept Dwight as my first name. They think Arthur was taken in by a family in Texas."

Griff scanned the papers. "Your biological parents have died, your adoptive parents are getting older, and you're an only child. After what, fifty years, you feel a need to connect with your only living relatives. Is that the story?"

"Only one other person knows the real reason, and he is my doctor. Before I tell my wife, I want to find my brother first. This is totally confidential, until the right time."

Griff arched his eyebrows. "At the office, I'm known as tight-lipped Griff."

Dwight folded his hands, ready to tell. "I need a new kidney. A transplant. I have had my evaluation, and the nephrologist tells me it's too soon to go on a donor list. But, my body is not responding well to dialysis. The doctor believes my best option is to find my brother. Siblings have the best chance of being a perfect antigen match, which means less chance of rejection."

Griff did not write that down. Dwight was glad when he folded up the notebook and shoved it back in his pocket. "Your brother may not be alive. How much older is he?"

Dwight's watch told him it was time to leave for his next appointment. "I have no memory of him. I wouldn't want this to interfere with your work. I'll pay for your expenses and time."

Griff rubbed his moustache with his thumb and forefinger. "My excess vacation is now six weeks, and I never take any. I'll make phone calls and so forth and let you know about expenses, but want nothing for my time. I need other projects besides work."

Dwight jotted a note on a piece of paper, then handed it to Griff. "My phone number and address in Great Falls. Feel free to stop by if you have questions or to report on your progress."

Griff placed the note in his shirt pocket. "Do you want me to call your office or home?"

"Take down my cell phone number. I'd rather not discuss these matters at court."

Griff wrote it on the piece of paper. Dwight walked around the desk, stuck out his hand. "I can't tell you what a relief this is. I'm uncomfortable with the private investigators who've testified before me. I had no idea who to ask, until your outstanding effort in finding Williams."

Griff returned the paper to pocket. "What time frames are we looking at?"

Dwight put his hand on the door knob. "As soon as humanly possible."

"I can take off part of this week. Even if it is my own time, I still should tell my supervisor I am helping you locate your long-lost brother. I'll leave out the need for a kidney."

Dwight nodded. "That sounds all right. Just so it goes no further."

"I'll write no official reports. What if I need to speak to your parents?"

"I'll ask them for you. I don't want them to find out. They would be devastated."

"Your Honor, one more thing. What is your blood type?"

An easy question. "I'm type AB."

An hour later, Griff drove with Eva to Rob's Deli and told her how he found Williams. "The envelope we thought was stuffed with money ended up being newspapers. Oh, and Jones rode to Great Falls Park on a bike and hid in a toilet stall in the ladies' bathroom. Can you beat that?"

Eva laughed. "Your genius never ceases to amaze me, Griff."

Uncomfortable with accolades, Griff simply shrugged. They had arrived in Columbia City. Griff parked behind the Deli. "Get ready for an awesome burger."

He thought buying her Rob's famous sandwich, the "Duffer," was the least he could do after cutting her short Sunday night. Inside, they gave their order to an extremely tall waiter, whose skin was as dark as black grapes. He was friendly and brought them fresh cups of coffee.

Eva filled him in on Scott and the kids. Rob brought the sandwiches to the table himself. He wore a green golf shirt and beige trousers, and his silver and black hair was swept back from his forehead. He set before them the large patties, steaming hot on grilled rye bread, with sauteed onions, Swiss cheese, and homemade Thousand Island dressing.

"If this isn't the best sandwich you've had, the next one is on me." Blue eyes twinkling, Rob gave a little salute and left their table to kibbitz with other patrons.

Griff savored a bite. "Are you working on any exciting cases, like last year?"

Eva wrapped her mouth around the Duffer and chewed. Then, she mimicked a sad face.

Griff set down his sandwich. "You don't like it."

She smiled. "I love the burger. My cases are lousy. All I've got is a fake import company that launders money. Pretty tame stuff."

"If ICE starts another task force, you can request me again." He launched into his burger. When Eva, his former supervisor at the task force, went on maternity leave for the birth of Martin, Griff did not care to break in a new supervisor. He asked to be reassigned to the FBI field office. The Bureau jumped at getting him back. It didn't like loaning agents to other agencies, war on terror excepted.

Griff had been back a couple of months, and now Eva had returned from her leave. On the cases they worked together, they really accomplished things. At the FBI field office, Griff picked up a few investigations, like he did the Jones case when Williams got transferred to Phoenix, but rarely anything he could sink his teeth into.

Wheat-blond hair tucked behind her ears, Eva shook her head. "Depends on Congress, if we get enough money in our budget. Before we merged into Homeland Security, Customs was a proud agency. Now, we're all but gutted. It will take a long time to rise to what we once were."

His sandwich gone, Griff ate sweet potato chips, a nice change from fries. "It would be great to be on the same team again. After Pendergast dismissed the case against Jones, I need a change."

She held the sandwich near her lips, which spread into a wide grin. "My instincts were right. There was a Russian behind the agent's disappearance."

Griff respected Eva's insights, which he had learned from more than once. "Just not the right one. But, what if your vision-thing of me in the woods was really Frank?"

Eva grew serious. "I thought of that."

"I don't think Frank will recover from being handcuffed for days. I'm sure he's done drinking for good this time."

She touched her lips with a napkin, then pulled two wrapped peppermints from her pocket. Eva handed one to Griff. "Grandpa Marty brought me a new stash from the Netherlands."

Their waiter refilled their drinks. He left the bill, and said in lilting English, "God be good to you today. This is the day he made for you."

Griff looked at the man's name tag. Wally sounded so American, but looked like he was from Africa. Griff asked where he was from.

He wore an engaging smile. "My home is here now. Rob gave me a job while I finish college. When I came from the Sudan, I had nothing. Knew not how to tie a shoe." He nodded. "Rob found an apartment for me and several others. Taught me to drive."

Eva looked up at the six-foot-six-inch man. "Are you one of the lost boys of Sudan?"

Wally nodded. "You heard of us, yes?"

Eva had. "My church is raising money for a medical clinic in the Sudan."

"It is greatly needed. May I bring you anything else?"

Eva shook her head and Wally left.

Griff had a question. "What is a lost boy from Sudan?"

"Our pastor played a video in church last month. They were boys when their parents sent them away to avoid conscription in the Sudanese military. Because of the civil war, thousands of boys, some as young as five, wandered all across the Sudan, to Ethiopia, then back to Sudan. Many died. Some were eaten by crocodiles. The ones who survived ended up in a refugee camp in Kenya."

Griff popped a peppermint into his cheek. "I need to look into it. Seems like Rob is doing a good thing for Wally. I forgot to mention Frank is on extended leave."

Eva ate the last bite of her sandwich, then swallowed. "I can't imagine something like that happening to Scott—" Her eyes flew to Griff's. "Sorry."

"Actually, Eva, I've been thinking a lot about you and Scott, how happy you are. Sue and I were, too." He shook his head. "To have that again seems impossible."

She lightly touched his arm. "You shouldn't try to find what you had with Sue. Because you won't. You don't see any woman for herself."

When his eyes met hers, he saw friendship. "How is Doctor Livingston?"

At this, Eva's eyes narrowed. "Why?"

Griff shrugged. He really had no idea why he asked. It seemed right, he guessed.

Eva snagged a chip from his plate. "June is a fine pediatrician. Took Andy off the medication for his asthma, and he's doing fine. He starts kindergarten in a couple weeks."

Griff smiled. "He is one terrific boy. You started to tell me about an award Kaley got."

Eva crunched a chip. "She wrote an essay on the founding of America. Won five hundred dollars. We're having a barbeque to celebrate. I've invited a few people. My folks are in Central Asia, but Grandpa will be there, and baby Martin, who you need to see more often." Her smile was warm. "I think June is coming. Will you?"

Griff extracted a twenty-dollar bill from his wallet. If he did go, it didn't mean he had to ask Dr. Livingston on a date. He could talk to her about her work with children. Eva looked so hopeful, he let down his usual guard. "Can I bring anything?"

Eva hooted, "Way to go, Griff. Come early. Scott wants to talk to you about doing a benefit for wounded soldiers. Some kind of a flying thing."

Outside, Griff opened the side door of the bucar for Eva. In just a few days, his life was getting busy. Eva might be right about getting out more, giving himself a chance. He dropped Eva at her office, promising to be at the party. His mind returned to the favor Dwight asked. With so little to go on, it would be a challenge finding his brother.

Still, if, because of Griff's help, the judge was reunited with his sibling and received a new kidney, that would be more rewarding than capturing a criminal. At the office, he traded the bucar for his Dodge Ram truck. It used too much fuel, the price of which had soared. Maybe it was time for a fuel-efficient car, especially if he logged in a lot of miles for the judge. He drove home with the window down. He was officially off the clock, and had to admit that it felt pretty good.

SEVENTEEN

Griff finished his Wednesday morning run by dawn. If he waited until midday, with its ninety-degree heat and high humidity, it would be insufferable pounding the trail at Nottaway Park. By ten, shady paths would give way to sun-drenched fields near the ball parks. Normally, he liked intense heat, but even he found this heat oppressive. Back home, a modest ranch house he bought after Sue's death, he toasted a bagel, scrambled eggs, and poured himself a glass of orange juice, his usual breakfast.

His shower over, he fired up the computer. He had the name of Dwight's brother and knew he was about two years older. Fine in and of itself, but what chance did he having of finding the right Arthur Bailey in a country as vast as America? Without a social security number, it would be nearly impossible to find him. Griff sipped some of the strong coffee he'd made.

How many more Arthur Baileys would he find this morning? He'd traced two in Florida—one in Titusville and another in Cocoa Beach. Both under the age of forty, they were too young to be the judge's older brother. For the next hour, Griff navigated various search engines on his computer for public records.

Sure enough, he found more Arthur Baileys in Florida. The one in New Port Richey was a resident of a nursing home and veteran of World War II. Griff scratched off his name. The number for Arthur in the Florida panhandle was disconnected. No new number was given. Another was a bum lead near Atlanta.

Griff checked the time. It was nine. He put in for leave until noon. After he ran down an Arthur in Tallahassee and Texas, he'd go to the FBI field office and try to get a new case to work on. Tallahassee was busy. He dialed Waco, Texas. The phone rang and rang. Finally, a woman answered, out of breath.

Griff introduced himself. "I am an FBI agent who is unofficially trying to help a friend of mine find his brother. Does Arthur Bailey live at this number?"

Her accent was pure Texan. "Yup, he does. But, he's at the livestock show in Fort Worth. Be back tomorrow."

"Ma'am, if I can ask some questions. That way if my Arthur is not your Arthur, we won't waste each other's time."

"Make it snappy. I'm canning tomatoes, and they're about done."

"How old is Arthur?"

"Fifty-six next month."

That sounded a little old, but then files could be wrong. They were only as good as the people giving the information. It was the right month. Arthur was born in August. Griff heard clanking sounds in the background. "My Arthur was born in Florida, and is close to that age. What can you tell me about your husband?"

The woman cackled. "Not my husband. He's my brother."

Oh-oh. Dwight's sister died. Was he wrong about that? Griff could not hang up on his best lead yet. "The Arthur Bailey I am trying to find lost both parents when he was a boy."

The woman, who had not told Griff her name, did not answer right off. He heard deep breathing, then, "Hold on. I've got to lift out my jars. I'm putting down the phone."

Clink. Clink. Sounds echoed for over a minute. She came back. "Can't fool with canning. Have to be precise or you'll poison yourself and your neighbors. Where were we?"

"You were about to tell me if your parents died."

Her voice became wary. "You say you're with the FBI? How do I know you're not trying to get our personal information to scam us? Happened down the road to really nice folks. Ruined their credit. They moved away. Had to start over."

Griff realized her anxiety was natural. "Ma'am, here's my FBI office number. Call me there this afternoon. I'm home now. As I said, I'm helping my friend on my own time."

"That sounds honest. I wrote down the number, so I can check you out later. I'll tell you this much, Agent Topping, our father and mother both died. We never found out how. We were raised by a pastor and his wife. Does that help?"

It sure did. Griff wrote down all she had to say. "So your birth name is Bailey?"

"Hold on. One of my lids is leaking." She plunked the receiver so hard it banged in Griff's ear. He'd like to meet this lady. She sounded like a real character.

She returned. "Kept our given names. Arthur Bailey. I'm Phyllis Bailey. Arthur's wife died of ovarian cancer a few years back, so he moved in with me."

Griff said that was what his wife died from. "It's a terrible disease. Strikes so fast, then they're gone. He has my sympathy."

Phyllis Bailey murmured, "You have mine, Mr. Topping."

They were quiet a moment, a kind of memorial to the departed. Griff drained the last of his coffee. "Do you have another brother that could have been adopted?"

"Not that I heard. Pastor passed on years back. It's Arthur and me now."

"Do you know his blood type?"

"Yup. He's type B and I am type A."

Griff swallowed. Dwight could use either of those types. "Did you ever live in Florida?"

"Not sure. I remember Texas."

"Maybe you moved as small children and don't remember."

"Could be."

Griff heard more banging in the background.

"My lids aren't sealing right. Can you call back?"

"How about you and Arthur talk when he gets home tomorrow, than call me at my office around this same time. See if you and he could have a brother."

"Oh!" She screamed this.

"Are you all right?"

"Yup. Just remembered. The old church secretary is turning ninety."

Griff smiled. She probably forgot to bake the cake. "That's something."

"Well it is," Phyllis agreed. "She might know about another boy. Mrs. Everson was with Pastor since he started the church."

It was interesting how she never said the pastor's name or called him father. "Can you speak to her before tomorrow?"

"Nope. Party is tomorrow noon. She's not good on the phone. Arthur and I will go to the party, then call."

"Phyllis, I may not be in the office then. How about I call you?"

"All right. To think we might have a long lost brother. All these years, not knowing."

Griff had to slow her some. "We're still not sure."

Phyllis clucked her tongue. "We're alone. Except for the animals. Does he have kids?"

He thought it would be all right to tell her. "Two."

"Boys or girls?"

"Girls."

Griff could almost see Phyllis's smile.

"Wait till I tell Arthur we've got two nieces."

She sounded confident, and Griff wished he was. "Maybe."

"You've got me going, Mr. Topping. You call at three. Should be home by then."

Before she hung up, he heard her whistle. He began to whistle a tune himself, one he made up. How great to tell Dwight that he not only found his brother, but the sister he thought had died.

This Wednesday morning, Dwight's court calendar was clear. Dialysis was at ten, so he stayed home to drink a cup of coffee with Christine. She shared with him the menu for the reception. Their altogether unremarkable morning was about to erupt.

The phone rang. Christine answered the portable by her elbow. As the wedding grew closer, it seemed the phone was permanently attached to her ear. She nodded, then her almond-shaped eyes snapped toward Dwight. "Yes, I'll tell him. Thanks for calling."

Christine got up. "Bernie says Ebbott and Longstreet is in an uproar."

Dwight drank his orange juice. "What about?"

"He said to turn on the news." She strode to the great room. Dwight hoped it was not another Native American press conference about Owen Jones, which should be old news by now. In fact, Jones had been arraigned, and a different federal judge was randomly selected to try the new case.

He picked up his coffee mug and joined his wife, who had on Fox News. "I can't believe it. Judge Cuttering's wife was hit in the face."

A federal judge's wife was assaulted? He should reset the security alarm. Earlier, he had gone out to get the paper and had not turned it back on. Instead he watched the Senate Judiciary hearing room come to life on the TV. Dwight watched as Senator Briggs condemned the violence. He looked truly outraged.

"Christine, what happened?"

She sat on the sofa. "Some protestor threw a cream pie right in Mrs. Cuttering's face."

"I saw a bit of the hearing last night when C-Span replayed it. Nolan handled himself well. Who would resort to such tactics?"

Their flat screen, which hung over the stone fireplace, magnified the offended face of nearly every U.S. Senator who served on the Committee. The camera zeroed in on Harry Briggs, the longstanding Judiciary Chairman. A former Air Force Colonel, his hearings were usually disciplined and well run. The minority party rarely got away with shenanigans.

As Briggs tapped the gavel, memories of Dwight's past week played tag in his mind. He'd used that gavel so many times. Mandy came in, stood behind him. She leaned over and whispered, "He'd never make it in your courtroom, Dad."

Voices flooded the hearing room, and Briggs drew his shaggy eyebrows together in a sinister scowl. The gavel landed again, this time with more gusto. "Order, I will have order." Large blue eyes darted about the noisy room. "Chaos from out in the corridor will not distract us from the business at hand."

Senator Briggs sounded frustrated. Dwight watched as the camera zoomed to Nolan. Drops of moisture glistened at his hairline, high on his forehead. Then, the camera panned out to reveal he was the sole occupant at the witness table. A glass of water and sheet of paper were in front of him. There was an empty seat behind him, no doubt where his wife sat before she was hit with the pie. First a federal agent was kidnapped, now a judge's wife was accosted at the Capitol. What was America coming to?

Senator Briggs folded his hands in front of him, his voice loud. "If we have security to protect us from people bringing guns into the Senate buildings, we should be able to screen for cream pies. Judge Cuttering, thank you for returning this morning to allow the Senators to complete their questions. Please accept my apologies for the offense to your lovely wife. "

Chuckles spread through the audience. Nolan swiped a hand through straight hair, parted on the side. The camera panned out, showing all the Senators, then stayed on the junior Senator from California. Other than the fact that Lars Zorn used to be an actor and Governor of California, Dwight knew little about him. In an intense conversation with an aide behind him, Zorn's handsome face shone, like he had just won an Oscar.

Christine turned to Dwight. "When do you leave?"

He glanced at the clock on the side table. "Pretty soon. I'd like to see—"

Nolan pulled the microphone toward his mouth. "Mr. Chairman, I have an additional statement to make, if I may."

Briggs looked puzzled. "Senator Zorn is about to ask you questions, but if he doesn't mind, I guess you earned that right."

The camera flipped to Zorn. With an accommodating smile, Zorn said he would yield to the nominee. A jurist with deep intellect, Nolan's opinions were studied for his wit and fine writing. Now at the witness table, muscles twitched on both sides of his face, and Dwight recognized the same intensity as when they served on a committee for courtroom security. A federal judge's home had been broken into and his son killed. Nolan wanted the U.S. Marshals, the agency in charge of security for judges, to do more.

Now that same judge, who lobbied Congress for an extra ten million to keep federal judges safe, had seen his wife creamed by a pie. Dwight twisted his fingers. If that happened to Christine, what would he do?

Nolan sipped some water. "Seven years ago, this committee sent my nomination for Court of Appeals to the full Senate. I answered your questions then, as I did yesterday, some of which have no bearing on my suitability to be a justice on the Supreme Court. You asked the name and party of every President I ever voted for, how much money I gave to political campaigns, and which charities I gave money to."

The nominee's hand gestured from left to right. "You ask these things to please interest groups and gain support back home. I wish I had not asked my wife to accompany me today. It is none of your business whom she volunteers for, whether it is a pregnancy clinic or an animal shelter. She is not the nominee." If possible, Nolan's cheeks beamed even more red.

All color drained from Christine's face. She grabbed Dwight's hand. "I feel for his wife."

Mandy jiggled keys in her hand. "Mom, are you coming with me to the caterers?"

"I'll stay with Dad, watch this a little while."

Mandy headed for the garage humming a tune. Nolan continued to lecture the Senators, his voice razor sharp. "After what you put me through, I can honestly say most of you are not interested in giving advice and consent to the President as the Constitution requires. Rather, some Senators and their staff, I will not name names, you know who you are, seek to destroy the Judiciary, our third branch of government."

Dwight sat back stunned. This wasn't the Nolan he knew. This was a lion on the attack against an enemy. Had he lost his mind? True, many federal judges felt the same way, but it was risky to say so at your confirmation hearing.

He turned to Christine. "He'll never be confirmed if he keeps poking them in the eye."

Christine seemed mesmerized, as if in another world.

Like a relief pitcher about to be called in the middle of a ball game, Nolan was getting warmed up. "You attack me for being a hunter, without telling the public my family eats what I shoot. My hunting club gives hundreds of pounds of venison to homeless shelters every year."

He sipped more water. "To you, my leisure activities are more important than my judicial philosophy. Senate staffers circulated negative talking points about me. Animal rights activists picketed my home. I was forced to obtain a personal protection order to keep domestic terrorists from stalking my family. Now, this morning, my wife is assaulted. I do not care if, as the ranking member said, it is just a pie. Next time it could be a can of paint or something worse."

Christine turned to Dwight, and tears clung to her lashes. Her voice was soft. "He's right."

Dwight tucked her hand into his.

Judge Cuttering folded the paper in front of him. "The attacks on me and my family are outrageous. I refuse to be a pawn, caught in the middle of a political battle between the executive and legislative branches. Chairman Briggs, I withdraw my name for appointment to the United States Supreme Court. During the recess, I called the President. He knows of my decision and tried to talk me out of it. I only hope that by this extreme measure, future nominees will not endure this circus."

The cameras followed as Judge Cuttering strode from the hearing room, head and back straight as a steel rod. Dwight's mouth hung ajar. "He just called me the other night and said nothing about a protection order. He can't withdraw."

The usually composed Senate panel sat in awkward silence, apparently with no prepared statement to read. Chairman Briggs banged his gavel a few times, puffed out his cheeks, before Senator Zorn made what Dwight thought was an insensitive statement.

"Mr. Chairman, because Judge Cuttering cut and ran, I am saved from having to question him and show how opposed he is to the values we Americans hold dear. I am glad he withdrew. What's a little pie? He doesn't have the stuff to be a Supreme Court Justice."

The news switched to the White House, where a reporter was asked for the President's reaction. In answer, he admitted that his network had no advance knowledge and was trying to learn if the President would hold a press conference. Dwight clicked off the set. He couldn't stand another minute of it. The gall of Senator Zorn to criticize Nolan so flippantly.

Christine's voice trembled. "I am glad your name is not on any list for the Supreme Court. If they came after me like that, I would go to pieces."

Dwight rubbed her hands, which were cold. "No, you wouldn't."

"Yes, I would."

He stood. "Rest easy. I'm not on the list, because I'm not a federal appellate judge."

Christine's blue eyes were wet. "Some day you will be nominated for the Court of Appeals. Then, they'll come after you like a pack of hounds."

Dwight's mind was a blank. He could only think to say, "There's no need to worry."

His wife moved to the sliding glass door, looked out on her immaculate garden. She spoke just above a whisper and he strained to hear. "What if they find out? We'll be ruined."

Dwight moved next to her, placed his arm around her back. A strong hand on her arm, he pulled Christine to his side. "That was a long time ago. If it happens, and I say if, we could handle the issue. You were young—"

Christine tore away from his hand, and raced up the stairs, away from him. He was glad Mandy was out of the house. His wife needed a few minutes to compose herself, then he'd go up and suggest they invite someone over for dinner. She loved to entertain, and that would take her mind off the past. Now was definitely not the time to share his secrets.

Griff waited until a few minutes after five to call Judge Pendergast. He figured most of the court staff would be gone. There was no answer. Sal sauntered into his cubicle. Griff waved him away.

Sal was not deterred. "What's up, man? You look all serious."

Griff held the receiver in his hand. "Can I help you, Sal?"

"If it's the Director, don't let me mess up your next promotion. I need Frank's address."

Griff hung up. "It's in the file. I know because I wrote it."

"The one in Phoenix, not Virginia. He's gone."

Griff's eyes widened. "Again? It's in there, Sal."

Sal mimicked a bow, shot across to his cubicle. Griff reached the judge on his cell.

"Your Honor, do you have a moment?"

"Yes, just one. I am on the way to do an errand for my wife."

"The individual," he was reluctant to say "your brother" on the cell, "that went to Texas, do you remember anything else about him?"

Silence met him. The FBI agent imagined the judge's mind reeling back and he wanted to ask, did they swing together, run around the yard? Out of respect, Griff waited. He heard a breath. "I was a baby. My mind can't grasp Arthur's face. It's like he never existed."

"I've done a cursory search on the internet, and come up with some possibilities." That was enough. No need to get his hopes up, yet.

Judge Pendergast sounded numb. "Call either number at any time."

"Count on me, Your Honor."

Griff hung up before the judge harangued him for not using his first name. He went to see if Sal needed help finding Williams. Griff was getting to be an expert at that. Sal did ask for his help. Without the victim, Frank Williams, the new Jones case was in danger.

By six, Griff was at Eva and Scott's garden party for Kaley, bearing cookies and balloons for the kids. He played catch with Andy, who was a natural athlete; his ball hit Griff's mitt every time. Griff invited Eva and her family to a Nationals game before the season ended, and ate one too many burgers.

He liked Scott's idea to use private pilots to give joy rides to the children of wounded soldiers. Eva's husband used his influence as press secretary to the SecDef to work with an association of private pilots, which in turn recruited pilots and agreed to underwrite the cost of aircraft rental and insurance. Intrigued, Griff promised to take some kids on short flights around Virginia next Saturday.

As it turned out, June Livingston did not make it to the party. His life was filling with fun things, even if his caseload was skimpy. Griff decided not to think any more about June. She was not meant to be.

EIGHTEEN

At their regular Friday morning meeting, Senator Zorn clapped Arnie on the back. "Did the police ever catch the person who hit Mrs. Cuttering in the face with the pie?"

Arnie bought the Senator a bottle of champagne to toast their success in forcing Cuttering to withdraw. "No. He was a smooth operator, whoever he was."

Lars hadn't touched the bubbly. It was a nice effort, but he never drank. Arnie knew that, but was making a point. They won. Round one anyway. The Senator's chiseled face hardened. "It's no time to slack. I know this President. He'll ram through the next nominee before we have a chance to derail him or her. Are we ready for round two?"

Arnie handed him a sheet, fresh off his printer. "Here are the top three names. My source is most credible."

Lars scanned the paper. "Are we collecting data to use against these three persons?"

His chief of staff grinned. "I will have a dossier by today's end for you to review."

The Senator rapped his knuckles on his desk, calculating his next victory. "I will so enjoy my lunch today with Senator Briggs. He is upset by my comment about Cuttering. That's too bad."

Arnie left to begin compiling his dossier. Lars straightened the knot of his silk tie, thinking how easy it would be for him to convince Briggs he was sorry, when in reality he was ecstatic that Cuttering's wife was smeared.

All day yesterday, Griff called the Bailey residence in Waco and got no answer. They must have stayed late at the birthday party for their old friend. Now it was three o'clock on Friday, and Phyllis's phone still rang. At last, an answering machine clicked on. Griff left his cell number, then got ready to leave the office to go flying. Sal was on the phone across the cubicle. Griff decided to wait a few minutes and ask if he'd found Frank.

He checked his e-mails. One was from Eva to confirm his flying time tomorrow with the wounded soldier's children. He typed an answer that he'd meet Scott at ten. That was the main reason he wanted to go up today. Get the kinks out, check the plane.

His cell chirped a single ring. The LED screen said it was from Texas. He guessed correctly—it was Phyllis Bailey. Her voice sounded like she was in a tunnel. It was hard to hear. He yelled into the phone. "Did you say something got loose?"

Sal stuck his head around the soft wall and gave him a wild look.

She yelled back, "Might as well have lost. I've got bad news. Mrs. Everson said we were born in Texas, like I said."

Griff lowered his voice. "She might be wrong."

The connection cleared and it was like Phyllis was in the room. "Mr. Topping, she's sharp as a tack. Said Arthur and me had no brother or sister, or anything. Arthur was ten months old when our folks died. I never did know for sure. Wasn't important."

She let out a dazzling whistle, like she was calling a sheep dog or something. A sharp ring reverberated in Griff's ear. His hearing would never be normal again, of that he was sure. So, it was impossible for them to be related to Judge Pendergast. "Phyllis, I wanted you and Arthur to find your brother. I am sorry for any trouble I caused."

"No trouble, except my canning is ruined. No matter. I'll start over this afternoon. Agent Topping, if you ever get to Waco, we would love to have you stop in. Try my pecan pie. The best around. And, Arthur and me, we respect our government out here."

He told her thanks. It was encouraging to hear she was a law-abiding citizen. After telling her that he'd like to meet them, too, he was back to square one. Griff got back on the computer, searching for Arthur. Sal came over to his cubicle and told him that Frank went to stay with his grandparents for a rest. Before leaving, Sal invited Griff over tomorrow, after flying. "Eat a few brats, watch the Yankees game. I never have been able to cheer for the Nationals."

Griff never said no to baseball, but he wasn't sure what time he'd finish flying. "I can call as soon as I touch down."

His notes stared back at him. Phyllis Bailey and her brother came to nothing, much like June Livingston. Logical sources revealed no close matches. Griff Topping was at a dead end. He wrote Arthur's name on a legal pad and everything he knew. It was as if he willed it, Arthur would reach out and call him, or send him an e-mail. He seemed that real.

The office was quiet, except for an annoying hum from the hall clock. Griff thought many times of disabling it, but never wanted it said he destroyed government property. He tried to put the irritating sound out of his mind. The longer Griff thought about Arthur, the more he was reminded that he found Williams by building on facts. When he had nothing to go on, he improvised, like knocking on the chalet's door and pretending to be a renter. Then, it hit him like a fast ball thrown hard in the glove. His logic was flawed.

Arthur was Dwight's brother in blood only. If two brothers were raised in different families, it was possible Arthur had no education, no advantages. He could have been adopted by poor parents, or not adopted at all. His sibling might have been raised in an orphanage, his last name changed—as was Dwight's. The what-ifs nearly forced him to give up. But, those two words did not exist in Griff Topping's vocabulary.

With his left hand, he toyed with the ends of his moustache. He had one more database to check, and this one was secret. He did not know why he hadn't thought of it before. A few strokes later, his monitor screen was emblazoned with NCIC. Law enforcement officers accessed the National Crime Information Center, which was operated by the FBI, because it contained names and biographical information for every person arrested. Submitted to the FBI by the arresting police departments, the information was shared with other law enforcement agencies. Griff found the correct search field and entered the name, "BAILEY, ARTHUR."

Within seconds, those arrested with that name filled one page, then another. So many men had the name of Dwight's brother. He scanned the voluminous list. How to narrow the scope of his search? Based on their dates of birth, some of these had to be pushing up daisies. Arthur was two years older than Dwight, as reported by the adoption agency.

Into the field for date of birth, he typed in a new search criterion—1950 through 1952. Griff hit "enter." Bingo. Three Arthur Baileys shot back. Griff highlighted the one born in 1951, hit enter again, which reduced the field to one Arthur Bailey, who was arrested four years earlier by the DEA in Tampa, Florida. Previous arrests were for mail fraud and theft.

On a list of federal agencies, he found the Bureau of Prisons. Instead of voice mail, a person actually answered. "This is the locator desk for the Bureau of Prisons. Can I help you?"

In his career, he learned some employees didn't care if a fellow employee needed help, they were rude to everyone. He tried anyway. "This is Special Agent Griff Topping with the FBI. I need to find an inmate."

Her pleasant tone surprised him. "Good afternoon, Agent Topping. Let's have the name and date of birth." He listened to the clicking of computer keys. "I am sorry. You can't go to prison to see Arthur Bailey."

"He died?"

She clucked her tongue. "Not that. He's been released and his file is transferred."

Griff got busy taking notes. "Can you tell me where?"

"Yes, sir. To the U.S. Probation Office in Panama City, Florida."

Not a total dead end. Still, he might be the wrong guy. "Thanks. You've been helpful."

"And you have a nice day, Agent Topping."

If Arthur's file was transferred to the federal records center, it would take Griff forever to get copies. He decided to try Panama City. A machine came on, said the office was closed. Griff did not want to leave a message. This mission was too sensitive.

It was after six in Virginia, the Florida panhandle was an hour earlier. He would have to wait until Monday. Griff shut down his computer, turned off the office lights. In his bucar, the heat was oppressive. He blasted on the air conditioning and for the first time in years, going home alone didn't appeal to him. A few miles from his house, he passed a sports restaurant that served spicy Tex-Mex food. Griff pulled in, but the parking lot was packed. The Nationals were playing against the Dodgers tonight. Even if he had a long wait, he really had nothing else to do.

From home on Monday morning, Griff called the Probation Office in Panama City. The receptionist promptly put him on hold while she found the officer who handled Arthur Bailey. Griff listened to soft music. His weekend turned out better than he thought it would. For one thing, his flying experience on Saturday was great. What a tremendous bunch of kids. He thanked Scott for including him and volunteered to help out again.

When Mr. Bailey's probation officer came on the line, Dawn Ahern confirmed she had a releasee by that name, since it was public information. But, she would not discuss her cases without proper identification. The file was confidential. She refused to verify Mr. Bailey's address or birth date.

Dawn spoke in a friendly, but firm tone. "Send me a letter on FBI letterhead, so I can talk to you on the phone."

That was an hour ago. Since then, Griff drove to the office, typed a letter, and faxed it on the FBI machine. No doubt if he faxed it from home, she'd accuse him of putting something over on her. He supposed precautions were a part of working with released prisoners. For the time being, Griff concentrated on a new stock fraud case.

By noon, when Ms. Ahern hadn't called back, Griff took Sal to lunch at Rob's Deli. He had researched on the net about the lost boys, mentioned it to Sal. Both FBI agents were amazed at the hardship the lost boys endured. As he hoped, Wally took their orders and brought their sandwiches, a "Duffer" for Griff and a "Birdie," for Sal, which was a crab-cake sandwich. Their orders came with fried sweet potato chips and iced tea. When Wally returned to check on them, Griff found out he was in his second year at a local community college. What came after, Wally wasn't sure.

Griff gazed up at the tall man. "I read that you boys endured tremendous suffering wandering around, and in the refugee camp. Would you ever write about it and tell others?" Sal's scowl made Griff think he crossed a cultural line. "I have a legitimate reason for asking."

Wally bent on his knees. "I tried to put the terrors out of my mind. It is not easy. We were beaten, robbed, and forced to walk hundreds of miles to find safety."

Sal ate his sandwich, but Griff could tell he was listening. His head was tilted, like he was memorizing everything Wally said. Sal had something close to a photographic memory. Griff's appetite disappeared. From his research, he knew things were much worse than Wally admitted.

Griff took an FBI card from his wallet, wrote on the back, and handed it to Wally. "I graduated from a private college in Pennsylvania, and I'm on their scholarship board. The college has a scholarship for students who survived great hardships in their lives."

Sal put down his sandwich. "Yeah. Agent Topping told me on the way over about you and the other guys. Some were reunited with their families."

Wally studied Griff's card. "My family was killed in the war. I am grateful to be alive."

A surge of compassion hit Griff. He was determined to help this young man. "You should consider applying for the scholarship. It would require giving details. The internet has many articles, and I could help you attach some to your application."

A look of sadness eased from Wally's face. "I should like to know more about your school and the scholarship. It helps me to see God has a plan for me."

Griff held out his hand for his card, then wrote down the college's website. "My phone number is on here, too. If the school looks good, call me. I will get the scholarship application."

Wally put the card in his front shirt pocket. "God is to be thanked for your kindness. You see, he arranged for me to meet you. I better check on the other customers."

After Wally left, Sal shoved the last of the Birdie in his mouth, then swallowed it with a gulp of tea. "With eight brothers and sisters, I thought I had it bad growing up. We were always scratching for enough to eat. Imagine him thanking God after what he went through."

Griff thought the exact thing, not because of eight brothers and sisters. He and his brother lived on plenty of everything growing up, especially baseball. Sal wiped his mouth, and Griff felt a need to give back. He took out a credit card. "Lunch is on me today, buddy."

His life was never clearer than at this moment. After Sue's death, he shut himself in a shell of work. That was respectable, he told himself. Except for visiting Gram in Cornwall, he kept his family at bay. Eva, Scott, and the kids poked through the armor at times, but only occasionally, like when he played ball with Andy the other day.

Griff never thought about God's plan for his life, as Wally did. With the way Sue died, that was impossible to believe. But, he could do something for others, besides putting bad guys in prison. He reminded Wally to call him. The young man smiled and waved, and Griff knew he would. He vowed to download the application and bring it to Wally himself.

Back at the office, Griff checked his messages. Ms. Ahern hadn't called after getting his fax. He got busy writing his final report on Owen Jones III. As he worked on it, Sal sauntered in.

"Guess what Daddy's boy is claiming now?"

Griff stopped writing. "It's cruel and unusual punishment to keep him in prison, because the new judge refuses to set a bond."

Sal smiled. "Besides that."

Griff shook his head.

"Owen Jones III claims he's got dirt on the White House. If we release him on bond, he'll divulge what he knows."

Griff leaned back in his chair. "Did he tell you that?"

Sal chuckled. "Well, he passed a note to a deputy marshal to give to me."

Griff wiped his moustache. He hesitated telling Sal what to do. "We work for the Bureau, and that guy kidnapped one of ours, held him hostage. Frank may never be the same."

A thundercloud passed over Sal's features. "Yeah. What if Jones was a patsy for someone higher? Frank arrested him before he could prove it."

"With Owen Jones's record, you have huge problems trying to present him as a credible witness."

"Believe me, I want Jones to pay. But first, I'll interview him, see what's on his mind."

Griff's intercom buzzed. Ms. Ahern was on the main line, instead of his private one. She must still be suspicious of his motives. After spending days tracking the judge's brother, he was not about to be derailed by a bureaucrat with ideas of power.

In a surly mood, he answered, "FBI Agent Griffin Topping. Who's calling?" Of course, he knew it was Ms. Ahern, but he made her give her name anyway. At her hostile tone, he clapped a hand over the receiver and sighed. Pride had no place here. This was for the judge. Sal rolled his eyes and returned to his cubicle.

"I assume you got my letter on FBI letterhead. Will you answer my questions?"

She cleared her throat. "With all the rain, I have a sore throat. I hope you can hear me."

Too bad she was sick. But, that did not excuse her waiting hours to call him back. Course, maybe she had to go to the doctor. "Loud and clear."

"Sorry to trouble you with sending a letter. I am careful, because some releasees have faked calling about themselves, giving pretend references for jobs and so forth. Why is the FBI interested in Arthur Bailey?"

"He's done nothing, as far as I know. Tell me about where he was born, his siblings."

Ms. Ahern was having none of it. "Agent Topping, why do you want to know?"

Griff rehearsed the angle he'd use. "I have no interest in him as a criminal. A colleague of mine was adopted, and now has a health problem. He needs my help finding his relatives."

"So, another FBI agent does not want to be the one searching. It is too painful if he does not find who he is looking for."

She sounded like a shrink, needing to know the reason for everything. He'd humor her without giving any details. He had to be shrewd, or she would drag the truth out of him like she did her releasees. "Not an FBI agent, but he is in the federal system."

"That sounds like code for a federal prisoner."

Griff set down his pen. This was getting nowhere. "Why do you think that?"

"Because of Skeeter's long history with crime."

"I know Arthur Bailey has a record. Who is Skeeter?"

Dawn coughed. "Just a minute."

Glad they weren't meeting in person, he waited for her to quit coughing. Her voice sounded rough. "Skeeter is Arthur Bailey's street name. He prefers it, so I call him that."

"Okay, save your throat. I'll talk."

He told her how he found Arthur in the Bureau of Prisons records, and she confirmed his file was in front of her. Did she know his blood type? Yes, type B, positive.

"And," she said, "it's interesting you should ask. In prison, Skeeter donated blood and indicated on the form he would be an organ donor. Many prisoners want to impress the Bureau of Prison employees that they are good citizens."

Griff was amazed that Dawn volunteered the information. "NCIC shows he was born in 1951."

"Correct, on August 13. It looks like he spent most of his life in Florida."

Excitement percolated within Griff. Was he getting close to finding Dwight's brother? When he asked about Skeeter's family, she poured cold water on his hopes.

"His file makes no mention of a brother." Dawn was silent a moment, and Griff imagined she was leafing through the records. "Wait a minute. Upon discharge from prison, he said he had a sister. An older sister, location unknown."

Griff slumped in his chair. "No brother?"

"No. Is it possible he was too young to remember?"

He made notes, but his heart was not in it. "My friend doesn't re-member much himself."

"Skeeter was in and out of foster homes. He is new to me. I can ask."

Ms. Ahern was getting ahead of him. Griff had another idea. "Can you fax a photo?"

"We take photos of all our releasees, but I don't know if I should send it."

Griff kept frustration under the radar. "You have my letterhead. Trust me on this."

Another cough. "Is tomorrow morning okay? I leave at three."

Gram always told him, "Griff, season your words with honey." He'd not done so with Ms. Ahern, and his conscience nagged at him. He liked to get along with everyone he worked with, so he said, "I hope you feel better." And he meant it, mostly because if she was sick, it might take another day to get the photo.

"Thanks, Agent Topping. I'll remember that."

That was nice, but would she remember to fax the photo? If not, he'd have to begin with Ms. Ahern all over again tomorrow, which did not appeal to him at all.

NINETEEN

Dwight would always remember it was the second of August when the call came, because it was the one that, like a bugle, began the hunt. Thirty minutes before he received it, he was at the neighborhood gourmet store, grinding coffee. As the aroma lifted around his nose, he wondered how close Griff was to finding his brother. He hadn't heard from him since that rather odd call last week. With his courtroom experience, he knew when an agent was holding back.

He paid for the coffee, then rushed back home, all the while digging deep in his memory to find some shred of Arthur. Nothing. When he pulled in the driveway, Veronica's car was nestled in front of his garage door. He parked behind her. In the kitchen, he kissed Christine on the cheek, held up the bag. "I got Hazelnut."

She took the coffee, measured it into a filter. "I almost didn't get home in time."

Dwight washed his hands, took a basket of rolls and set it on the dining room table, where Stuart was holding Veronica's left hand with his right. Her face glowed with expectant motherhood.

Mandy sat across from them, talking about a five-piece band she hired for the reception. She should have said he hired them, because Dwight was paying every nickel. He'd ask Christine after dinner how much it cost. Then, he remembered her tears last week when Nolan withdrew. He'd keep his mouth shut. It was only money.

Besides, the wedding was supposed to be a happy event. Tonight, if they stayed on that topic, no one would bring up the idiocy of news coverage since he dismissed the Jones case. Not only did the Lake Michigan tribe hold one press conference, they had a second one where other tribes criticized him before the microphone. A regular circus, and he was the bearded lady. He paid little attention to any of it. He despised himself for thinking that one good thing came from Nolan's withdrawal—the media had left Dwight to cover a new catastrophe.

Christine brought in grilled chicken and vegetables. Fresh basil leaves adorned the center. Dwight dished it up on the white china plates. In tall crystal glasses, strawberries floated in her homemade lemonade. Veronica brought a spinach and tortellini salad. Surrounded by his loving family, the voices of Dwight's critics evaporated.

Mandy picked at her chicken. "At first, the music will be classical." She smiled at Christine. "In your honor, Mom, then they'll move into a couple of sixties, for Dad."

The phone rang in the kitchen. Dwight was chewing. "Let it ring."

Whoever it was hung up. The answering machine did not come on. He took another bite. "See, a sales call."

Christine's light eyebrows knit together. "We're registered on the do-not-call list."

Dwight was buttering his roll when the phone struck again. This time a voice he did not recognize said on the machine, "It is urgent I speak with you."

It might be connected to Christine's parents in Austria. He got up, nearly knocked over his chair, to grab the phone. "This is Dwight. May I help you?"

The caller identified himself, then asked an astonishing question. Dwight replied, "Yes, I am available to meet, and nothing has happened since we last talked that reflects adversely on the President." He kept his voice calm but inside he felt excitement. "Thank you."

Dwight returned to the table. "Monday, I have a meeting at eight o'clock."

Veronica stared at him. "What was that about the President?"

His eyes scoured Christine's face. She managed a smile, but Dwight's appetite had disappeared. "Jasper Collins wants to see me. It's routine for a judge aspiring to the Court of Appeals to see the Chief of Staff."

Veronica was unconvinced. "I work at the White House, remember? This sounds like something more."

Dwight studied his family. Of course, he trusted them. "Keep this quiet. When the President announces the new nominee for the Supreme Court, he may elevate me to the vacant circuit position."

Christine's fork landed on her plate. The clanging sound covered up her nervous laugh. "I hope we don't move."

"Not before my wedding anyway." Mandy stood. "Chad is coming, we're going to the tux store for measurements." She left the room.

Veronica touched his arm. "Whatever it is, you'd be great. I could tell that to the President."

Dwight laughed. "Let me have the meeting first."

Veronica laughed. "Okay, if you say so. I'm cancelling my vacation this week and going back to work in the morning."

Stuart's face was pensive. "What if Bernie asks how you're doing?"

Unfortunately, Bernie could not keep a secret. To him, information wielded power, and he used it often. Dwight toyed with his unused knife. "Don't mention it. I am sure this is no big deal."

Christine rinsed the dishes, put them in the dishwasher. Dinner was over. Veronica and Stuart just left, and she was tired. The bones in her feet ached. Dwight was in the living room, watching the news. She sat with him a few minutes, but had no interest in the headlines about the latest terror attacks in Europe or whom the President would nominate to the Supreme Court.

Tomorrow would bring new demands. Mandy wanted Christine to select her dress for the wedding. Somehow, she had no desire to shop for a pink mother-of-the-bride dress. She leaned against the counter, massaged her temples. Louis and Naomi Sumner graciously offered Mandy their home near Mount Vernon for the wedding. The yard was twice as large as theirs and could easily hold two tents for the reception. It was a sweet gesture, one for which Christine felt indebted.

When Chad picked up Mandy, he stayed less than one minute. Rattled his keys the whole time. That boy—he was barely old enough to be called a man—never relaxed. Maybe Mandy liked that high energy, but Christine didn't. When she grew up, her father, the Austrian Ambassador to the U.S., was rarely home. Her childhood, with no chance to develop relationships or sink roots in one place, left scars. Not the surface kind on her forehead, which she concealed with makeup, but deep, emotional ones that lasted a lifetime.

Maybe that was why she fell for Dwight so quickly, and so hard. He became her family. Because Christine hungered to understand everything about human emotions, she pursued a doctorate in psychology. Scraps of chicken and zucchini went down the disposal. The grinding sound made her wince. At her age, she now saw that the more she learned, the further she was from knowing anything about anyone.

Her life began to feel like one of Bach's somber cantatas, and tonight she needed something soothing, not troubling. Christine popped in a CD of violin music. Her passion for classical music began as a child when she learned to play the violin, but it had been years since she touched her instrument. Strains of Bach mingled with memories of her sweet grandmother playing the great man's music on records. Gradually, pains in her head subsided.

She squirted liquid soap in the dishwasher. Her mind veered from the routine to her youngest daughter. Should she caution Mandy about living with a man so much like Christine's father, someone who was always on the edge? Chad was only twenty-three. Still, character formed in younger years often hardened into a dysfunction as one grew older. She snapped shut the door and was about to turn the knob to wash when the phone rang. It seemed they were on everyone's call list.

The crisp voice on the other end sounded like a sales lady, but it belonged to Rita Spitzer. "How is Mandy's wedding coming along?"

Christine was not up for talking. "Hectic. And Linda's?" With Winston being the grandson of the founder of Bernie's firm, it would be interesting to see how family dynamics played out. Seemed to Christine that Bernie was trying to build a type of dynasty. Rita prattled on about the guest list, which included members of the President's cabinet.

Christine asked polite questions. "Who is coming?"

"Secretaries of State, Defense and Interior, so far. Oh, and Jasper Collins, the President's Chief of Staff."

"Quite a list of politicians." Christine did not tell Rita there was no way the Secretary of Interior, Mr. Owen Jones, II, would be invited to Mandy's wedding. Not after Dwight's dismissal of the case against his son caused such a furor among several Native American tribes. Christine kept her own counsel, and listened to the growing list of celebrities.

When Rita drew breath, Christine interjected, "How is it going for you, Rita?"

"Fine, until Bernie got this new scheme going."

Christine sighed. "Which new scheme?"

Rita's chuckle sounded like a casserole exploding in the microwave. "You should know, you talked him into it. So, instead of being ahead of the curve for Linda's wedding, I am behind. Next time, keep your ideas to yourself. It was so false of you, Christine."

As her friend became hotter, Christine fought to remain cool. "If I offended—"

Rita blurted, "That huge house at the lake. The one you took us to see last time. You knew Bernie would want to buy it."

Christine's voice rose. "It was for charity. I thought you enjoyed the tour. If you imagine it was more than a social night out, you are seriously mistaken."

With Rita's escalating snide remarks, Christine doubted her protestations were getting through. Rita held fast to her version of events for years, even when she was wrong.

Rita lobbed another shot. "Maybe Bernie said it was your idea. I forget. It's too late now. We signed the papers, but I'm not happy. The distance to Smith Mountain Lake is farther than the Chesapeake, where I wanted to buy. Besides, Annapolis is more fashionable."

"I am sorry you feel that way." Her headache roared to life. From her junk drawer, Christine pulled out a blank sheet and started her to-do list for tomorrow.

"Christine, what should I do about my party for Judge Cuttering on Saturday, the one to celebrate his confirmation? Since he withdrew, I am unsure what to do."

Christine had forgotten that invitation. "If it was my party, Rita, I would call everyone you invited and see if they want to come to support Nolan and his family. They need it."

Rita sighed. "I wished I never planned it. Bernie told me you weren't going to have one, so I felt he wanted me to."

Christine shook her head. Why did it always come back to her? She refused to accept blame. "I'll ask Dwight. He and Nolan are friends." She hoped that would clue Rita to end the call. It worked.

Rita said, "Good idea. Let me know," and hung up.

"Ask me what?"

Dwight had just walked into the kitchen. Christine leaned against the counter. "That was the strangest call from Rita. She practically accused me of secretly arranging for her and Bernie to see the house they're buying. Remember the night we went there on the charity tour?"

Dwight drew her into his arms. "That's absurd. Don't worry about it."

Easy for Dwight to say. He was not the accused. Christine tried valiantly to put it out of her mind. "Oh, I nearly forgot. She asked for your advice about her party for the Cutterings."

He gave her a squeeze. "My advice is for Rita to ask the Cutterings what they want and for you," he touched her nose with his finger, "to stay out of it."

That was a perfect plan. She would call and leave Rita a message tomorrow, when she might not be home. Christine did not want to even hint to her that Dwight had a meeting at the White House. What would Rita say if she knew?

For a fleeting second, Christine relished the idea of having one up on Rita. Elation soon dissolved into guilt. She did not need to elevate herself by feeling she was better than Rita. Besides, a more important question saturated her emotions, one that needed an answer before tomorrow. How did she really feel about Dwight getting promoted to the circuit bench, and what would she tell him?

A few hours later, Dwight had waited up for Mandy, and now reset the alarm. With a heavy burden, he walked up the stairs where Christine was getting ready for bed. She may not be in favor of a move, but he missed the mental rigors of being an appellate judge. Presiding over trials was interesting, even demanding, but it did not invigorate his mind like deciding how *stare decisis*, settled case law, applied to modern conflicts.

Until Jasper's call, he didn't realize how much he enjoyed the camaraderie of discussing law with other judges on the panel. A trial judge had little interaction with other judges. Dwight loved to blow dust from old legal volumes, and find that a 1930s case held the key to an appeal. His love of history permeated all things he touched, from his study of George Washington, to his classic car, "The Judge," to the law.

Upstairs he found Christine sitting on their bed, staring out the window across her garden, probably at nothing. It was almost dark. He sat beside her, covered her hands with his. "The President may want me on the Fourth Circuit. We won't have to move. Since I was confirmed to the District four years ago, and was a state appellate judge, I should sail through."

She turned to him. "You want it, don't you?"

Dwight walked to the window, folded his arms on the ledge. No doubt, his life was great. But, was this all there was? If he turned down the President, he'd not get another chance to serve on a higher court. He reached for his wife to join him at the window. She folded her arm inside his, laid her head against his shoulder.

Dwight stroked her hair. "Christy, for a lot of reasons, I do. The more I preside over cases, the more I tire of reining in defense attorneys. I long to engage in a deeper application of the law. If the President asks me to the Fourth Circuit, I want to say yes, with your blessing. If you aren't sure—"

"Sshh." She touched his lips with her fingers. "You have it. You deserve every good thing."

These were words Dwight longed to hear. He hugged her tightly. "We'll see what tomorrow brings."

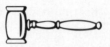

TWENTY

By noon the next day, Griff had seen the photo of Arthur Bailey, a.k.a. Skeeter. After he got over the shock, his immediate reaction was to fly to Florida, interview him right away. Dawn Ahern was against the idea, but promised to think it over. Eager to jumpstart his plan to find out if Skeeter could help the judge, Dawn was the one glitch. She was supposed to call this morning. Now, it was almost lunch time. Should he skip eating to wait for her call?

Griff had not yet told Dwight that Skeeter even existed. He first wanted to meet the man, size him up. Because of his criminal record, the judge might not want his kidney, even if they were related. His cell phone rang.

It was Eva Montanna. "Scott said you had a blast flying the kids."

"I'm glad you called. Remember Wally, the lost boy we met at Rob's Deli?"

She did. Griff told her he was taking Wally a scholarship application. "Want to join me?"

Eva's laugh was rich. "You got me hooked on Rob's. The only day I can go is today."

Griff checked his watch. Guess that clinched plans for the next hour. Dawn Ahern would have to wait, unless she called on his cell. Thirty minutes later, he and Eva were seated in a booth at his favorite lunch spot.

Wally served them Duffer sandwiches, with extra Swiss cheese for Eva. When Griff handed him the application, the young man was very appreciative. He told them he explored the college website, but he did not want to bother an FBI agent with his life.

When Wally left to get them more hot coffee, Griff's cell phone rang. He checked the LED screen. It was Panama City. "Ms. Ahern, what have you decided?"

When she replied she would allow him to interview Mr. Bailey, if she arranged it and went with him, Griff felt his brows rise. "Okay. I fly my own plane. What day is convenient for me to arrive? Not next Friday."

Eva munched her chips, looked around at Rob's golf memorabilia. He agreed to fly down tomorrow. The weather was supposed to be clear.

He switched the phone to his left ear. Because of firing his gun, the hearing in his right one was impaired. "I already mapped out my flight. Can I call you back this afternoon with details?"

Dawn agreed to arrange a time with Skeeter. Griff folded his phone.

It was Eva's turn to lift her delicate brows. "Sounds like an interesting case. Won't the FBI pay for your ticket to Florida?"

Griff took a couple bites of his sandwich, not liking to keep things from his former partner. Thankfully, Wally came back holding a pot of coffee. He refilled their cups, then left. Eva was done with her sandwich. Griff knew her mind was not distracted by hot coffee, although she loved the stuff as much as he did.

Her hands cradled her cup, blue eyes searched his face. "I think this is not a case at all and Ms. Ahern is someone special, who you would rather not talk about."

Oh, brother. When Eva got onto something, she never let it go until she knew all. He had to say something. He tried the old line he used on Dawn. "I'm helping an adopted colleague find his bio-family. I can't say more."

She drank her coffee. "Or won't."

That hurt. "Eva, it's confidential."

Her features eased. "I believe you." She changed the subject. "Wally was happy you brought the application. Do you think he needs help filling it out?"

That was a thought. He called Wally over. "I'm happy to come back, go over it with you."

Wally dipped his head. "It would be good if you could read what I write."

One plan in place, Griff hoped his trip to Florida tomorrow went as well.

The flight to Apalachicola was rough. Griff took off from Virginia on a beautiful clear day but hit turbulence over the mountains south of Asheville, North Carolina. When his Skyhawk began to bounce precariously, he deviated in search of kinder air. He finally found what he was looking for and, as he neared Panama City, right on the Gulf of Mexico, the blueness of the water startled him.

Thankfully, his touchdown on runway two-three was smooth because he really needed to get out of the plane. He hoped Skeeter's PO had not gotten sick of waiting for him. The air traffic controller handed him off to Panama City International Airport's ground controller, who directed him to the general aviation section of the airport. Griff wiped sweat from his forehead and taxied to a stop in front of the fixed base operator's building, known as the FBO, and turned off his engine. The propeller stopped abruptly. The cockpit's vibration ended, just as it was supposed to.

His headset off, Griff enjoyed the instruments' final whine. Already the cabin of the Cessna 172 Skyhawk was stifling. Griff quickly climbed from the plane, bent to touch his toes, then straightened. His back felt better. He stretched out both arms, turned from side to side. It was good to be out of the cockpit where he'd been confined for five hours, except for one stop to refuel. With all the vicious wind in the sky, he almost decided to head back, but the strong desire to meet Arthur Bailey made him soldier on to the Gulf.

On the ground, it was easy to feel that was the right decision. However, there was something he had to do before he found Dawn Ahern. Inside the FBO lounge, a computer tuned to the weather channel was on the service counter, which wrapped along one side. He wanted to check the weather for tomorrow, but hurried past the TV in the corner, its sound on mute. A lone woman was engrossed in a magazine. Her purplish hair, which looked fake, caused his heart to sink. The probation officer described her hair as black.

Griff approached her. "Ms. Ahern?"

The woman scowled at him from behind her magazine. "I don't know you."

He stepped back. "You're not Dawn Ahern?"

She pursed her lips, shook her head and went back to reading.

Relieved the uptight woman was not the PO, he mumbled. "Excuse the interruption."

Griff spotted the sign he was looking for and, on the way, he nearly ran into a petite woman coming out of the ladies' room. They stopped, two inches from a major collision. Both said, "Pardon me."

This woman's long black hair was drawn into a thick braid. Its clean shine complemented the exotic features of her face. He took a breath. "Do you happen to be Ms. Ahern?"

Her face lit up at the sight of him. She extended a hand. "You must be Agent Topping. Call me Dawn. How was your flight?"

"I'm Griff. The plane I flew didn't have a restroom, so I'm looking for one. Excuse me."

To the sound of her twinkling laughter, Griff walked to the counter and asked the clerk to have the Skyhawk refueled, then headed for the men's room. Back in the lounge, Griff found Dawn seated in a distant corner of the room, her file open. Griff sat in an adjoining fabric chair.

From his rear pocket, he took out his credential case. The gold badge on the outside gleamed in the light. "Since you insisted on a letter, I assume you want to see these."

Dawn's smile was like sunshine over water. "Not necessary. Only the FBI would care enough about my offender to fly here."

He noticed she didn't mention Skeeter's name in public. Professional, but overly-cautious. So far, she had not coughed, which was a good thing. An accordion file on the table was presumably Arthur Bailey's.

"Want to look through his file?"

Griff wrenched his eyes from her bright smile, a pleasing contradiction to her earlier suspicions of him. He skimmed the papers. "I should be familiar with the man before I meet him."

Dawn handed Griff the data sheet on Skeeter. A small photo was attached to the lower left corner. It was a miniature of the one she faxed, only this one was a color digital. Griff could not believe his eyes. It was Dwight Pendergast looking back at him. A worry-line across the forehead, just like the judge's. His brother had similar diamond-shaped ear lobes, and high cheekbones. Gray hair was tucked behind his ears. Griff reacted just as he had yesterday as the photo printed over the fax. The similarities between Arthur Bailey and the judge were plainly eerie. Arthur might be two years older than Dwight, but his lifestyle added many more.

There was no doubt that Arthur Bailey, this felon and Dawn's releasee, was Dwight's brother. Griff would wait until after he met Skeeter to decide how to break the news about him to the judge, as well as what happened since they were separated. He sensed Dwight would not take it well. Dawn seemed to watch him, taking mental notes.

No reason to waste time. "Ready when you are."

She gathered her file. "He is expecting us."

Griff led the way to his plane. Intense August heat reflected from the asphalt. By now, the temperature in the Skyhawk would be even hotter. With a hand, he waved to Dawn. "You may get in. I need to check something first."

He used a tester to make sure the newly added fuel was not contaminated. If it contained water, they'd have to pump the tanks. Because Griff never got fuel from this operator before, he had no confidence the guy followed the strict guidelines for filtering fuel. At his flying club at Manassas, the fuel operator was legitimate, so it was never a problem.

Dawn walked around the plane like a pilot would. He was curious about her, a strong type, yet feminine. A bit like Eva. This thought put his mind at ease. Perhaps she was cautious by nature. Eva was. After Dawn demanded his letterhead, he wasn't sure what he had gotten into. Better put his eyes back to the fuel test or they'd never take off.

He let out a stiff breath. The fuel passed inspection. "Okay," he called.

His passenger walked to the correct door and waited for him to help her into her seat. Griff handed her a headset. When Griff slid into the left seat, Dawn's headset rested around her neck, properly plugged in.

Griff opened his window. Dawn's was already opened. She must have flown before in small planes. "You seem comfortable in here. Am I right?"

"I have flown for years."

With her attention to detail, she probably made a fine pilot. "Really! Are you licensed?"

"Yes. If you give me the checklist, I'll help you go over it."

Even though it was hot and he would usually be in a hurry, Griff had to know more. "Can you fly a Skyhawk?"

"Not just the Skyhawk, Bonanzas, too. I learned to fly in Hawaii."

So, she was Hawaiian. Dawn was talking. He'd better listen.

"My husband was an Air Force pilot. He encouraged me to keep up my license."

So, she was married. That was always the case. Griff finished going over the list.

She looked at him, headset around her neck. "He died two years ago. I try to keep current."

So, she was a widow. The strain in her voice told him she was still grieving. Well, as a widower, Griff could relate to her pain. "Dawn, I am sorry about the loss of your husband. I know how hard it can be. My wife died from cancer eight years ago."

He gazed into her face. She blinked back tears. Headset over his ears, he asked, "Ready?"

Dawn dabbed her eyes, then nodded. Griff adjusted the throttle, craned his neck to look beyond Dawn, then behind the aircraft. He leaned toward the open window and yelled, "Clear."

With that he turned the key. The Skyhawk's engine leapt to life. Dawn placed her headset over her ears and adjusted her microphone close to her lips.

Griff spoke into his microphone. "Up in the air, we'll get relief from the heat." In seconds, an idea came to him, and he never stopped to think he might regret it. "Do you want to fly us to Apalachicola? By my calculations, it's a twenty-minute flight."

Dawn rewarded him with that mesmerizing smile. "I would love it."

She handed the laminated checklist back to Griff. In his headset, he heard Dawn's soft, yet competent voice as she gave the aircraft tail number, displayed on the control panel, to the Panama City tower. "Preparing to depart for Apalachicola via VFR. Request permission to taxi."

The tower responded with the last three digits of the Skyhawk's tail number. "Two Lima Gulf, you're clear to taxi to runway zero-two-three and hold short."

Dawn repeated his instructions. Without hesitating, she increased power. The plane moved slowly toward the taxi way. At the intersections, Dawn looked left, then right. She stopped short of the runway and maintained pressure on the toe brakes.

Griff called off the checklist items and Dawn verified them. As she turned her yoke right and left, then in and out, she checked the response of the controls. She increased the RPMs and asked Griff to turn the key to check the magnetos. The list completed, Griff heard her in his headset, "Panama City Tower, Two Lima Gulf ready for takeoff on zero-two-three."

The tower told them they were cleared for takeoff on that runway, then added, "Turn left and maintain a heading of zero nine zero, and altitude of two thousand feet."

Dawn echoed, "Two Lima Gulf is cleared for takeoff on zero-two-three, maintaining a heading of zero-nine-zero and altitude of two thousand."

Griff had listened carefully. She's right on the money. After looking over her shoulder for incoming aircraft, Dawn powered up and turned onto the runway. Just like Griff would have, while still rolling, she applied full power and the aircraft sped down the runway straddling the center line. At sixty-five knots, she pulled back on the yoke, and the Skyhawk lifted off the runway.

As Dawn ascended to two thousand feet, Griff kept chitchat to a minimum. He watched her operate the controls, and something like pride swelled within him. Dawn was the first woman he'd seen since Sue who could handle an airplane with confidence. Griff's headset crackled as Panama City tower called.

"Two Lima Gulf switch to Tyndall approach at 124.15."

Immediately Dawn responded to the tower, then switched her radio frequency and contacted the Tyndall controller, who handled approaching aircraft. They told her how to skirt around the restricted area of Tyndall Air Force base. A short time later, Dawn neared Apalachicola Airport. She announced her intentions on channel 122.8. Griff marveled at her flawless approach and landing on runway zero-two-four of the uncontrolled airport.

The windows opened for cooling, Dawn shut down the engine, and removed her headset. "How are your nerves after flying with me? Will you make it to Skeeter's?"

Griff swiped his moustache with his hand. "Very well done. I enjoyed flying with such a skilled pilot." If it wasn't so corny, he wanted to add, "And, we're off to a flying start."

Griff borrowed the courtesy station wagon the airport kept for visiting pilots. With Dawn pointing, he drove the beater to Arthur Bailey's house, three blocks from the shrimp docks. He turned off the car, lowered the windows.

Griff checked his watch. A quarter to two. "So, you'll interview him, take a urine sample to see if he's being a good boy and not doing drugs. Then, it's my turn."

She gathered her file from the backseat. Fingers on the door handle, Griff saw her nails were short, as if she bit them. Did she sleep nights or stay awake, thinking of her husband?

Dawn faced him. "While you interview Skeeter about a possible organ donation, I'll walk to the Outrigger to meet the manager who claims he does odd jobs."

He liked her eyes. "After flying here, you could drive this heap with ease."

"I need the exercise. Besides, it's only two blocks. When you're done, come get me." She supplied directions.

"Don't forget to tell Skeeter about me."

This forced a tight smile on her lips. "The real you or the pretend you?"

Griff thrust a hand through his hair, which always swelled in humidity. "An organ researcher will do, thank you."

Dawn's laugh made his day. His year in fact. She stayed on point. "I will remind him that he gave blood in prison, signed up to donate an organ, and you are going to interview him about it."

When she opened the car door, it gave a definite squeak. Griff knew by now, Skeeter had gotten rid of anything incriminating. Well, Dawn had called yesterday to let him know they were coming. Griff shrugged it off, and watched her walk up to the front door. He found her attractive, and seeing her in person wiped out the negative feelings built up after talking with her on the phone. At the screen door, she knocked.

Would she turn to look at him? His mind urged her to, but then a man with graying hair, which fell below his chin, opened the door. That had to be Skeeter. Dawn stepped inside without turning. Oh well, it was not like this was some date.

To learn about the ex-con who might save the judge's life, Griff scrutinized the yard and exterior of Skeeter's house. Built on low piers, the structure was in need of some repair. A few dark-green lattice boards nailed around the base were broken, leaving holes big enough to permit creatures to take refuge beneath the house.

No way Griff would crawl under there to fix a sewer or water pipe. Just thinking of it, a sweat broke out on his forehead. He bounced out of the wagon, stretched his legs. He could face down terrorists, rappel out of a moving helicopter, and shoot Glocks or Sig Sauers and hit his target. But, being confined under that house would be sheer torture. Add to that snakes, gators, spiders, and armadillos, and Griff would pay a professional a hefty premium to make the repairs.

From the peeling paint on the window sills and untrimmed shrubs clinging to the house, Skeeter probably let his pipes leak. Was it possible he really was the judge's brother? He'd heard of babies being switched at the hospital. But, that photo of Skeeter did not lie. They were brothers all right.

Skeeter's vehicle must be parked in back. A lone metal chair, rusty at that, was on the front porch, with a foam cooler opened next to it. An empty flower pot on the front step suggested Skeeter wanted to make this place home, but didn't quite know how. A sago palm drooped in the front yard. Even the tropical storm that blew through the area the other day did not help the shriveled grass.

Back in the wagon, Griff reviewed his notes, including a list of questions for organ donors that he got from George Washington Hospital. If Dawn kept to her word, he'd meet Skeeter in five minutes. So far, she impressed Griff as not only good at her job, but forthright. The door squeaked. On the porch, Dawn waved.

It was a neighborly gesture, like they were all going to share fried oysters and greens. Griff knew better. He brought his senses to full alert; he was going in undercover. In the living room, Dawn introduced him to Skeeter, who averted his gaze. It took a lot of discipline for Griff not to stare, for looking at Skeeter was like looking at Judge Pendergast, only different. It was clear Skeeter was a man who traveled mostly wrong roads.

What a shame. His brother was a great man. Fine lines etched his face, especially around his eyes, which were the same shape, but lighter in color than Dwight's. Like the picture, the forehead bore the groove across the middle, only deeper, and the earlobes, there was no mistaking those. Griff shook his hand. Calluses told him Dwight's brother did some honest labor. Dawn held her file in one hand and, in the other, a small packet—presumably with Skeeter's urine sample.

She stopped by the door. "Remember, talking to Mr. Topping is voluntary. I am not requiring it in any way. But, when you donated blood, you said you would donate an organ. Mr. Topping, I will see you in fifteen minutes."

Dawn was gone. Griff looked around, impressed. Skeeter's house was cleaner than he'd imagined. The torn chair and card table were definitely not purchased at any tourist shop in downtown Apalach. It must be difficult for releasees to afford anything but essentials.

Griff nodded in an offhand way. "Can you spare a few minutes? I won't take much time."

Skeeter shrugged as if to say he had no better prospects, then pointed to the tattered card table. Two metal chairs, without rust, sat at ninety degree angles. Griff sat in one, opened his portfolio. "Ms. Ahern told you I am helping people find organs in time to save their lives. When you signed the form in prison, maybe you thought of pledging an organ upon your death. Many organs come that way."

Skeeter still would not meet his gaze. Maybe he guessed he was an FBI agent. Offenders sensed it when law enforcement officers were in their presence. It wouldn't matter. That was not why Griff was here.

He finished his rehearsed statement. "Out of a sense of caring for their fellow man or woman, some people donate a kidney. We can live with one kidney, if our health is all right. Are you interested in learning more about being a living donor?"

Like tiny bees, Skeeter's eyes darted between Griff's face, his file, then back to Griff's eyes. "I'm glad you said that. I was a wonderin' if you thought I cared enough to let 'em put me down, so they could get my organs. I've seen on TV that we're gettin' more liberal about medicine and death. I thought maybe it had gone too far."

So that was why he was evasive. He believed Griff wanted to hook him up with a doctor death. "Mr. Bailey, I am sorry. That is not my intention. I'm looking to find a living donor with the right blood type and so forth. To match you with someone who needs a kidney."

"Call me Skeeter, would'ya? I don't remember Mr. Bailey."

Griff turned to notes on a legal pad. "I have some questions to help decide if you are a suitable donor."

Skeeter again looked uncomfortable. He leaned forward, and his hands slicked back a strand of hair that fell in his eyes. "If I can be a donator, what's in it for me? Has my kidney got a dollar value to make it worth my while?"

Surprised by his bold question, Griff felt like a beggar looking for the ultimate handout. "Mr. Bailey, while it is illegal to sell an organ, and I'm not assuming you or anyone else wants to sell one, you can be reimbursed for expenses. It is my experience that people who donate do so because they care."

At the word illegal, Skeeter stiffened in the chair. "Oh, I care, Mr. Topping, I care. What do you mean, my expenses?"

Griff smiled. He was drawing Skeeter in, as he hoped to. "There are provisions to cover all of a donor's expenses, such as time away from your job, medical costs, things like that. Costs to donate a kidney can be great."

Skeeter nodded. "It don't hurt to answer your questions. I consider myself a caring person. I want Ms. Ahern to know I am, too. Say, call me Skeeter. Mr. Bailey sounds like my father."

This was the opening Griff wanted—to ask about his father. He moved down the list. Attentive, Skeeter edged closer to the table. Things might work out for Dwight after all. All too soon, Griff learned Skeeter knew little more than the judge about his family background.

Never adopted, Skeeter moved in and out of a foster home and had many fights with their tough-acting son. No mention of a blood brother. Griff asked Skeeter the medical questions. He confirmed he had type B blood, which was a possible match for Dwight, who was AB.

Griff picked up a legal pad to check off the next answers, which was on top of his notes about Dwight, his childhood, and so forth. Griff was careful not to pick these up. Skeeter moved his chair even closer. He never had polio, tuberculosis, heart trouble, or high blood pressure. What Skeeter said next nearly knocked Griff from his chair.

"If you want someone to testify to my good health, talk to my sister."

Griff stopped writing. "Your sister?"

Skeeter nodded proudly. "Eleanor is two years older than me. I tracked her down. Based on her good health, I should live to be an old man. She lives on an Indian Reservation in Florida."

"Are you and Eleanor Native Americans?"

Skeeter put a cigarette in his mouth, but didn't light it. "Eleanor lived there with some missionaries and just thinks she's an Indian. I don't."

Griff pointed to the cigarette. "Do you smoke?"

He shook his head as if it was connected to an electrical circuit. "No, sir. I just like the feel of the thing in my mouth."

Griff made a note, then moved on. The rest of the interview was routine. In a few minutes, he picked up his file, and shook Skeeter's hand. "If you are a match, what is the best way for me to reach you?"

Skeeter hesitated. "When you gonna call?"

Griff was not sure, in a week or two. Skeeter gave him a new number. "I may change it again. Ms. Ahern will always have my right one."

Griff left the house, hoping he hadn't forgotten anything important. It might have seemed suspicious to ask more about Eleanor. He did slip in a question about drug use and, as with his smoking, found Skeeter's denial hard to believe. On the way to the Outrigger, Griff thought about how to ask Skeeter's PO about his sister, without tripping her red flags. Griff had learned that Ms. Ahern's antennae were super-sensitive.

TWENTY ONE

On Monday morning, Dwight sipped tomato juice in an air-conditioned suite at a safe house, a street north of the White House. It was called a safe house because the media did not know of its existence. At least, not yet. Surrounded by paintings of Washington and Jefferson, which set him at ease, he sat alone in the spacious room, going over the judicial nomination form that he was handed nearly an hour ago. One item intrigued him: State your judicial philosophy in less than fifty words. That would take some brevity.

Most were general in nature. List all the speeches you have given in the last five years. Explain any area of your life that might cause embarrassment to the President. Dwight would say, "None." Once he read through the thick document, he rehearsed what he would say to the President.

Barbara Jo Houston, the President's Special Assistant, had greeted Dwight at seven, and promised he would be done in thirty minutes. A mantle clock, which looked like a precious antique, chimed 8:00 a.m. When he left home, he asked Christine to reschedule his dialysis for 9:00 a.m. His cushion of time was getting razor thin.

Ms. Houston walked in, carrying a small tray with another juice and apple Danish, which she set on a coffee table. He seized the chance to quiz her on his prospects of seeing the President. "I reviewed the questions the President will ask. I presume I will see him sometime this morning."

Her accent was as Southern as ham and red-eyed gravy. "I am sure it will be a few more minutes. Make yourself comfortable."

Comfortable! Dwight did a slow burn. If it was anyone but the President, he would have left long ago. Dwight rarely waited longer than five minutes. Except once, when he waited for Veronica to appear in her wedding dress so that he could take her to the parish church and walk her down the aisle. Of course, he forgave his daughter for keeping him waiting sixteen minutes.

He waved off the snack. "Thank you, I never eat sweets." His voice trembled. "I do not mean to sound agitated, Ms. Houston," she insisted he call her that, "I have another appointment at nine. Should I push it back?"

Dwight snapped on his reading glasses and double-checked the time. He would have to be on the machine by ten, at the latest.

Ms. Houston turned her head sideways, as if she were the matador and he were a bull. With her sleek hair lobbed off at her chin, she reminded him of a younger version of Constance Ingles, a self-assured career woman. "Judge Pendergast, I will notify the Chief of Staff that you have an appointment more important than the President of the United States."

She turned on three-inch heels and shut the door with a definite click. Why couldn't he learn to soften his tone? Christine cautioned him that some people mistook his desire for timeliness as something else—impatience. Dwight stood. Who was on the other side of the door? Even if it was Barbara Jo, he owed her an apology.

Dwight opened the door quietly to find her talking on a phone in an office near the front door. "Yes, Jasper, that is what the judge said. Either you get the President here or he would leave. His ego is bigger than the Potomac."

"That is simply not true, Ms. Houston." Dwight stood in the doorway.

She turned, the phone's receiver a few inches from her ear. Most people got red when caught in a lie. She did not. Her eyes narrowed and her cheeks burned white.

Dwight held out his hand. "May I please speak to Jasper?"

Even when not wearing his black robe, Judge Pendergast was persuasive. Christine told him that his effect on people was powerful—they found it hard to say no to him. It was not something that he honed, it was natural.

Ms. Houston did not relinquish her phone, so he was left standing there, hand held out. Phone to her ear, she glared at him. "Jasper, Judge Pendergast found his way into the hall and is listening to our conversation. Do you want to say anything to him?" Her eyes were narrowed so tightly, they looked like two paper cuts etched in her face. "I'll tell him."

She hung up the phone in triumph, her eyes never leaving Dwight's face. He lowered his hand, but did not go back into the suite. He wanted to hear what this young woman had to say. In all his years as a judge, a lawyer, and even a student helping his dad navigate the land mines of the Defense Department, Dwight never retreated from a fight.

He was not about to be intimidated by a "Schedule C" politico, who got her job the day after graduating from college. So what if her father was a heavy contributor to the party? Dwight had a lifetime appointment as a federal judge. Besides, Christine would not mind if he never had another confirmation hearing.

Dwight folded his arms, took a step toward her. "What does Jasper want you to tell me?"

The Special Assistant to the President snapped, "He is coming to deal with you." Her fists curled into small balls. Dwight thought any moment she would stamp her foot. "You may be a federal judge, but you have no right to throw your weight around. Do you intimidate your wife in this fashion? I feel sorry for your law clerk, whoever she is."

Dwight sucked in a deep breath. It was up to him to defuse the situation. "Ms. Houston," he stepped closer, "I apologize if you thought I was being short with you."

Barbara Jo Houston held up both hands. "Do not, under any circumstances, come closer. You are a typical male, offering a conditional apology. *If* you made a mistake. All I can say is, there was no need for you to act like a bully."

Bully? What was she talking about? The front door opened. Jasper Collins breezed in. Dark curly hair smothered his head. In a gray pinstripe suit, starched white shirt and smart tie, the President's Chief of Staff looked every bit like a successful lawyer. On television, he always wore an engaging smile. Dwight was relieved to see he smiled now.

He also sounded like the consummate Washington insider. "Judge Pendergast, sorry to keep you waiting. So is the President. A national security problem with North Korea, I can't say more, prevents the President from keeping his appointment with you."

Dwight held out his hand. Jasper grasped it warmly. He was getting on firmer footing every second. "I tried to explain to Ms. Houston I have a medical appointment I have to keep."

Ms. Houston pulled herself up even taller. "Jasper, this guy is all yours. He never mentioned a doctor's appointment. I suggest you find out what it's for. I'll be back in my office, in the West Wing."

No doubt, she emphasized *West Wing*, to be sure Dwight knew she worked for the most powerful man in the world. On the black-and-white tile floor, her heels dug in hard.

Jasper motioned Dwight back to the suite. "Don't mind her. She's a bit new. Working in the West Wing has, ah … Shall we go in?"

Dwight smothered a laugh. Jasper was all right. "She reminds me of a four-star General my dad tangled with once. No matter what Dad said to repair things, the hole got deeper. How much time do you need? I really can't skip this appointment, even though it is routine."

That was true, as far as it went. Dwight had decided not to go into detail about his dialysis or medical condition until he knew more about the President's plans.

From the coffee table, Jasper picked up the papers Dwight reviewed. "I trust you had time to read these."

Dwight nodded.

"The President wants you to write out the answers for him. Can you get them back to me," Jasper looked at his watch, "say Wednesday at this same time?"

"No problem. I've a light schedule. I can drop them off by eight."

"If I am not here, give them to Ms. Houston."

Dwight decided to ask, he had nothing to lose. After the run in with Barbara Jo, Dwight's name might slide to the bottom of the candidate list for circuit court, if not off completely. "For which appellate position is the President considering me?"

Jasper raised his eyebrows, dark against cappuccino-colored skin. A quizzical look framed his face. "Since the President has not yet announced the new nominee for the Supreme Court, I cannot tell you. Not that I think you'd leak it to the media, but we have to be careful."

Dwight took the papers from Jasper, folded them in half, and slid them into his lower suit coat pocket. "Better give whoever it is a chance to prepare his or her arsenal. Every lawyer I know would view achieving an appointment to the highest bench as a pinnacle to his or her career."

"You say that as if you do not."

Dwight did, but heat for the top job was a thousand watts hotter than for other benches. "Jasper, you're a lawyer. What do you think?"

Jasper's smile was electric. "I think you would be good under cross-examination. Bring these to me on Wednesday, and plan on at least an hour for that meeting, from eight to nine."

Was Dwight getting paranoid, or was that Jasper's attempt to scold him for the earlier disagreement? He put that behind him. Tonight, he'd have to haul in boxes of old papers from the garage, but no matter how long it took, he would have the lengthy questionnaire to Jasper on time. With his left hand, Dwight gave a partial salute. "Assure the Commander-in-Chief, my time is his time."

The two men walked out the front door. In the bright sun, Dwight was thankful on two fronts. The media weren't camping out front, and Barbara Jo Houston was nowhere in sight.

The following day, Dwight decided to take "The Judge" for a ride to the auto parts store. It wouldn't matter if he bought anything, he'd enjoy the ride in the GTO and familiar smells of rubber tires in the store. Last night, Dwight carted in some boxes from the garage and stayed up late, working on the summary for the President. He was tired, so it was a good thing nothing unusual occurred in court—he sentenced a dentist to two years in prison for Medicaid fraud. He set his keys on the kitchen counter and picked up the mail, which Christine left lying in its usual spot. She would be interviewed at six o'clock about a grant her organization received to link children from the District with adoptive homes.

Reading glasses at the edge of his nose on this steamy August day, he sifted through junk mail and those with address labels from Christine's friends. One letter in a gray envelope had an uneven hand. Addressed to him, it bore a Panama City, Florida, postmark. They knew no one in that city. Dwight turned it over, then put aside his misgivings. Inside was a sheet of lined white paper, torn from a spiral notebook. Written in the same uneven hand, his eyes consumed the two paragraphs:

Dear Dwight:

I understand you ain't feelin too good. There is a chance I can maybe help you. I donated blood to people who needed it. I'm also willin to give a kidney. I dont like to think of anyone bein so sick. Maybe we can help each other. Could you cover my expenses if I give you my kidney?

Because I own my own sucessful business, I'd hafta hire people to run it while I was recoverin. There's travel expenses to where your at, doctors expenses, and travel for my recovery. Think nothin of it. I talked to a medical man who said my costs might be two hundred thousand dollars. What's not covered by your insurance, you could maybe git from family members. I'm travelin a lot, but you can reach me at my P.O. Box in Apalachicola, Florida. The address is on the envelope.

The letter was signed "Mr. Skeeter."

Who on earth was Mr. Skeeter? Whoever he was, he knew Dwight's address and all about his medical needs. This could not be! This should not be! Except for his doctor, only FBI Agent Griff Topping knew of his quest for a kidney.

No way Griff was behind this. The paper trembled in Dwight's hands. Fierce anger and fear clashed in his mind. The way the letter was written told him that this Mr. Skeeter, a man of little education or sophistication, was trying to bleed money from him. He reread the letter. There was no mistaking it. Mr. Skeeter wanted money from Dwight in exchange for a donated kidney.

He must know it was illegal to sell an organ. The letter was crafted to make it seem the money was for expenses and inconvenience. It was one thing to be reimbursed for time away from work, but one would have to be the CEO of a Fortune 500 company to expect two hundred thousand dollars. Misspelled words and poor grammar suggested the man had no job, let alone "a successful business," as he claimed.

He picked up the phone. When Agent Topping's voice mail connected, Dwight left a message that it was urgent they talk. Dwight banged down the phone, unsure what to do next. There was only one thing he felt like doing. He scrawled a note to Christine in case she got home before he did, set the security system, and opened the garage door.

"The Judge" welcomed him. He would miss Christine's interview, but he had to get away. Drive somewhere, but where? A place to blow off steam. On the back roads in northern Virginia, he reached hunt country where large farms and horses dotted the roadside. He tried to put out of his mind that Griff still had not called and decided to go to Middleburg. The historic feel of the place usually set his mind to rights.

With all four windows down, air rushed over his face. The warm breeze was toxic, the kind that stoked a temper. George Washington apparently struggled his whole life to regulate his temper. Dwight normally succeeded, but at this moment blood pulsed in his ears. That letter was extortion, pure and simple. Of course, there was nothing pure about such a despicable act.

By the time he reached The Red Fox Inn, a stone eatery and hotel that had graced the town for decades, Dwight made up his mind. He wouldn't pay the fellow one dime. Dialysis for the rest of his life was better than giving in to threats. He secured his classic car and strode inside.

Thankfully, cool air welcomed him, and he found a seat at a carved table. A couple drinking wine in a far corner paid him no heed. Paintings of horses and fox hunters in red jackets hung on the walls. From a young woman in period costume, Dwight ordered fish and chips and iced tea with no sweetener. The tea was brought immediately, and he took a long drink of the delicious brew. In a few minutes, his food arrived. The fish was tender and mild, just as he remembered it.

He was nearly finished when his cell phone chirped. Dwight grabbed it from his shirt pocket, and his hello was returned by an apologetic Griff.

"Sorry, your Honor. I was meeting with Agent Domingo on the new case against Owen Jones, but I won't bother you with that. Your message sounded urgent."

The reality of the agent's job dampened Dwight's fury, somewhat. "It is. Could you meet me at my house in an hour? I would rather not discuss it on the cell. You have the address?"

"I am at the FBI field office, but I can be there within the hour."

Dwight signaled for his check. All the way home, questions for Griff thundered in his head. It was all he could do to keep from speeding. But then, the idea of the media harping about a federal judge getting caught in a speed trap restrained his foot.

It did not stem the thoughts careening in his mind, which at the moment felt like the Autobahn, that highway in Germany where cars flew along at whatever speed they wanted. When he arrived home, the house was empty. Dwight stalked to his study, and waited for Griff, to explain how a letter demanding money for a kidney arrived at his home.

Although Judge Pendergast had led him promptly to his study, Griff now stood there alone. Right after he arrived, Dwight received a phone call and left the room. Griff looked around, but was thinking of what Sal told him about his interview with Owen Jones III. Jones signed a waiver, met with Sal without his attorney, and claimed the whole thing was instigated by a man who knew the President. This man, whom Owen refused to name, called and threatened to harm Secretary Jones if Owen did not pay money to Lev Federov.

Owen Jones claimed the whole kidnapping scheme was Lev's idea.

Lev was the one who demanded money from *him*. It was predictable Jones would claim to be a victim. Griff had tried to warn Sal. Just then, he spotted an autographed photo of the Nationals. The judge must be a baseball fan, too. They had something in common besides the law after all.

The door opened. Griff was about to ask if he thought the Nationals had a chance to enter the playoffs, when the intense look on Dwight's face stopped him. The judge pointed to a leather chair. "Please sit."

Griff did, but felt awkward, like he was back in Pendergast's courtroom. What had he been thinking to help a federal judge? Even though the FBI Director approved it, such favors were bound to turn sour. Sal once tried to help a state judge discover if his son gambled. He did. Because Sal knew of embarrassing information, that judge never spoke to Sal again. Passed him in the hall without even a nod.

Dwight unlocked a desk drawer, handed Griff a letter. "I need an explanation."

Griff silently read Skeeter's letter. With each word, conflict raged within him. He had waited to tell Judge Pendergast about finding his brother because he hadn't resolved how to tell him that Arthur Bailey, a.k.a. Skeeter, was a criminal. Now, the hopes of getting a kidney from his brother had turned to dirt. More like mud.

He looked at Dwight, but instead saw Skeeter. Words caught in his throat. Okay, so the brother had hazel eyes, long hair, and a felony record. It was unnerving to see the resemblance between the two men. What was Griff supposed to say? The man who calls himself Mr. Skeeter is Arthur Bailey, your long lost brother. The one you want a kidney from. While you went to college and law school, he's lived a life of crime. Not only is he an ex-con, he's a current one, willing to help you for money.

The judge stood and stared at him. His arms moved by his side like it took a tremendous effort to control himself. He obviously expected something from Griff.

Griff swallowed, then rose. It would be nice to have a soda or something, but he'd never ask. "Your Honor," he noticed this time Dwight did not correct him, "I cannot believe this. Mind if we sit?"

They did, and Griff explained, "My investigation took me to Florida. With the help of a federal probation officer, I interviewed a man named Skeeter to try and find your brother. I didn't tell her or Mr. Skeeter about you. He thought I was researching organ donors. He must have seen my notes in the file, but it was in my sight the entire time."

Dwight's arms were crossed on his chest. "How did he get my name and address?"

Griff nervously raked a hand over his moustache. "It is maddening. I can only conclude he reads upside down, then memorizes what he's seen. An FBI agent told me many prisoners pick up that skill. I should have removed the notes before I went into his house."

"That goes without saying, but it's too late."

"I agree and we need to do something about it. Before we proceed, you should realize I need to keep working through this man to find your sibling. Precipitous action could ruin my chances and yours. Are you comfortable with my taking the letter and handling it for now?"

Griff was thinking of Skeeter's sister Eleanor. If he could find her, she might be a better match. Dwight closed his eyes, and Griff felt he had to add, "As I said, he knows nothing about you. If you'll notice, the letter is not addressed to Judge Pendergast."

Dwight leaned forward. "Will you tell his probation officer? I want this Mr. Skeeter fried."

Griff arched his eyebrows. If he informed Dawn, she would violate his release, and that would fry his chances to find Eleanor. "Yes, when the time is right. It may be difficult to prove Mr. Skeeter meant to extort money from you. He asked to be reimbursed for expenses. They're exorbitant, but a jury might believe him."

Dwight's cheeks puffed, and he blew out the air. "What do you propose?"

Griff told him he had a plan, but gave no details. That was because his plan was not even a skeleton. But, he would think of something. "Justice will be done. Do you trust me to continue?"

The judge pursed his lips, stared Griff in the eye. "I do."

Relieved, Griff took the letter and left, a different man from the one who walked in thirty minutes before. Humbled, he had to find a way to salvage the damage Skeeter had done, not only to Griff's reputation, but to his giving the judge a kidney.

A few minutes after the agent left, Dwight heard the garage door opener clatter. Christine! How he longed to talk to her about what was happening in their lives. It was strange, because he was the one who kept from her that he had a brother and why he so desperately wanted to find him. His independence in making judicial decisions, consulting no one, had seeped into their personal lives. He saw now that there were too many secrets. Even Christine had remained silent about that blue letter he found clutched in her hand, which Dwight had forgotten until now.

He opened the back door for Christine, who was collecting packages. When she came around her car, both hands filled with bags, his heart went out to her. "Let me help you, honey."

Her smile, a phantom, was there and gone. She looked tired. Dwight relieved her of a few bundles. "Looks like you bought out the stores. How was your interview about your adoption program?"

They were in the mudroom now. She dropped her packages on the white bench and slumped down. "You didn't see it?"

He shook his head. "I'll tell you all about it."

As if she had not heard, Christine waved a hand in the air. "A funny thing happened at lunch with Mandy today. Do you know who showed up?"

Dwight was about to say Rita, when she answered, "Chad. With a 'See you later Mom,' Mandy took off." She sighed. "I don't know, Dwight. She gives in to his slightest whim. He is more than demanding. I think he even encourages her to give up her friends."

His wife seemed down, depressed. He had an idea. "Would you like to go for a drive with me, in the GTO? We'll talk over dinner at one of our favorite restaurants." He decided not to mention he had eaten not too long ago.

Her blue eyes, rimmed with red, searched his. "I can't think of anything I'd rather do. Let me freshen up. I can be ready in ten minutes."

As Christine trotted upstairs, he retrieved his adoption file from his desk. Out of deference to his parents, he had never talked to his wife or daughters about his birth parents or his brother. It was time for that silence to end.

TWENTY TWO

Dwight passed the tree-lined community of Langley, home of the headquarters for the CIA, and carefully picked his way through traffic speeding on the George Washington Memorial Parkway. At eight o'clock, Jasper would meet him at the safe house. There was one problem. All he could see ahead of him was a solid line of cars in all lanes.

His foot had a permanent resting spot on the brake. At fifteen minutes to his appointment time, he reached the Theodore Roosevelt Bridge. A passenger jet landing at Reagan National Airport rumbled overhead. He should have left home earlier. One never knew how long it would take to get to the District; travel in these parts was more imprecise than forecasting the weather.

He stayed up late last night—it was early morning before he went to bed—answering questions about his cases and his health. Plus, a multiple-page ethics questionnaire required his financial data. Assets, debts, loans, investments. Standard stuff, but Dwight was up until one going through stacks of old files to make sure he got it right. At midnight, Christine crossed her eyes at him and went to bed.

There was no use racing the engine of his mind, but he did it anyway. To keep the Chief of Staff waiting would compound the bad footing he achieved for himself on Monday with Ms. Houston. As he cleared the bridge, traffic eased. Dwight sped up, only to grind to a crawl again behind a flower delivery van, which he could not see around. Before he knew it, he missed his street. Three long blocks later, Dwight found a parking spot by a meter. The watch on his right wrist read four minutes past eight. He was late.

He grabbed the manila envelope marked for Jasper, ran to the entrance, and knocked on the painted red door. It was opened by a compact African-American female, in a black pant suit and glasses.

Her smile warm, she stepped aside, and let him enter. "Judge Pendergast, Jasper told me to expect you."

Dwight drew in a breath, happy that Barbara Jo was not the keeper of the door. Such a thought was beneath him, but he felt it all the same. He'd never allow so erratic a person to work for him. If Dwight was her boss, Ms. Houston would have already been fired, no matter who her father was. He tapped the envelope. "I'm a few minutes late. I hope Mr. Collins was not kept waiting."

The woman showed him to the same room from Monday. "He has not yet arrived."

Dwight strode into the airy room. A second later, his countenance fell. Barbara Jo faced him, held out her hand. "I see you have completed the questionnaire. May I have it?"

He retreated, and with the corner of his eyeball, searched for the woman who let him in. Though she had not identified herself, she seemed a safe harbor. But, like smoke, she had disappeared. "I prefer to wait for Mr. Collins. I am supposed to meet with him."

Ms. Houston flashed a peculiar look, as if she'd eaten sour candy. "According to my watch, you are late. Did you expect a man as busy as the Chief of Staff to wait for you?"

The woman needed a tongue transplant. Dwight ordered himself to take a deep breath. Pretend she is your daughter, who received sad news. He shuffled back into the entryway, feeling better knowing he could escape out the front door.

A soft voice behind him asked, "Judge Pendergast, may I get you anything?"

He turned his head. It was the woman who let him in. "I didn't catch your name."

"Nicole Driver, Special Assistant to Mr. Collins."

Dwight had reached the hall. "Ms. Driver, is Mr. Collins coming soon, do you think?"

Barbara Jo barreled toward him, a tornado at warp speed. "Nicole, as the President's Special Assistant, I have been assigned by Mr. Collins to the Judge, and you are to assist."

Dwight spied a long, padded bench and sat on it. "I am fine waiting here."

Nicole stood her ground, but Barbara Jo was not finished. "The Chief of Staff instructed me to take your answers. He has been called into a meeting with the President and the entire Cabinet, which is going to last," she dramatically arched the watch on her slim wrist, "at least two hours. Did you want to sit there for that long?"

Dwight had no choice but to hand over his documents, which he had photocopied, to Barbara Jo. He held out the envelope, making sure his one and only witness, Nicole Driver, had a clear view. Then, a thought struck him. Under the circumstances, it was a reasonable thing to ask. "Ms. Driver, would you assist Ms. Houston by writing out a receipt for me."

"Sure, Judge Pendergast."

Before Barbara Jo lodged an objection, Nicole scurried to a side room. She came out again with a handwritten receipt. Meanwhile, Barbara Jo thumbed through his answers. "All right, it's in order. You can give him a receipt."

Dwight plucked it from Nicole's fingers, walked to the door. "Good day, ladies." He rushed into the fresh air. When he got to his chambers, the first thing he'd do would be to call Jasper Collins and tell him that he would never again meet with, talk to, or be in a room alone with Barbara Jo Houston, even if the President of the United States asked him. She was a time-bomb, waiting to explode.

A day passed since Griff had read Skeeter's letter. In a fury, he had driven back to his office and called Skeeter. When he didn't answer, Griff left a message, giving the main number for the northern Virginia FBI office. He wanted Skeeter to be shocked to find that, Griff, researcher of organ donations, really worked for the FBI. Would he even call back? If Skeeter thought there was money in it, he might. No doubt, the ex-felon was working several angles at once.

When he did not hear back from Dwight's brother this morning, against his better judgment, Griff called Dawn. Had she heard from Skeeter? No. He hinted her releasee got it in his mind he could get money for his kidney. They talked about it, and Dawn confided that DEA Agent Nick Tascoda called her some weeks ago. According to Nick's informant, a man who called himself Grady was involved in setting up a sale of cocaine. The man called Grady, who Nick thought was really Skeeter, escaped—and there was no evidence to prove his involvement.

Griff was just about to ask her if she had flown recently, when the secretary called him on the intercom. Her voice had a distinct Brooklyn accent. "I got a mystery call. A man asked if this was the FBI office. Did Griff Topping work here? When I offered to connect him to you, he hung up in my ear."

No doubt Skeeter was afraid to talk to Griff. "If he calls back, connect him right away."

Griff returned to his call with Dawn, but ended it quickly with a promise to keep her informed. He punched in Skeeter's phone number in Apalachicola. The answering machine again. This time, Griff was ready. After the beep, he bellowed, "Pick up the phone, Skeeter. It's Griff Topping. You call here, hang up on my secretary."

Because he didn't know how long the device would record, he hurried, "I've got the letter you sent. Preserving it as evidence. It's illegal to sell an organ. You call me back by tomorrow, or I'll be down there. You won't like that, because you'll be in handcuffs. On second thought, maybe I'll send it to your PO and let her drag your sorry carcass off to jail."

About to slam down the phone, Griff heard a squeal, then Skeeter's voice. "Is this some sick joke?"

He had Skeeter's attention. "Look who is talking about sick. What guy would try to sell a kidney to a federal judge?"

"What you talkin' about, man?"

"You must be stupid. That letter you sent? It went to a federal judge."

Silence. Another squeal. Had Skeeter turned off the machine? "His name and address were in my notebook, and you thought he needed a kidney."

Skeeter's voice shook. "You really an FBI agent?"

"You called the FBI's number didn't you?"

"Why did you come to my house askin' about organ donors?"

Griff decided to use the information he got from Dawn to scare the ex-con. "I came to see you, after you were identified as Grady. It seems Grady, who was really you, tried to sell cocaine in Homosassa. Shame on you for sending an extortion letter to a federal judge."

Skeeter didn't deny the cocaine or the letter. "You're an agent, what can I do now?"

That was the question Griff hoped he'd ask. Still, he could not help wondering how Skeeter, with his poor life choices and criminal activities, could ever be reconciled to Dwight. "I won't contact your PO, yet. Keep doing what Ms. Ahern tells you and promise me you will not send any more letters."

"Do I have your word you're not gonna tell Ms. Ahern?"

Typical criminal. Always trying to forge a deal for himself. Skeeter was in no position to deal. "No. You promise me and I will do what is necessary to resolve the mess you're in. The way I figure it, conspiracy to deliver an illegal drug will send you away for life."

Skeeter breathed into the phone. "Yeah, you're right."

"I want your word, Skeeter, you will stay of out trouble." His word might not be worth much, but it was all Griff could do for now—until he put in place some missing pieces.

This time Skeeter did not try to wiggle out of it. "I will."

"One more thing. You said you had an address for your sister."

"You gonna get her involved?"

"I won't tell her about your latest scam, if that's what you mean. But, I have a feeling she is an important link to turning you around. You told me that yourself."

Silence, then, "Just a minute." When Skeeter returned, he gave Griff an address for Eleanor Bailey. "It's old, though."

Griff agreed to call back next in a couple of days, and check on him. He felt one positive thing came from meeting Skeeter. His search for Eleanor, the sister who Dwight thought had died, was about to begin.

The rest of Wednesday, and now Thursday morning, Griff tried to find an Eleanor Bailey at the address Skeeter had given him. An hour ago, he learned that neighborhood had been demolished. In its place was a retail development. He was no closer to finding her or justice for Skeeter, as he promised the judge. He was still at his computer when the office phone rang. Griff did not need to hear Skeeter's name; his lazy speech pattern gave him away. Today, he sounded panicky.

Griff leaned back in his chair. "What's so important?"

Skeeter snorted into the phone. "Your guys were here last night to tempt me. I told them I'm not in the business any more. Agent Topping, tell my PO that I called you right away."

Griff had no clue what Skeeter was talking about. Experience taught him not to say so. "Skeeter, how do you know it was me or my people?"

Skeeter snorted again. "Cause it was like the last time with Nick Tascoda. He's DEA. A guy I know shows up, with a guy I don't know. Wants to cut me into a deal that he claims will make me a bundle. Last time, all I got was a bundle of time. You use a snitch who knows me and he brings along one of your undercover agents."

The revelation that Nick arrested Skeeter was a surprise. Dawn referred to his narrow escape from Nick, but Nick must have also nailed him on the earlier drug conviction. Was Skeeter calling to find out if the visitors were undercover agents? If he had a connection into a drug conspiracy, this could be the answer Griff had searched for.

Nick was in a picture on Griff's shelf. As Skeeter vented about the men who tried to trap him, Griff took it down and looked at the odd assortment of rookie FBI agents, all much younger. Shorter than Griff, Tascoda stood a row below. The sight of his face cinched Griff's idea.

Tough and smart, Tascoda taught Griff the language of the street, how to blend in undercover. During FBI training, Griff learned a lot from Nick, a former homicide detective with the Baltimore Police Department. Griff heard he'd transferred to the Drug Enforcement Administration, but had lost track of him.

"What makes you think I was involved last night?"

Skeeter ignored his question. He just talked fast. "This guy wants to use my shrimp boat to git cocaine from Colombia into Florida. But, I can't be with felons, my PO said so."

What Skeeter meant was, if he helped the police as an informant, which could involve him with felons, it would violate the terms of the supervised release. The old catch-22. Griff rubbed his chin. POs like Dawn learned the hard way that some criminals pretended to help law enforcement, but operated their own scams. If caught, they claimed their criminal acts were for the police, when in truth they weren't.

"Skeeter, when you told them you weren't interested in their plan, what did they say?"

"Left a number, case I changed my mind."

That was something to go on. Griff got the number and told Skeeter to write down everything about the two men. "Fax it to me, today. Send a copy to Ms. Ahern, and call her."

Then Griff called DEA Agent Nick Tascoda, who was out. Griff was left with the worry that if the local police had a bead on Skeeter, there was not much he could do as a federal agent. At least, not until he reached Nick. And if Skeeter was arrested again, Judge Pendergast could kiss his new kidney good-bye.

TWENTY THREE

Thursday morning began for Judge Pendergast like other days, but it would end like no other day of his life. Oblivious to Griff's dilemma with Skeeter, Dwight was once again at the safe house. Yesterday began miserably and finished on a worse note. Dialysis took longer than usual and, when it was over, the nurse told him he should come more often.

He'd mentioned it to Christine but did not tell her that he'd have to go on a transplant list soon. Last night, Jasper had called to complain his file was incomplete. This rattled Dwight because he knew he'd answered all the questions. Jasper assured him number ten was missing, and he wanted Dwight to bring it this morning to the safe house.

Dwight's answer to question ten explained his medical condition, but that page was apparently now absent from his packet. Did he somehow fail to include it, or had it been removed? Dwight knew why Christine wanted him to reveal the kidney problem to the President. She was happy with their lives and wanted no changes. Zero. Except for getting a new son-in-law, Chad the speedster. Although lately, she had begun to question his character, as did Dwight.

He slid his cell phone out of the leather case, set it on silent mode. Dressed in a tan suit, ivory shirt, and navy tie, he was ready to meet with the President, which is what Jasper promised when he came into the suite, took Dwight's paperwork, then left him alone. That was fifty minutes ago.

Once during his nomination to the federal bench, Dwight shook the President's hand. More of a perfunctory meet-and-greet, the President had asked about his alma mater, Georgetown. That was it.

The Attorney General and his staff vetted him for the U.S. District Court. Dwight could not help but wonder if this would be the same kind of meeting. If so, what was the real purpose? Maybe to look him in the eye, size him up as a jurist.

Today, he had no conflicting appointments. Still, he felt unsettled. Ten cups of coffee could cause jitters and, yes, he drank a whole pot of regular. His doctor berated him to lay off the caffeine. But, he loved a strong cup of coffee. His one vice. That, and his obsession, fishing.

A door slammed nearby. Please, let it not be Barbara Jo Houston. When Jasper called last night, Dwight hinted strongly Jasper should be the one to meet him. Dwight played with the back of his hair. For some reason, his cowlick was as ornery as a northern pike on the end of his line. What would the President offer him? Or would he?

Jasper Collins rushed into the suite. With great anticipation, Dwight looked past Collins to see if the President followed. His hopes were dashed. All alone, Collins walked over to an old-fashioned telephone, punched in some numbers. "Sir, Judge Pendergast is here. Yes, I will."

He held out the receiver. "The President will speak with you now."

As much as he prepared for this moment, adrenaline spiked through Dwight. The President was waiting for him. He took a confident step forward, grabbed the phone and pressed it to his ear. "Mr. President," was all he could think to say.

The President's voice boomed as if addressing a crowd at an airport in Ohio. "Good of you to be patient, Pendergast. I wanted to meet you personally, but the Chairman of the Joint Chiefs and the National Security Adviser need to brief me in two minutes. China is making noises over this North Korea thing. But, I'll skip the international intrigue. Pendergast, what I am about to ask, needs an answer as soon as possible. You are my pick for—" He stopped. "One more minute."

Dwight caught his breath.

"For Associate Justice of the United States Supreme Court. You have what the country needs. You have a stellar reputation serving on two courts. My advisers prefer another, but I want you. Are you with me?"

Dwight could not have been more stunned. The Supreme Court of the United States! The highest court in the land! In front of the camera—and now behind it, Dwight was learning—the President was a man of few words. There was something anticlimactic about the way he blurted out his intention and demanded to know if Dwight was "on the team."

How could Dwight say no? He should not delay, even for a moment. The President might change his mind and go with his advisers' other choice.

"Sir, Mr. President, I am honored by your trust in me. I am able to tell you, here and now, I accept your nomination to be the next justice on the Supreme Court."

"I knew you would not let me down. Told the Attorney General we could count on you. Jasper will give you all the details. You and I will have breakfast the morning we announce your candidacy, 'er, I mean your appointment."

"Thank you, Mr. President."

"Godspeed."

The President hung up, and Dwight realized his life was changed, at the speed of sound over secure telephone wires. Supreme Court Justice. Sure, he thought of it, every lawyer in Washington, D.C. had. But, Dwight never thought it would happen.

A thought shot through him like lightning. What would Christine say? He had to talk with her before the news leaked. Constantly speculating about the future nominee, each day the press hauled out a new victim to mangle and harass.

Jasper clapped him on the shoulder. "Well, done, Judge. We've a lot of work to do. The President and his team combed your dossier. Everything looks in order. You may inform your family, but they must pledge to tell no one else until the President makes the announcement in the Rose Garden, with you at his side."

"When will that be?"

"We will let you know on your cell phone. Timing is critical. Make sure we know your trial schedule."

The whole thing seemed unreal, like a fabulous dream he would wake up from, only to find his life was the same as yesterday, reeling in out-of-control defense attorneys. Then, all his hopes rushed out of him like a leaky balloon. His kidney dialysis. Had the President seen his explanation in the paperwork he brought over this morning? Had there been time? His ascension to the Supreme Court would be over before it began. Christine was right. He was not meant for a higher court. Not in the cards.

Dwight stepped away from the phone toward Jasper, and willed himself not to toss away this chance so cavalierly. He opened his mouth to speak, but no words came. Dwight never felt more wretched in his life. How had he let it get this far without even mentioning his kidney? The last time he was on the list for Court of Appeals, he had not been sick with more than a cold. He still had his gall bladder and appendix, which was more than Bernie or Louis Sumner had.

"Mr. Collins," he began, "there is something I meant to tell you this morning, but it was lost in the rush of time and the President's sudden telephone call. I explained all this in my answer to question number ten, but you said it was missing. Of course, I brought it today, but you might not have had time to see it. You will want to notify the President at once. My name cannot be announced."

Jasper's boyish face drooped. "You wrote an opinion trashing *Roe v. Wade?*"

Dwight shook his head. "No. I ruled on one case upholding the parental notification in Virginia. You know about that. I followed the law."

"You have a secret gambling problem?"

"No! I have a medical condition."

Jasper's face fell a notch lower. "You are HIV positive, and your wife doesn't know?"

Jasper sat, and Dwight did, too. "It's a long story." Dwight took a deep breath and began.

"I love to fish. In a bass contest last fall, I did something stupid."

"Out with it man. This may work with a jury, but I need to know. Are you saying you cheated and used illegal bait?"

Dwight suppressed an absurd jolt of laughter. "I fell from the boat, inhaled brackish water, and got sick. Terribly sick. It was too late when they figured out it was from some toxic bacteria called Aeromonus. Wrecked my kidneys. I've been on dialysis. My doctor says it's not agreeing with me and I need a transplant, but I'm not yet on the list."

Jasper clutched his arms around Dwight's file. "You need a kidney transplant."

Dwight sighed. "Yes. Probably pretty soon. Otherwise, I'm healthy and fit."

"That's it? There's nothing else you neglected to mention?"

"Cross my heart." A smile tugged at his lips as he refrained from finishing the phrase: *hope to die.*

Jasper stood up. Dwight expected him to pick up the secure telephone and call the President, but he did not. Slowly, Dwight found his own legs, and he was ready for them to be cut out from under him by Jasper's next words.

Jasper tucked the file under his left arm. "I confess, I didn't look at what you brought over, but I will. If what you wrote matches what you just told me, no problem. You go to dialysis and we'll put a press on the hearing. It'll be over with before you go on the transplant list, right?"

Dwight thought that over. Was it ethical to keep his medical condition from the President and the Congress? He voiced aloud his concern.

Jasper had a way of putting him at ease, whereas Ms. Houston had a knack for the jugular. "The Senate's role is to advise and consent on the nominee's ability to be a justice, to decide cases according to the Constitution. Your medical history is none of their business. The President will be briefed. Now that he has selected you, our President is loyal to his team. He will stick with you."

Dwight was unsure. "I would feel better if I could speak to the President about it personally. I do not want him to think I sandbagged him on this."

"Judge Pendergast, leave it to me. If the President has an issue, he will reach you."

Before they left the suite, the two men shook hands. Moments later, Dwight stood outside on the sidewalk, blinking in the bright morning light. Heat rose from the asphalt. He took off his suit coat, slung it over his shoulder. It was hooked on his thumb as he walked toward his restored GTO. He'd jumped one hurdle he was worried about. But, there was one more. Christine's blessing the other night aside, she would not be as easy to convince as Jasper.

A few hours came and went before Griff heard from Nick Tascoda, who was back from an early morning raid. Griff enjoyed the few minutes of small talk at the beginning of the call, reminiscing with Nick about FBI training and catching up on the years since then.

Nick thought Griff would by now be in charge of the FBI's office in Los Angeles or New York. "I knew you'd do well at the Bureau."

"I'm happy right where I am. Funny, I grew up in New York, but I have no interest in moving back. I wasn't surprised when you left the Bureau for DEA."

Nick's laugh, deep like a tuba playing, reminded Griff of a prank he, Nick and some other classmates had pulled. They stayed at a local motel the night before they were to report to Quantico and returned from dinner, to smells of marijuana wafting down the hall. It was Nick's idea to run down the hall, bang on all the doors, and yell, "Police, Search Warrant! Open up."

They had all laughed at the sounds of feet running and toilets flushing. Griff reminded Nick how much money was washed away that night.

"Those were fun times, Griff. You know I'm a proud former Marine, but DEA's basic agent school was harder than the FBI academy, not because I was older. Every bit as grueling as Marine boot camp, it nearly killed me."

Sal appeared around the half-wall, but Griff waved him away. "But, you made it."

Nick explained how he had been at the Chicago FBI field office, doing background investigations on applicants. "I hated every minute and longed for action. DEA offered me a position. Now my life is action packed."

Griff had really enjoyed the times he worked undercover and told this to Nick, then got to the reason behind his call. "Thanks to Skeeter, we may get to work together."

Nick took it from there. "He's a likeable guy, but breathes the wrong air. A few years back, I arrested him during a marijuana case."

"Skeeter is worried you are still trying to catch him doing something wrong."

Nick had an easy answer. "A few weeks back, I posed as a buyer of cocaine. The supposed cocaine dealer dove through a window and escaped. I think he saw me. We got the middleman, who described a man that fits the description of Skeeter. Only he went by the name of Grady, so I'm not positive it was Skeeter."

"Did you show your middleman a photo lineup?"

"Yes, but he couldn't identify him."

How much could Griff divulge? He told Nick about the two guys that came to see Skeeter and gave Nick the telephone number they left.

Nick agreed to check it out. "You've piqued my interest, Topping. I should get back to you soon."

Griff took that as a promise. He did not want to leave Skeeter on a long leash. Before Nick hung up, he asked Griff about Sue and whether they had any kids. The words didn't catch in his throat, as they usually did. "She died of ovarian cancer, eight years ago. But, that's better left for another time."

An hour later, the display on Griff's cell revealed a call from Nick, who made short work of his promise. Griff smiled. His respect for Nick made working with him satisfying.

Nick traced the phone number that the men gave Skeeter. It was the same one known by the DEA Tampa office. "Wish I had more. It belongs to a prepaid cell phone."

Griff noted that it was the same kind of cell phone that Owen Jones gave to Lev when he kidnapped Frank Williams. Sal had mentioned just this morning that he was going to see if Owen Jones would take a polygraph, to see if his claims about a man calling him and Lev demanding money held a kernel of truth. Griff seriously doubted it and turned his attention back to Nick and the investigation at hand. "Those prepaid things are almost impossible to trace."

Nick agreed. "We know that someone in the U.S. has the phone with that number, and it is being called by some heavy duty cocaine suppliers in Barranquilla, Colombia. We think these guys have been involved in shipping airplane loads of cocaine to the U.S."

Not an expert on the drug business, Griff looked to Nick to educate him. "They want to use Skeeter's shrimp boat for something. He backed off, so he has no details, yet."

Griff thought a moment, then added, "Nick, you need to know he made a stupid move in my case. When I accused him of being involved in a cocaine case in Homosassa Springs, he didn't deny it."

Nick whistled softly into the phone. "That I would like to know more about. It could be the Colombian cartel." He paused, then added forcefully, "I *know* he was Grady, I just can't prove it."

They discussed how to deal with Arthur Bailey, a.k.a. Skeeter, a.k.a. Grady. Skeeter might be an embarrassment to Dwight, but he was a necessary source of family history and Griff's only lead to Eleanor. Nick saw him as a key to interrupting a big cocaine smuggling operation. This was shaping up to be one popular guy.

Griff summarized. "You and I both want his help. Our problem is, how do we get past our agencies' policies against making Skeeter an informant because he's under the supervision of a federal probation officer?"

Nick's idea thrust Griff deeper into the problem. "Simple. You approach the PO and ask."

Griff had wrangled his way into Dawn's oversight of Skeeter in order to help Judge Pendergast. He didn't care to reveal to Nick his concern that Dawn Ahern might think the whole organ donor thing was a pretext to get Skeeter as an informant in the drug case. So, he hedged. "Nick, you called her first. You ask her."

Nick's booming laugh was having none of it. "You have the ongoing relationship. You're the logical agent to supervise Skeeter."

"No, I'm not."

The DEA agent chuckled. "I say you are."

This back and forth was wearing thin, so Griff told Nick, "When I met with Skeeter, I messed up. Somehow, he saw the name and address of U.S. District Judge Dwight Pendergast in my notes. He made an assumption about the judge and wrote him a letter, which arguably broke the law. Now, Pendergast wants Skeeter supervised up close and personal."

Nick whistled again into the phone. "All I can say is, with that muscle, you call Ms. Ahern about Skeeter. Tell her that *I* say either he telephones the suspected smugglers for DEA or returns to prison."

Griff could predict how Skeeter would decide. He was not sure about Ms. Ahern. He thanked Nick for getting him in deeper, and called her number. Once again, she was not in. That gave him more time to develop a scenario he thought Dawn could accept.

TWENTY FOUR

D wight merged onto Georgetown Pike. He was heading home
early. After handling a motion on a civil case, he gave Gladys
the afternoon off. Christine's words of last week bounced off
the walls of his mind, "You deserve every good thing." If she felt so
positive about an appellate judgeship, then he hoped she'd agree to his
going one step higher.

He passed the turn for Great Falls Park, where Owen Jones III had
been cornered. It was meant to be, he guessed, that another judge
drew the new case. Dwight could put that defendant and his audacious
father behind him. He had other concerns, like planning his confirmation strategy. And neither Jones the elder nor junior would have any
part in that.

His hands gripped the wheel. When Nolan withdrew, one pundit
remarked that the next nominee best prepare for a nuclear war. What
did that mean for him, his family? Judges were supposed to be nonpo-
litical and, in his legal decisions, Dwight was. In recent years, getting a
seat on the federal appellate bench was like running for Congress—the
judges who wrote popular decisions were confirmed. So, it followed
that a nomination and confirmation to the Supreme Court would be
as robust and bloody as a run for the Presidency.

In that light, Dwight questioned his sanity. Was he ready, physically
and emotionally, for such a pitched battle? His mind sought the logical
road. The potential outcomes, while not deadly—like they could have
been for General Washington in the Revolutionary War—would affect
the country for many years to come.

The Supreme Court's decisions touched the life of every American. How far could a President go in pursuing the enemy in time
of war? Could Americans be held indefinitely as enemy combatants?
What rights did the states have to pass laws that required parental consent before a minor could get an abortion? Dwight pondered a recent
decision by the Supremes that caused a firestorm across the nation. It

upheld the right of local governments to condemn private property—even raze entire neighborhoods—solely for economic development that would enrich private developers.

He reached his driveway, then nestled "The Judge," which Bernie affectionately called a relic, into the third stall of the garage. Dare he hope he could correct the recent ruling on eminent domain, and return the judicial system to something closer to George Washington's vision, a system that strengthened and did not divide the nation? He slid out, pushed down the door lock on the window ledge. While holding his thumb on the outside door handle, he slammed the door. He could not help being conscious of criminals, even in his own neighborhood. A suspicious nature came with the territory of living and breathing the law.

Except for the time when the U.S. Marshal insisted on doing a security assessment of their home. Christine wanted a security alarm, Dwight was against it. No big surprise, he lost. But, all her arguments in favor of the alarm turned out to be wrong. The goofy thing tripped by accident five times the first year. Since then, they got used to it and Dwight learned to live in the bubble.

He punched the code, disabled the alarm, and opened the back door. At least, there were no alarms at the lake. No doubt that would change when he reached the high court. In the mud room, he stopped. Faint smells of smoke tickled his nose.

In the gleaming gourmet kitchen, Christine scraped a black mass into the sink. The odor of burnt food was everywhere. Not a good sign. Neither was what he did next. He gave her a hug, then sneezed all over her neck.

Her voice was strained. "Oh, please. It's not that bad in here."

She sounded hurt by his sneeze. An accomplished cook, she rarely ruined even delicate meringue desserts. When she did not turn toward him, he suppressed an urge to reply, "It's not like I planned it" and instead made his voice extra friendly, "Christy, it's great to be home."

In reply, Christine finished scraping, turned on the water. In the garbage disposal, she ground up whatever was hidden down there. Dwight decided it was best to motor on by. He set his briefcase on the built-in desk, pulled open the fridge. A bowl of cut-up strawberries, kiwi, and melon looked good. He reached for the bowl.

Christine shut off the disposal. "Don't touch the fruit. We're having company for dinner."

Oh, oh, she sounded grumpy and he had wanted to tell her about his conversation with the President. Dwight opened the cupboard, found some raisins. "Who's coming?"

He shoved his hand into the box. Christine walked over, put her hand on his arm and looked him straight in the eye. "Don't eat too many. You'll ruin your appetite, just like I ruined the chocolate cake I was making. Have you forgotten that today is Bernie's birthday? He and Rita are coming to dinner. I also invited Louis and Naomi."

Dwight was used to her lectures about what and when he should eat. He usually ignored her well meaning advice and did what he wanted. Today was different. He needed her to be in a good mood when he told her. So, he plucked out three raisins, held them in his hand for her to see, then popped them in his mouth, one at a time.

After he swallowed them, practically whole, he took her hand. "It's not like you to burn things. What's on your mind?"

She stared at him, stress lines around her mouth. Even without makeup, Christine was beautiful. That she fell for him, as he had for her, was a miracle. Of course, Mom called him nice looking, but Dwight never believed her. His face was broad, his skin too amber.

Her eyes darted to the oven and back to his. "Lots of things. Book deadlines, Mandy's wedding, your mother called. Nothing really."

Lots of things suddenly turned into nothing. This was definitely not the time to talk about the Supreme Court job. But he had to, and soon. Dwight realized she neglected to ask about his meeting with the President. Things like a Supreme Court nomination did not stay quiet for long in Washington, D.C. Keeping a secret there was like having a fire without smoke. It was impossible.

And Bernie made it his daily mission to glean political news and use it to maintain his power base, which was why he remained managing partner at Ebbott and Longstreet. Besides, Bernie had many contacts at the White House. By dinner time, he would know what supposedly only Dwight, Jasper Collins, and the President knew.

He glanced at the digital clock on the microwave. "What time is dinner?"

Christine's hand seemed to sag in his. "Seven."

Dwight drew her to him. "Why invite people when you have so much your mind? I hate to see you stressed."

Her head rested on his chest. "I promised."

These precious moments with his wife leaning on him didn't happen often. His arms cradled her head. "A few weeks back, Louis and I found a superb restaurant. Let's order shish-kabobs and the fixings for six. All you'll need to do is the rice, boil water for tea. How does that sound?"

When she said "Okay," it sounded like she choked back a sob. Dwight gently pulled back. "Tell me what is wrong."

Her wet eyes looked like melting ice, and he knew her heart was troubled. She sniffled. "Our baby girl is getting married. I feel so—"

Dwight fixed a smile on his face, filled with hope. "Honey, a lot's been happening lately. You probably need to take a few days off and just rest."

He led Christine by the hand to the leather sofa in the great room. Inwardly, Dwight practiced his opening statement and closing argument, all in one. "You told me I had your blessing, and today, the President offered me an appellate judgeship."

A smile wavered on her lips. "That is fabulous, darling."

Dwight knew better than to return her smile. "Not the D.C. Circuit."

She blinked and a tear rolled down her cheek. She wiped it away. "Is it the Ninth? I knew we'd have to move to California. Dwight, there's no way I can do that before the wedding."

She jumped up from the couch, walked to the bay window, where Dwight joined her. The garden bloomed with a patriotic theme. Red geraniums encircled white and purple petunias, all around a bubbling fountain. Oblivious to the flowers, he placed his hands on her upper arms. "It's not California."

Her eyes remained fixed out the window. "Then it must be the Fifth Circuit. I can tell by your tone, we're moving to Texas."

Dwight gently lifted up her chin. "I have even better news." His blood pressure rose, pounded against his eardrums, and he felt as giddy as the day he and Christine got married. "Christy, the President is nominating me to the United States Supreme Court!"

There, he told her! A parade in his honor might march past any minute. He'd call his folks, tell Veronica and Mandy before the whole world found out. Christine hadn't said a word. Her bottom lip trembled. Big tears sprang to her eyes.

When she got angry, her nostrils flared. They were now at full bloom. "And you said yes, didn't you, without talking to me first? I may be happy for you, Dwight, but not for us. How would you feel if I took a job as a university president without speaking to you?"

The first thing that bubbled into his mind found its way to his lips. "But, we don't have to move. I thought you'd be happy for me."

Her hands flew in front of her. "Oh, I am. I know how you love the law. This must be a dream come true. But, I have two issues with you." She held up her index finger. "Number one, you could have said, 'Mr. President, I am honored, but my wife is part of my team. Can I let you know tomorrow?'"

Her hands flew around her head in expansive, barely controlled gestures. "Did my husband consider my feelings? No." She held up two fingers. "Number two. What I have struggled to overcome with years of therapy will be gossip on the nightly TV. Did you stop to think how I would feel to hear, 'Americans should know our new Supreme Court nominee's wife is a murderer?'"

Her voice was shrill, her cheeks glowed. Dwight reached for her. She escaped his grasp. "Leave me alone!"

"You're not a murderer. How can you say that? Dr. Filo said you were ready for others to know."

Her eyes flashed. "He meant our children, people close to us."

Dwight stepped toward her, only she retreated, her hands balled into fists. "You saw what happened to Nolan Cuttering. Because he talked about his faith, his wife was hit in the face with a pie. What do you suppose the advocacy groups will do when they find out I killed someone?"

How to calm her down? He never imagined anguish had sunk so deep within her. "You were sixteen. You couldn't have known a homeless man would lurch into the street in front of you. The federal prosecutor didn't think you did anything wrong. He never charged you."

"Dwight," she nearly screamed his name, "my father was the Austrian Ambassador. We had diplomatic immunity. I was driving too fast. I should have been able to stop."

She was sobbing now. Dwight tried to comfort her. "That was thirty-five years ago. You need to get over it. No one will care."

"Agghh. Can you guarantee me that? Does the President know about it?"

"No. Come to think of it, I was more concerned about my—" He stopped.

Christine wiped her face with the palm of her hand. "Your what?"

"My dialysis," he fudged. "Jasper promised to tell the President. Remember, you encouraged me to tell him and I did."

"Yes, I do. But, your not talking to me about it before saying yes is what hurts. It's not like you."

He shrugged his large shoulders. "I'm sorry. Try to imagine the thrill to be asked. An adopted kid like me. When the President of the United States asks, you say yes. I couldn't help it."

Christine made a fist of her right hand and smacked it into the palm of her left. "I know you're sorry, but what are we going to do? I can't handle it, Dwight." She started crying again.

As much as it hurt to say it, he had to. "Then our future is simple. The President has not announced it publicly and will not until tomorrow. I will call Jasper Collins and tell him right now that I am not their man. My health is an issue. You need never come up."

Then, Dwight could avoid telling her about the transplant for a while. He wanted to tell her today, but with her emotions cascading faster than Niagara Falls, he would not risk it. "I'll order the food. We'll have our dinner party and Mandy will marry Chad. We'll go on as before, and live as if I had never been asked. You are the most important person in my life."

Christine then did something unexpectedly. She screamed. A mild one, but still a scream. She covered her mouth. "Don't you dare blame this on me, by putting me first! When you asked me to marry you, you knew all about my accident. You promised it would never come between us!"

Dwight just stood there, transfixed by her agony. "What am I supposed to say or do?"

Her voice shook, "I wish I knew. I cannot be the reason you turn this down. You deserve it. You love appellate work. I know that. The President does, too. Dwight, please help me!"

Now, he rushed to her, held her. If he was turning it down, he had to call Jasper soon. "Honey, we'll decide together."

He meant it, but he did not know how. Then, an idea scratched at the surface of his mind. Louis prayed about things. Dwight had no clue how to approach God, especially since he was not positive that God even existed. But, maybe Louis would have some idea out of this dilemma. Christine liked Louis, agreed in principle with his beliefs, even if she did not practice them. "Would you mind if I called Louis, asked if he would pray for us?"

Her sobs started to subside. "Okay. I want to be in the room, so I know what you say."

"I will tell him that no one knows about the nomination and not to bring it up tonight."

She nodded. They went to Dwight's study. Louis's secretary said Judge Sumner was sentencing a drug-dealer. Dwight gave their home number. Christine's face was blotchy. He told her, "You hop in the shower. We will see this through, no matter what happens."

She left the room and Dwight watched her go. He felt terrible. He'd have to withdraw his name. There was no other solution. He was crazy to consider it in the first place. Christine was right. When they married, he promised that the death of the man—Dwight didn't even know his name—would not hinder their lives or their love. His standing in the safe house, talking on the telephone to the President, had turned his head, made him forget his promise.

Griff and Nick Tascoda tweaked their plan to use Skeeter to infiltrate the drug smugglers. Griff cradled the phone to his ear, leaned back in his chair. He was getting caught up in the hunt. Then a problem surfaced. An issue of jurisdiction. "The crime must be prosecuted where it occurs. In the Eastern District of Virginia, we've got tough judges. Their sentences live up to the crime."

Before Nick could object, Griff relented, "But, I know there's no way you can steer the case up here. Even though I'll supervise Skeeter, you should get credit for a big drug bust. After all, you work for the Drug Enforcement Administration."

Nick let out a giant laugh. "I always liked your judgment, Topping. Listen to what I've been working on. You get Skeeter a new cell phone, issued in the Florida panhandle near where he lives. The FBI pays for it. The number is registered to Skeeter at his address. But, the invoice is mailed to you at your office."

Griff grasped the plan immediately. "Skeeter accepts a free phone. I'm on the books as the owner, and create the PIN. That way, I check on the account, see who he's calling."

"Simple, huh. The ACLU may not like it, but it will help you keep track of what he's doing, at least by his phone calls."

And it *was* after all a way for Griff to keep his word to Dawn to watch Skeeter closely, but he kept that to himself. "When should we have our first meeting with Skeeter?"

"In two days. We'll set up in Crystal River, Florida. That way, we all travel, but it puts us in my district."

Griff never heard of the place. He hauled out an atlas, turned to Florida. It took a minute to find the tiny dot. "Tampa looks like the closest airport, right?"

"I will meet you there when your flight arrives."

"Skeeter is expecting my call, but it may take him a while to go along with helping the DEA infiltrate a smuggling group."

Nick grew serious. "Buddy, time is of the essence. These guys have eluded us for too long. At our meeting, you'll give the phone to Skeeter, and he'll call the smugglers."

That made sense to Griff. Since Skeeter's call would come from the Middle District of Florida, the conspiracy would land in Nick's jurisdiction. Then, Nick could follow it, wherever it went, across jurisdictional or state boundaries. No wiretap was necessary. All they needed was Skeeter's consent to record his conversations, and Dawn's okay, which Griff had better get soon.

When Louis returned the call, Dwight was in his study. He yelled for Christine to pick up the extension in the master bedroom. After Dwight explained their dilemma, Louis's reaction caught him off guard.

"You have my congratulations. A serious decision lies before you. If you accept, your private lives will be torn open. Not only will I pray, I would like to do so now."

Christine sounded puzzled. "You mean out loud, on the phone?"

Dwight swallowed. It had been a mistake to involve Louis.

"Sure. Naomi and I regularly pray over the telephone, especially if I have a grueling case. Don't misunderstand, not about the case, but for energy, wisdom. Besides, if we are able to hear each other over wires we cannot see, isn't it possible the creator of the universe hears us?"

At that idea, Dwight was silent. He supposed anything was possible, but it did seem farfetched.

His wife was not as skeptical. "You make it sound possible."

Whatever helped Christine get through the present crisis, he'd agree to do. It was hard to admit, but that included withdrawing his nomination. He fervently hoped he did not have to.

Louis cleared his throat and prayed, "Lord of heaven and earth, give Christine and Dwight wisdom to decide what to do, and the courage to follow through. The Bible says that, where two or more gather in your name, you hear our prayers and answer them. We pray especially for them to have peace. In the name of your son, Jesus. Amen."

Dwight felt strange. From his fingertips, up his hands, to his arms, he saw and felt goosebumps. It was as if the air conditioning was turned down too low. Only it wasn't. With a free hand, he rubbed one tanned arm, then another. It was no use. He was freezing. The bumps, a reminder of Louis's prayer, prickled his skin. If asked, Dwight would be unable to explain his reaction to what on any other day he'd describe as kind words. Christine sniffled on the other end of the telephone.

He should say something to break the uncomfortable silence, but Christine talked for both of them. "Louis, thank you. I don't know what we'll do. You and Naomi are coming for dinner at seven. You'll be happy to know my husband is helping me."

Louis chuckled. "That I want to see. Never knew you were a kitchen guy, Dwight."

The chill in his body had not subsided. Were his kidneys shutting down? He was not due for dialysis until tomorrow. Dwight had to get warm, so he ended the call with, "Thank you, Louis. We'll see you at seven," then he walked upstairs. At the master bedroom door, he heard Christine say, "I know you believe God has a special purpose for each of us."

Dwight stopped short of entering, to listen for clues of how she felt. He imagined she was sitting on the recliner chair next to the bed, her bare feet up, as Louis explained the tenets of his faith. Christine had more natural curiosity about spiritual matters than he did. Several times she had asked Dwight to go to church with her. She wanted to attend the same church as Louis and Naomi. Dwight always declined. Christine had not gone, either.

Did his reluctance keep her away? He did not like to think so. She was an independent woman, did what she wanted with her career. In the hall, he shivered. Loath to disturb Christine, he waited thirty more seconds. He was about to go in when her soft voice reached his ears, her Austrian accent more pronounced than usual. "Louis, you know what Dwight is like. Once he makes up his mind, to change it is like dismantling Mount Rushmore."

Dwight was aghast. She was talking about him to his best friend, telling him things she had never said to Dwight. He kept listening.

She laughed. "Louis, you understand. I'll tell Dwight what you said." Christine actually giggled. "See you both later."

He heard her hang up the phone, the chair squeak. He made himself wait five more seconds. Dwight found himself counting, one, two—

This was silly. He should go in and ask. He turned the corner and ran right into his wife. Her left arm and shoulder thudded into his chest.

"Ooh, that hurts."

Dwight massaged both arms. "Is that painful?"

"My arm's okay. It's my shoulder." She rubbed her left one. "It feels like electricity."

Dwight was no longer freezing, he was burning. A living wreck. This kidney thing could really go bad. His doctor said there were no guarantees. Maybe Christine was opposed to his nomination for logical reasons. Dwight now felt ashamed at his selfish attitude.

Filled with concern, he forgot her cryptic statements to Louis and steered her to the bed. "I'll get you some aspirin. We'll talk after I get the food from Gus the Greek."

Christine laid her head against the pillow. When Dwight returned from the bathroom with two aspirin tablets and a glass of water, she sat up and took them. "I don't know why I am so tired."

She closed her eyes and Dwight slipped from the room. His insides felt like molten lava. Downstairs, he called the restaurant. In the half bath, he ran cool water on a washcloth and put it on the back of his neck. After drinking a large glass of orange juice, he felt better physically but, like a dog at his heels, doubts nipped at his mind.

He had two options. Go with the President, accept the nomination—of course, he already had—and put his wife through the meat grinder of Washington politics. Dwight had thought that Christine was recovered from the guilt and shame of that accident. She never spoke of it. Dwight rinsed his glass. The food would be ready to pick up in ten minutes.

As he started the car, his mind turned over the other option, maybe the only one. Ask Jasper Collins to remove his name from consideration as Justice to the United States Supreme Court. At the end of the driveway, he exhaled. His mind approved that plan, a surgical strike against future pain.

TWENTY FIVE

On the way to the restaurant, Dwight's mind told him, No! Don't give up this easily. He turned left. If there was another course, another road to follow, he would take it. A few minutes later, as he pulled into the restaurant parking lot, he saw two men who were taller than he, wearing casual clothes, walking on the sidewalk. Their arms were full of flowers.

Dwight watched one man open a heavy looking wooden door to an old church. The other stepped in, and the first man was swallowed inside. The sign said it was an Episcopal church, the kind his parents had taken him to on Easter and Christmas.

Before he knew what he was doing, Dwight stood by the wooden door. An intense desire to peek inside propelled him to open it. Then he stopped. He could not just walk in on some wedding or funeral. Dwight gripped his keys so tightly that a deep groove etched his palm. For a man obsessed with control, he felt his life was careening near the edge of a precipice, a speeding car with no brakes.

It was crazy. He wasn't religious. Dwight turned away from the church and got within fifty feet of the restaurant when he started to sweat. Beads of moisture formed on his forehead, under his arms and back. It wasn't that hot today, only about eighty degrees. A third option crossed his mind. Drive straight to the hospital and admit himself. He pictured Christine waking up to a phone call that her husband was at the emergency room.

The internal debate was drowned out by a triumphant melody that floated to his ears. His hand on the restaurant door handle, Dwight glanced back at the brick church. Green ivy grew up the side, reminding him of the English countryside. Dramatic music from an organ met Dwight where he stood, and he was drawn to the beauty of it. Thankfully, no one entered or left the restaurant. They would think he was a kook.

He recognized that it was an organ playing because he and Christine had watched a television program about a woman who played historic pipe organs around the world. If the organ was old, it might be worth seeing. He unfolded a handkerchief from his back pocket, wiped his brow and neck, and ignored a fresh crop of sweat that formed. He left the restaurant.

Inside the church, it was cool, the lighting dim. One of the men he saw earlier affixed a sign to a stand.

The man noticed Dwight. "Are you here for one of the sessions?"

Dwight did not want to bother him. "I was intrigued by the music."

The man's face lit up, like he was standing in sunshine. "My partner's wife has a great musical talent. She also plays the piano and flute. My wife's down in the kitchen making dinner. We'll have over a hundred people here in an hour."

"You mentioned you have a partner. What kind of business are you in?"

The man held out his hand. "I'm Wendell Cochran, partner in a small law firm, Cochran and Golden, not far from here. We take off every Friday afternoon to serve at this church."

Dwight introduced himself by first name. "I'm a lawyer, too." Before Wendell asked where he practiced, Dwight asked a question. "How do you leave your law firm for a few hours?"

Wendell laughed. "When my partner suggested we help the downtrodden, I was skeptical that we could volunteer and keep the firm going. But, God is faithful. Since I began doing this last year, my clientele has doubled, and I mean with *paying* clients."

The judge was now impressed by more than the music. "What do you do here?"

Wendell adjusted the sign. "Briefly, we run a legal clinic, give free advice every Friday afternoon for the poor in this church and community. We provide a meal and have a worship service, where we give thanks to God. Another lawyer drives folks over from the homeless shelter. We're a network of attorneys who are believers."

Wendell pulled a card from his wallet and gave it to Dwight. "If you want to have lunch sometime, I can tell you more about sharing the love of Christ with others. Now, duty calls. I have to set up chairs." He ducked through a low doorway and was gone.

Dwight shoved the business card into his front shirt pocket without looking at it. He pondered the fact that a fellow lawyer would give up his Friday afternoons to help the poor. A memory stirred Dwight's mind, a memory of independent study class, his last year of law school.

Dwight had been proud of a paper he'd written on poverty law. When his father read it, he told his son such a topic was linked to the other political party—the one that he and his father didn't belong to—and his career in Washington would be over. Dad convinced him not to submit the paper. So, Dwight investigated and wrote about the legal aspects of using space for commerce. His father's boss praised it as ahead of its time and passed it around to upper level management at Jenkins and Richter Space Industries. Dwight snagged an internship.

Without telling his dad, he did pro bono work for a veteran's organization after graduating from law school. When he became a partner at Ebbott and Longstreet, however, he assigned younger associates to do most of the free cases.

He listened to the organ crescendo. Choices in life influenced one's future. If Dwight had not listened to his father, he might be a bearded lawyer setting the guilty free, instead of where he was today. And where was he exactly? About to decline one of the most coveted positions in the legal field. That seemed like bitter justice. And, if Louis and Wendell's God had a part in that, Dwight wanted no part of him.

A little past four, Dwight was back home. He set the take-out food on the counter and found Christine in the dining room, arranging the table with crystal and their best china. She looked up from a bowl of pink roses and smiled. He let out a low whistle. Wow!

She looked rested. Her blond hair shone, her cheeks held a faint blush. This was definitely not the same Christine he left tired and upset more than an hour ago. He wondered what caused such a transformation. Dwight planted a light kiss on her lips. "Your nap refreshed you. To look at you now, I'd never guess that a little while ago you were dragging."

She bestowed another smile upon him. "I slept twenty minutes, when I heard music. I thought Mandy was in her room. She was not there. It was a beautiful organ piece by Bach, being played on an old organ. But, it wasn't on the TV or radio. It was playing in my mind."

Dwight stared at her. Hearing music in her mind? Things with his wife were worse than he thought. "How do you feel now? Let's sit and talk."

He pulled out a cherry-wood chair, which she ignored. "I've got to chill the salad, and the kabobs. What took so long?"

He told her briefly about the church and meeting Wendell Cochran, who worked with the homeless. "Guess what his wife was doing? Cooking dinner for a hundred people."

Christine leaned toward him. "You were in a hurry. Why go into a
church?"

That was a good question. Dwight rewound the tape in his mind's
eye. He saw the men carrying flowers and thought it was a funeral.
Then he heard music. Organ music! Was it Bach? Unlike Christine,
Dwight was no expert on classical music. But, he might recognize it.
"Which piece woke you? Do you have it on CD?"

Christine began to turn in a circle. "I can find it in my classical col-
lection. It may take a few minutes. Put the food in the fridge."

Dwight did as she asked, then ran up the steps to change into his favorite pair of shorts until it was time to get ready for dinner. He could
not bring himself to tell her about the symptoms of hot and cold he'd
been experiencing all day. In the bedroom, Dwight opened a drawer
to the tall cabinet, where he kept his watches and cufflinks. Christine
stored earrings and necklaces in the second drawer.

He placed his watch in the drawer and closed it. Christine's drawer
was ajar a few inches. He moved his hand to close it, then for a reason
he could never explain, pulled it open. Her jewelry cases were lined up,
all but one. The abalone case contained a fire-opal necklace he bought
her last year for her birthday.

Dwight snapped open the case to admire the stone. Where the case
had been lay a folded piece of blue paper with Christine's name on it.
A vision of his wife gripping blue note paper invaded his memory. This
was the paper he'd seen her holding recently when she was sleeping.
He shouldn't pick it up, but did. The paper was a heavy bond, not like
any he used.

It was addressed to "Christine," not "Mom." So, it wasn't from the
girls. Maybe it was from her father and mother in Austria. A question
gnawed at him. What if it was not from them? With his right hand,
which he did not often use, he grabbed the top of the letter as if he
would flip it open. Music drifted up the stairs. He listened. It was the
song he had heard in the church!

Dwight dropped the letter into her drawer, put the case on top and
shut it. Never before had he snooped on his wife. What had gotten into
him? He was no spy. Besides, he trusted Christine completely.

Back downstairs, Christine stood in the middle of the living room.

Eyes shut, her face soared upward, and her hands were folded in front of her as if in prayer. But, Christine did not pray. What was she doing?

"Christy," he spoke louder than the music, "Is this the piece you heard?"

She opened her eyes. "Yes. It gave me, gives me, a feeling of peace I can't describe."

Dwight folded her hands in his, looked down into her eyes. "It's a strange coincidence. When I walked into the church, it was because of music playing on an organ."

Christine's hands flew from his, to cover her mouth. "You don't mean—"

"I do. The very same one. Not only that, it was on an old, restored organ, which was being played about the same time you heard it."

She shook her head. "You were eight miles away, in town. It is impossible that I heard the same organ you did."

Sweat trickled down the middle of his back. "I can think of no physical explanation."

Dwight and Christine were married more than thirty years. They knew each other's thoughts, finished their sentences. But now they simply stared at one another, speechless.

Christine spoke. "I have never believed in miracles. Your hearing this song in a church, where you'd never been, at the same time I hear the identical song in my mind, is more than astonishing. On top of that, you meet an attorney who helps homeless people, when it's telling others about the homeless man I hit with my car that's my problem with your nomination. I can only think all of this is linked with Louis's prayer to God."

Dwight noticed that she didn't say "Louis's God," which was how they used to refer to him.

Her smile was breathtaking. "When you left, I intended to hide my face in the pillow and cry my eyes out. Instead, I fell asleep and woke to the strains of Bach. Dwight, God exists. That much I now believe. I intend to tell Louis tonight."

Not sure he should ask, he plunged ahead. "Does that mean you're okay with the media coverage surrounding my nomination? Because if I'm out, I should call Jasper Collins."

Christine reached for his hands. "I know it will be rough, but I cannot live my life under this shadow. Until the President asked you, I did not realize how it has been weighing on me, invading my sleep, robbing me." Christine's voice broke. She wiped her face with her hands, then began again. "Robbing me of being able to love my daughters as I should."

Dwight wanted to say, *you mean Veronica*, but didn't. That was probably what she meant.

"Let the President make the announcement. Do you want to tell Bernie and Rita tonight, since Louis already knows?"

He kissed the tips of her fingers, each one of them. "Thank you. Thank you." Dwight drew her in his arms. "Let it be our secret a bit longer. Now, I should shower."

He released her, and headed upstairs with a new lightness in his step, when, like muddy feet on a clean kitchen floor, the thought of that blue letter stomped all over his happiness. On the landing he called over the music, "Christine, have you heard from your folks lately?"

"I checked on them after the call at the lake, remember. They are fine."

Right. He had to know. "Any letters?"

She came into the living room and looked up at him. "No. Why?"

"Um," he decided not to fracture the peace they had. "I wondered if their health was up to our news. The media should have a hard time finding them in the Alps."

"Dwight, I never thought of that." She paused. "I have an idea." She held out her hand. "You told me an attorney, Wilbur Coltraine, gave you his card."

"Wendell Cochran."

"Please call and tell him that we, or at least I, want to help his wife serve the homeless. I don't know why it's taken me all these years to figure that out."

Dwight found the card. "Being a judge, I don't think it's right for me to help at their clinic. Their case may come before me."

Her face lost its color. He held up a hand. "I mean I'll peel potatoes." He would, too, if it helped Christine. And he had to wonder, was there some purpose to the organ music and a lawyer who helped homeless folks for free?

TWENTY SIX

That evening, Louis and Naomi arrived first. Dwight thanked Louis for his earlier help. Naomi scooped ice into crystal goblets, looking quite summery in a rose-colored skirt and white blouse. Naomi Sumner radiated kindness, and tonight was no exception. When Rita and Bernie arrived, the talk turned to their new home at Smith Mountain Lake. Rita was planning a large party to celebrate.

Rita sounded giddy. "You're all invited. Judge Sumner, you and your wife, too. Since Nolan asked me not to have a party for him, I decided to have one anyway and just change the date and the reason."

Christine could not even feign interest in Rita's plans. She walked between the kitchen and screened porch to fill glasses with lemonade and ice. Even with the fans whirring on the porch and the air conditioning on in the house, it was sweltering. Drops of sweat beaded on her forehead.

Lamb shish-kabobs heated on the grill, and everything else was ready, but the peace she felt over Dwight's nomination had begun to fray around the edges. A letter she received in the mail that morning disturbed her. The printed words danced before her eyes, in her heart. It was the second one she received on the same blue paper in a little over two weeks. The first one was addressed to her in childlike writing. She had thrown it away, and never told Dwight, dismissing it as the ravings of a disgruntled viewer of one of her television appearances.

This second letter was different. It was personal, and she could not dismiss it as a prank. The address on the envelope was typed, with no return address, and it bore a postmark from Washington, D.C. Who sent the unsigned letter, with its vengeful lines? Lost in thought, Christine watched Dwight use tongs to take meat and vegetables off the grill, put them on a platter while her guests chattered and laughed.

Back in the kitchen, she removed the rice from the microwave and ladled it into a scalloped china bowl. She took the platter from Dwight, seated the guests around the table, and lit two candles. Dwight asked

Louis to say grace. Her head bowed, she listened to him pray for the second time that day.

"Almighty God, thank you for the food we are about to receive and for the hands that made it. Your bounty is beyond measure. In your son's name, Amen."

Despite thoughts of the letter, fresh peace filled her. There must be something powerful about prayer, which she had never known. Christine read about people of faith who were healed of disease for which doctors had no explanation. Dwight was speaking. What did he say? She looked across the end of the table.

"Christine, Bernie asked you to pass the rice."

"I'm sorry." She handed Bernie the bowl of brown rice and toasted almonds. As they ate, conversation veered from the law to weddings, but Christine mindlessly transferred food from plate to mouth. She made a mental note to put on the coffee for dessert. It would be unkind to put a damper on Bernie's birthday.

Christine thought about the circumstances that led them all here tonight. She hadn't given a dinner party in more than a year. When they were at the lake and Dwight left the room to take the phone call from her parents' housekeeper, Bernie complained that Rita never celebrated her birthday or his. Christine had replied, "That's too bad." Then Rita exclaimed, "Christine, you give such great parties, I can't possibly compete with them."

Christine took the hint and tonight was the result. She dipped a piece of lamb in mint sauce and put it in her mouth. Bernie clinked down his glass. "A fabulous meal." He patted his stomach. "You have outdone yourself, Christine."

She swallowed, sipped lemonade. "I'll let you in on a secret. Dwight helped."

Her eyes searched her husband's. They sparkled as he smiled.

Rita seized on this, "Christine, are you turning over a new leaf?"

Dwight placed both of his hands on the table. "It's time I learned to be a servant." He pushed himself up, and asked, "Who wants coffee?"

The extent of Dwight's culinary know how was to make toast, spread it with peanut butter, and pour a glass of milk. This would be interesting. Louis rose, too. "Dwight, I like what you said. Let me get the cups."

The two men disappeared. Naomi stood. "Should I clear the dishes?"

Christine waved for her to sit. "It's too much fun being waited on." She turned. "I'm sure this is in your honor, Bernie."

Rita set her fork and knife on her plate. "Did Dwight help you frost the cake?" Her tone was so forceful, she managed to blow out one of the tapered candles. Christine glanced at her friend. She had acted strange all evening.

Christine excused herself to get the igniter to relight the candle. In the kitchen with coffee brewing, Dwight was telling Louis about Wendell Cochran's legal aid clinic and how he and Christine planned to serve there next Friday. Dwight linked an arm around her waist. "It was her idea. You'll be happy to know we've agreed to allow the President to announce I am the next nominee for U.S. Supreme Court."

A voice behind her growled, "What?"

Christine peered around Dwight's back. Bernie held plates in both hands, a stunned look on his face. The dishes rattled in his hands. "Let me get this straight. Did you say that the President is nominating you to the high court? Why am I just finding out?"

Dwight rushed over, eased the dishes from his hands. "I was going to announce it over dessert."

"You told Louis."

Dwight stammered, "It slipped out, I guess."

Christine thought Bernie had tears in his eyes. Were they from happiness for her husband or something else? She never knew with him. While he'd been Dwight's friend for years, she was not totally at ease with his reactions to Dwight's achievements. She didn't think Bernie was jealous over Dwight's being a judge. It was something else altogether. She had an idea—she was not sure—so she'd never discussed it with Dwight.

She placed a hand on Dwight's back. "You men go back to the dining room. I'll get coffee and dessert. Then, Dwight can make a proper announcement." Christine smiled at the guest of honor. "And Bernie, thanks for your help."

"You're welcome, Christine."

Dwight shrugged, went off with Louis. Bernie lingered, as if he wanted to tell her something. Christine asked him about his daughter's wedding. At least, that was something they had in common, and it seemed to take the edge off whatever hurt he felt in Louis finding out first.

She poured coffee into cups, set them on a tray along with creamer

---

and sugar. Bernie talked about the guest list, which she had already heard from Rita. Aware he watched her every move, Christine was glad Dwight never hovered like that. She placed silver spoons on the tray.

Bernie was all kindness. "May I take in the tray?"

"That would be nice, but it's your birthday. You're supposed to relax."

"Nothing would please me more than to serve you after that wonderful meal."

Good night, would he quit with the compliments! She smiled as brightly as she could. "Be my guest."

He picked up the tray, smiled back at her and made for the dining room. Christine busied herself wiping the countertop.

Bernie seemed so appreciative for the party, she began to feel guilty about not preparing the meal from scratch as usual. It would not hurt to be friendlier to Bernie. He was Dwight's best friend, or had been until recently. Lately, Dwight seemed to prefer Louis's company, and she was not sure why.

Christine returned to the dining room. Dwight stared at her, like she had food on her chin. The tray sat in the middle of the table. Where was the dessert? That was why Dwight had looked at her so funny! She hurried back to the kitchen and retrieved it from the fridge. Dwight had taken the store-bought pastries from their box and arranged them on a tray earlier to complete the subterfuge of their "homemade" dinner.

Now she realized that the pastries looked all wrong for a birthday celebration. Was her life a sham, like the store-bought food? The letter suggested it was. She had forgotten about the letter during dinner, but now its accusations came flooding back.

She rummaged in the junk drawer and found some candles left over from Mandy's last birthday. Well, it was pink candles or nothing. She stuck one in each pastry and lit them.

In the dining room, Louis was deep into a tale of sailing the Florida Keys. Someone had poured coffee, everyone had a cup. Except Bernie. He sat with arms crossed, staring into space.

She put the tray of pastries in the center of the table. "It's not flaming cheese, so I won't ask you all to cry 'Oopa!' But, I would like us to sing happy birthday."

Christine led them in the first verse, skipping the "How old are you?" verse. None of them were getting younger. Bernie made a fuss about blowing out the six candles. When she sat, her body ached. No doubt about it, she was exhausted from all the stress. It might be good to get away for a few days.

Bernie's voice grew loud. "On Saturday, Rita and I thought we'd head up to Pennsylvania to tour Fallingwater. We have room for everyone in the SUV." He plunked down his fork, looked at Dwight, then Christine. What had gotten into him lately? First, lingering by her in the kitchen, now this. Was Dwight aware of his attentions? She'd never told Dwight that she dated Bernie in college before she met Dwight. Bernie claimed he never told him, either.

Christine searched her husband's face for any sign that he thought something was up with Bernie. A couples road trip to the Frank Lloyd Wright house in Pennsylvania was not the getaway she had in mind. Dwight wore a forced smile, which meant he was uncomfortable. Rita ate her dessert without looking up.

Louis was the first to reply to Bernie's invitation. "Naomi and I are taking our grandkids to a farm in Maryland. Another time, Bernie." Naomi nodded, finished her pastry.

Rita helped herself to more coffee in the carafe. "Christine, these are interesting little cakes. Gus's Greek restaurant has delicious ones, just like it. Ever been there?"

Christine had not, and truthfully said so. But, that was where the takeout came from. She felt caught in a lie. She never said she made dinner, only that Dwight helped, which was also true. Why were friends so petty sometimes? Why couldn't they all be happy for each other's joys?

As she thought of being hit in the face with pie, a shudder rippled through her body. Dwight seemed to notice. His eyes held a question mark, like he wanted to ask if she was okay.

Bernie asked again about Fallingwater. "Will you and Dwight come?"

Christine set down her fork. "Dwight can decide. At some point, the President will make the announcement. He did not tell me when that is."

Rita drew together her painted brows. "What announcement?"

Naomi smiled at Christine, a knowing smile. Louis must have told her. She realized neither Dwight nor she had asked him not to.

Bernie stood, raised his water glass. "I propose a toast to Dwight, the next justice of the United States Supreme Court."

Rita gasped. She stood up with the others, but more slowly.

Bernie continued, "To the best friend a man ever had. We've been through a lot over the years. May your confirmation be swift, not too painful, and your tenure on the bench long and successful."

Louis chimed, "God bless you."

Christine clinked her glass against Naomi's, but she kept her eyes on Dwight's face. She wished she knew what he was thinking. He was so strong. His face looked tan, against smiling white teeth. If anything ever happened to him, she'd be lost. Tears stung her eyes. Her life with him was real. Why had she ever believed otherwise?

Whoever wrote that letter was trying to make trouble. How odd that it should come on the same day as the offer from the President to become a justice to the high court. Did whoever write it already know it? She tried to feel happy, but knew she wouldn't until Dwight read that letter.

It was after midnight when Christine trudged up the stairs. Naomi and Louis stayed until eleven. Bernie and Rita lingered for fifty more minutes. Mandy had been home, asleep, for hours. Dwight was downstairs locking up. Christine's muscles hurt, her feet throbbed.

Dwight walked into their bedroom, whistling like his life was on easy street. Without one word, she pulled open the second drawer on the tall chest, moved aside her jewelry case, and drew out a blue letter.

She handed it to Dwight. "This came this morning. You know I shred envelopes, but it had a D.C. postmark, no return address. When you read it, you'll see why I burned Bernie's cake. I should have told you earlier, but with everything—"

She stopped. Dwight seemed eager to read it. He snatched the folded paper from her trembling hands. She watched him unfold it, read the few lines, which by now she had memorized: *Your life is false. Your husband only married you to have a baby to keep from going to Vietnam. It is possible you will learn about other ways that he deceives you. What will you do then?*

Dwight dropped the paper on the bed as if it were a letter bomb, and went into lawyer mode. "We need to put it in a plastic s bag, right away. Whoever typed this may have left fingerprints. I am going to show it to the U.S. Marshal."

"Is that all you can think about—evidence? What about what it says?"

"Christine, we'll find out who sent this and they'll be sorry they did."

"What do you mean, sorry?"

"They'll be caught and arrested for making a threat."

She collapsed on the bed, not touching the letter. Her head was beginning to hurt. "It's from someone who doesn't like me. That's what shook me, thinking they might make trouble for you."

Dwight grabbed a tissue from the carved wooden box on the nightstand and picked up the letter with the tissue. "I'm going downstairs to put this in a plastic bag."

She stopped him. "Wait. I want to talk about what it says."

He folded his arms over his chest. "Why? You don't believe it, do you?"

"I never wanted to."

Dwight's arms fell. So did the letter. "Christine, it was not like that and you know it. How can you think I married you for such a reason? After more than thirty years, don't you know me?"

Christine put a finger to her lips. "Sshh. Mandy will hear." Tears blurred her sight. Her mind was a fog. It had been such an emotional day. Words felt like knives as they left her throat. "Did you marry me to stay out of the draft? Did you want a baby right away to make sure you wouldn't have to fight in Vietnam?"

Dwight sat on the edge of the bed and reached for her. "No! I loved you then, love you more now. Christy, don't cry."

The wall she built for so many years burst free. He sat beside her, and she told him everything, almost. That she and Bernie dated in college. That she had confided in Bernie about the accident. That, when she wrote to tell him she was marrying Dwight, Bernie wrote back, saying that Dwight was only marrying her to avoid the draft.

Dwight bolted off the bed and stood up, towering over her. "You never told me about you and Bernie. Why?" His tone was hurt, angry, accusing.

Christine wiped her eyes, blew her nose into one tissue, then another. "There was nothing to tell. You and I agreed not to talk about who we had dated before."

"But, Christine, all these years. He's been my law partner, my friend—and you both kept it a secret? Why did you have to hide it?"

How could she make him understand? "Bernie liked me a lot. We went out a few times, a play at the Ford Theater and dinner. I told him

I saw him only as a friend. After that, we hung out, had coffee, studied. That's all. When I met you, my whole world changed."

Dwight's next question forced her to confide in him a secret pain. "Why did you never tell me about Bernie's allegations?"

Her nose was getting congested. "His letter came just before we were married." Christine felt broken in two. "All these years, I worried that, maybe it was true."

Dwight sat back down, his warm hand found hers. They held each other for a long time. He whispered, "If only you had let me know your pain. I thought you and Veronica were just different, couldn't see eye to eye. I thought it was a mother-daughter thing. Now I wonder—"

Christine cried into his shoulder. "I knew it was wrong, but I could not feel the kind of love I should for her."

Dwight's words were hard. "All because of Bernie. If he sent you that letter today, I'll never speak to him again."

She picked the note up from the bed, read it again, holding it with the tissue, then pulled back from Dwight. "It doesn't sound like Bernie. I got another one of these a week or so ago, same paper, but in a child's scrawl. I tossed it out. It can't be Bernie, he's your best friend."

He gently stroked her hair. "Maybe he didn't write this one, but I find it hard to forgive Bernie for writing you all those years ago, making you distrust me."

She looked into his eyes. "But, I was wrong to take it out on a little baby. As Veronica grew independent, like me, I guess I blamed her. Bernie was injured in Vietnam. He thought you took me away from him."

"Okay, forget Bernie for now. What are you going to do to make it up to Veronica?"

Christine blew her nose. "I can never tell her what I thought. Maybe, if we follow what Louis did for us today, we might find the answer."

That night, shades drawn and holding hands, Christine and Dwight did something they had never done in all their lives. They prayed together for God's help and healing.

TWENTY SEVEN

B efore breakfast, Dwight donned mechanics' coveralls and headed for the garage. Now was his chance to forget that stupid letter and spend some happy moments working on the Judge. Although it had only been two thousand miles since the car's last oil change, Dwight would empty out the old and put in fresh.

He raised all three overhead doors to let in the greatest amount of light and fresh air. After running the front wheels of his baby on low ramps, he placed jacks under the frame. It didn't hurt to be careful. On a mechanic's creeper, he slid under the car, then gathered his filter wrench and oil catch pan into position. No sooner was he under the car, when he remembered what happened the last time.

Dwight slid back out and retrieved from his tool box his customized half glasses. They had a large plastic arch between the lenses where they rested on his nose. With his bench grinder, he'd made a new indentation on top of the nose piece, and switched the temples to the opposite sides. Proud of his invention, he put on the glasses, which were upside down. They might look strange, but when lying on his back beneath the car, he could see above his head to loosen his oil pan plug and filter.

Old oil drained, a new filter sealed in place, and oil added, Dwight crawled under again to check for leaks, his feet sticking out from his classic Pontiac. A female voice startled him.

"Good morning. Is that you, Judge?"

Immediately, he knew that high-pitched voice did not belong to Christine or Mandy. Besides, they never called him Judge. Wearing a ball cap with no visor, and upside-down glasses on his oil smudged face, Dwight rolled out expecting to see his neighbor, who still addressed him as Judge. He sat up on his creeper, and looked up into the face of a smartly dressed woman. He could not believe his eyes. He recognized the TV reporter that had been hounding him—that Kat woman.

She held a microphone toward his face. A cameraman was right behind her, balancing a television camera on his shoulder. "I am Kat Kowicki from Channel 14. People would like your reaction to the news you've been named by the President as the next Supreme Court Justice."

Kat kneeled down, as though she could interview a sitting judge, but Dwight leapt to his feet, brushed dirt from his coveralls. She moved in, placed the microphone near Dwight's face. "Were you surprised the President picked you, even though you've not been on the U.S. Court of Appeals?"

Ambushed by a reporter in his own garage, Dwight was shocked. In the initial confusion over how to respond, the feeling of weakness made his blood boil. With every nerve jangling, he wanted to throw her out. Of course, a camera was recording his every move.

He backed away from the microphone. "I am impressed, Ms. Ko-wicki, with your effort to get a story, but I know of no such announce-ment by the White House. Therefore, I have no reason to have a reac-tion."

Dwight turned his back on her, walked toward the house. His hand reached up, fingers ready to punch two of the garage door openers. "I do not know how you got my home address. The U.S. District Court and the Marshal's service go to great lengths to protect us. Since you are trespassing, I suggest you leave my garage, unless you want to spend the weekend in there."

His fingers pressed the buttons, and two doors began to clank shut. Tethered to the cameraman by her microphone wire, Kat looked at Dwight, a defiant glare in her eye. She held out a business card. "Sir, if you returned my calls, we could arrange an interview in your cham-bers."

Dwight stepped inside his house, the camera still shooting, and hit the third button. As the opener clattered near the ceiling, the final ga-rage door started closing. The cameraman beat it to get out from under the door, dragging behind him one Kat at the end of the microphone. Her business card fluttered to the garage floor.

Dwight made sure there were no body parts trapped beneath the overhead door, then snuck to the front door. He did not want the cam-era to take a picture of him through a window. As he passed a gilded mirror in the hallway, one for which Christine paid a fortune, he nearly scared himself. His glasses were on upside down, and his cheeks and nose were smudged with grease. In his visor-less cap, he looked like a demented man.

This would be the nation's first glimpse of their newest Supreme! He could not let that happen. Dwight glanced out through the small window above his front door. Kat was doing her news piece with his home as backdrop.

Dwight ran back to the mirror, tried to imagine a farmer over coffee, or store clerk reacting to that ugly mug on television. He'd be out before the President ever made the announcement. He reversed his glasses and his finger did some walking in the phone book. There! The number for Channel 14.

As much as it pained him, he knew it had to be done. At the station, he asked for the manager. Instead of solving his problem, there was a new one. The station manager was nowhere to be found. Portable phone dangling in his pocket, Dwight hauled out to the garage, scooped up Kat's card and did what he'd said he would never do. He called a television reporter.

Kat answered, still in front of the house. Dwight promised to give her an exclusive interview. Only then did she agree to hold off running the film she just shot.

Dwight breathed a sigh. "There are two conditions to my interview. We'll do it after the President's announcement and you cannot leak it to any other news source."

Kat was indignant. "Why would I do that, when our station has the exclusive?"

Dwight watched the van pull away. "I guess you wouldn't, but you know what they say. In Washington, one cannot trust even his dog."

"Judge Pendergast, you have my word."

"Thank you." Dwight hung up, wondering what on earth that was worth.

Griff Topping was in his office before eight, wanting to clean things up before he left for Florida to meet with Skeeter. The plan for making him an informant in Nick's drug case was in full swing. His private line rang. He asked Dawn Ahern if she was doing any flying over the weekend.

Her voice was crisp, not as friendly as the day they flew to see Skeeter. "No, are you?"

Griff toyed with his magnet tower. "Recently, I flew some kids of wounded soldiers. I think you'd be interested."

Dawn didn't seem to be in the mood for small talk. She launched into the reason for her call. "What is your real interest in Arthur Bailey?"

Her abruptness brought to mind their first call, when she insisted on seeing a request on FBI letterhead before she talked to him about Skeeter. He thought they were beyond that in their professional dealings.

Before he mustered an answer, she continued, sounding more perturbed. "Skeeter sent me a note saying that he had contact with felons and you know all about it. Are you in the habit of using the court's officers to make contact with potential informants?"

Not surprised by her question, Griff was stung by her frigid tone. Where to begin? With the truth, he guessed. "Did Skeeter admit I told him not have contact with criminals, and to report the visitors to you?"

Dawn's tone softened, slightly. "No. He mentioned you initiated contact by telephoning him, blowing your own cover. He accused me of bringing a ringer to his home. I could only reply that all I knew was that you were interested in his donating an organ, as you claimed to me."

Griff detected an accusation behind the words, that he was lying to her. Dawn knew Skeeter tried to get money for his kidney, but no other details. Griff swiftly calculated how much to reveal of Skeeter's latest boneheaded scam, then reminded her that he was interested in finding Arthur Bailey for an associate who wanted to find a relative. "I am not at liberty to divulge his or her identity. I can't violate my word to keep it confidential."

"Okay," was all she said.

To convince her, Griff took a small step further. "Skeeter saw some notes in my file that included the name and home address for federal judge Dwight Pendergast."

"How do you know that?"

"Because he admitted to me he read the name upside down and memorized it. He assumed Judge Pendergast was the person needing the organ, thought he could make some money. The judge received a letter from Skeeter, which came close to offering to sell a federal judge an organ."

She unloaded on Griff. "And you brought this upon him by interviewing him for an organ. Was that your purpose, to trip up Skeeter, so he'd be forced to work as an informant?"

Griff was on a tight rope, walking a fine line between being angry with her and currying her favor. "Judge Pendergast is incensed about the letter. Believes I fouled things up, and I did. Not only do I have to assuage his concerns and your concerns, I have to rectify it. Imagine my predicament."

Dawn calmed again. "I would *not* want to be in your boots."

She was coming around, but would she agree to the plan he and Nick discussed? "You and I have to work together. The judge is convinced Skeeter's actions violate the law, but agrees with me that it is not a matter the U.S. Attorney will prosecute, if there is another way."

Dawn was not buying it. "I sense whatever you have in mind, I won't approve. You realize Skeeter cannot associate with felons, which he will do if he works as an informant."

Boy did he. He'd thought of little else. Griff wished they were face-to-face, not talking over the phone. Since they were on a hardwire phone connection, Griff continued his sensitive negotiations with Dawn. He told her how he appreciated her hard work to turn Skeeter around; he did not want to hinder her, but truth was, Skeeter had done it to himself.

Griff put down the metal nut, and fingered the end of his moustache. If his next argument failed to sway her, he was done for. "If you agree, the Department of Justice will, too. Here's why. There is an exception to the policy that releasees can't have contact with felons. The DEA is pursuing a high-level target and Skeeter is their only alternative to infiltrating it. Can you trust me to put this together?"

Not superstitious, Griff did not cross his fingers, but he did hold his breath.

A little sigh escaped from Dawn. "He has to have some consequence for writing the letter. If only he asked me about it, but he didn't. I guess he is not making the progress I hoped for."

Before he could think better of it, he plunged in head first. "Skeeter will introduce an undercover DEA agent into a cocaine smuggling ring. I will supervise him as an informant. He'll be in a tricky position, and I suspect Skeeter will be too scared to venture into criminal activity of his own."

"You mean you're doing this for his own good?"

Griff wanted to laugh, but that might set her off again. "Once the smugglers know he is cooperating with agents, they'll never trust him again. He'll have to hide from them and anyone else who learns he's a snitch."

Her next question was natural. "If it's that bad, why would Skeeter help you infiltrate the group?"

"He knows the alternative. You'd try to terminate his supervised release and Judge Pendergast will want him prosecuted for attempting to sell an organ. Either way, the devil you know is better than the devil you don't. He'll agree."

At last, Dawn consented. Despite the back and forth, he respected her professional attitudes. Talking with her made him want to recapture what they experienced on the flight back from Apalach. Two thousand feet above the earth, Dawn opened up about her life, how hard it was to raise a son after losing her husband. How she prayed for strength and courage. God was faithful and saw her through to the end of the tunnel. Griff listened, shared his feelings about grieving for Sue. How he depended only on himself. Dawn offered to pray for him. They landed before he could ask what she meant.

He knew one thing—she had touched a place in his heart he thought had died. With great risk, he let uncharacteristic words tumble from his lips. "Dawn, I'd like to switch gears, away from Skeeter."

Her guard went up. "Oh?"

Griff drew back. A part of him said *hang up*, while another part wanted to get to know her at a different level. "I was wondering if we could talk again, like we did in the sky. I enjoyed"—that was not the word he wanted to use, but there it was—"your company."

He stopped, waited for her reply, which he thought would never come. Then, an opening. "I enjoyed yours, too."

Relieved, Griff figured that was enough for now. He gave her a few more details about the sting, then hung up. Not only was the plan he crafted with Nick about to become a reality, his creativity was going to be challenged again. But, there was another hurdle. He needed the FBI Director's approval. One person who could help came to mind, and Griff wasted no time calling Judge Pendergast to ask a much-needed favor.

After his run-in with Kat, Dwight showered and changed into his black suit, which seemed appropriate after the morning he'd had, and headed to work. Now he exited the Capital Beltway at the Eisenhower Connector and headed for the courthouse, where he had a full calendar of motions and sentencing hearings. His mind hovered on Kat. She was one reporter with gall. The radio was tuned to NPR. He turned onto

Elizabeth Lane, and waved to the guard. As the security gate raised, Dwight heard a report that a new source claimed to have met with Secretary of Interior Owen Jones II and offered to pay for the federal designation of the Michigan White Pine Indian tribe.

Dwight raised the volume, but as he descended the ramp beneath the building, the signal faded. Such an allegation was not made in the Jones trial. Who was this media source? Was this going to be "casino-gate?" He marveled at the timing of the scandalous report, a Friday morning. No doubt, the White House would have to react quickly to keep the story from consuming the weekend shows. Was it possible this new accusation would obstruct his nomination to the Supreme Court?

As he entered his outer office, Gladys was just hanging up the telephone. Words poured from her mouth like salt from a shaker. "That was the White House. Jasper Collins wants you over there. You are not to delay one minute."

Dwight just knew it. Jasper heard the rumor, and wanted to grill him about why he let Owen Jones off the hook. The President would want to know if Dwight's dismissal could come back to bite him. He set his briefcase on the edge of her desk, his hands gripping the handle. The thought struck him that maybe she had more to tell. "Did Mr. Collins say what it was all about?"

Gladys's face had an aura of having talked to the President himself, rather than his Chief of Staff. "Judge, he was in a hurry. What do you think he wants?"

Dwight spoke slowly, so as not to reveal the terrible anxiety he felt. "I think you should call Mr. Collins, let me talk to him."

Gladys pulled out her sheet of important numbers. "Maybe it has something to do with your moving up a notch, to the appellate bench. The President will announce soon who he wants to put on the Supreme Court, and there may be an opening for you."

Dwight nodded, but said nothing. Gladys soon learned that Jasper was not in. She was transferred to another number. She put her hand over the mouthpiece. "They put me through to Barbara Jo Houston's voice mail. Should I leave a message?"

He wasted no time. "No! Hang up!"

TWENTY EIGHT

The next two hours were a blur. Dwight called Christine at her office, asked if she could join him at the White House. Did she have time to go home and change, she asked? No. He had Gladys cancel all the hearings before him. On the drive to the White House, he caught more NPR news talk, and found out it was Frank's informant, the casino operator who first introduced the FBI into the Jones case, who was now talking to the media. Apparently, with the Jones case dismissed, the informant felt secure in his immunity from prosecution.

The informant claimed he offered a bribe directly to Secretary Jones. When offered the money, the Secretary became indignant, refused to take it. But, here the informant threw in a new twist—Secretary Jones referred the casino operator to his son, Owen Jones III.

While Judge Pendergast waited for Jasper Collins in his West Wing office, Dwight called Christine on his cell. She was just getting out of a cab on Pennsylvania Avenue and was about to enter the White House gate. She told him not to worry, the future was not theirs to see.

Jasper walked in then, so Dwight folded his phone, slid it into his pocket. Jasper looked harried. "Judge, in light of your dismissal of the Jones case, what do you make of this accusation about Secretary Jones? Will it come to anything?"

As Dwight feared, his nomination was about to vaporize. What could he do? He tugged on his ear lobe, and offered the best defense he could, knowing it was too little. "There was no evidence in the case that the Secretary was involved. The government could not prove the charges. I had no choice but to dismiss the matter against the son."

Jasper paced from the desk to the window. "Here's the plan."

Dwight waited for him to tell him to do the decent thing, and withdraw his name. Instead, Jasper said, "In two minutes, the President will take you into the Oval Office, for a private chat."

That was it then, the President would ask him to bow out. Why not get it over with, instead of driving him nuts. Jasper picked up a folder, motioned for Dwight to follow. "Then, the two of you will go to the Rose Garden, where he will make your nomination official."

His nomination official? Had he heard correctly? Numb, Dwight walked beside Jasper. Just outside the Oval Office, he explained something else. "FBI Director Kirkwood told me the same thing you did. I arranged for him to appear on two of the weekend talk shows. Kirkwood will say the informant never told the FBI he met with Secretary Jones. Nor did the FBI's investigation find that it happened."

Dwight breathed deeply. "Does Kirkwood think the informant is lying now?"

Jasper suppressed his famous smile. "Apparently, or he would not be going on the talk shows. Just be prepared."

Dwight's feet stopped moving. He stood in the hall outside the Oval Office and waited to hear if Jasper knew of some other bomb about to drop.

"Before nightfall, you will hear it or see on internet blogs, that there is a nexus between the dismissal and your appointment."

There was no such thing, and Dwight told Jasper so, defended himself outside the Oval office. "I would like to know who dares to make such a claim about me."

Jasper grabbed his arm. "Don't worry. I have complete confidence in you, as does the President."

Under the circumstances his words rang hollow, but Dwight believed he was sincere. After all, the President could dump him here and now, if he wanted to. "I appreciate that, Jasper. You wanted to be the one to call Kat Kowicki and schedule the exclusive interview I agreed to."

Jasper opened the door. "That's all taken care of."

In yellow dress, pearls, and eggshell-colored shoes, Christine, Austrian immigrant, mother of two, and wife of Dwight Pendergast since she was barely twenty, sat in the front row of the Rose Garden. She was absolutely awestruck, a lump in her throat and tears threatening to well over, as she watched her husband, a real smile on his face.

There he was, standing next to the President, being nominated for the highest court in the country. A million thoughts galloped through her mind, but she managed to focus enough to hear the glowing words the President was saying about Dwight, "… ethical judge … confidence in his judicial philosophy … not an activist on the court."

Her heart overflowed with many emotions, the least being pride. The love she felt for Dwight was a deep and lasting kind, the kind that comes when two people face the greatest storms of life, and survive. She would love him even if he were not a lawyer and a judge. When she saw him that morning, car grease on his forehead and face, she laughed and they had a silly time while she helped him wipe off the marks. Now, look at him. So tall, so handsome, in his tailored black suit. The white shirt set off his dark hair and black eyes.

Christine regretted that, with the short notice, neither Mandy nor Dwight's parents were here. She had called them before she left her office. They would all come to the confirmation hearings, and watch today's events on television.

With her office in the building next door, Veronica easily made it and now sat next to Christine, looking pregnant and happy. She squeezed her daughter's hand and was happy to be sharing this moment with her. Veronica turned to her, there were tears in her eyes.

Christine whispered, "Isn't this exciting?"

Dwight stepped to the podium. The air was warm, but Christine did not notice. His smile was for her, she knew. He graciously thanked the President for the wonderful opportunity, thanked his parents for their encouragement. "And, I would not be here today, if not for my wife, Christine."

She felt her whole body tingle. Her fears and worries dissolved in the enormity of this moment. Dwight had finished talking already. She missed much of what he said. She hoped he'd written his remarks so that she could study each word.

As her husband and the President walked back into the White House. Jasper Collins approached her, held out a hand and smiled. "Please come with me, Mrs. Pendergast."

He took her to a plush room filled with sculptures and paintings of Theodore Roosevelt. Bright lights were aimed at Dwight, who sat behind a massive walnut table, being interviewed by Kat Kowicki. Two cameramen recorded these moments to be broadcast on the evening news.

Christine quietly took a seat along the back of the room and lifted up a silent prayer for Dwight not to be tricked by the reporter. At that moment, she realized they needed, *she* needed, a spiritual component to her life. After praying the night before, she had taken time to talk to God herself. It was hard to explain how she felt afterwards, like she was not alone with her troubles. That the creator of the vast universe cared about her.

Jasper sat next to her. In a low voice, he explained, "This is the only exclusive interview before the weekend. Then, for the talk shows, we'll have Senator Briggs and Senators from our party appear for Dwight. You and he should avoid all media contact, unless it is arranged by me."

Christine nodded, and went back to observing Dwight. He looked calm, and Kat sounded more casual then Christine expected. Her questions were open ended, not cloaked with venom.

"Judge Pendergast, I know one of your favorite pastimes is working on your Classic 1971 Pontiac GTO, which coincidently is known in car buff circles as 'The Judge.' How else do you relax?"

His hands tented, Dwight beamed for the camera. "I spend time with my family, and am a student of our first President, George Washington. You and your viewers might be interested to know Washington appointed eight Supreme Court Justices and three Chief Justices. In fact, Chief Justice Oliver Ellsworth was the first to write a single opinion as the ruling, instead of nine separate opinions."

Kat smiled as though talking to a friend. "If you had your choice, would you rather have been nominated today, or many years ago by George Washington?"

His eyes sparkled. "That's a tough choice. If I had been nominated by Washington, I would not have had a chance to be interviewed by you." They both laughed and Christine knew that would go over well on television.

He unfolded his hands. "On the other hand, back then I would not have to endure eighteen to twenty hours of questioning by the Senate."

Christine wanted to add *nor would your wife have to endure being hit with a pie.* Of course, she stayed quiet for the five minutes the interview took. Dwight introduced her to Kat, who asked, "Would you mind if we take your photo? I promise not to ask you any questions. We'll slice your picture in, as if to get your reaction to one of my questions."

Out of the corner of her eye, Christine spotted Jasper looking at her. Perhaps she should decline. But, then he nodded. Christine was used to appearing on television, so this was nothing unusual. But, she had a feeling that, from now on, the other reporters would not be as gracious or understanding as the one known as Kat.

On the way back from lunch with Sal, the tang of sauerkraut and Swiss cheese on his tongue, Griff heard the news on the car radio about Judge Pendergast's nomination to the Supreme Court. He was dumbstruck. This totally ramped up his search for Eleanor. He'd put the drug case and Skeeter ahead of finding the judge's sister. All the way back to the office, he was quiet, and Sal asked him if he was feeling sick. Griff just said, "No," and continued thinking.

At his computer, he spent the next hour on various public sites on the internet. No Eleanor Bailey of the correct age in Florida. He was about to run NCIC, when his supervisor told him to report ASAP to Director Kirkwood at FBI Headquarters. Then he made a snide remark about what Griff did to get called downtown. True to his nickname, tight-lipped Griff, he said nothing.

Simply drove his bucar to the Bureau on Pennsylvania Avenue and parked in a garage a few blocks away. Few street-level agents met the Director, unless it was a special occasion. The previous year, Griff shook Kirkwood's hand at an award ceremony for a case he worked on with Eva Montanna. Rain began to fall. It was a brisk walk; he'd left his umbrella in the car. Too much hassle taking it inside.

At the entrance, Griff flipped open his credentials. The security guard allowed him to walk around the magnetometer so that his gun wouldn't set it off. With other agents he didn't know, Griff rode the elevator to his floor, where he was the only one who exited. Outside the Director's office, a guard checked his name on an appointment list, then buzzed him in to Kirkwood's inner sanctum.

A blonde woman wearing a navy suit greeted him, offered coffee. Not wanting to juggle a cup with his file, Griff declined. Director Kirkwood came out to meet him, and Griff shook his hand, only this was no award ceremony. Why was he here? An inch taller than Griff, the Director was youthful in a gunmetal suit. His carefully combed reddish hair had no gray.

Glad he had at least worn a jacket over slacks, Griff knew some agents resented Kirkwood because he was the former Deputy Director of the CIA. Griff appreciated his take-no-prisoners style. Where others before had failed, he installed a new FBI computer system that actually worked, nothing short of miraculous.

Griff was cautious. "Good afternoon, sir."

On the plush carpet, Kirkwood silently moved to his office, and Griff followed the former spy. No one else was present. He felt a little like being called to the principal's office, but because Griff had "suggested" that Judge Pendergast speak with the Director, he was not as intimidated as he might be. He thought he knew what this was about. But, then, Kirkwood could have something else in mind.

"Let's get right to it, Topping. I have a meeting with the Attorney General in ten minutes."

Fine with Griff. It would not cost him a fortune to park. They did not sit.

"I want you to nail down this thing. First, I have a question."

"Sir?"

"I've read the reports from the Owen Jones case. You chose not to notify the court that you found the missing FBI agent until after you captured the kidnapper. You did fine work, but what I need to know is, was your decision influenced in any way by Judge Pendergast?"

The question took the seasoned FBI agent by surprise. What was Kirkwood driving at? Griff stood tall. "Not at all. I knew that waiting to tell the judge about finding Agent Williams could result in a dismissal. Still, I strongly believed that if I notified him too early, Pendergast would have an ethical obligation to tell the defense attorney, which might prevent us from finding whoever was behind his disappearance. If I were to do it over again, I would make the same decision."

He wanted to add, "Hindsight is twenty-twenty," but that sounded defensive. The Director studied Griff's face as if he were a specimen under a microscope. "Agent Topping, do you believe the Secretary of the Interior was involved in a bribery conspiracy?"

Griff knew that Frank's informant had told the media Secretary Jones *was* involved. Did Kirkwood know more? The Director had myriad sources, and being ex-CIA, he might have inside intel, but Griff had seen no evidence to implicate Secretary Jones, and he told the Director so.

Griff wanted to tell him something else, but the tricky part was saying it without adding another smudge to Frank's career. "Sir, when I took over the Jones case as lead agent, I was uncomfortable with it. The judge's dismissal was consistent with the evidence. I felt Jones Junior was scamming the Native Americans out of their money, and if charged with fraud, could have been convicted."

Kirkwood's eyes were riveted to his, so Griff kept going. "I never met the initial informant who now claims that he offered money personally to the Secretary. Frank did have the informant polygraphed at the beginning of the investigation, but none of the questions focused on the Secretary, because he didn't make that allegation back then. Without probable cause, it would have been unfair to target a Cabinet member just because his son is a criminal."

Kirkwood dropped his eyes, straightened his tie. "Agent Sal Domingo is working with the IRS to fully investigate the informant. Did you ever tell Pendergast of your misgivings about the Jones case?"

Griff felt his face grow hot. He was used to being questioned; his problem here was, he had no control over where Kirkwood was headed. "That would have been inappropriate. O'Rourke, the federal prosecutor who took over a couple weeks before the trial, knew I had doubts."

The Director took off his gold-rimmed glasses and put them in his suit pocket. He lifted his chin, looked Griff in the eye. "Do you suspect Judge Pendergast was motivated by any political considerations when he dismissed the case against a Cabinet member's son?"

Said like that, the Director must be worried there was some kind of quid pro quo. If Owen Jones III meant to embarrass the President and Judge Pendergast, his plan was succeeding. Griff could not help wondering how much power Owen Jones III and his father really had. How far did their schemes reach?

Griff did not have an opinion about the White House, but set the record straight as far as the judge. "The Pendergast I know would resign from the court before being a party to anything like that. The agents I know think he's on the right side of justice—a real boy scout."

Tension lines eased from the Director's forehead. He nodded. "Okay, Topping. Glad to hear you say so. I went out on a limb with the White House and told Jasper Collins the same thing."

Kirkwood put his glasses back on. "Summarize what you just told me in a statement and deliver it to my office in a sealed envelope. With regard to the adoption matter, treat it as ancillary to the judge's confirmation. Write no progress reports. When it's over, give me a concluding memo about your special assignment."

Griff nodded at the Director. His CIA days showing through, Kirkwood continued in the same vague way. "All your expenses are covered by the Bureau. Questions?"

"Does my supervisor know the background of this, or should I speak to you?"

Kirkwood checked his watch. "My car is waiting to take me to Justice. Keep it between you and me. I will handle your expense voucher. That's it, then."

In the outer office, Kirkwood told his secretary to call his driver, he was on the way down. The Director rode in a secure elevator, while Griff got on the public one. He descended, totally ignoring a woman and two kids, his mind calculating how many other secret investigations were approved by the Director, for Congress, or the White House.

At the back of his mind, he heard the woman shoo a small kid away from the buttons. He started to cry, but Griff tuned him out. Director Kirkwood had given him a gift. As part of his new mission, he could fly privately or commercially, and the FBI would pay for it. Cool.

Just then, the boy reached up, pushed the red STOP button. The elevator lurched to a stop, then bounced. Griff banged into the back wall.

Griff's chest tightened in panic. The worst possible thing happened! He was stuck in an elevator. It might as well be a cave with no light. The alarm bell shrieked. Within moments, sweat poured from under his arms. His claustrophobia was in full reign.

He lashed out, "Kid, what do you think you're doing! Get him away from that panel."

Griff pulled off his suit coat and, throwing it over his arm, reached toward the control panel. The woman screamed and grabbed her two children. She must have seen the gun in his holster. Griff quickly reached for his credential case, flipped open his badge. "I'm an FBI agent."

She looked as terrified as he was uncomfortable. Once, when Griff was very young, his mother took him to see his father at a large office building. The elevator stopped in between floors. Alone with Griff, his mother flew into a panic, crying, shaking. It took over an hour for the doors to open. By that time, Griff was traumatized. No matter how old he got, he could not shake the fear of being caught in tight places.

If he was a praying man, he'd pray. That is what Dawn would tell him to do, and his fevered brain uttered a kind of plea for help. Then, he stared at the red button as if he'd never seen it before. What was he supposed to do? Finally, his mind cleared and he grabbed the outer plastic ring and pulled it toward him. Instantly, the bell quit ringing and the cubicle began, thankfully, to move.

At the first floor, Griff darted from the elevator, hurried past the guards, and lurched through the glass doors. Outside, he breathed in the hot, sultry air. Pelts of rain on his head felt cool. He did not care how wet he got. He was free.

At four that afternoon, in plenty of time for the Friday night news, the media gathered in the Senate Press Gallery to cover the Senators' spin of Dwight's nomination. When Senator Zorn arrived with Arnie for his reserved time, they found Chairman Briggs still taking questions from reporters.

Lars nudged Arnie's arm. "I don't like having to wait, but there are more reporters to hear the Chairman."

Arnie cupped his hand near his mouth. "I'll circulate, alert them Senator Zorn is waiting."

Minutes later, Briggs took a final question, then the junior Senator from California got his chance to step behind the microphones. Lars stood directly in front of the Senate seal, his smile grave. "I will carefully consider the President's latest choice to fill the Supreme Court vacancy."

He looked at news crews folding up their equipment. Didn't they care what he had to say? He talked louder and faster. "I was disappointed by Judge Cuttering's withdrawal for such a trivial reason, but today," he paused for effect, "today, I am more disappointed. This nominee, with no federal appellate experience, is even less qualified."

Lars knew very well the power of the camera to broadcast his beliefs and ideas to millions of homes, all prospective voters in the next Presidential election. From within, he worked up a visible outrage, which he hoped would resonate with those voters. "I assure the nation, I will do all I can to protect Americans from closed-minded judges sitting on the Supreme Court. Pendergast has proven time and time again he favors the rich against the poor, the powerful against the weak. But, I will keep an open mind—maybe the judge will surprise us all."

Senator Zorn buttoned his suit coat. "Now I am happy to answer any questions."

He smiled at two video photographers. All the reporters had left. There were no questions. Lars stepped from the podium. Now, he really was disappointed. All that attention for the Chairman and none for him. All that rage, and no one to listen.

Arnie joined him, chattering about Briggs's comments. Lars couldn't care less. As they descended the steps to the Capitol basement where they would hop on the tram to the Dirksen Office Building, Lars twisted the button on his suit coat, and nearly tore it off. "We had Cuttering on the ropes. Now, we have to start over again. I want to know what Pendergast eats for breakfast, who he entertains, where he travels. Arnie, leave no stone unturned, my man."

Where was Arnie? Lars looked over his shoulder. His staffer did not seem able to keep up. At six-foot-three, Lars took enormous strides. He lived as he walked, large. He was the first to reach the tram, so they could ride through the tunnel and avoid the rain. Arnie finally caught up with him, breathing hard.

"Senator, I will pull out all the stops. I've heard he is an avid fisherman. Maybe the animal rights groups will see him as a threat."

"I don't think we can expect an encore. Find some dirt, some weakness. I want something no other Senator will have."

The duo walked around the security perimeter and took a seat in the front of the electric tram. To give the Senator and his aide privacy, security officers held back several tourists with a guide. As the conductor started the trip back to Dirksen, Lars leaned over to Arnie. He meant to speak low, so his voice wouldn't echo off the concrete walls, "I remind you, this is my only term in the Senate. I do not intend to run again. You do a superb job here, and you will help me select future nominees"—he paused to relish the words—"when I'm in the White House."

Arnie stared at the track, but his somber nod convinced Lars that he understood what was at stake.

TWENTY NINE

After his meeting with Kirkwood, Griff's investigative wheels turned fast. Dawn gave her okay for Skeeter to drive to Crystal River, about three hours from Apalach, provided he stayed in touch with Griff on the way. He called Skeeter, who tried to sound casual, but Griff sensed fear around the edges. In a short time, he got back to Nick. All was arranged.

Griff sat back in his chair. The victory seemed empty. There was really no one to tell he'd be gone for a few days. Who cared? Eva and Scott did, but they were on vacation for a long weekend. He wheeled his chair around the wall, saw Sal's back. He went over and found him writing a report. As Griff neared, Sal flipped over whatever he was working on. Something confidential, no doubt.

Griff hadn't told Sal he just saw the Director, so he took it in stride. "Hey, Sal. I'm working on a case with the DEA in Florida."

Sal turned so he could see him. "You assigned to drugs now?"

He sounded interested, so Griff explained he had come across a man released from prison who could help the DEA. "Nick Tascoda and I go way back to the FBI academy."

"Then he jumped ship to work drugs. You thinking of doing the same?"

Nick's excitement had infected Griff with the idea, until he found out about the grueling training. "I'm Bureau to the bone. But, it will be fun to work this case with Nick. A real prankster, like you. Hope you meet him sometime. You'd hit it off."

As Griff prepared to leave, Sal tapped the paper on his desk. "I need to ask you something. Were you interviewed by FBI agents updating Pendergast's background investigation?"

Was Sal's question connected to the report he'd just turned over? Before Griff could ask, Sal added, "The Bureau does a background investigation on every nominee to the federal bench. A couple of days ago, an agent from the Washington Field Office interviewed me."

Griff leaned against the half-wall. "Wow, that was before today's announcement. Do you know Pendergast?"

"No. They asked something that bothers me."

Griff's thick brows shot up on his forehead. Sal's exterior was tough, like rawhide. "Oh?"

Sal scratched his chin. "Yeah. They want me to prepare a report about what happened when we arrested Federov. They hinted that they want to know what influenced our decision not to notify the judge as soon as we found Frank. You know, Lev's trial is next month."

"Seems like his lawyer would want to postpone the trial until after he testifies against Owen Jones. Try to get the best deal for his client. When is Jones going to trial?"

Sal shrugged. Griff thought about what the Director asked him earlier. So, he sent some FBI agents to check up on them and Dwight. He didn't like the tone of their inquiry. Maybe Sal was overreacting. "Do they think we delayed telling the judge because he asked us to?"

Sal whipped his report face up. "I don't know what they think. I wanted you to know they interviewed me and may come after you as well. It's a good thing you're leaving town."

That sounded funny, but Griff knew what he meant. "Thanks for the warning. You seem kinda testy about it. At the time, you and Roger Gant agreed we should postpone telling the judge."

Sal rubbed his eyes. "That's exactly what I'm telling these backgrounders."

Griff relaxed. Sal was emotional over nothing. "Time to shove off, I guess."

Sal stood. "I'll give you a ride to the airport. When you flying out?"

Sal made a note of Griff's flight arrangements, and Griff returned to his work area, picked up his portfolio from his desk, and left the office. The exchange with Sal revealed a comforting truth. His fellow agent was concerned for him. Griff's parents were, of course, but that was different. They knew he was an FBI agent, but that was as far as it went.

When Griff reached his car, he decided to call his folks, but he'd keep quiet about going to Florida. Not having worked on a drug case with Nick before, he wanted to be careful. He drove home, looking forward to the "action-packed" life that Nick promised, if only for a few days.

In the West Wing, Barbara Jo paced her office floor. Jasper had treated her abominably. He'd handled this morning's interview between Pendergast and the Channel 14 reporter, while she was made to stand outside the doorway to the Roosevelt Room. Of course, when it was over, she stalked away as fast as she could. She had no wish to speak to Pendergast. But, Jasper didn't know that. Or did he?

She had helped Arnie uncover the truth about Cuttering. That judge was a nut who believed the earth was made in six days by some intelligent designer. With those beliefs, he didn't deserve to be on the highest court. He was a violent man who killed animals. Barbara Jo detested meat eaters herself, but she kept her beliefs private. In college she had carefully avoided joining any extremist groups.

If it was possible, Barbara Jo felt in her entire being that Pendergast was worse than Cuttering. He exuded something more than confidence—a dangerous clawing for power. Barbara Jo saw it in his eyes that first time at the safe house. The judge wore an evil glint like her father's, one that said he mowed down minorities and women. But, she refused to think of her father. Right now, her enemy was Dwight Pendergast.

Her therapist believed that her intense dislike of the judge was misplaced anger at her father for rejecting her. Barbara Jo dismissed these truths as inconvenient. She knew in her heart that Dwight Pendergast must be stopped. Wasn't his arrogant daughter, Veronica Fife, proof that the Pendergast family's quest to control ran deep? Barbara Jo was working on her own special plan when the phone rang at her desk.

A male caller said, "Meet me at Union Station at six. Our usual spot. It's urgent."

"You must have read my mind. I'll be there."

On her computer, Barbara Jo checked the President's schedule. He was on Marine One, to Andrews Air Force Base, from where he would fly on Air Force One to Yellowstone National Park to give a speech on protecting the nation's parks. She snatched her purse, then locked her drawer.

She left the White House and strode to the security gate, intending to catch a cab to Union Station. Impervious to the wind gusting and the dark clouds looming overhead, Barbara Jo was laser-focused on putting Judge Pendergast in his place, which was off the court entirely if she had her way.

Dwight and Christine basked in the glow of success. What a day! From a reporter in their garage in the morning, to the Rose Garden in the afternoon, then to a church supper for the homeless. They even washed dishes with Wendell and Hazel Cochran in the church basement, joking about the contrasting scenes that day had held. Then Dwight convinced his wife to escape with him to the lake.

They had tossed a few essentials in an overnight bag and were now speeding along Interstate 81. Dwight tried to keep it five miles over the speed limit, but it felt like he was going fast. A sixties station played on the GTO's radio, and Christine's head rested against the seat cushion.

Orange streaks in the sky, like strokes from a giant brush, beckoned them to the mountains. The last few days had been overwhelming. Dwight was just beginning to feel his system return to earth. Maybe this was what it was like to venture into space, orbit the globe. Christine snapped up her head. "I forgot. Did you ever ask Bernie about that letter?"

The happiness he felt turned to sludge, the oozing kind he sank in sometimes when stream fishing. Why did she bring that up now? Couldn't she float with him on air for a little while? "Christy, I haven't even talked with Bernie since your party."

"It was not my party."

"You know what I mean."

She sat up now, tilted her seat forward. "You are still upset because I never told you I had a hamburger once with Bernie in college."

"No, I'm not. I simply haven't talked with him. Consider my schedule. I never even got to my office today. Next week, I'll call him. But, not this weekend." He reached over and patted her hand. "I want only to sit on the dock and be with you."

Christine tilted her head and looked at him doubtfully. "With or without a fishing rod in your hands?"

Rats. She'd snagged him, and reeled him in. Now his planned fishing weekend was a bust. "When I said *with* you, I meant it. We'll do whatever you want. Go for a boat ride, shop for the wedding. Pick out baby clothes for the twins. We'll have a real getaway."

Dwight did not mention his alternate plan. He'd fish when his wife was sleeping. She always slept late on Saturdays.

Christine squeezed his hand. "Sounds great. I'll get up early with you, make coffee, and we'll watch the sun rise over the lake. Just the two of us."

THIRTY

S aturday noon, Nick met Griff at the flight arrival area at Tampa International Airport. It was good to see each other after so many years, and on the way to Crystal River they caught up on their lives and events leading up to their drug case. From the window of the government vehicle Nick called his G-car, a Cadillac Escalade, Griff saw things he never saw in Virginia. Pencil thin palm trees, a black buzzard on a light pole, and flock of white egrets flying overhead.

He felt out of his element. "I know nothing about shrimp boats."

Hands steady on the wheel, Nick glanced at Griff. "You don't need to."

 Griff shrugged, gave Nick his impressions of Skeeter, but kept mum that he was the brother to the new nominee for the Supreme Court. Minutes later, they reached Denny's restaurant, their trysting place, some miles from where Skeeter dove out the window to avoid being arrested. Nick parked next to a pickup truck with huge tires. Griff shook his head. That behemoth belonged in some arena packed with fans screaming as it went airborne over another monster truck.

Griff spotted Skeeter sitting at the counter. He tapped his shoulder and whispered, "Come with us." Skeeter picked up his coffee and followed the duo to a booth in the rear. Nick shook Skeeter's hand, then asked, "Hurt yourself jumping through the window?"

Griff suppressed a grin. Nick was letting Skeeter know that he knew what Skeeter was up to. The ex-con may have gotten away with it for a few weeks, but now he had to face his crime. Their backs to the front door, Griff slid into the booth, Skeeter next to him. Nick sat across from them, with a clear view of the front door.

A skinny waitress, blond hair pulled back in a net, gave them menus. Griff scanned it for the biggest burger he could find, a double-decker with fries. He glanced at Skeeter, whose eyes flitted to Nick, back over his shoulder toward the door, then to his hands that were clasped on the table. Nick's eyes simply bored into Skeeter's.

At times, even Griff found the DEA agent's direct gaze intimidating. Skeeter must feel like the accused in the presence of his interrogator. Still, it was imperative that Griff get them working together. Baseball was an icebreaker. "Skeeter, how about the Devil Rays? Think they'll make the playoffs?"

The waitress returned with coffee and took their orders. Skeeter unrolled his fork and knife from the napkin. He set down the fork, but held onto the knife. Griff sensed he was in a panic. With the toe of his shoe, Griff nudged Nick under the table. "You used to be a baseball fan."

Skeeter turned his head sideways. "Agent Topping, you known him long?"

Griff cradled the cup. "Since agent school. He's one of the best I've ever known."

That seemed to settle the man a bit, because he put down his knife. Conversation got down to business. Skeeter whispered how two guys showed up at his home in Apalach. One man he'd known in prison brought along Rusty. Nick made notes in a notebook. Griff kept it all in his mind. Skeeter said Rusty did all the talking about smuggling cocaine.

Skeeter glanced sideways. "That's when I got scared and thought you was settin' me up with an undercover agent. Rusty kept askin' to use my shrimp boat."

Nick quit writing. "Of course, you assured the guy you had no interest in doing anything to violate the conditions of your release."

Skeeter nodded his head up and down. "You got that right. No way, I'm goin' back to the big house. I told 'em the Dora Ruth was leased to a friend. I wasn't gonna use her for smugglin' and have her seized by the feds." He shrugged, looked apologetic.

The waitress returned juggling four plates of burgers and fries. Skeeter dove into his extra plate of fries, and Griff guessed he was done talking for now. Nick continued probing Skeeter to fill in the blanks. "When do these guys want to use your boat?"

Skeeter cast his eyes over his shoulder, then to the front. "Soon."

Nick started writing again. "For how long?"

Skeeter chewed and talked. "One night."

"One night!" Nick seemed surprised. His dark eyes held Griff's, his voice low. "Sounds like they want to use his boat to transfer a load in the Gulf, then bring it into port." He drummed the stubby pencil on his notebook. "Or, it could be an airdrop."

Skeeter's head bobbed up and down, while Griff mulled over the smugglers' intent. Nick ate some fries, then explained, "If an unfamiliar boat comes into port, it receives enhanced scrutiny. Keen locals might notify the police. But the shrimp boats are in and out of the ports and rivers daily. No one pays much attention to them." Skeeter kept eating when Nick asked him, "What kind of money did they offer for Dora Ruth?"

Skeeter opened his mouth to say something, but the waitress came with their bill. "I see you're busy. Let me know if you need anything." Griff reached across the table and grabbed it.

Skeeter finished his fries. "They want me to drive the boat, 'cause I know the Gulf. We didn't discuss what was in it fer me. I thought they were feds. If you're expectin' me to help these guys, I want to know what I'll git from the deal."

Nick leaned toward Skeeter. They were eyeball to eyeball. "We're not talking about what you're going to get, other than staying out of prison. Understood?"

Like a disappointed kid, Skeeter's head drooped. "I don't want to get stuck with a bunch of fuel bills and other costs, and then be runnin' for the rest of my life, lookin' over my shoulder."

Griff had stayed quiet to let Nick settle the score, but it was time to regain control of his informant. He pushed away his empty plate. "Skeeter, we expect you to do everything you can to introduce us into this group. We'll keep your involvement to a minimum, because we don't want you in the picture any longer than necessary. In the end, Nick will advise and I decide when you have done enough to stay out of prison. Is that clear?"

Skeeter stared into the cup he held in his hands.

Griff nudged his seat mate out. "We're going to find a quiet spot, where you can call your pal Rusty on your new cell phone. You agreed we could record the conversation, right?"

Skeeter blinked his eyes. "Yeah."

Griff paid the bill, leaving the waitress a generous tip for giving them privacy.

At a shopping mall parking lot, Nick parked the Escalade a distance from other cars. It was so hot outside he kept the motor running, the air blasting. Besides, with the tinted windows up, no one could see in. Griff moved to the backseat with Skeeter, who grumbled about the mess he was in.

Griff fired a warning. "Be ready to leave a message. Rusty might not answer a call from an unknown number."

With the cell phone connected to Griff's recorder, Skeeter keyed in the numbers. As Griff predicted, Rusty didn't answer. "Hey, this is Skeeter. You came to see me in Apalach. Call back."

He left his new phone number, and Griff turned off the recorder. They would wait. Griff hoped Skeeter was not deceiving them about Rusty, making up a story about helping DEA. If Skeeter was lying, the letter that Skeeter wrote to Judge Pendergast could not be ignored. Skeeter would have to be brought to justice.

It wasn't long before Griff learned Skeeter wasn't lying. Rusty called back. Nick turned around in the front seat to listen, and with the monitor in his ear, Griff could hear both sides.

"Rusty, good to hear from you man."

"Skeeter, you on a cell phone?"

"Yeah."

"Careful what you say."

Skeeter snorted. "I'm not stupid. You want to charter my boat. I'm behind in my payments, so I'm lookin' for work. When do you want her?"

Rusty's reply was unintelligible.

Griff flashed Skeeter a thumbs-down. Skeeter nodded. "What did you say, man?"

Rusty cleared his throat. "I said, do you know a port or river we can use to unload the boat and a building to store my shrimp?"

Griff scribbled on Nick's note pad: *You'll check around.* Skeeter delivered the line as prompted.

Rusty's voice kept breaking up, but Griff made out, "Skeeter, you'll make enough on this catch to pay off your boat loan. Have another guy you trust on board."

Griff wrote: *Ask why.* Skeeter did.

Rusty was full of himself—and answers. "You'll be out one night. It'll be raining shrimp. The shrimp buyer will have his man on board to protect his interest, but don't expect him to do any heavy lifting."

"Okay. I'll get a man and pay him. I can tell that's what you're gettin' at."

Rusty's laugh echoed in Griff's ear. "I knew you was smart."

"Yeah? I want an advance. Gotta make a payment, buy fuel. You can't use my boat for less than two hundred thousand dollars."

Rusty was all ease. "We'll talk money and future work when I come down in a few days."

Griff wrote hurriedly: *Demand the day and time.* Skeeter and Rusty agreed it would be in four days. When Skeeter hung up, Griff turned off the recorder. He would wait to debrief with Nick until Skeeter was out of the SUV.

Nick was on top of it already. "It's going to be an airdrop. Skeeter, Griff and I will be in Apalach for the meeting."

Skeeter looked like he wanted to escape. "What about findin' a building and stuff?"

Nick started to roll out of the parking spot. "Griff and I will make those arrangements."

"Like what? I want to know."

Griff disconnected the cell phone from the recorder. "You'll know what we tell you."

Nick jammed the brakes, turned and pointed at Skeeter's face. "That's right. You want to stay out of prison, you do what we tell you. When Rusty asked you to have a man aboard to help, you will. He'll be your new crew member, an undercover DEA agent."

Skeeter ran his fingers nervously through his hair, and he yelped, "I can't take along a fed! These guys will spot DEA right off. I don't want to git killed."

Griff recognized his informant's anxiety. He put a hand on Skeeter's arm.

Nick softened his tone. "Skeeter, when you were dealing and met me several years ago, did you recognize me as DEA?"

Skeeter hung his head. "Nope."

Nick laughed heartily. "Neither will these guys. Our undercover agent has more years in drug dealing than you or Rusty."

Skeeter relaxed and Griff removed his hand. "If you get another call from Rusty, tell him someone is there and you have to call him back. Then, call me on my cell." He showed Skeeter a piece of paper with the number on it. "Memorize it."

"Okay. Now what?"

Griff crinkled the paper, put it in his pocket. "If he calls, I'll hook up the recording device on my phone, and call you back. You'll establish a three-way call to Rusty, and I'll record it. Got it?"

"I guess so." Skeeter slumped against the back window.

Griff gripped his shoulder. "You can do this, Skeeter, and turn your life around."

He returned to the front seat and, for two hours, they drove around bayous and ports. Wherever Dora Ruth docked after the airdrop had to be near the Gulf and used by shrimpers. Finally, they found a perfect place. Yankeetown was a remote outpost on the Withlacoochee River, and an abandoned shrimp dock was for sale. On Nick's pad, Griff wrote the number. He saw another benefit to this river, but he decided to wait to tell Nick until after Skeeter left the car.

Once Skeeter reluctantly agreed to bring the Dora Ruth through the Gulf to Yankeetown, Nick drove him back to his truck. Without a goodbye, he got out and slammed the door. Seconds later, he roared away in the high truck with giant wheels.

Griff chuckled. "What a character. I hope he doesn't fold on us."

"He won't. He's a tough old bird."

Nick drove Griff back to his hotel at the Tampa airport for his morning flight back to Virginia. As they got closer to Tampa, Nick wove in and out of snarled traffic. Griff liked being in Florida, but the heat and drivers were worse than back home.

Along the way, Griff suggested that Rusty was just one member of a larger conspiracy to ship drugs through the defenses of the U.S. government. "I presume when he said raining shrimp, he meant drugs. Are you going to be the undercover agent on board?"

"I'd love to be, but no. I'll supervise capturing the smugglers without losing the cocaine. Once the cocaine is in the government's possession aboard the Dora Ruth, my most important mission is to ensure that it doesn't return to the supply chain."

Griff played with the edge of his moustache. "It's probably better to use someone without your past relationship with Skeeter."

"Thanks. Means I'm doing my job. Tony Snyder's an agent with over fifteen years of undercover experience. All drugs. I don't want any risk that the cocaine will slip away. There are some agents who are remembered because they lost a load and it got back on the street."

They drove awhile in silence. Griff respected his friend and what he did as a DEA agent. The dangers were real. Drug dealers protected their loads with guns and violence. If things went as planned, Nick might get a promotion.

Now looking out the window, Griff saw no palm trees. Although darkness would not descend for hours, he wasn't looking at the scenery. He was focused on Skeeter's letter demanding money from Judge Pendergast for a kidney. Maybe the ex-con couldn't be rehabilitated, but if Skeeter could help them seize a large quantity of drugs and dismantle part of the drug cartel—even just to keep himself from going back to prison—Griff would have something more—a sense of confirming justice.

THIRTY ONE

Early Wednesday, severe weather returned to Northern Virginia and at sunrise a twister tore the roof off a shopping mall and barely missed Mount Vernon. In the West Wing, Barbara Jo was safe from the aftermath, but not from the tempest boiling within her. She slammed down the telephone in disgust, not even saying goodbye to Arnie. Who did he think he was, ordering her to come through or she could forget the gala honoring the Prince of Sweden? He even threatened that she could forget their future.

Arnie was always in such a panic. He needed to be more calculating. She vowed to help him, and she would. She intended to attend the biggest event of the summer. Everyone who was anyone would be there, even POTUS and the First Lady. To be left behind would wreck all of her plans. Her formal gown had been created for her at designer prices. The delicious white dress, with beaded hem and periwinkle blue sash, was hanging in her closet at home. An actress who played Queen Victoria wore one just like it in a movie. Once Arnie saw her in it, he would propose, of that she was sure.

Besides buying the dress, she scheduled an appointment with Hector to do her hair. He took months to get into. She wanted to make as many high-powered connections, for Arnie's sake, as the evening allowed. He had a lot more going for him than slaving for Senator Zorn. Barbara Jo had her sights set on Arnie running for Congress from Maryland.

As she fumed about her reluctant boyfriend, Jasper Collins buzzed her on the telephone. She lifted the receiver, then answered his question. "Yes. Senator Briggs will meet with the President today at two o'clock. Is there a problem?"

She thought, but was not sure, that Briggs was meeting about the nomination of Judge Pendergast. Why hadn't she told Arnie? The voice in her head taunted her, *because he's treating you like a fool.* Barbara Jo closed her eyes. With her therapist's help, she had trained that voice to leave her alone. Now, it was back. Jasper was talking over the intercom, but it was as if he was in her office. "They're going to discuss the head-count in the Senate for Judge Pendergast."

Barbara Jo was interested. "Will the Senate Judiciary vote him out of the committee?"

Jasper was curt. "We never know until after the hearing. Several new groups are crawling out from under rocks. Come to my office."

Barbara Jo bounced from her chair, picked up a blue and gold port-folio with the White House seal, and walked into Jasper's office. In her silk blouse and black linen suit, she felt particularly sharp. One had to act and look the part in the West Wing.

Jasper was talking into the telephone. He put the person on hold to speak to her. "It's the senior Senator from Arizona. The Big Sky tribe is supporting the White Pine tribe from Michigan. They're holding a rally demanding the President withdraw Pendergast's nomination. It won't be long before it erupts on the news."

Jasper held out a file. "There's an updated case list from the judge. Make sure it gets into the proper section. I want the President to have it for his meeting with Briggs. As soon as you're done, bring it back." He held up a hand in caution. "Don't let it out of your sight."

Her boss returned to his call, and Barbara Jo picked up the file. Back in her office, in less than seven minutes, she completed her assignment. It took another two minutes to do something extra, something Jasper would never know. He was still on the telephone when she returned the confidential White House file on Judge Pendergast. Jasper nodded to her and Barbara Jo went to call Arnie. It looked like she'd be going to the Swedish gala after all.

Griff flew into Tallahassee aboard a commercial flight. The hurricane season was not a time to fly the Cessna to the Gulf. Nick Tascoda and fellow DEA agent Tony Snyder met him in the pickup area. Griff fig-ured Skeeter's eyes would bulge when he got a glimpse of Tony, and his thick neck. His brawny build fit his role as a deck hand on a shrimp boat, and Griff figured he must spend hours at the gym. Not Griff's thing. Give him a path to run any day. On the way to Apalachicola, Tony and Nick made Griff feel that he was an equal part of their case.

Griff leaned in, so they could hear him. "Tony, do you know much about Skeeter?"

Tony turned over his shoulder. "I've read the files on him. What's your impression?"

What did Griff think of Skeeter? "A bit slippery, always on the look-out for a scam."

All three agents laughed. Griff raised a new concern. "He called last night. A car was parked down his street, and Skeeter wanted to know if we were having him watched. He sounded nervous."

Nick looked in the rearview mirror. "That ought to keep him on the narrow road, for a few days anyway."

Tony craned his head toward Griff. "Don't worry. I'll keep a tight reign on Skeeter."

They traveled along Route 319, past dense pine forests, each man lost in his own thoughts. Nick played the radio, and Griff realized that Nick thought there were two kinds of music, country and western. As they neared the Gulf of Mexico, the pure white sand made Griff think about moving from Virginia.

Then, he saw a rare sight, rare to him anyway. Alone at the top of a dead palm tree was a bald eagle, scanning the water for fish. He was about to point, when Nick interrupted to say that he contacted the Panama City DEA office. "Told the agent-in-charge about our investigation, and that cocaine smugglers are meeting in Apalach. They're sending two agents to help."

Extra sets of eyes would be crucial in watching Skeeter. All things seemed in order, and Griff enjoyed the fresh new landscape unfolding before him. The sun's golden rays spread across Apalachicola Bay. No wonder Dawn loved it here. He doubted they'd get a chance to fly together for a while.

With all he had to do to find Eleanor Bailey and justice for Skeeter, he'd best remove Dawn Ahern from his mind altogether. Yesterday, she called Griff to find out about "our guy." Just when it sounded like she wanted to talk about other things, Skeeter called on the other line.

Now, Griff used his cell phone to call him. "Hey, Skeeter. This is your substitute PO. Are you there alone?"

"Yeah."

"Battery Park is half a mile from your house. Do you know it?"

Skeeter did. Although his voice was shaky, he agreed to meet them in twenty minutes.

Griff folded his phone. "He's scared, but will see us there."

Three hours later, Skeeter fidgeted in the Dora Ruth's pilot house. He and Tony were waiting on Rusty, who was late. The windows were open, but no breeze relieved the heat. He must be out of his mind to entertain a DEA agent on his boat. If things turned sour, and they always did for him, he'd just forget about prison and kiss his life goodbye. It hadn't been much of a life anyway.

The agent stood a head taller. Skeeter only knew him as Tony—no last name. He was a giant, more like a bear than a man. Skeeter made sure he stayed an arm's reach away from Tony's broad shoulders. Just looking at Tony's biceps, he felt his body getting weak. Skeeter wiped clammy hands on his pant legs. "Ya' know, I'd never suspect you was a DEA agent."

Tony touched the visor of his Harley Davidson ball cap. "Nice of Nick and Griff to introduce us."

"What I'd like to know, is how long have I known you?"

Tony twirled the ends of his handlebar mustache between his thumb and forefingers. He grunted. "We don't want much known about ourselves. Tell Rusty I worked shrimp boats before I became your man for pot."

The fear Skeeter felt roiled in his stomach like a meal of bad shrimp. "If Rusty asks, I told him I'm payin' you for this gig, out of my part. He talks like his people are picky."

Skeeter looked across the street. There were Griff and Nick, at a picnic table in front of the Outrigger, drinking something cold. Why'd they involve him in this thing? Course he knew. All because of a stupid letter he wrote to a federal judge.

Tony seemed to follow his eyes. "Don't worry, Skeeter. I've done hundreds of drug deals, so has Agent Tascoda. Rusty trusts you, so he'll trust you to involve me. Besides, I'm armed and not going to let anything happen to either one of us."

"What if he doesn't show? I taped a note to my door, like Griff said, so's he could find me here."

Tony shrugged, walked around the Dora Ruth liked he owned her. Within a minute, a convertible Ford Mustang, its top up, parked its nose toward the Dora Ruth. The driver slid out, the passenger stayed inside. A pint-sized man with red hair strode onto the boat. Even though his shades were on, Skeeter recognized Rusty. In slacks and a shirt with palm trees all over it, he looked like he sold cars.

With both Rusty and Tony on his boat, Skeeter couldn't think of a worse moment since he left prison. All he dared hope was that the next thirty minutes flew by like the wind. He breathed in deep. "Rusty, this here's Tony."

Tony stuck out his huge hand. "Hi. I'm Skeeter's partner."

Rusty looked Tony up, then down. "You know Skeeter's paying you out of his share."

Tony's head snapped toward Skeeter, but he said nothing. Skeeter tried to stay cool. He'd told Tony about the payment. Why didn't he answer Rusty?

Instead, Rusty took charge. "Skeeter, you won't get a dime until the charter thing is over."

Skeeter hated this deal. He edged away from Rusty, to the step that would take him off the boat. "You're refusin' to advance me money? I told you from the git-go, I didn't have none."

Rusty just looked at Skeeter and said nothing, then he turned to Tony. "You're his partner. We have a big investment in this deal and Skeeter wants us to put up all the cash."

Skeeter was surprised at how Rusty thought Tony knew everything. Worse, Tony was silent like a big rock. As soon as he opened his mouth, Skeeter wished he hadn't.

Tony pointed to Rusty's car, flexing his biceps in Rusty's face. "My money says Rusty's Mustang is rented. If it isn't, it should be. The police can only seize what Rusty owns." Tony put a muscular arm around Skeeter. "You say we're partners. Yeah. Me and him go way back."

A pain stabbed his shoulder. Was it Tony's way of telling him to keep his mouth shut? Well, he would. No problem there.

Thankfully, Tony released him. "He's putting himself at risk. He can't rent a shrimp boat. He owns this one," Tony stamped a booted foot on the wooden deck, "and it can be seized from him. I told him he's crazy to work this gig with you."

Rusty stared Tony down. Cold fear froze Skeeter's blood. He didn't dare move, didn't dare flinch. Tony got right into Rusty's face. "You should front him some money."

Just when Skeeter thought he was finally done, Tony challenged Rusty more, "If I'm gonna help Skeeter, I wanna know what the product is and how much it weighs. I need to know I'm getting paid what I deserve."

Rusty glared at Tony, and Skeeter's stomach rocked. He should have eaten breakfast instead of drinking all that coffee. Tony held his ground, while Skeeter almost lost his. He was too old to be messing with drugs. He saw that now.

Rusty looked over his shoulder at the guy in the Mustang, then turned back. "We need you to go to a certain location in the Gulf. You'll get coordinates when it's time. Our plane will drop coolers filled with coke. Four hundred kilos. You pick them up, bring them to port. Remember, you need a storage building where we can transfer."

Skeeter felt his head nodding, but Tony wasn't in agreement. He spit as he talked, "Four hundred kilos of coke are the same as eight hundred eighty pounds. That's worth about six million dollars! And you want to pay Skeeter a lousy two hundred thousand? If we're handling that much coke, I expect a hundred thousand for me—and I don't own the boat."

Both Skeeter and Rusty began to protest at the same time, but Tony wasn't through yet. "I've worked on deals where the going rate for off-loaders is ten percent. You're cheating Skeeter, and I'm not working for peanuts."

Rusty had enough. "You've probably killed this deal." He held up a finger, like they were to wait a minute, and stalked off the Dora Ruth. Maybe, he was going to get a gun. Skeeter jabbed a finger at Tony. "You can't push them guys around like that. My one chance to git out of a jam, and you mess it up."

Tony grabbed his finger. "If we did it too cheap, they'd think we were beginners, or police."

Rusty stood by the passenger's window, talking and gesturing to the man inside. Skeeter had no idea who he was. He had his dark glasses on, too. Tony walked to the edge of the Dora Ruth. "Time will tell, Skeeter. We'll wait."

His own arms shaking, Skeeter tapped Tony's biceps. "Hey, Rusty's carryin' a black bag."

It must be a gun. He soon found out it wasn't a gun, but a vinyl bank deposit bag, which Rusty held out to Skeeter. "My partner doesn't want to meet you, but he agreed to give you twenty thousand. You'll be paid half a million, and that's our last offer." Rusty avoided looking at Tony. "If your partner isn't satisfied, get yourself a new one. For someone having trouble making his boat payments, you're not in a position to demand ten percent. Agreed?"

Skeeter looked past Rusty to Tony, who nodded his head. Skeeter crushed the bag to him with his left hand, stuck out his right and shook Rusty's hand. "Deal. So you know, I wanna port the Dora Ruth at Yankeetown."

"Okay. The drop will be at night. You'll retrieve it, get to port, and hand it off to the buyer before daylight. Do a dry run. Let people see your boat. I'll get back with the date."

Rusty turned and left. Before he was behind the wheel of his car, Tony walked into the pilot house, and Skeeter followed. He wanted to know what the DEA agent was gonna do. Tony talked into a small device like a walkie-talkie. "Things are set. Never met the passenger, who's the main guy. Don't know where they're going from here."

Skeeter heard Nick's reply. "Copy that. PC units, stay with the Mustang to its destination. We need to ID these people. My guess is that's a rental car."

Some other agent Skeeter hadn't met, responded, "10-4, We'll stay with them, get back to you with details."

Tony poked Skeeter's money bag. "We're meeting Nick and Griff at Battery Park. They'll decide how much you get to keep for fuel and stuff. You drive."

Skeeter locked the pilot house door and led Tony to his truck. Even with twenty thousand in his hands, his future belonged to this giant, and Skeeter was getting a glimmer of respect for him. For a federal agent, Tony sure knew how to set up a drug deal.

THIRTY TWO

Since their return from the lake house, such a media frenzy whirled around Christine and Dwight that they finally unplugged their phone. Dwight continued his rounds on the Hill, meeting with Senators who had been handpicked by the majority and minority leaders. Just before dinner last night, Chad arrived to take Mandy to dinner. When they argued over the choice of a restaurant—he wanted Italian, she seafood—Chad squealed off in his little red car and Mandy ran upstairs crying.

Dwight urged Christine to let their daughter work things out on her own. She ignored his advice, and went upstairs, where she and Mandy talked for more than an hour. Dwight went out to the garage and tinkered on his GTO. Christine found him there at ten o'clock and explained her idea for screening phone calls; she was going to change their phone number. No word about Chad, which was fine with Dwight. The last thing he wanted was that hothead for a son-in-law.

By eleven o'clock on Thursday morning, Dwight conferred with three Senators in the majority party. Their questions were probing, but courteous. A date for his confirmation hearing would be announced tomorrow, after Dwight called upon the ranking member of the Judiciary Committee and three Senators in the minority party. He expected those meetings to be more hostile.

Back in his office, Bernie called, wanting to have lunch. Dwight put him off, but gave him their new home phone number. He also called Griff Topping with his new number, hoping to find out more about the search for his brother, but he got Griff's voice mail. Dwight arranged with Wendell Cochran to work at the church again on Friday. He and Christine both felt like it was important work, and Christine seemed at last to be healing from the scars of her long-ago accident.

Gladys had put a bowl of flowers on his desk. When he asked her in to thank her, her eyes were watery. She had a young granddaughter;

maybe something happened to her. Dwight waved her to sit. "Is there anything I can do?"

His secretary lifted her head. "Judge, Constance Ingles was here, and said when you take your seat on the high court, you'll leave your staff behind." Gladys sniffled, but looked right at him.

Constance Ingles sure thought she knew a lot about everything. "Don't be silly. Of course you'll go with me as my secretary, if you want to."

The weight of the world seemed to slide right off her shoulders. Dwight felt guilty. "I should have mentioned it before now, but with everything going on, I forgot. Let's not get too far ahead of ourselves. I still have to be confirmed."

Gladys almost waltzed out of his office. "You'll be confirmed. You're too good not to be."

Dwight wished he was as confident.

Griff's computer was on, but the screen saver had taken over. It had been awhile since he touched a key. His cell phone rang, which gave him a good excuse to forget the report he was supposed to have finished yesterday.

Eva Montanna sounded chirpy. "I have good news. Want to hear it?"

He wanted to shuffle the report to his drawer, but that would make the federal prosecutor unhappy. "It's got to be more interesting than what I'm working on."

Eva gave a little chuckle. "Okay, I'll bite. What's so bad?"

Griff leaned back in his chair. "Sal and I are about to round up parents who fled without paying their court-ordered child support. For the FBI to be involved, they have to owe huge sums."

"That's important work, Griff. Local law enforcement has no way to cross state lines to get the parents who aren't paying."

Since he and Sal needed to get going, he started to shut down his computer. "I know, but I've got a drug case heating up and I'd rather see it finished first."

Eva was not sympathetic. "You know my rule, get done today what you want to do tomorrow."

Griff locked the report in his top drawer. "You said you called with good news."

"I hope you think so. What do you think of my having a reunion for everyone we used to work with—Earl, Robbie, even Trenton? Scott's promised to fire up the grill. Will you come?"

Lately, Griff really missed working on the task force with Eva and the others. "When is it? This drug case is about to erupt."

Eva was silent, as if thinking. "If I make it in two weeks, would that work?"

"I hope. Send me an e-mail."

Eva signed off. Griff checked his Glock and got out an extra ammo clip. You never knew if some parent would flake out and pull a gun to keep from going to jail. His desk phone rang.

Nick Tascoda's voice boomed in his ear, "Our agents served a subpoena on the corporate office of the car rental agency. That Mustang was rented by Buzz Watkins, who was previously arrested by DEA."

Griff put the ammo clip holder on his belt. "It's a peculiar name. Do you know him?"

Turned out Buzz was arrested years ago with marijuana on an airport runway in southern Georgia. He flew aboard a twin engine Cessna and was unloading the stuff when a sheriff's deputy drove into the airport and made for the plane. The pilot took off, leaving Buzz to take the blame.

Griff wanted to know more about Buzz, but time was short. Nick agreed to do more digging and call Griff tomorrow. Maybe by then, Rusty would have called Skeeter with the date for the airdrop.

Over at Sal's cubicle, Griff found him staring into space. Griff knocked on the wall. "Ready?"

"You mean our assignment? Yeah, I can't wait to grab those loafers off the street."

But, Sal lingered in his chair. Griff was hungry and wanted some lunch before their team met at one. "Sal, what gives?"

He swiped his eyes. "My son just got accepted to Michigan State University."

Griff thought he understood. "You must be proud. That's where you graduated from."

Sal stood. "Proud is only half of it. The kid is going to be twice the man I am. He's not only brilliant, he cares about healing people. Sal Junior wants to be a doctor."

With no child of his own, Griff was happy for Sal, but he realized he did not know the depths of the man's happiness. He clapped a hand on his back. "Let's go get those dads who don't hold a candle to you."

Five hours later, after Griff and Sal helped a crew of FBI agents net delinquent parents, he was back in his office. Along with eleven delinquent dads, Griff arrested a woman who failed to pay the custodial father more than a hundred thousand dollars in child support. While he'd not want to work these cases every day, he felt a measure of success. It was fitting that Sal left soon after to celebrate his son's good news.

On his voice mail, he found that Nick had called an hour before. Although it was already six o'clock, Nick answered, "Nick's desk."

Griff growled, "What d'ya mean, Nick's desk? Why not just say, this is Nick?"

"I never know if I want to talk to who's calling, so I pretend I'm just someone walking by his desk."

Griff laughed at Nick, the prankster. "Okay weirdo, want to talk to me?"

"We sent out leads to learn all we could about our man, Buzz. Answers are flooding in."

From Nick's tone, it must be good news. Then, he remembered Eva might send an e-mail, so he fired up his computer. Griff missed a sentence or two of what Nick said, but gathered that after Buzz got out of prison, he moved to Augusta, Georgia. Griff had two e-mails. "Augusta's near South Carolina."

"Forget that. We subpoenaed his credit card records. Recently, Buzz bought fuel at Ft. Lauderdale Executive Airport for a twin engine Cessna 404."

Nick began talking faster than Sal. "The tail number was changed. It came back registered to a different plane, a Cessna 182. Smugglers switch the numbers to keep law enforcement from finding the true tail number. We got lucky, because the fuel attendant saw shadows of the original number, wrote them on the fuel ticket. Our guys worked on both numbers and found the Cessna 404 was leased by Watkins. He paid cash for the plane rental, which I say suggests criminal intent."

Griff connected the dots. "This guy has done these trips before."

"Right. I think we may have worked our way inside a monster case, and I'm glad to be working it with you. I contacted the owners of the dock on the Withlacoochee River."

Griff recalled the spot, near the Gulf at Yankeetown. Nick found out the owners used to be shrimpers, with no known criminal background. He rented it for a couple months.

"I told them I wanted to see if I could make a go of a shrimping business."

Griff printed the e-mail from Eva so that he'd remember the party, folded it and put it in his pocket. When they scouted out Yankeetown, he had seen a U.S. Coast Guard station near the entrance to the river. "Nick, I meant to mention this when you drove me back to the airport. See if the Coast Guard consents to let us use the station as an observation post. The locals are used to it, so our presence won't seem like too much heat."

"Griff, I hadn't thought of that."

Glad he had workable ideas, Griff was about to ask Nick about other developments when Nick threw in a ringer. "It's time to have Skeeter bring the Dora Ruth to Yankeetown."

Griff did not disagree, so he rang Skeeter and the men had a three-way conversation. It was now up to Skeeter to call Rusty and firm up the date.

Hours later, Skeeter called Griff, and he sounded shaky. "It's a good thing you had me call the guy. He wants me there for the drop in three days."

Griff did his best to calm Skeeter. "I'll meet you in Yankeetown. Tony will be with you on the Dora Ruth the whole time."

"If that's supposed to make me feel better …"

His voice trailed away and Griff promised to call him again in the morning. He felt like a regular babysitter. In another hour, he firmed up his plane reservation, then called Dawn. She had given him her home number so that she could be kept in the loop.

For a few minutes, they made small talk. Griff asked if her son would keep his job at the hardware store when he started school.

"Brian floored me today. He wants to go to college out your way."

That was surprising. Virginia was a long way from Florida. "What's the connection?"

"Virginia Military Institute."

She sounded tired, like she'd had a long day tracking criminals, just like Griff. "So what does his mom think about that?"

"Glad he has a goal. Thankful it's a few years away. His father flew Air Force fighters, so I guess it's natural he wants to follow in his footsteps."

Like father, like son. Just like Sal. Griff would probably never experience it. "I'd love to talk, but I fly out early in the morning. I'm heading south."

She was quick to ask, "Are you coming to the panhandle?"

Was she asking because of Skeeter? "No. I'm checking the phone calls to and from the cell phone I gave Skeeter to use, and I see no evidence he's associating with felons."

Dawn was silent, like deciding what else to ask. He didn't expect what came next. "Agent Topping, I am concerned that by allowing Skeeter to help you, you give him the idea he can commit a crime and get away with it."

Back to calling him Agent Topping. Well, they were professionals with a business relationship. It was time to get some sleep. Once the deal went down in Florida, he might not get any for days. "Skeeter isn't getting away with trying to cajole money from the judge, if that's what you mean. As I said before, he's getting us inside a drug smuggling group, but for the rest of his life he'll face the prospect of these violators looking for him, with vengeance in mind—"

She interrupted, "I know—"

Griff interrupted right back. "Now, I really must go." He was about to hang up, when she asked, "Will you call me from Florida?"

"Sure." He replaced the receiver on the phone. Why so irritated with her? Dawn was doing her job. Maybe his touchiness sprang from personal feelings, which by now he could see she did not share.

THIRTY THREE

With a white towel wrapped around his waist, Dwight peeled potatoes in the basement of the Episcopal Church. He and Christine were helping prepare dinner for low income folks. Some might also get free legal help in accessing veterans' benefits, seeking a personal protection order against a violent roommate, or avoiding eviction, but Dwight steered clear of the clients.

Christine spread foil over three casserole pans and put them in the ovens. She had already carved a niche for herself with Wendell's wife, Hazel Cochran, by introducing her to strawberry lemonade and a chicken-cashew dish, which she and Dwight donated for today's meal. She picked up a potato peeler, and sliced off peel twice as fast as Dwight.

He bumped her hip with his. "Hey, you're cutting into my job."

Christine's lips parted. "I'm not threatened by you." She plunked a potato in a pan of cold water. "It's a joy to see you out from under 'The Judge,' and being so domesticated."

"Ouch, that hurts. I hope you're not going to get high and mighty once I'm on the Supreme Court and make me get rid of my baby."

She pointed to a green spot on a potato. "Dig that out with the top of the peeler. They're toxic. Dwight, I love your car. With the pressures on us lately, working in this kitchen is the most fun we've had in days."

Hazel came in, her pretty face tense. She looked at Dwight, then Christine. "There was a news alert on the radio." On the verge of tears, Hazel's lips trembled. "I don't believe it, but a group called Justice for America is saying there's a picture of Christine's father in a Nazi uniform, and that he recently spoke at a Nazi rally in Austria claiming the Holocaust never happened."

Dwight threw down the peeler. "Impossible!"

Hazel reached for Christine's hands. "There's more, I'm afraid. The announcer said it is a crime in Austria to deny the Holocaust and that your father could be arrested."

Christine's face, which moments before had glowed with happiness, lost its color. She held her stomach. "Dwight, I'm going to be sick."

"Hazel, could you take over here? I'm taking Christine home to call her parents."

Christine ran up the steps to the narthex and outside to the car, holding her mouth. Dwight drove home, the towel still around his waist. "Christy, your father and mother aren't Nazis."

His wife tapped his arm. "Please, don't go so fast around the corner. My head is spinning."

Dwight eased off the gas. "We'll urge your parents not to talk to the media. It can make things worse. We'll get Bernie to help us." He glanced at Christine, who looked tormented. He realized there was too much going on, and he'd still not asked Bernie about the letters. And, he needed to hire a lawyer to issue a press release.

His hands gripped the wheel. After he called his in-laws, he should talk to Jasper Collins, too. Things were not getting easier. Christine then asked the very things on Dwight's mind: Who hated them so much to make up vicious lies, and were they connected to the letters she'd received? He wished he knew.

Sunday night, Griff packed his bag, toothbrush, and extra clothes, ready to spend a week or more in the Tampa area, which was a good six to seven hours from Panama City, where Dawn worked. He resisted the urge to call her and just talk. The night passed and Griff slept little. Mostly, he thought of Skeeter and whether the ex-con had a heart of courage or brains of straw.

At five o'clock Monday morning, Sal pulled into the driveway to take him to the airport. Out the front window, Griff saw that, thankfully, he was in his bucar, not that bondo job he drove. He did not want to break down on the way to the airport and miss his flight. Griff locked the front door, not knowing when he would be back home.

By ten, Griff reached Florida and was picked up by an agent on Nick's team. They reached the Tampa DEA office in time for Griff to get a five-minute tour, then Nick ushered them into the conference room. The briefing for Operation Igloo was about to begin. Blinds drawn against the searing Florida heat added an air of even greater secrecy to the business at hand.

Griff did a quick tally of the agents and officers. Twenty-two in all. The only person Griff recognized besides Nick was Tony. Nick welcomed everyone to the planning session and introduced Griff. Nick passed around an attendance sheet, which came to Griff last. He saw that everyone had written their identifying info and code name they would be called on the radio.

Like Nick, most were DEA agents. Some were with the Florida Department of Law Enforcement, others county police officers. But, because everyone wore jeans and short-sleeved shirts, Griff couldn't tell them apart. Since it was a drug smuggling case, and ICE had authority to enforce smuggling laws, Griff made a note to talk with the three ICE agents, see if they knew Eva.

Griff handed the list to Nick, who informed the whole group for the first time of their mission. "Griff's informant is inside a major drug smuggling group. Tomorrow night they're going to use an airplane to drop cocaine into the Gulf."

As murmurs rose throughout the room, so did Griff's excitement level. Nick raised his voice to be heard. "We'll have constant observation of the drop, arrest everyone involved, and seize the cocaine. We hope to get all the money intended to pay for the cocaine."

A few whoops around the room. Griff was pumped, but years of experience told him to be on the lookout for the unexpected. Nick pointed to a large Florida map, hanging on a white board, and his magic marker rested on a spot in the Gulf.

"This is about twenty nautical miles west of Yankeetown. If we trust the bad guys—and none of us do—" Nick stopped long enough for the laughter to die down. "Okay. Tomorrow night at midnight, an aircraft will release four hundred kilos of cocaine to a shrimp boat waiting below. Aboard the Dora Ruth is our informant, one smuggler, and," Nick nodded to Tony, who stood at his left, "Agent Snyder. The informant knows his identity."

Everyone, Griff included, was handed a copy of the list of assignments, so each agent knew what the others were doing. Most were assigned to Crystal River, where the smugglers would meet Skeeter and Tony before departing to the drop zone. As the smugglers moved, Nick would command their surveillance teams over the radio.

Griff couldn't find his name on the sheet. He listened to Nick's instructions for a clue. "Stationed in the second story of the Coast Guard station, two agents overlook the river upstream from where it enters the Gulf. They'll do a couple of things—report on movements of the Dora Ruth and, using a portable radio repeater, will enhance our radio signals."

Griff didn't think he would be in the Coast Guard Station. Right, he found those agents' names on the list. Nick finished his overview. "For the safety of the undercover agent, we've planted a hidden microphone in the warehouse where the smugglers will get their drugs. Agent Topping and I will signal the correct time to make arrests."

Great, he would be paired with Nick for Operation Igloo. An ICE agent asked, "What kind of aircraft and where it will come from?"

Nick motioned Griff to the front. "Our pilot and airplane expert will take that one."

Griff raised his fact sheet. "DEA found that the brains behind this deal, Buzz Watkins, used a twin engine Cessna 404 in the past. We think he'll use that plane. His photo is in your packet. ICE aircraft will try to place them inbound. They'll probably fly low, to avoid tethered balloon radars anchored along the Florida coast and FAA radars."

Nick warned, "Be alert. We're not sure if the smugglers will move the load of cocaine to the building we rented, or if their customers will be waiting in the area with the cash. Report any contacts. Griff and I will signal you via radio when there's probable cause to make arrests."

Tony raised a hand. "How many arrests can we expect?"

Nick tapped the marker on his palm. "Everyone Rusty and Buzz have contact with are targets. It's easier to grab and release them, than to try to find them days later. Your team leader will tell you where and when to meet tomorrow. You should all get sleep today."

Griff knew why. They were about to pull an all-nighter. The briefing over, he called Skeeter, who was on the Dora Ruth, near Crystal River. That was a relief. He had worried that Skeeter would take his boat in another direction, like Mexico. Griff gave Skeeter the code, "The charter trip is set," so Skeeter would know Griff and Nick were leaving Tampa and due to arrive in his area in a few hours.

Skeeter put the Dora Ruth to port at Crystal River to top off his tanks. From what he could tell, there was no fuel at Yankeetown. If he'd left yesterday, when he knew a squall was coming, he would have been smack in it. The waves were still kind of rough, but nothing he wasn't used to and nothing his boat couldn't handle. Skeeter wasn't happy about coming so far, even if it was Rusty's money he was using for fuel.

On the other hand, to keep out of prison, Skeeter would drive to Alaska and back to please Nick and Griff. His face windburned, Skeeter refueled, but watched every penny. Whatever was left from Rusty's money, he planned to keep.

Skeeter motored the Dora Ruth back to the Gulf and up the Withlacoochee River, to the wooden dock Nick rented in Yankeetown. No one was around. Lots of water and buildings, but no Tony, who was supposed to meet him, and act like he really was his deckhand.

Thoughts of facing Rusty alone made Skeeter want to smoke. He'd quit in prison, but started after escaping from Nick a few weeks back. He lit one now, the kind with low tar. As bad as it was to help the feds, this was his last chance to have a life. He blew out a smoke ring, watched it float off. It tasted like burnt toast. He ground out the cigarette under his sneaker.

Griff seemed decent. The law had been Skeeter's enemy, but now, helping them the way he was, it almost made him feel respectable for the first time in years, since he took the Dora Ruth on her first voyage. He pulled a water bottle from the cooler, guzzled it half gone. When he put down the bottle, he looked up. There was Tony, staring him in the face, wearing his Harley Davidson cap. The scary thing was, he never heard him step aboard.

The two men drove into Yankeetown in Tony's truck. The road wound along the river, and every now and then the trees cleared and Skeeter saw the water. It looked calm. Nice homes were built across the road, even bigger ones along the river. Skeeter snickered at a dumpy mobile home, it was so Florida. At least, people used to build whatever they wanted. Not since all the hurricanes. Now, a home near water had to be on stilts, and big-time developers were tearing down mobiles to put in condos.

Well, it wasn't his problem. His house was going to stay. They hit a more traveled street and soon were in tiny Yankeetown. Tony pulled into the gravel parking lot of the town's only restaurant. It had white shutters against cement walls painted yellow, like it was someone's small cottage, and purple flowers grew in pots on the sidewalk. Skeeter just hoped the food was decent. After the long trip from Apalach, he was hollow.

Inside, two big pool tables separated the bar and eating area. The staff knew everyone, except Skeeter and Tony. That's why Tony wanted to come here. Hang out, get to know the locals. They took a booth, and a chubby waitress with black pigtails plunked menus down. They both wanted iced tea. Skeeter drank his with lots of lemon. He tried to talk to her, like he was from the neighborhood. Found out her name was Nena, she had two boys.

"Me and him," Skeeter nodded toward Tony, "are shrimpers. Know what we want to eat?"

Nena didn't smile, but guessed, "Shrimp."

Skeeter cackled. "Righto. Extra fries, hold the slaw."

Tony asked for a cup of clam chowder and broiled grouper, not shrimp.

Skeeter wrinkled his nose. "Does the platter come with hush puppies?"

She put her hands on her aproned hips. "You want extra?"

Nena was all right. Maybe this would be an okay place to start over. Course, his PO, Ms. Ahern, would have to approve him living here, and she'd never want him out of her sight. He nodded. "We're working out of the river for a while and need to eat up."

In minutes, Nena brought their food. The lightly fried shrimp were delicious. The grouper on Tony's plate was pale. Skeeter decided to look around Yankeetown. Some of the older houses were small, and Nena wore no wedding ring. Maybe, she'd be interested in going out sometime. After the case was done and everything.

He wanted to get to know Tony, but the undercover agent wouldn't tell about his real life. Skeeter shoved a shrimp in his mouth, watched the big man eat.

"Tony, how do you like your Dodge truck? I might want to get rid of my Ford."

Tony ate what was called dirty rice. "She's a beaut, but I'm glad Uncle Sam's paying for the fuel."

Skeeter stumbled on something the big man could talk about. They talked of trucks and fish until Nena brought the bill. No way Skeeter was paying it. "What time's breakfast?"

Nena turned. "Six o'clock. I'll take that up for you, when you're ready."

Skeeter was not ready. Tony was still eating that funny-looking rice. Skeeter drank his tea and, finally, Tony reached for his wallet attached to his belt. When he drew out two twenties, Skeeter smiled. Now if he could just get Tony to buy his breakfast, he'd get lunch and still be one meal ahead.

Tony called Nena over. "Keep the change." Her face lit up and Skeeter realized he blew it. Tony looked like the big tipper. Well, maybe he would pay for breakfast.

"Come on, Skeeter. Let's go for a ride on the Dora Ruth. It won't be dark for hours."

He followed Tony, but didn't really want to get back on the boat after being aboard her all day. Skeeter just wanted Rusty to call, get it over with. Course, if he never called, that would be even better.

THIRTY FOUR

D wight leaned back in his chair, his mind focused on his wife. After hearing the absurd allegation that her father was pro-Nazi, Christine called her parents. They were shocked, then angry, at the news. Right now, she was upstairs crying in her pillow, and he was trying to make it right, to ask the White House to issue a statement in support of him, his family. But, so far his efforts had failed.

Desperate to reach Jasper Collins, Dwight kept getting voice mail. On the next try, a woman answered. When she said her name was Ms. Houston, hope turned to dread. Dwight was tempted to hang up in her ear, but of course he didn't.

True to her difficult self, she refused to put him through to the Chief of Staff. "He is in the Oval Office, with the President."

Dwight mustered a congenial air. "I understand. Please, I need to speak with him right away."

Her voice was as sharp as ever. "He can return your call after he and the President finish meeting with Senator Briggs."

His mind was alert. "Oh?"

Barbara Jo's voice cut like a knife. "They are discussing you. They did on Wednesday, too. Makes one wonder whether your nomination will ever reach the Senate floor."

Dwight was stunned. Surely Jasper would have called him if the President had second thoughts. He must get through, explain that the report was pure slander, but he said none of this to Barbara Jo.

She was not finished twisting the knife. "Maybe you won't be confirmed. I will tell Jasper you called."

A buzz at the end of the line told him that he had to trust that Jasper would call before anything drastic happened. Bernie was next on his call list. His secretary said he was in with a client. Strike two. Dwight then phoned Neal Longstreet, the founding partner of his old firm.

Neal instantly agreed to issue a press statement, but suggested Dwight needed what he referred to as a "media survival plan." Dwight arranged to be at the firm the next morning at seven to form a strategy.

On the way out of his study, he stopped. He should be upstairs with Christine now, but his feet were mired in place. As her friend and husband, Dwight was at a loss for how to comfort her. Still, he must try. After all, she was going through this because of him. Why did his enemies attack his family rather than go after his court rulings, his legal opinions? One reason jumped ahead of all the others. They were nothing but cowards.

In Yankeetown, Skeeter and Tony took the Dora Ruth for a practice run into the Gulf of Mexico. Not too far, just enough to be seen around. When they docked her, Skeeter's cell phone rang. Almost as if whoever it was saw them return. It was Rusty. He wanted them to come to the Guest Inn on Route 19 in Crystal River, close by Skeeter's hotel. Tony called to tell Nick, who said he and Griff were in town and would park across the street, where they'd watch from Nick's SUV.

When Skeeter and Tony got to the motel, Rusty wasn't in his room, where he said he'd be. Skeeter shrugged. "Now what?"

Tony banged on the door again; still no answer. Skeeter just knew there wouldn't be. Back at the truck, Tony grabbed the front of Skeeter's shirt and hissed in his ear. "Hope he didn't get cold feet because he thought we're the police."

Tony lifted that same strong fist he pounded the door with to Skeeter's face, and being so close to that powerful grip made Skeeter's heart race. He needed Tony on his side. "I didn't say nothin' to give it away, I promise Tony. I'm with you all the way. If they thought otherwise, I don't think I'd still be standin' here. They know where I live."

"True." Tony gazed around. "Look over there."

Skeeter saw Tony's thick finger point to a restaurant, attached to the motel. That made sense. It was dinner time. He could eat.

They found Rusty slouching on a chair, at a table for four. The corner was private. With one other couple in the place, Skeeter's hopes for a decent meal fell. A good place should be packed at this time. He'd order his old standby—grilled cheese and fries. He could live on fries.

Then Skeeter glimpsed a skinny guy sitting by Rusty at the table, and suddenly nothing on the menu sounded good. A big gold loop earring hung from his ear lobe. His head was shaved, but little stubbles poked over it like weeds. Baggy cargo pants and an oversized jersey with the sleeves cut out told Skeeter he was trouble. Looked like a pirate in a Gasparilla parade.

On the drive to the motel from the boat, Tony had told Skeeter that Rusty was bringing together the players, and that included the buyer for the cocaine. To Skeeter, the skinny guy didn't look like he had the stuff to be the buyer. Rusty was dressed the same as before, just without sunglasses.

As he got closer, Skeeter saw Mr. Skinny had not tucked the jersey top into his pants, which meant one thing. He was armed. Because he was "on paper," Skeeter never carried a gun. Too dangerous. He took a seat closer to Rusty and let Tony sit next to Mr. Skinny. Then, Rusty introduced them to the guy—his name was Vince.

Skeeter guessed that Vince was the smugglers' guy on the Dora Ruth, to protect their interest in getting the drugs aboard. Rusty said Vince would use his cell phone to contact their boss. On the way over, Tony had asked Skeeter if he knew a cocaine supplier named Buzz Watkins, so Skeeter figured that was the boss Vince would call. Skeeter had never met Watkins and never wanted to. It was enough to know he was the man in black shades who came with Rusty in the 'stang when Skeeter got the twenty thousand. The way Rusty kept saying, "our boss" and "our main man" made Skeeter wonder if Rusty even knew Watkins' true name.

Vince didn't look healthy enough to be working on a shrimp boat, but Skeeter didn't dare say so. "I got an extra pair of gloves. We'll try to make it look like you're part of the crew."

So far, they hadn't ordered any food. No waitress came either. That was fine, since Skeeter's appetite vanished at the thought of a gun under Vince's shirt. He knew Tony had a weapon, but Vince was a different animal, and for some reason, he wasn't taking to Skeeter or his idea about wearing gloves.

Vince reminded them it was his boss calling the shots. Oh yeah, Skeeter knew that. It was like Vince wanted them to know how important he was. When Vince pounded the table, Skeeter glanced at Tony, who was his quiet self. Tony didn't move any of his big muscles, just looked past Vince as if he wasn't even there.

Vince talked like he was from up north, not Florida. "I've got the coordinates, but won't give them to you 'til we're out on the Gulf. Once you get them, no one's making any cell phone calls, understood? I'll have contact with the plane and will tell you exactly when to move into position." Skeeter raised his eyebrows at Tony as if to say, "This guy's done this before." When Tony blinked, Skeeter knew he got his message. Rusty stood, and nodded to Vince. "Now's a good time for you guys to head out to sea. Get your things, Vince. You'll ride with them to the boat." He turned to Skeeter and Tony, who had scraped their chairs back and gotten up. "Wait there by your truck, he'll be right out." Then Rusty did something that really got to Skeeter. He slugged him on the shoulder. "See you early in the morning, when we should all be closer to being rich."

Vince and Rusty headed for the motel, while Skeeter and Tony hiked over to Tony's truck. Skeeter rubbed his shoulder and gladly got in the back seat. Tony made a call on his cell. "Nick, we're leaving for the boat. The thin guy is Vince. He'll have contact with the plane. We'll get the coordinates at the last minute."

Tony was silent for a moment. Skeeter tried to hear what was being said. He couldn't, so he watched cars and one truck like his with huge tires tear by on Route 19. Tony kept looking at the motel. Skeeter told him, "I'll let ya know when Vince comes out."

Tony nodded, then said to Nick, "Okay, be careful, too."

Skeeter looked back to see if Vince was coming. He wasn't. "I don't like that guy, Tony. I guess we'll pretend to be shrimpers until the plane arrives. Want somethin' to eat?"

"Skinny Vince is no problem. We'll drive around for a while. See if Rusty is having us followed."

Vince sauntered over, wearing the same loose top. Skeeter hissed, "He's got a gun."

Tony started the truck. "Don't worry, I've got mine. Vince will sit up front, where I'll keep both my eyes on him."

Glad he was sitting behind Vince, a man with something to prove, Skeeter couldn't help thinking he wished Nick and Griff were in the truck, and that tomorrow could not come fast enough.

An hour later, Tony was on the Dora Ruth along with Skeeter and Vince. To Tony, Skeeter acted nervous. At the helm, he did okay guiding the boat away from the dock, but his eyes were glued to Vince. As they chugged down the Withlacoochee River, and Vince hovered near the pilot house, looking up the river, Tony was not too concerned. He knew karate and could put him down with no trouble. He had other options if it came to that but, in his whole undercover career, Tony had never shot anyone, which was nothing short of miraculous.

At the hotel, he assured Skeeter he had a gun. This was not exactly true. His .38 caliber S&W was in his ankle holster. But, he had a second gun, a 9-millimeter Glock, a fifteen rounder, in a holster beneath his oversized tee shirt, which hung over his jeans. From his crate, he had a perfect view of Skeeter, Vince, and the wake rolling from the stern.

The sun flamed more orange than yellow; it would set in about two hours. They passed expansive docks that belonged to upscale homes tucked away from the moving water. Trees grew thick along the bank, so the river seemed more narrow than it really was. Tony liked being on the water. An expert sailor in his real life, he loved to sail on the Gulf. Seasickness never bothered him, which was one reason Nick asked him to act as Skeeter's deckhand. He knew boats and the mysteries of the Gulf, just in case.

They glided past a Coast Guard patrol boat, and Vince looked furtively away from it. Skeeter held the wheel and said, "Steady." He steered them beyond the dock of the Coast Guard station. Tony watched Vince step behind the pilot house. Did the Coast Guard boat make him nervous, or was he relieved it was not out patrolling the Gulf?

On course to the open water, Tony was glad that Nick and Griff were not far away. He tore into a bag of burgers they'd brought along and grabbed a chicken sandwich. He handed the bag to Skeeter, who took a cheeseburger. Vince passed. No wonder he was so thin. Tony munched another chicken burger. It would be a long night, with no food until morning.

At dusk, Skeeter lowered the outriggers into place. To any aircraft or other boats, it looked like he was actually shrimping. A few pelicans followed the boat, looking for scraps. Since they weren't really shrimping, the birds got wise and flew off.

The sun wove pink and gold across the sky for another hour. Faint stars came out. The men didn't talk, and Tony used the quiet to turn over the plan in his mind. There was maybe one flaw, but it was too late to rectify it now. They should have another boat in the Gulf, as backup.

When blackness surrounded them on all sides, Skeeter ordered Tony to raise and secure the outriggers. Vince got a call on his cell and said one word, "Bingo." Tony went back to planning. At midnight, Vince got another call. He checked his GPS and gave their coordinates to whoever was on the other end. Tony assumed it was the pilot.

Vince folded his phone, then ordered them to turn on the spotlight. "Point it directly into the sky. They'll be overhead in ten minutes."

Tony checked his waterproof watch and, nine minutes later, he heard the distant whine of aircraft engines. He looked in the direction of the sound, strained to see. Because the plane was flying low with no lights, he couldn't see it, but they were coming.

He knew another plane was tracking its every movement. According to plan, a U.S. Customs Citation jet equipped with FLIR, forward-looking infrared radar, was high overhead. Its monitor would reveal heat emitted from the Cessna 404's engines, even in total darkness.

If everything went as they planned—and there was always an "if"—Customs would monitor the airdrop, then follow the 404, until they vectored Air Force F-18 interceptors. The F-18s would tell the Cessna smugglers they flew too close to the nuclear power plant north of Crystal River, then escort them to the panhandle and order them to land.

Engines revved closer. Tony shadowed Skeeter by the wheel, squeezed his upper arm for one second. He hoped Skeeter understood that the squeeze meant, "Don't panic and do what you're told." Skeeter turned to Tony. In the strange light, with darkness all around them, the informant's face was haggard and worn, which wasn't surprising with the life he'd led.

Adrenaline pulsed through Tony, his heart accelerated. He was ready. His wife was home, praying for him, even as the engines slowed. There was no way he could do this kind of work, undercover in the underbelly of society, without the power of prayer. Tony felt the main reason he was still alive was because the God of heaven and earth, who set the stars in place, had his eye on him. They didn't talk about it much, but he and Nick went to the same church. He felt a little easier knowing Nick was calling the shots.

Skeeter turned the Dora Ruth. Griff had briefed Tony on the Cessna 404, with its clam-style cargo door that could be opened by the copilot at slow speed. Above his head, the pilot banked the aircraft left and flew in a circle around the boat. Any second, Tony expected the copilot to push containers of cocaine out of the plane.

He was thankful he was on the water and not in that plane. In total darkness, the pilot did not have a good view of the horizon. With the drag of flying with the door open, the plane's altitude might drop, then crash into the Gulf.

Bang! Splash! Splash! Tony lost count as the plane's engines drowned out the sound of coolers landing in the water. He raced to the side. So did Vince. A minute later, as quickly as they started, the drops ended. The roar of the engines increased, then became quieter as the airplane climbed and banked north. Skeeter shut off the spotlight.

Difficult and dangerous work began. Bright strobe lights flashed in the water, lighting up coolers of cocaine bobbing all around them. It was their job to capture them all, every single one. This wasn't as easy as Tony had planned. He hoped that, before the smugglers were all arrested, worse pitfalls did not await them.

It had been nearly an hour since the cocaine rained from the sky. Vince organized the recovery, as though he had done it many times before. He perched on the bow and aimed a handheld spotlight at the containers. Skeeter steered Dora Ruth alongside each one. At the back of the boat, Tony used a gaff to snare floating bundles and yank them aboard. Being physically fit was a prerequisite for this deal. Each one weighed about eighty pounds.

When he pulled the first one aboard, Tony discovered that, for a bunch of coolers, the system was pretty sophisticated. Each container was a camping cooler, wrapped tight with duct tape. Then, it was wrapped with a life jacket, which was held in place with more duct tape. Each life jacket bore reflective tape, plus a strobe light that automatically lit when the life jacket made contact with the water.

As each cooler was hauled aboard, Tony disabled the strobe and stacked the load at the rear of the Dora Ruth, keeping an accurate count. So far, he told Vince, they recovered nine coolers. Vince waved the light around the black water. "There's thirteen. Keep looking!"

Gently rolling seas kept the boat separated from the remaining coolers. When it took another twenty minutes to find the next three, Skeeter voted to forget the last one. Waves were building, rocking Dora Ruth. He insisted the airplane dropped only twelve. Skeeter's anxiety reached a peak as he shouted, "Thirteen's an unlucky number!"

Tony agreed they should quit, which left Vince standing there with his light, finding nothing. Tony wanted off the water, not because of superstition, but the unknown. Others might know about cocaine being on the Dora Ruth, those with intent to rob and injure. Out there in the dark, on the vast Gulf, they were sitting ducks.

He said none of this to Vince, only, "Are you sure there are thirteen?"

The boat shifted on a wave. Vince lost his footing, and grabbed an outrigger. "We've got to find it. Each one is worth half a million dollars. Men are killed for losing less."

Fear laced Vince's words. Tony wasn't afraid, but Vince was right. The missing cargo was worth a fortune. They had to find the lost cooler, if there was one, even if it took all night.

Tony walked over to Skeeter at the helm. He kept his voice low, "Keep searching."

An hour later, far off to the east, Skeeter pointed to a flashing strobe. "There!" He turned his boat to retrieve the final cooler. Tony stowed it below, with the others. They made for the river, which was safer than being on the Gulf. As they neared the Coast Guard station, Tony sighed pure relief. He stood where he could be seen. In moments, Griff and Nick would receive word that the Dora Ruth and all three men were on the river. Phase two of Operation Igloo was about to begin.

THIRTY FIVE

At three o'clock in the morning, Griff and Nick received word over the radio from the agents assigned to the Coast Guard station that the Dora Ruth moved past and headed up the river. The citizens of Yankeetown were sleeping, oblivious that Operation Igloo was in full swing. Griff drove there so that Nick could work the phone and radio. They left to other agents the surveillance of the smugglers who had taken up residence at the Guest Inn Motel.

Griff found his body armor not only hot but bulky. A mere five minutes up Route 19, the radio crackled, and agents reported Rusty and Buzz were talking in the parking lot at the Guest Inn.

Nick spoke into the microphone, "Alert us when Rusty does anything besides talk."

Griff lifted his eyebrows. Things could get tricky. "Vince must be making calls from the Dora Ruth."

Nick put down the mic. "Everyone seems to be in place. Let's go to that closed gas station a mile from the warehouse."

In another five minutes, they pulled into the gas station. No overhead lights were on. Again an alert broadcast over their radio: Rusty and Buzz were spotted in a white Tahoe at a shopping mall on Route 19. That was eight miles south of where Nick and Griff were parked. Nick asked the surveillance agents to keep them advised of Rusty's movements.

The next report was the unexpected that Griff knew was bound to occur: A green Subaru Outback tailed the Tahoe to the mall, then parked on the opposite side of the highway.

Griff slunk low behind the wheel. "Do you know anything about that Subaru?"

Nick held the mic, ready to give commands to the various teams. "The Outback might be on counter surveillance and looking for police. Or it's someone going to steal the cocaine from Rusty and Buzz, or maybe rip off the money from the buyer."

Griff did not like the sound of the additional vehicle. "Either way, it complicates things."

Nick used the radio to alert the rest of the team, then added, "We're the only traffic out here and the police patrol division is not aware of our presence." He set down his mic and told Griff, "Can't take any risks for leaks."

Before Griff could reply, they heard from an ICE agent at the Coast Guard station. The Cessna 404 was forced to land at Panama City, Florida, and the pilot and copilot were being held. The Customs crew got infrared footage of containers falling from the plane.

Griff gave Nick a high-five, then the radio leapt to life: a thirty eight-foot motor home, with Virginia license plates, pulled next to Rusty and Buzz in the mall parking lot. The driver was described only as a man wearing glasses. DEA agents saw the passenger, a man wearing a cowboy hat and boots, get out and go over to the Tahoe.

Griff felt for his Glock, to be ready. "Sounds like our buyer has arrived."

"Exactly." Nick keyed the mic and told the other teams. As Nick fielded all the pieces thrown at him, Griff was impressed by his acuity. In minutes, their suspicions were confirmed. Surveillance agents saw the three men go to into the motor home and, in five minutes, Rusty, Buzz, and the cowboy returned to the Tahoe. The trio headed to the motel, leaving the driver in the motor home.

Griff realized no one knew the men in the motor home. Another agent was calling DEA to run the motor home's license plate. A short time later, the DEA HQ radio operator called. Griff and Nick heard the encrypted report: "That plate is registered to Sierra Cooper from Columbia City, Virginia. Be advised we have a C1, Tyler Cooper, at the same address."

The report ended, but Griff had to ask, "What is a C1?"

Nick chuckled. "That my friend, is the highest level cocaine target there is."

Griff's heart beat faster. Then, he heard voices inside the warehouse. Things were closing in. The excitement level bumped up another notch. Over the receiver from the listening device, Griff recognized Tony say, "I don't like sitting here with this stuff. How long we gonna wait?"

Now Skeeter. "Yeah, I want my money. All of it."

Another voice, which Griff didn't know. Maybe it was Vince, who laughed, "Be patient. I called Rusty. He's bringing the buyers to look at the shrimp."

Nick turned to Griff. "I wanted to park here in case someone tries to steal the drugs. They'll have to go past us."

Griff tilted back the driver's seat. "What about the guy in the motor home?"

Nick set the passenger seat to recline a bit. "I suspect Tyler Cooper took Rusty and Buzz inside the motor home to see bundles of cash. Once they're satisfied each is on the level, the exchange will occur."

"Since the addresses are the same, Cooper must be the driver of the motor home."

Nick shrugged. "Or Cooper could be in the cowboy hat. We won't know until we arrest them. My guess is that Sierra is a woman, and she is not present."

Griff sensed the next few minutes would not only be key to arresting the suspects, but packed with danger. First the green Outback, now the motor home. He was right. The radio snapped. The man in glasses left the mall parking lot and drove the motor home to an RV park north of town. The motor home was tailed by the green Outback.

Before Griff had a chance to ask Nick if the teams were prepared to split up if those two vehicles went their separate ways, the radio crackled again. "A red Suzuki 4x4 just pulled out of the RV park driven by a man wearing glasses. Is anyone in position to follow it?"

Nick keyed his microphone. "Is anyone on that 4X4?" There was silence. "Okay, watch for the Suzuki, it may be in the wind."

The red 4X4 was probably being driven by the man from the motor home, maybe Cooper. Griff wished he was on it right now, but had to stay put with Nick. Quickly they learned that Rusty and Buzz were back at the Guest Inn, and Nick rallied the troops. "Keep on all three vehicles. Be alert. The green Outback could be preparing to rip off the money, or could be the smuggler's guy and the money will be given to him. Rusty and Buzz may leave the motel again."

The radio went quiet. Over the speaker in the Cadillac, Griff heard noises inside the warehouse. A cell phone rang. Vince answered. "Yeah? Everything here is cool. We're waiting for instructions." A pause, "See you then."

Vince must have ended the call, because he started talking. "Skeeter, my boss, Buzz, has seen the money. Rusty's bringing him and one of their guys here to see the product. If they're satisfied, they'll move it from here."

Immediately, Nick was back on the radio. "Tahoe may be heading toward the dock. Be on the lookout." He looked at Griff. "Get ready to move."

Moments later, Nick got rattled by a report that came over the surveillance team's radio: "Rusty, Buzz and the cowboy left the motel in the Tahoe and they're being followed by a white panel van. It pulled out suddenly from behind the motel. Both vehicles are headed toward Yankeetown."

"Stay on them!" Nick snapped over the radio.

Griff pushed up his seat, put his hand on the key in the ignition. "What's with the white van? I need a play book to keep track of all these people." Griff was getting antsy, sitting in the Escalade, hearing it all, but not being able to see anything.

Nick propelled his seat forward. "I expected these smugglers to have a large contingent, but I don't like the additional numbers. Makes it harder to control. So far our team's been able to cover them, except the Suzuki. We'll see what happens."

Ten minutes later, the Tahoe shot past. Griff gestured, "Look! The white van's behind it."

Both vehicles turned west onto Route 40. Nick radioed to surveillance that his car would take over the point, then said to Griff, "Go, but hang back."

Griff followed the two cars south to the river at such a distance that he couldn't see taillights ahead. A quarter mile from the warehouse, the speaker in Nick's SUV came alive with screeching noises. It sounded like metal sliding on concrete.

Griff eased his speed. "Sounds like the sliding door on the warehouse opened. Now, it's closing again."

Nick growled in agreement. Griff pulled in behind a closed-up cottage, a block from the warehouse. He turned off the lights and engine to listen to the speaker. Tony was talking. Griff saw Nick reach behind his seat and pull out what looked like a submachine gun. It was dark, so he wasn't sure, "Is it an AR-15?"

The DEA agent wedged the butt between his feet and held the gun between his knees, the muzzle pointed at the ceiling. "This is the River Rock Carbine, created especially for DEA. It fires a steady stream of two-twenty-three caliber Remingtons. It's meant for serious business." When the warehouse door opened for the second time, Tony was the first of the three men inside to hop off his crate. Skeeter stayed on his, but, when Rusty sauntered in, Vince jumped to attention. Tony hadn't

seen Vince act that respectful with Rusty before. Then he looked beyond Rusty and saw the man walking behind him. So that was the guy
who made Vince jump.

This guy, with his bulbous head and nose, must be Buzz Watkins.
Tony had studied his arrest photo. His aggressive stance, the way he
held his head, told Tony this man was in charge. That confirmed what
Tony suspected—Rusty was the middleman who arranged for Skeeter's
and Tony's services. Tony glanced over at Skeeter, who seemed frozen
to his crate. Probably hoped that acting like a mannequin would keep
him from being seen, or shot.

Buzz walked over to the Igloo coolers. Now, a third man strode
into the warehouse, wearing a cowboy hat and boots. Square and squat,
he reminded Tony of a football tackle from his high school days. His
bleached blonde hair stuck out below his cowboy hat—a real piece of
work. Tony stepped closer to the coolers, figuring what was coming
next.

Buzz jerked a finger at Vince, then pointed at the cowboy. "This guy
represents the buyer. I've seen the money. Now, he wants to see our
product before money changes hands."

So far, everything was standard operating procedure for the drug
running business. Still, Tony's eyes swept the place. His mind and body
were ready. The buyer's man took a knife from his pocket and sliced
through the duct tape on one cooler. He tossed back the top and drew
out a square packet the size of a cigar box.

It was really a plastic bag, wrapped in more duct tape. With his knife,
the cowboy stuck open the package, peeled back tape and plastic, and
smelled the contents. Tony watched him stick a little finger into the
hole, scoop out a small amount of cocaine, then rub that finger on his
gums. So far, the guy was all action, no words.

Next, the cowboy moved several coolers off the pile, opened one at
the bottom of the stack, and took out another kilo of the cocaine to
test. Tony's arms tensed to strike or reach his gun.

The man was done taste-testing. He counted all thirteen coolers,
turned to Buzz. "Okay. Let's move it."

Rusty walked over and slid open both doors. The white van backed
into the warehouse, and Rusty closed the warehouse doors. The van's
driver stalked to the rear, opened wide the double door to the van. His
movements quick, he pulled out a gun. The van door exploded open.

Four men with guns jumped out, yelling, "County Police. Hands in
the air."

The driver waved a badge around. Working undercover, Tony felt he must comply. Up went his hands. He had no time to look for Skeeter. The four men wore badges on chains around their necks. One came up to Tony, grabbed the gun from his waist. "On the ground."

He shoved Tony with his foot to the cement floor. So, this was what it felt like to be on the other side of the law. If Tony blew his cover, said, "Hey, I'm one of your guys," Skeeter was dead for sure. Handcuffed, he found himself lying next to Skeeter on the concrete. Skeeter moaned, like he'd been hurt.

"You okay?"

"They slammed my shoulder."

"Shut up over there!" The police shouted orders and one of them hauled Tony by his arm away from the others, shoved him back on his belly. From what he could see from the ground, Vince, Buzz and the cowboy were all handcuffed and down, too. But, Rusty he couldn't see. Tony had no way to contact Nick or Griff. Surely they must be able to hear what was happening through the microphone. If he yelled, that would compromise him and Skeeter. Tony stayed quiet, tried to figure what to do.

A block away, Griff and Nick had heard it all on the speaker. Griff started the Escalade and put it in gear, but his foot stayed on the brake. "Nick, you said the local police didn't know we were coming. How can this be happening?"

"I don't know. We covered all contingencies."

Through the speaker, Griff heard boxes being moved and piled, voices shouting. Griff was haunted by the question, how could DEA go forward without coordinating with local police? Now, his whole case had imploded. And with all those guns. Suddenly Griff heard the van engine start inside the warehouse. Then the same sound as before, the large doors being opened.

Nick must have heard, too. He ordered Griff, "Pull into the gate, block their exit!"

Griff spun tires as he drove away from the house, raced down the street. From under the front seat, Nick hauled out a magnetic red emergency light, opened his window and placed it on the roof. He jammed the cord into the cigarette lighter.

Over the radio, he yelled, "All units, we have a problem at the warehouse. I repeat, move to the warehouse."

Nick grabbed the carbine with his left hand, placed his other hand on the door handle. Griff skidded in front of the gate opening. The white van rolled toward the gate, aimed right at Griff and Nick, like it would run them over. The next second, Nick flew out the passenger's door, while the Escalade was still sliding on the gravel.

Nick stood, legs apart, and pointed his carbine at the van. When the van kept coming, Nick opened fire. Griff's head snapped back as he watched a stream of bullets penetrate the windshield in a horizontal line along the top near the roof. The next burst went vertically down the center, obliterating the rear-view mirror. The van skidded to a stop.

Everything happened at the speed of sound. Griff had no time to think. He ran around the front of the Escalade to tackle Nick. He'd gone berserk. Out of the corner of his eyes, he saw Rusty run toward the Tahoe. Wait! Rusty was one of the smugglers, he should be under arrest.

Griff aimed his Glock at Rusty, shouted, "Freeze. Put your hands on the hood of the car!"

Rusty jerked up his arms and did exactly as Griff commanded. Griff cuffed him with the help of a DEA agent who had just gotten there. Other task force officers ran into the lot. Nick steadied his rifle at the van and barked orders. "Arrest everyone who's not one of our guys."

During the next few minutes, Griff helped the team arrest five men in the van, all uninjured by Nick's marksmanship. Each wore fake badges, and none had law enforcement credentials. With Rusty cuffed, Griff checked the back of the van. Sure enough, he counted thirteen coolers, then motioned Nick over and showed him. Nick shook one. "It will take a while to check and make sure all the cocaine is in them. Will you safeguard the load a minute?"

Griff guarded the six-million-dollar bounty, while Nick returned to the Escalade and ordered the surveillance team in Crystal River to seize the motor home and arrest the people driving the Outback. When everyone was in custody, they would assemble at the Coast Guard station. With the so-called police in handcuffs and under guard in DEA vehicles, Griff and Nick returned to the warehouse.

Tony was flat on his stomach, hands cuffed behind his back. Griff knelt and used his handcuff key to release him. When Tony sat up, blood spurted from a large gash on his forehead. Griff took a handkerchief from his back pocket, handed it to him. "What happened?"

Tony pressed the cloth to his head. "I wish I knew. The others are behind the crates."

He got up and, with Griff, went over to Skeeter, Vince, and Buzz, who were on their stomachs, hands cuffed behind their backs. Griff didn't move to release any of them. It might be good for Skeeter to suffer—and not tip anyone that he was the informant. Tony towered over the men on the floor, then pulled the .38-caliber revolver from his boot, and steadied it on them.

"Someone should keep an eye on these dirt bags, read them their Miranda rights."

Nick bent down, read them their rights, then Tony pulled him and Griff outside. In the light from the warehouse, Tony's neck muscles bulged. Griff could see he was angry, but the big man kept his voice under control. "Nick, tell me please. What is going on here?"

Nick wiped beads of sweat from his forehead. "I thought we crossed wires with the local police. But I had called their narcs, who assured me they had no operations going down tonight. I told 'em we did and asked them not to alert the patrol division, to keep leaks to a minimum."

Griff ran a hand over his moustache. "How did you know they weren't legit?"

Nick gripped Tony's arm. "When these guys arrested you, no one gave you Miranda warnings, so I figured they were robbers, posing as police. Since Rusty was free to leave in the Tahoe, he must've been working with the guys in the van to steal the cocaine from Watkins."

Griff shook his head. With everything happening so fast, he hadn't noticed the lack of police procedure that tipped Nick. "Good for you, Nick. I've never been involved in anything so bizarre. I thought for sure you went nuts."

His system in overdrive, Griff felt himself calm down. He slapped Nick on the back."My friend, you need to spend more time on the range with your River Rock Carbine. All those shots and you didn't hit anyone."

Nick grinned. "Well, that was the idea."

Griff strode over to Skeeter, who was still on the warehouse floor. To the DEA agent guarding Buzz and Vince, Griff said, "You transport those two, I'll take this guy."

He helped Skeeter to his knees, then to his feet. Griff noticed the floor was moist beneath Skeeter and the front of Skeeter's jeans was

wet. He must have been scared to death. Griff took him over to the
Escalade in the shadows, where he removed Skeeter's handcuffs.

In a gentle tone, he explained what happened. "Skeeter, there is
constant danger in drug cases. I hope you never think about getting
involved again."

He stuttered, "Do you think I'm crazy? All that shooting. I'm not a
violent guy."

Griff tucked the handcuffs over his belt, behind his back. "Do you
want to take the Dora Ruth back home?"

Skeeter was too badly shaken. "Not in the middle of the night. Can't
I stay at your motel? There's guys out there who are gonna look for me
when Rusty and Buzz don't see me at jail."

That made sense. "Stay out of sight until these smugglers and robbers are transported. I'll be awhile, but you can come with me to Tampa. I'll get you a room."

An hour or so later, the entire Operation Igloo team assembled at
the Coast Guard station. Despite a few scary moments, the teams arrested nine men at the warehouse, and two from the green Outback,
who had been waiting for a signal from Rusty to steal the money out
of the motor home.

Griff learned that the mystery only deepened because, when the
agents seized the motor home from the RV park, they found none
of the cash. The park manager confirmed that two men in the motor
home had been towing a red Suzuki 4x4, which had since vanished.
Since Tyler Cooper wasn't arrested, it appeared he just might be the
man in glasses who got away. Griff could not wait to sink his teeth into
his trail and see if it led all the way to Virginia, along with the money.

THIRTY SIX

The next morning, after the debacle with the media about his father-in-law, Dwight worked with Neal Longstreet and Jasper Collins to fend them off. Jasper arranged for retired Senator A.J. Button to show Dwight the ropes. From now on, A.J. accompanied Dwight on all his rounds with Senators on Capitol Hill. While landing a trophy fish thrilled him, Dwight abhorred the thought of being somebody's catch.

The last Senator on his schedule was Lars Zorn. Zorn was so cordial—the warmest of all the minority Senators—that, as their time drew to a close, Dwight lowered his usual guard. In fact, Lars asked none of the questions Button predicted he would. Lars even had a television crew take their pictures shaking hands.

They were all chatting, about ready to leave, when Senator Zorn showed Dwight some photographs from his movie days. Dwight concluded that Lars was so enamored with his own career, he'd have little interest in derailing Dwight's.

Lars pointed to his photo with Senator Briggs. "I'm proud of the bipartisan relationships I forged on the Judiciary Committee, and I will work with the Chair to get you through."

The Senator again shook Dwight's hand for the benefit of the camera crew. Then he said softly, so softly Dwight was positive no one else heard, "I hope your wife is not as sensitive to a little opposition as was Judge Cuttering's wife." He smiled for the cameras as though he'd just paid Dwight a compliment.

Dwight took the warning to heart. It was all he could do not to give Zorn a verbal thrashing right there in the Senator's office. Maybe the someone who started a whisper campaign against Christine's father was Zorn. Last night, Fox News had confirmed that the photo of Mr. Schweitzer in a Nazi uniform was a phony, and there was no evidence he disputed the Holocaust. Jasper Collins had called Dwight that morning to say the Austrian Prime Minister told the President her father would not be arrested.

In the doorway of Zorn's outer office, Dwight felt like washing his hands. He turned to the Senator, still smiling for the cameras, and intoned, "I look forward to answering whatever questions you have for me." Dwight walked out, ready for battle.

Griff had gotten a room for Skeeter at the airport hotel where, he guessed, his informant was now sleeping, but neither Griff nor Nick— nor any other agents—got any sleep. An hour before lunch, Griff was reviewing his notes, still running on pure adrenaline. The action Nick promised had come all right, but reality sunk in fast. After a big raid like last night's, there was a mountain of paperwork.

And, what a night it was. Griff was still so keyed up, he didn't notice he was tired and hungry. All around him, the DEA office buzzed with agents and officers trying to move that mountain. They fingerprinted the eleven prisoners, weighed and sealed the cocaine, and wrote reports about the evening's events to the predawn hours, all to be presented to prosecutors.

Later, Nick would bring the prisoners before a federal judge, where they would be charged with conspiracy to possess cocaine with intent to distribute. Buzz and Rusty would also be charged with operating a CCE, a continuing criminal enterprise, for which they faced life in prison. Griff planned to watch these initial appearances—he wanted to see if the judge released any on bond. If he did, he was crazy.

Pains in his stomach compelled him to stop writing his notes and go refill his coffee cup. The coffee, which kept him awake, also wreaked havoc on his insides. Half a cup of coffee and two paragraphs later, Nick tapped his arm.

"I'm going to check on the motor home. You ought to come."

All of a sudden, exhaustion threatened to override his curiosity. Plus, he hadn't finished his account of what happened and what was said by the defendants. He stifled a yawn. "What's up?"

Nick swallowed some coffee, rubbed his eyes. Cup in hand, he sat on the edge of the desk. "Our team got a warrant to search it. They're holding Mr. Cowboy—"

Griff laughed, "The guy in the cowboy hat, you're telling me his name really is Cowboy?"

"Nah, it's some long hyphenated job. Anyway, I think you were right, the guy who got away probably is Tyler Cooper, from Virginia. Customs brought a drug dog to check out his motor home. Now, they've sent for a second dog. The first one alerted for drugs hidden beneath the bed in the rear. The problem is, we couldn't find any."

Griff inserted his notes in a folder, set the pen on top. At the mention of Virginia, Nick had him. It meant more cases for Griff back home. "Cooper's the one who took off in the red Suzuki."

Nick held the back door open for Griff. "Right."

Griff strode beside Nick to the expensive-looking motor home. A U.S. Customs Border Patrol vehicle was parked next to it. The white Crown Victoria had the words "K9" on the rear quarter panel, and a large cage filled the entire back seat. A uniformed CBP officer stood next to the vehicle, holding a leash. At the end of the leash sat a black Labrador retriever, a red bandana around its neck and pink tongue hanging out of its mouth. Griff knew nothing about dogs, but this one appeared relaxed and compliant. He knew enough not to pet or talk to the animal because it was "working." The CBP officer, Bart Kearney, introduced the handsome Lab as "Cowboy" and Griff chuckled at the coincidence.

"Does Cowboy know we arrested his relative last night?"

Bart Kearney looked confused. "What?"

Nick laughed it off. "One of our defendants was arrested wearing a cowboy hat, and we took to calling him Mr. Cowboy. No disrespect to the real one. Has Cowboy had a chance to inspect the motor home?"

The officer leaned over and stroked the dog as though they were best friends. "Cowboy says there's drugs or drug money beneath the bed."

Griff was intrigued; he had not worked a case with drug dogs. "How does he say that?"

Bart, who probably got the same question every day, patted his dog's head. "My dog is trained to alert to the smell of marijuana, cocaine, heroin, and several other drugs. He holds the record for seizures in Customs. When he smells drugs, he scratches at the location. That's what we call a positive hit." He pointed to the motor home. "In there, Cowboy scratched at the base of the bed. When we put him inside the bed frame, he scratched at the floor under the bed."

Nick let Cowboy smell the back of his hand. "So, drugs were under there."

The officer shook his head. "Not necessarily. Cowboy's sense of smell is so powerful, he can detect drugs on items that simply touched drugs. Say, a suitcase that once held drugs was stored under the bed, this beautiful Lab could smell it."

Griff liked the look of that dog. If he was not gone so often, a dog like Cowboy would be great company. If Cowboy's smeller was that sensitive, Griff wondered, where'd the money go? Had the driver of the Suzuki taken it from of the motor home?

The surveillance agents had said Cooper, if it was Cooper, pulled the motor home in and left right away. It was very curious. Maybe the cash was there when Rusty and Buzz saw it, then they took it with them along with the man in the cowboy hat, ole-what's-his-name. If so, where did it go?

Kearney gave Cowboy more lead. "I should get him some water."

Just then, another CBP K9 unit pulled into the lot. Kearney nodded. "This will be Kahlua. She's called the 'determinator.'"

Another CBP officer opened the rear door of his unit. Out stepped a shiny golden retriever that could have been named "best in show" at Westminster. Kahlua walked next to her partner, head held high.

The officer led Kahlua into the motor home, but Bart stayed outside with Cowboy. "Kahlua is not trained to sense drugs. She detects the unique ink used to print currency, and she's found millions of dollars being smuggled out of the U.S. to Colombia."

The three men chatted while Kahlua worked inside the motor home. Soon, she descended the steps of the motor home followed by her CBP officer, who wore a big smile. "Kahlua says there's currency in there."

Now Nick looked confused. "But, the agents searched under the bed and found nothing."

The officer nodded. "That's what they said. Kahlua doesn't make mistakes. She says it's there."

Nick grunted, then, without telling Griff what he was doing, he walked to the rear of his Escalade. Griff continued to watch Kahlua and Cowboy. These highly trained dogs were not straining to play together. In fact, each seemed oblivious to the other. Griff realized he had not paid much attention to dogs, which were wonderful assets to law enforcement.

Nick came back carrying a canvas satchel of tools. "I have an idea. If you officers have time to hang around, we'll let you know."

Griff followed Nick inside, wondering what he was up to. The luxurious interior was something like what a rock band might travel in. Countertops made of marble, crystal lamps on the walls, and ceramic tile floors in the kitchen. In the bedroom, the entire mattress and platform on which it rested were raised like the hood of a car, and held aloft by hydraulic pistons.

Nick, along with Griff and two DEA agents, circled the bed, all peering at the same thing—an empty cavern with a carpeted floor. Nick was carrying a crowbar, which he held up to the outside base of the bed to measure it, and then compared that measure with the depth of the recessed area inside the bed base. Griff saw no difference, which meant there was no hidden compartment.

As Nick pressed down on the compartment's floor, his voice grew excited. "It's not secured, it's moving. Griff, grab two pairs of pliers out of that satchel. Get on the other side. This carpet is probably held down by tack strips, so it should be easy to pull."

With the pliers, Griff and Nick lifted up much of the carpet. What Griff saw next astonished him. The entire carpeted floor beneath the bed rose silently, pushed by hydraulic pistons similar to those that raised the bed. Snugly underneath it all was exactly what Kahlua said was there—stacks and stacks of one-hundred dollar bills. The entire secret compartment, which lay between the floor and the frame of the motor home chassis, held six million dollars.

It was an unbelievable sum. "Nick, you're brilliant!" His friend's next command reminded Griff what a terrific agent he was. Hurray for DEA, but too bad the Bureau lost him.

Nick told the team leader, "Have the money counted by two agents. It is to be sealed in evidence bags by the same two agents. Have the rest of your team do the paperwork to seize this motor home. I want Mr. Cowboy before the judge. The government should argue for no bond."

Outside, Nick saluted the CBP officers and their canine partners. "Your dogs were right. Before we do inventory, let's have you take Cowboy and Kahlua inside to get a photo taken with the evidence." Nick turned to Bart and said, "I'm going to buy both dogs a steak, and Griff here will buy one for each of you officers."

The thought of shoveling out forty bucks for a couple of steaks did not faze Griff in the least. Except for a few tense moments, when he thought Nick was going to kill some local police, Griff had not had so much fun working in a long time. He turned to Nick. "Last night was unbelievable. Is it always this way at DEA?"

Nick smiled. "On any given day, it is. I've developed many good cases like this. But, God has kept me safe and I thank him for that every day."

So, Nick believed that God protected him. Griff would think about that, later. For now, he wanted to track down Tyler Cooper and his Virginia connections, then get forty—or even fifty—winks.

Back at his borrowed desk, Griff studied a report he'd printed of Tyler Cooper's earlier arrest in Virginia. DEA had done its job, just like last night, without the hoopla of a press conference. They quietly made their arrests—well Nick's submachine gun fire was a little loud, but otherwise it was pretty quiet—even though hardened criminals endangered their lives. The whole scenario made Griff proud.

Last night a major smuggler was arrested, taken off the streets. Buzz Watkins organized a small army to move four hundred kilos of cocaine. Another high-level distributor, the man in the cowboy hat, was in custody; and, if he talked, he could lead them to Tyler Cooper, the man who drove the motor home with the six million dollars—and maybe to others even higher. Tyler and his wife lived in Columbia City, Virginia, not far from Griff's home.

The kingpin of them all was Rusty. The little man with red hair who looked like a car salesman had orchestrated a scheme even more devious. With the sellers and buyers in such proximity to each other, he and his counterfeit police officers almost stole it all—four hundred kilos of cocaine *and* the six million dollars that Mr. Cowboy and Tyler Cooper had brought with them to make a buy.

Griff leaned back, and grabbed the end of his moustache. All the arrests and seizures were possible because Rusty was introduced to Skeeter, whose boat they needed. Griff met Skeeter because he was helping Dwight look for his brother, who he was trying to find because he needed a kidney. All the time Cooper dealt drugs right under Griff's nose in Virginia, and now he was going to get to arrest him. That was the plan, anyway. All the threads seemed to connect. Maybe Nick figured it right—there is a God who cares about these things.

But Griff had no time to reflect on all this now. He wanted to get moving on a more tangible plan. It didn't take long for Nick to agree with his idea. Five minutes later, Griff called and gave Sal the license number and description of the red Suzuki 4x4. "Can you help me, Sal?"

"For you, Topping, I would even quit working on my arrest statistics report, which, as you know, is my favorite thing to do. Leave it to me. When you coming back?"

"Call my cell soon as you know anything about Cooper. I won't fly in for a few days, but thanks for asking."

Eager to find the missing smuggler, Sal hung up. Jocelyn, the DEA secretary, buzzed Griff. "A pushy attorney called twice. Says he's from Washington, D.C. and insists on talking to the agent who is detaining his client's motor home. Nick said you should talk to him. Will you be here, in case he calls back?"

"Yeah, right here having fun. What's the lawyer's name?"

She paused. "You know, he didn't leave it. Both times he called, Nick was outside in the motor home with the dogs. I didn't tell him that, though."

"Good job. He calls back, send him to me."

She took his order for a sub sandwich, a meatball with extra cheese, and Griff went out to give her a ten-dollar bill. Hot food was what his stomach needed for the hours of work ahead. He hoped the lawyer did call back. It would be fun to see what information he could pry out of him.

All the paperwork was finally done at 4:30, and Nick brought the defendants before a judge. Griff stayed at the office in case the lawyer or Sal called. At five minutes to five, he started asking around for a ride to his hotel. His brain had all but melted. Like every agent on the smuggling case who'd been working for thirty-two hours straight, he desperately needed sleep.

Plus, he needed to check on Skeeter at the hotel, who after last night was so scared, he was afraid to return to Apalachicola. Griff put him in the room adjoining his.

Jocelyn found Griff near the tech room, where he'd just gotten a promise of a ride. She lowered her voice, as if about to reveal a secret. "Your Washington attorney is on line three."

"I guess I don't leave after all." At the first desk he came to without an agent, Griff picked up line three. "FBI Agent Griff Topping. What can I do for you?"

"This is Attorney Bernard Spitzer calling from Washington on behalf of my client."

Griff cut through the suave voice, which suggested a steep hourly rate. "Who's your client?"

Spitzer went right on, as if Griff had not uttered a word. "She told me her motor home is being detained by your office in Tampa. Apparently, it was stolen. I am trying to get it back."

That was a neat story, a stolen motor home. "Could you hold a moment?" Without waiting for a reply, Griff put the attorney on hold and walked back to the desk where he left the printout for Cooper's Virginia arrest. He expected Bernard Spitzer was representing him or his wife, Sierra. Griff went back to the attorney. "I ask again, Bernard, who do you represent?"

The lawyer hesitated long enough for Griff to think there was more to it. "Agent Topping, I'm known as Bernie. You may call me that as well. My client is Sierra Cooper, and her motor home was stolen. It may have been driven by some criminals. I'd like it released."

Since Griff knew no criminal attorneys in D.C. named Spitzer, he'd feel him out. If he had realized Bernie was Dwight's friend and former law partner, Griff might have stepped more lightly. But, he didn't, so he treated Spitzer the same as any other lawyer who defended criminals. "Ms. Cooper must have some idea how the motor home ended in Florida. Did she file a stolen vehicle report?"

Griff heard a long-suffering sigh. If the attorney was irritated with him, all the better.

"Not that she mentioned to me."

Wound up from no sleep and all that coffee, Griff let her rip. "I suggest you find out if she loaned it to anyone. Possibly a family member, like her husband, used it."

The lawyer became agitated. "Agent Topping, it is not my job to help authorities. I am only interested in returning the motor home to my client before it is damaged."

Griff chuckled. "Bernie, you may find it interesting to learn that your client's motor home is being held so that we can get a warrant to search it thoroughly, if it means tearing it apart."

Bernie Spitzer went beyond frustrated to outraged. "I insist you not search that motor home. My client does not want it damaged. Who is the Assistant U.S. Attorney handling this? I will file a motion to suppress your warrant and prevent the search of that motor home."

Griff leaned back in the chair. "Don't worry Bernie. If the warrant is issued without probable cause, it can be remedied in the Court of Appeals."

"Agent Topping, you are in Florida, but surely you've heard of Judge Dwight Pendergast, the new Supreme court nominee?"

Griff jerked forward. Why was Bernie invoking Dwight's name? "Sure, but I don't think *he's* got a claim to that motor home."

"Of course not. He is my personal friend and former law partner. If you do not return the motor home, I will have no choice but to involve him. Tell that to the prosecutor."

Griff changed his tack. "Why didn't you say so? I can help. Have Ms. Cooper call me and, after she answers my questions, we can probably release the motor home to her."

"I cannot allow her to answer your questions. You see, I'm not sure what the case is about."

Griff was weary with Attorney Spitzer, so he laid out his cards. "I'm guessing you haven't handled many criminal cases. The motor home was used by drug dealers here in Florida. Tyler Cooper was seen in it just before others were arrested. If he is here in Florida, I suspect he left Virginia in violation of his bond in the drug case there. We'll find out how deeply he's involved. Meanwhile, the motor home is seized by the U. S. government for facilitating the sale of cocaine."

Suddenly, Bernie got subdued. "How could he be there without his wife knowing?"

To Griff, that was totally naive. "He must have called his wife, because you're now calling me, or Tyler Cooper called you and asked you to call me and report the vehicle as stolen."

Spitzer did a great job backpedaling. "I represent him in the other case, but he hasn't called me."

Griff was surprised to learn that Bernie was a lawyer on a drug case. For a high-powered and high-priced attorney, he seemed out of his element on the call with Griff. Griff almost felt sorry for him, being deceived by his criminal client—almost. "I hope you charged a hefty retainer, because when Tyler's motor home was seized, we found six million dollars in it. Of course, we seized the cash, too."

Bernie stammered, "Agent Topping—" He took a deep breath. "Thank you for sharing that. I may not continue to represent either of the Coopers. Goodbye."

Griff stared at the phone. Bernie was in over his head. Whichever federal judge had allowed Cooper out on bond would have it thrown back to him or her in double doses. During his career, Griff witnessed many ironies, but this one was a keeper. Bernie invokes Dwight's name, whose unknown brother sets up the arrest of that same attorney's client. He wrote down everything Bernie said. Now, it really was time to get some sleep.

THIRTY SEVEN

E arly the next morning, Dwight was up and dressed in a summer-weight jogging outfit. His black suit was in a bag over his shoulder—he was on his way to dialysis and he would change into it when done. He was about to set the security alarm to leave the house when the phone rang.

Bernie Spitzer was out of breath. "Dwight, can we have lunch today?"

Dwight calculated the next four hours. After dialysis, he had a meeting with Jasper Collins at the White House to discuss the Senate confirmation hearings. And, he promised to take Christine to lunch in the Senate dining room with Chairman Briggs. No way could he change that. "Bernie, I'm sorry, but today I'm booked solid."

"We never get together. Are you avoiding me?"

His friend sounded anxious, and hurt. Dwight realized he might be avoiding his old friend. He had not sought out Bernie ever since he read that letter claiming he married Christine to stay out of Vietnam. There just hadn't been time to get together, and it wasn't something you could discuss on the phone. Resigned, he sighed. "We should talk. How about later this week?"

They arranged to have breakfast on Wednesday. Dwight picked up his suit and white shirt, gold tie threaded through the collar, and headed to the city. As he drove, he tried to figure out the best way to approach Bernie about the letters. He wondered if Griff was making any progress in finding his brother. He hadn't heard from the agent. If only he could know before his confirmation hearing if there was a suitable kidney donor. Lately, he prayed it might be possible, but it all seemed to be out of Dwight's hands.

After a good night's sleep, Griff sped east along I-75 in a Jeep Cherokee borrowed from the DEA office. He passed mangled signs and damaged roofs, unhealed scars from hurricanes that in the previous year had traumatized this land and people. Going to the Seminole reservation was Skeeter's idea. Since he hadn't slept one hour while left alone in the hotel, Skeeter snoozed in the passenger seat, his head against the headrest.

Griff, on the other hand, woke early, refreshed by the prospect of renewing his search for Eleanor. She seemed the last family option for Dwight's kidney. Skeeter took himself out with that ugly extortion letter. While Eleanor was a few years older than Dwight, she was young enough to donate a kidney to her brother—if she were still alive.

Off the interstate, Griff turned north on a two-lane road. It didn't take long to see he was on a road less-traveled. There was no oncoming traffic. Skeeter's head flopped left, then right. He began to snore. Griff shook his shoulder. "We're about to enter the Seminole Big Cypress Reservation. Wake up and have a look at it."

Skeeter moaned and reset his seat to see. Moments later, he pointed and let out a low whistle. "That's the biggest gator I ever seen."

A thirty-foot wide creek ran alongside CR-833. Griff slowed to take a look at the biggest gator *he'd* ever seen, as well. It was lying on the bank with its head pointed toward the water. He wanted to stop, but there was no shoulder. Besides, they had an appointment to keep.

The alligator behind them, Griff marveled at the vast pasture lands—dotted with palm trees and various kinds of cattle—that stretched on both sides of the road as far as he could see. "Skeeter, I didn't think the reservation would be this serene." Griff had navigated Seminole websites on his laptop last night at the hotel. Two facts stuck in his mind, which he now told Skeeter. The Seminole Indian tribe had one of the largest cattle herds in the nation and, after the Seminole wars, they never signed a peace treaty with the federal government.

For miles and miles, they drove past grazing cattle and horses. No buildings or homes interrupted the tranquil scene. When they reached a small community with houses, churches, and two gas stations, Griff saw the sign for their next stop, the Ah-Tah-Thi-Ki museum.

"This is it." He parked in a paved lot across the street, then walked with Skeeter on the boardwalk over a pond. It was Griff's turn to point. "Small alligator, in the middle, its nose in the air." Skeeter shouted at the gator like it was an enemy, and the reptile slunk below the water.

Inside the museum, a woman with coal-black hair and wearing a blue-striped dress and white beads welcomed them. Skeeter signed the guest log, but Griff didn't. At the gift shop, he paid their admission. They watched a short movie of the history of the Seminoles on a panoramic screen. At the end, when a Seminole warrior disappeared offscreen and encouraged them to go in the same direction, they did, and passed exhibits of Seminoles fishing and tanning deerskins.

By the Green Corn Dance exhibit, Griff checked his watch. It was12:15 p.m. Time to meet the librarian in the archives. Glass windows revealed stacks of magazines, books, and a computer. They were met by a woman in a wheelchair. She wore a bandana around the neck of her blouse. When she spoke, her voice was soft and clear, as if she were reading a book to school children.

"You said you are looking for Eleanor Bailey, although you are not certain if she has a married name."

Skeeter edged in the door, and removed his Tampa Bay Buccaneers ball cap. Griff was astonished by his act of politeness. He might have one or two redeeming attributes after all. Skeeter placed his cap over his heart, like he was singing the National Anthem at a baseball game. "Ma'am, Eleanor is my sister. The last I knew, she was unmarried."

"Call me Sallie. I'm Sallie Bird, of the Bird clan. Are you a Seminole?"

Skeeter nodded, then jerked a thumb at Griff. "He's not, but he's helpin' me look for my sister. He's FBI."

Griff wished Skeeter hadn't mentioned that, but Sallie's smile did not fade. She rolled her wheelchair from a table. "Come and sit. Do you know your mother's name?"

Skeeter took a chair beside her and Griff sat next to him. Skeeter rubbed his chin. "My father, Joseph Bailey, fought and died in Korea after the war. I guess he was not Seminole. After that, my mother was killed in a car accident. I was a kid and don't even know the year she died. I went to foster homes."

Sallie looked at Skeeter with large dark eyes that held their own sadness. Maybe she'd too been in foster care, but Griff would never ask.

She nodded pleasantly. "Do you know your mother's clan? There are eight now. Panther is the largest. Besides Bird, there's also Bear, Big Town, Deer, Otter, Snake and Wind. When a woman's line dies out, that clan is gone. Alligator is no more."

Skeeter shook his head, shrugged. "Nah. I know nothin' about that. My sister Eleanor was cared for by our aunt after the accident. Clara someone. When she died, Eleanor came to visit me at juvenile detention, wanted to get money for us to be together. It was the last time I saw her."

Sallie rolled back, got out a spiral-bound notebook from her desk. "After Mr. Topping called, I set this aside. You can look through this—it's a biography of many important members from our past. Let me know if you have questions."

Skeeter took the book and gingerly laid it on the table, a great treasure. Griff was somewhat amused. When Skeeter had told him Eleanor thought she was Seminole, Skeeter said he didn't believe it. Griff knew one thing. At this rate, finding Dwight's sister Eleanor would take not days or weeks, but months. He had been careful to let Skeeter think he was only helping him. The judge's name never came up.

While Skeeter looked through the book, Griff slipped out and returned to the gift shop. The woman there, the one who took his twelve dollars for admission, had a head full of white hair. Perhaps this lady, who was older than Sallie Bird, knew more about other Seminoles.

She smiled as she put a price tag on a handmade doll. "How do you like our museum?"

Griff smiled back. She wore no name tag, so he just said, "Fine," and explained his search for Eleanor Bailey. "My friend is in the library with Sallie. She doesn't know anyone by that name."

The woman set her doll behind a glass case. "There are Seminole reservations in Hollywood, Tampa, and Brighton, Florida—in addition to one in Oklahoma."

As she talked, Griff watched her face closely. Her skin was honey-colored and unlined, save a few crinkles around greenish-brown eyes. She spoke some words that Griff did not understand.

"Excuse me?"

"That is the Creek language. I speak Creek, Mikasukee and English."

Griff could barely master English and said so. Her face lit up, as if the sun and the moon lived in her smile. "I remember an Eleanor Panther. She was gone, came back. Many do. She lives on the Brighton reservation, off Road 721A, about thirty minutes north of here."

It was a lead, a start. "Where is her place?"

"Look for a bright yellow fence on the side of the road, right after you turn. You'll see a sign, Solid Rock Farm, by a rock as big as a small car." The lady smiled again, reminding Griff of Gram Topping. He had an urge to visit her in England and vowed to fly to Cornwall as soon as he wrapped up this investigation.

"You can't miss it."

"You're a lifesaver." Griff knew she had no idea he really meant that, especially if Eleanor Panther was Eleanor Bailey, Dwight's sister, and could give Dwight a kidney.

He found Skeeter in the library, tears running down his ragged cheeks. He looked up at Griff. "I'm reading about my people. One Seminole woman was part white, like me. Her uncle saved her from being killed, and her mom fled with her. They lived on berries. When she was fourteen, she moved all the way to North Carolina, and she was the first to go to school."

Skeeter wiped his eyes. "I thought I had it bad."

Griff walked over to the table, rested a hand on his shoulder. "You can come back another time. We've got someone to see, who might help us. Let's go."

Griff was getting good at keeping secrets, too good. But, if Skeeter was crying already, how would he react if he knew they were on the way to see a woman who might be Eleanor? He'd be a wreck. Better let him see her first. Maybe they'd recognize each other. Then again, maybe it would be a false start, just like Phyllis in Texas.

Eleanor Panther started the Solid Rock Farm six years ago. On her green and brown quad runner, she drove from the barn, its four knobby tires throwing bits of dirt and grass into the air. The quad helped her navigate the many acres of her farm. An auto accident when she was a young girl left her with a limp. The broken right femur bone never set right. To compensate, she paid for special boots to be made with the right sole a half-inch thicker.

She headed from her horses to her fifteen acre ponds. To say this farm, where she raised tilapia and turtles for sale, was her whole life would be missing a larger part of who she was. Her farm was a means to make money, to help needy children, to help her church. She glimpsed her manager, Felix Tidewater, and raised her hand to wave.

Felix was sent to her by God. Of this she had no doubt. His degree in aquatic engineering combined with a knack for business were just what the farm needed. Since she hired Felix three years and eight ponds ago, she began to make money. He was kneeling to check the oxygen level of the water, so he didn't see her wave.

As she drove nearer, he straightened. Eleanor parked her quad next to his by the pond. She had no particular purpose in seeing Felix, just a routine check to see if everything was going smoothly. They were nearing the end of the third quarter, and sales were high enough to pay him and other employees a bonus.

She pulled a bandana from her pocket and wiped her face. Because Eleanor liked to feel the breeze on her bare neck, she kept her black hair, now turning silver in the front and along the sides, clipped short to her chin. "Tomorrow I'm taking some teens from church to the wild mustang show. They love the horses, and I can use a day off."

Sweat glistened above his upper lip. "On Friday, I'm driving over to Indiantown to meet with a state fishery expert. Our oxygen levels have been dropping."

"Is it a problem?"

Felix swatted at a fly hovering near his cheek. "I'm not sure."

Felix was the hardest working man she'd ever met. His work ethic paralleled hers—no sleep until the columns balanced, and the dishes and her quiet time complete. Because she lived with chaos as a child, she drove it from her adult life as the reservation cowboys drove their cattle. Having a spirit of calm around her made up for deficiencies in her life, and she was relentless in achieving it.

She stayed on the quad. "I don't know if I'll be back before your meeting on Friday. Tonight is prayer meeting."

Back at the house, a ranch with two bedrooms, a skylight in the kitchen and large screened porch, she was surprised to see a strange Jeep in the driveway. Two men, one tall and clean-cut, the other wearing a ball cap, stood looking at her vegetable garden, where she grew pumpkins, squash, and cabbage, like the old ways. At the sound of her motor, they turned to her.

The tall man was lean, with reddish-brown hair and moustache. He looked successful, even behind dark glasses. The shorter man was older, with gray hair pulled behind his ears. Eleanor drove straight to them; she didn't relish walking in front of strangers. "May I help you?"

Before either of them spoke, she saw something familiar about the older man. His face was bronze. His ear lobes were diamond-shaped, before they merged into his jaw line. Could it be Artie?

She shut off the machine, slid from the seat. The taller man held out his hand. "I'm Griff Topping and this is—"

Eleanor did not listen. She hugged her brother, whom she had not seen for years and years, and held him. "Artie, it's me, Eleanor."

The circle of her life closed, complete for the first time. With her hands on his upper arms, she pulled back and lovingly looked at his

face. He wore it all, years of disappointment and shame. If only Artie
could feel the joy and love that she felt. She wished with her own
hands she could wash away his hurts, but that was impossible.

"Artie—" She used the name that she called him as a little boy.
"We've lost so much time. How come you never answered my letters?
They started coming back, stamped 'addressee unknown'"

Skeeter flinched, like she hurt him anew. "I don't know."

With a firm hand, she stroked his cheek. It was wet. Eleanor heard
a door slam. The other man had climbed back into the Cherokee. His
kind gesture would give her and Artie a chance to get reacquainted.
But, it was too hot in the sun. She took her brother's hand and walked
him inside, where she poured him lemonade from lemons she grew
herself, on trees behind the house.

He sat on the stool by the counter. Eleanor gave him another hug.
"I'll be right back."

She walked outside, went over to the car window, and knocked. The
man lowered it.

"Excuse me, I was so shocked to see my brother standing in my yard
after all these years, I missed your name. But, any friend of Artie's is a
friend of mine. You look like a nice man."

He offered his right hand. "Griffin Topping. I haven't known Skeeter long."

Eleanor had to laugh. "So, he's kept that nickname. Our mother said
he was her Skeeter boy, because he was always buzzing all around her,
like a mosquito."

She invited him in from the heat, but Griffin declined. He said
she and Skeeter needed time to share memories. For the next thirty
minutes, they did. Cried on each other's shoulders, and tried to build a
bridge from the past to the future.

Their cry over, she fixed Skeeter a plate of leftovers—fried cabbage,
baked beans and Indian fry bread. Eleanor marveled at his presence in
her home. She could not guess why her prayer was answered today, but
she gratefully accepted it for the miracle and blessing it was.

Eleanor sat across from her brother, watching him eat, her heart
overflowing with concern. When she asked what he had been doing,
he shrugged, looked far away and asked her all kinds of questions about
the farm. She refilled their lemonade. "It's nice of Griffin to bring you
all this way to find me. He must be a good friend. You said he works
for the FBI."

Eleanor was puzzled by their connection and why he didn't come inside. He'd driven all the way from Tampa to find her, so it must not be because he was prejudiced against Native Americans. No, he remained outside for some other reason.

Skeeter cleaned the last bit of baked beans from his plate. "Sis, I know this was leftovers, but it's really the best food I ate in a long time."

"Artie, would you like some more?"

He set down the fork and smiled. "Your fry bread was real good."

She laughed as he smacked his lips. "You're still a character, little brother." Eleanor took several pieces of the fry bread and warmed them in the skillet. As she did this, she heard a knock on the front door and saw Griffin standing on the other side of the screen. Towel over her shoulder, she opened the door and welcomed him. "Please take some refreshment."

Griff took off his sunglasses and followed her into the kitchen. "I had the air on in the car, so it wasn't bad. I called back to my office, had a bunch of phone messages to return." He took a seat at the table across from Skeeter. "It smells wonderful in here."

Skeeter beamed. "You should taste my sister's Indian bread."

Eleanor swelled with happiness. She wanted to ask Artie about his life, if he had a faith in God, but it seemed he'd built many walls. Walls that thick did not come tumbling down in an hour. And, she was not the prophet Joshua who fought the battle of Jericho.

Her faith in God was strong. A verse in the Bible was the cornerstone of her belief that this meeting with her brother was not a coincidence. Romans, chapter eight, said that all things work for the good of those who love God and are called according to his purpose. If she said that to these men, she sensed they would either laugh or say something sarcastic. So, instead, she fed them her special bread.

Griff refilled his lemonade. "Skeeter is right. Fry bread is delicious. What's the secret?"

"I was telling my brother I learned to make it as a young girl from Aunt Clara. Artie, do you remember she brought me to visit you at your foster home?"

"I remember you, not her so much. It's fuzzy. You wore a long braid."

Eleanor sat by him now, placed her hand on his tanned forearm. "She promised to come back for you and was petitioning the court to care for you, when she died." Her throat constricted and her eyes flooded with tears.

Skeeter covered her hand with his. "That dream became my nightmare. I got your letter tellin' you were being cared for by missionaries. I still have it after all these years."

Eleanor pulled a tissue from her pocket and blew her nose into it. Griff chose that moment to uncover another old wound. "Skeeter told me on the way over he has a hazy memory of another brother. If you're interested, I may be able to help you find him."

The years fell away, like when she peeled the rind off a lemon. This fruit was sweet, not sour. Eleanor was holding her baby brother Dwight in her arms at the hospital. He was two days old, she was about four. His little face was soft, shiny, and his black hair was thick. She kissed him over and over until Mother told her to stop. Eleanor must have seen him again, but her car accident wiped out any memory of it.

Eleanor looked at Griffin. Why was he so ready to help them? She guessed the reason was not important and decided to trust in the purpose. "Tell me, is it possible to find him? I was injured badly, broken ribs and leg, and a collapsed lung. It was all Auntie Clara could do to care for me. I got better, but when she died, I was too young to know what happened to little Dwight. He was named for President Eisenhower you know. Skeeter, Father looked upon him as a hero."

Griffin held his lemonade glass between two hands. "Eleanor, I haven't even told this to Skeeter, but I have a lead. It may not pan out, but would you like me to follow it and let you know?"

Skeeter scraped back his chair and stood. "I only remember Eleanor. She came to see me, wrote me, cared about me. Have you ever heard from our brother, Eleanor? Because, if you haven't, I have no interest in him if he has no interest in us."

His voice shook and Eleanor feared for his soul. A plan formed in her mind. "Artie, don't say such things. He was a baby and may not even know about us. Griffin, I want to know the results of your search. Let me give you my phone number."

Griff pulled a notebook from his back pocket and wrote in her number and address.

Eleanor walked over to her brother and hugged him again. "My guest room has a bunkbed. Would you like to stay over and be my guests tonight? There's a prayer meeting at church."

She was so happy when both men answered, "Yes."

THIRTY EIGHT

Griff set their bags in Eleanor's guest room, took time to wash off the road dust, then returned to the kitchen. Skeeter was setting the table for dinner. Her invitation to spend the night would accomplish two things. First, it gave Griff a chance to learn about Eleanor so that he could tell Dwight, who still believed that his sister had died. Second, it kept Skeeter away from the Dora Ruth and any friends of the smugglers who might want to get even for their recent arrest.

For Eleanor's sake, Griff tried to show respect for Skeeter, but it was hard. Several times he had to corral his tongue. Eleanor handed him a bowl of rice and steamed vegetables. To be polite, he asked about her church.

She poured more lemonade. "I keep food cooked, ready to reheat, because folks from church come by, all hours of the day and night. That's why I'm going to prayer meeting tonight. We are all praying for a center to help troubled families that Pastor wants to build."

Eleanor set the microwave to cook. "You sit. Skeeter, will you pour the coffee?"

Griff grinned as Skeeter did exactly what she asked. She was an engaging woman. Her eyes, while more green in tint, were the same shape as Dwight's. Something about her jaw and chin confirmed they were siblings. The judge should be happy to know she was alive. Plus, she ran a thriving fish business, and Dwight loved to fish. So did Skeeter, come to think of it.

Griff sipped the delicious brew. "Thanks, Skeeter."

His informant stopped, spun around, as if to see if he meant it. Griff smiled, so did Skeeter. The man appeared relaxed for the first time since they met. Perhaps because for once he wasn't scamming someone or getting in trouble with the law.

Eleanor gave them each a hot chicken drumstick. Skeeter picked his up. He was about to bite into it when Eleanor sat at the head of the table and held out her hands. "Will you join hands with me as I return thanks to the provider of all things?"

Skeeter dropped his chicken leg, as if he'd been caught stealing it. Sheepishly, he wiped his hand on a napkin and took her hand. Griff took each one of their hands and, for a moment, felt enormous satisfaction about bringing them together. Eleanor had a different idea, one he'd think about in the days to come.

Her prayer was brief. "Lord, thank you for richly blessing us with this meal. Thank you for using Griffin to reunite me with my brother. To you be all glory and praise. Amen."

Prayers to God were not something Griff had learned. He was familiar with saying grace, because Eva and Scott prayed before they ate, but it wasn't something he'd grown up with. Holding hands around the table with Eleanor Panther and her brother like they were doing right now, however, felt right. A truth crept into his mind. Just as the carpet was peeled back in the motor home to reveal hidden currency, Griff saw that, despite all that had happened in her life, Eleanor seemed to tap into a hidden source of strength. She radiated peace and contentment. Not only did she believe God used Griff, she told this to her God.

He did not understand it. Was Eleanor Panther some kind of angel? He had just touched her hand, and she was flesh and blood. Eleanor passed him the rice, then said something that he found remarkable. "I sense you have an interest in spiritual things."

She gazed directly at him, and the peace he saw in her eyes unsettled him. Griff Topping, undercover FBI agent who infiltrated the criminal world, was confronted by another world he knew nothing about. How to answer? Yesterday, he wasn't interested in spiritual things. Five minutes ago, he cared less about his inner being. At this instant, it seemed nothing else mattered. He found the words. "Yes, I am."

Skeeter shot him a look that asked, Are you nuts?

Eleanor smiled. "Then, tonight will be special for you."

Skeeter looked toward the extra bedroom. "I'm tired and not gonna go."

Eleanor didn't stop smiling. "Artie, please? You might find an answer. If not, you will get to be with me awhile."

Griff ate his chicken in silence, but wondered what it would be like in church. Probably uncomfortable, but surely not as dangerous as Yankeetown. Bottom line, he shouldn't take his guns, so he'd better lock both in the borrowed DEA Cherokee.

Thirty minutes later, Griff turned Eleanor's car into the parking lot of the Seminole Living Water Baptist Church on the Brighton reservation, just a mile from her house. In the front seat, she gave him directions. He felt strange wearing jeans, as Eleanor was dressed in a yellow striped skirt, red blouse, and beaded necklace. When he saw the church, a simple whitewashed building with a steeple, he felt less tense. Griff turned off the van, handed Eleanor the keys.

She placed them in a leather pouch around her waist. "Thank you for driving, Griffin. I'm speaking tonight and those few minutes helped me gather my thoughts."

Griff turned in the seat and grinned. "Ready, Skeeter?"

Skeeter flashed him a cross look, took his time getting out. In a car next to them, a man and a woman were talking to two young boys. One raced up to Griff and offered him a piece of gum. Griff reached to pull a stick out of the pack, and it snapped his finger.

A genuine laugh rose from Griff's belly. Apparently, his sense of humor didn't have to be parked at the church door. Sounds of piano playing grabbed his attention. He caught up with Eleanor and Skeeter, who held the door open for him.

It was only the third time Griff had entered a church. The first was for the funeral of his grandfather, Admiral Topping, at St Paul's Cathedral in London. It was a sad occasion, and the only thing he remembered was holding Gram's hand. The second time was when his brother's son was christened in a Catholic Church. Both churches were large, the ceremonies symbolic. Griff walked out both times and went on with his life, not being changed.

Tonight, a woman played the piano and the music stirred something within him. Every one of the twenty people who assembled there greeted him with a shy smile, but their handshakes were firm and friendly. Eleanor introduced her brother, Artie, saying God had used Griffin to answer a prayer she had prayed every day for over thirty years.

Eleanor guided them to the first pew. Pastor Charles Billie led them in a song from a book. Griff read lyrics about Christ being a solid rock on which they could stand. He recalled that Eleanor's farm was called the Solid Rock Farm.

Pastor Billie stood up and spoke to God, asking him to help many people. Griff didn't know any of them, but their plights were universal. A son without a job. A wife with cancer. And a grandmother who needed nursing care. He closed his eyes—it was more private that way—and listened. A part of him joined in lifting up a plea for God to hear, a plea that somehow the burdens of these people would be lightened.

Tomorrow morning he'd leave with Skeeter and never know if the cancer was healed, if the son found a job. But, he was convinced that Eleanor would know, and that she'd keep praying for them all. Prayer time ended and Pastor Billie invited Eleanor to the front.

She carried a book and opened it. "The Bible is God's word to show us his plan for our lives, to sustain us in all things. Many of you poured out your hearts tonight. There is hope for our struggles and pain. Look at chapter three of Ephesians, verse eighteen. The Apostle Paul prays that we will grasp how wide, and how long—" she paused, "—how high, and how deep is Christ's love. Can you feel it?"

Eleanor closed her eyes. Griff tried to picture what she was talking about, what it all meant. He really couldn't.

She spoke again. "I found Christ's love for me, after I suffered much. Both my parents died, then so did my auntie who cared for me. I was separated from both my brothers. But, today, I thank God for bringing one of them back to me."

Her voice broke. Griff saw tears glistening in her eyes. "We will not always have happy times but, through it all, I know Christ loved me enough to die for me. Because he rose again, he is my source of strength."

She started singing a song, not in English, but an Indian tongue. Others joined in. To Griff's ears, it was haunting, like wind on a dark night. He wanted to ask Skeeter if he knew the words, but from the blank look on his face, he could tell he didn't.

The song ended, but a sense of needing something or someone more played on in Griff's mind until they left the church and he was back in Eleanor's quiet house, lying on the top bunk. Thankfully Skeeter was willing to sleep on the lower bunk, although at the moment he and Eleanor were in the living room catching up on the lost years.

Under a light Indian blanket, Griff raised both arms under his head, his mind a beehive as he contemplated all that had happened in the past month. The drug raid nearly falling apart when the men tried to steal the cocaine. Nick figuring out they weren't police and busting them. A drug case bringing him to Tampa, which was much closer to the Brighton reservation than Apalach. Skeeter wanting to go to the Seminole reservation to find his sister. The Ah-Tah-Thi-Ki museum lady knowing Eleanor, then Griff finding her an hour later.

But, really, he had to go further back. Agent Williams going missing; Griff rescuing Frank from the chalet in the woods; capturing Owen Jones, the mastermind behind the kidnapping plot; Dwight asking for his help, then, because of Skeeter, Griff meeting Dawn. Dawn! He should call, let her know the drug case was a success.

He had to bring Skeeter back to the Dora Ruth, too, even though he'd love to stay on the reservation another day. It was so peaceful, which gave him time to think. Even now, he heard crickets out the window. It wasn't just adrenaline that kept him awake, it was a question. Did these things go his way because of happenstance, or was a higher power orchestrating it? The answer was not as far away as he thought.

In Virginia, Dwight and Christine were also awake. They tried to sleep but, after tossing and turning, they both got up and went downstairs. In the kitchen, Christine fixed hot cocoa and Dwight sat on a stool, watching her pour liquid into cups.

"Be careful, Christy."

Steam rose around her face, curling little edges of her hair. "I'm all right." She set the pan back on the stove, and handed Dwight his cup.

He sipped the chocolate and it was delicious. "Thanks. This should help me sleep."

They were quiet a moment, Christine leaning on the counter. "So, at breakfast this morning, you mentioned the letters to Bernie. And he claims to know nothing about them."

"I believe him. You should have seen how crushed he was. He said that, although he once believed I married you to avoid the draft, he realized he was wrong. Bernie is humiliated that he even told someone back then, who he thinks might have remembered it all these years and is now out to get us."

Christine sighed. "But, he can't remember who he told?"

Dwight drank the cocoa. "That's right. I think we should forget it. I gave the one letter to Agent Topping and mentioned both of them to Neal Longstreet. As our attorney, he'll keep it confidential. Neal does not think they are related to the slander about your father."

Christine rinsed out her cup. "How did he reach that conclusion?"

Dwight joined her at the sink, put his arm around her shoulder. "From forty years of political experience in Washington. Come on, let's sleep. Tomorrow, I'm going over my testimony and need to be mentally sharp. The Department of Justice attorneys are threatening to cross-examine me just like a hostile witness."

THIRTY NINE

The next morning, before the sun rose, Eleanor fed Skeeter and Griff a breakfast of sausage, biscuits, and fresh-squeezed orange juice. She scrambled eggs, sprinkled with green onion. Griff hadn't eaten so much in a long time. After the meal, he thanked Eleanor and said, with real regret, "We'd better get going, Skeeter. It's a long drive to Tampa to pick up Nick so we can take you back to Crystal River and the Dora Ruth." Skeeter's fears ran so deep that Griff had agreed to go along on the Dora Ruth when Skeeter took her back across the Gulf to Apalachicola.

Eleanor shook his hand. "Griffin, I cannot thank you enough for all you have done for me." She looked at Skeeter, who lingered on the front porch. "For both of us."

"I've done nothing. I think your God may be the architect of your reunion. One day, you may meet your other brother. I hope to call soon."

Skeeter and Eleanor cried and hugged and promised to stay in touch. Griff wondered if Skeeter was capable of it. He climbed into the passenger seat, and chattered all the way to Tampa about anything that flew into his mind. Shrimp. The Chinese flooding the markets. No more contact with criminals. Eleanor's cooking. He wanted to help on her farm. His incessant talking was worse than Sal's.

After a while, Griff blocked out his words to mull over how best to tell Dwight he had found Eleanor. No doubt, it would be emotional. On the way, he called Nick and gave their location. When they reached the Tampa DEA office, they waited for Nick to come down and drive them to the Dora Ruth.

On the way to Crystal River, Nick handed Griff a file folder. "We put a copy of Tyler Cooper's arrest photo from Virginia in a photo spread and showed it to the RV park manager." Nick snapped his fingers. "He ID'd Cooper as the driver of the motor home, and the guy who got away in the Suzuki."

Skeeter moaned from the back seat. "I never want to hear from those jerks again." He slammed his hands over his ears, reminding Griff of the "hear no evil" monkey. Griff ignored Skeeter and tapped the file on his knee. "Let me guess. In here, you have a warrant for Cooper, and I get the pleasure of arresting him."

After all they'd been through in the past couple days, Griff liked the sight of Nick's smile. "I thought you might like to tie this one up for us."

Griff opened the folder. "Consider it done. I'll call you when he's in custody."

At the Dora Ruth, Griff and Nick said their goodbyes. They would next see each other when the drug case against Rusty and the others went to trial. He and Skeeter boarded the boat and motored down the Withlacoochee River.

When they were well into the Gulf, it happened. It was so sudden-like, it caught Griff by surprise. Skeeter was staring out the window in the pilot house, the boat on auto pilot. Griff joined him and Skeeter slouched into the Captain's chair. His hands shook so, he couldn't hold them on the wheel. "I'm gettin' away from this."

"You want to sell the Dora Ruth?"

Skeeter stuck an unlit cigarette in his mouth, tried to talk with it hanging in the corner. "Yeah, Yeah. Sell her, move away, far away. Change my name."

Griff prepared himself for what Skeeter would want to make that possible. "If you want to enter the witness protection program, I'm here to tell you that life is no Hollywood movie."

The Dora Ruth rose and fell over gentle waves. A cigarette drooping from his lips, Skeeter reached back and held onto his ponytail like it was a life preserver. "No way. I talked to Eleanor about my life. She wants me to come live with her, give me a new start."

Griff considered it, but wasn't sure that was best for Eleanor. "Doing what?"

"There's stuff I can do, grow lemons, help Felix Tidewater with the fish."

Griff watched a gull fly overhead. With no obvious destination and far from any shore, the bird soaring over the water made Griff realize that he, too, had no firm direction for his life. He shouldn't condemn Skeeter for wanting what Eleanor had—vision, energy, a purpose. Griff had something, at least—a nearly perfect job. It paid well, gave him the satisfaction of helping society, and it wasn't boring. Yet, for the past couple months, it wasn't enough.

Eva had seen it before he did. Tried to tell him that he needed a change. Still, June Livingston wasn't the answer. He had to find it inside himself. So did Skeeter. Before he could ask Skeeter how he would like going to work every day, Griff's cell phone rang. It seemed strange, way out here in the Gulf. There was enough light to see it was Sal.

"Hey, Sal, did you get a bead on Cooper?"

In between the static, Griff heard Sal say something instead about Lev Federov. "His father called, is flying in from Russia. Wants to meet tomorrow. Can you give me backup?"

Griff shouted, "I'm in Florida, on a boat. I'll be back tomorrow night."

Sal growled, "That will be too late. All right, I'll find somebody."

The call ended as abruptly as it began. Griff would have to call Sal later. He returned to Skeeter. "If Eleanor is willing to have you, it makes sense. Are you ready to work for what you want?"

Skeeter broke the cigarette in two. "Eleanor says us kids were all enrolled in the Seminole Tribe by Aunt Clara in 1957. Because I'm a member of the Tribe, I can git a monthly dividend from the casino profits."

Oh, so that's how his mind worked. "How much?"

Skeeter put another cigarette in his mouth, but didn't light it. "Eleanor wasn't sure. She's not for gamblin', but thinks maybe a thousand a month."

Griff lifted a foot onto the footrest, leaned his arms on his knee. "You need Ms. Ahern's permission to move. Since I know your sister, your PO will want my recommendation."

Skeeter tossed the cigarette out the pilot house window, eyed Griff. "What will you tell her?"

"Eleanor Panther is a fine woman, with a strong work ethic and faith."

Skeeter seemed pleased. His lips spread into a big smile. "Yup, that's my sister. So, you're gonna tell her I should go."

Griff weighed his words carefully. Eleanor could put Skeeter to right, if any human could. "I will tell Ms. Ahern that you should not go if you're going to be involved in gambling. I am not talking about your share of the dividend. If the Seminole tribe gives that to you, then you deserve it, I guess. I mean how you spend your time and money. You say you want to do right, Skeeter, but you have not disciplined your life as Eleanor has. I'm concerned about how you're going to keep away from your old ways when you've had fifty years of practice. And whether you're going to be a help to that fine woman or a heartache. What's your answer to that?"

Skeeter looked out over the water and stared for a long while. Griff left him alone to think about what he'd said. Griff had his own questions to answer. When he called Dawn this morning, she agreed to meet him at Skeeter's home and take him to the airport. There were things he wanted to tell her, but would he?

He stared at the moving water, silver and gray, listened to the hum of the Dora Ruth. Griff was enjoying the ride, but he didn't like dwelling on the unknown. Finally, he made one decision. He'd tell Dwight about Eleanor, but not about Skeeter. Not yet. Skeeter had no idea the man he had sought money from was his own brother. Even when Eleanor had mentioned the name Dwight, Skeeter didn't seem to make any connection. And Griff wisely kept his mouth shut.

Darkness fell, but they didn't reach Apalach for a few more hours. An arch of lights across a towering bridge beckoned them to the entrance of the harbor. The breeze vanished, and stars dotted the sky like tiny diamonds. Griff joined Skeeter in the wheel house.

A cigarette still dangled from his mouth. "What if I signed a paper that says I won't gamble? Bein' at some slot machine or poker table is not for me, I'm an outdoors man."

Griff slid in a question he'd been meaning to ask. "How did you like Eleanor's church?"

Skeeter rubbed hair away from his face. "The Creek song was cool." He stopped, looked at Griff. "What'd you think of it?"

"It was all new to me. I had a good feeling about it afterwards."

Skeeter nodded. "Okay, then. I'll go to church."

Griff held up his hand. "Wait a minute, Skeeter. That's not why I asked. It's a big part of your sister's life. If you reject it, I see you going in separate directions from her. Period."

"Yup, Griff. I can do it. No gamblin'. I'll go to church. You tell that to Ms. Ahern."

Griff said nothing. Most likely, Dawn had heard it all before. An ex-offender finds religion, goes straight, for a few months. Still, if he had strong family behind him, caring what path he took, it could make a difference. And Skeeter had something more. He had a praying sister.

The next morning, Griff headed downstairs to the hotel lobby for a continental breakfast, a new lightness in his step. He poured hot coffee in a foam cup. Warm cinnamon buns looked good. He put one on a napkin, and carried breakfast upstairs, avoiding the elevator.

In less than a minute, he ate the bun, then swallowed his coffee. After Dawn finished meeting with Skeeter, she was taking Griff to the airport. She said she wanted to find out what her releasee learned from helping DEA. Griff knew Dawn was good at getting information—well, out of him, at least.

He brushed his teeth, swiped a comb through his hair, and checked himself in the mirror. A few gray hairs edged out by his temples. Probably Dawn hadn't noticed him as a man, let alone his white moustache hairs. Maybe he should shave it, wipe out the invaders. No time now.

Griff checked the room for personal items. Nothing but yesterday's paper. He left the old news behind, picked up his suitcase, and walked to the lobby. Dawn wasn't out front. He set the case by the sliding doors and took a minute to grab another cup of coffee. There were fresh rolls in the warmer. Griff took one and ate it in four big bites. So much for breakfast.

He waited outside by a cluster of palms. The sun, still low in the sky, was not yet unbearable. Griff breathed in the salty air that blew over this coastal town. Last night, the weather forecaster predicted a squall line moving from Texas toward the panhandle later today. He hoped his flight got out ahead of the storm.

As he turned to go inside for a weather update on the approaching storm, a car horn blared, making him jump. It was Dawn. When she rolled down the tinted window he could see her laughing at him. With her hair in a trim braid and her vibrant smile, she made him feel like he was someone other than an FBI agent being driven to the airport by an associate. He tossed his bag in the back, then slid into the passenger seat.

"Hi, Griff. We have to hurry to get you to the airport on time. Sorry I'm late."

She had not called him Agent Topping. He buckled his seatbelt and she roared away.

"Hey Dawn," he joked, "we're not in a Skyhawk on the runway. You don't have to get up to liftoff speed."

"I would feel terrible if you missed your flight."

He felt her speed diminish a bit. "I can think of worse things. I like Florida. Skeeter could always take us for a jaunt on the Dora Ruth."

This time, Dawn smiled. "He's the reason I'm late. Your drug caper shook him pretty badly. Skeeter wants to live with his long-lost sister, who's not lost anymore, thanks to you." Her smile made him feel great.

As she turned west onto Route 98, Dawn glanced at Griff. In that look, he imagined he saw respect. "If all your cases are like the one Skeeter was involved in, you have a very dangerous job."

Griff nodded. "He was more afraid than anyone I've seen in a long time. Hopefully, it scared him away from crime."

"Another time, I'd like to hear how you found Eleanor so quickly. I wonder if it has something to do with your search for organ donors. But, tell me what you think of her."

Hmm. Sounded like she wanted future conversations. He did, too. "Eleanor Panther can greatly influence Skeeter for the better. She works hard, runs her own business. Seems smart and honest."

Dawn kept her eyes on the road, but tilted her head. "A good beginning. Tell me more."

"Their mother, a full-blooded Seminole, was a laundress. She met and married an airman stationed at Homestead Air Force base, near Miami. Mr. Bailey died young, then right afterward, the mother died in a car accident. Eleanor, Skeeter, and a younger brother were in the car. Eleanor was injured, but the two boys weren't. An aunt took care of the three kids, but with Eleanor's injuries, it was too much. Eventually, the boys were placed in foster homes."

Griff looked over at Dawn's hands on the steering wheel. She wore a silver bracelet around her right wrist. A starfish charm danced every time the car hit a bump. It was hard to believe she was going to drop him at the airport and he might not see her again. "Did Skeeter already tell you about his family?"

The way she tilted her head to look at him, while at the same time concentrating on the road ahead, was disconcerting. He wanted her to stop the car, tell her he was not ready to go, just yet.

Dawn passed a truck that spewed diesel fumes. "Glad to get past that wreck. I'd like to get the details from you, since you're the ace investigator."

Griff returned to talking about Skeeter, the reason they had met. "Eleanor always wanted to find the boys, and once she even did find Skeeter, who she calls Artie. For some reason, they got separated again."

Dawn interrupted, "Skeeter told me he was ashamed of being caught for stealing shoes from the foster family. They had him charged. He thought his sister would think he was unworthy."

"I didn't know that."

She laughed. "Of course not. You're a federal agent. He would never admit it to you."

Griff raised an eyebrow. Dawn had sharp instincts. "Anyway, you should see her farm."

Just then he noticed the wedding band on Dawn's left hand, gleaming in the sun. She was talking, but he had to force himself to listen. "Skeeter will not be transferred and permitted to live with his sister until she is totally vetted. Do you think she has any criminal record or associates?"

"No, and I think you should interview Eleanor. You and she have things in common."

Dawn spun her head, gazed at Griff. "What—that we both want her brother to succeed?"

Griff had done it. Her tone was an echo of when she demanded he prove he was an FBI agent. "For one thing, you and Eleanor are strong women. You are both religious. Maybe Skeeter told you, she took us to church. I sensed he was uncomfortable there. If he moves to Brighton, it will have to be with his eyes wide open."

Dawn slowed to pass through the small town of Mexico Beach, but said nothing. Griff turned his head to watch people in beachwear eating ice cream cones. Things were easier here, not so frantic. The surface of his soul felt calm, but inside he was churning—about his future and his feelings for Dawn, and the things he saw and felt at the Seminole church.

Barely through town, Dawn accelerated. "I'm curious. Why do you think I'm religious—because I said that God protects me?"

Maybe he shouldn't have said it like that. His tongue felt glued to the roof of his mouth. Oh, for a cup of java. "From the start, Eleanor talked of her faith. She wouldn't let us eat until she said a blessing on the food. She reminded me of you, maybe because you have her air of confidence. You told me your faith helped you heal from your husband's death. After Sue died, I had nothing to help me, except work."

Griff glanced at her wedding band. "Have you gotten remarried since we first met? I don't remember that you wore a ring before."

She twisted it with her right hand. "No," was all she said. But then she asked a piercing question. "You said Skeeter didn't seem comfortable in church. How about Griff? What was his reaction to the experience?"

How to explain that meeting Eleanor, who believed he was an instrument of God, well, changed him? The way the whole thing went down was not of human hands. Had anyone but Dawn asked that, he would have jokingly said he loved to try new things. But, he was not the same Griff he was even a week ago. "To tell you the truth—no, wait, let me start again. I tell the truth." He was really fumbling. "This will take a couple hours. Maybe we could talk over dinner."

"Your flight leaves in less than two hours. There's no time for lunch, let alone dinner."

Her reply left the door open. "I don't have to be back today. You could take me to a hotel. We're almost to Panama City. Some shut-eye sounds great. Haven't had much of it. I'd like to buy your dinner." He laughed, "After all, you saved me the price of a rental car."

"I have a son, you know."

"I'd love to meet Brian. Maybe he can come, too."

Dawn tapped her fingers on the wheel. The next thing, she pumped the brakes and turned the car around in a marina parking lot. "He's old enough to stay home alone. That way, you and I can talk freely. I want to hear what made Skeeter so fearful, and Brian should not know that. I'll get him a pizza."

The rest of the way, they talked about their jobs, what they liked and didn't. Griff felt tensions evaporate. She dropped him at an inexpensive hotel off the beach, with a promise to pick him up at six o'clock. Griff told her to make reservations. In his room, he changed into a pair of shorts and running shoes. He had some serious running and thinking to do on the beach, before six o'clock.

FORTY

Part of Neal Longstreet's strategy to win Senate votes was for Dwight to be available to the media. Neal conducted a focus poll. The results indicated that people liked Dwight's interview with Kat Kowicki, the way he came across as genuine. When Kat called Friday, Dwight assumed she wanted a follow-up story. He didn't want to offend her by having A.J. present, when he didn't the first time, so he arranged for her to come to his office at five-thirty. Gladys agreed to wait, in case anything arose he needed help with.

Kat was punctual. Gladys offered her tea, she declined. Dwight saw no cameraman this time. In his office, she took a seat, and he went to his chair behind the desk.

She went for his jugular, which nearly knocked the breath right out of his lungs. "I got a letter today that says your wife killed a man in Washington, D.C. I am not sure I believe it, so I thought it best to talk with you immediately."

Dwight was more than speechless. He felt ill. Silently he prayed for wisdom in dealing with this. The last thing he should do was exactly what he felt like doing—throwing Kat from his office. But, he knew that truth was the best course. She had proved to be a straight arrow, even if she was relentless in getting the story. Her interview had even helped him, and he had helped her by giving her an exclusive. Maybe she'd be reasonable now.

"I appreciate your coming to me. I assure you it's not what you think. May I see the letter?"

Kat pulled a thin light blue piece of paper from her folder and handed it to Dwight. His eyes darted over the few typewritten, hate-ridden lines. Of course, it was unsigned. He handed it back to Kat.

"Christine will not mind my telling you what really happened. One night, when she was sixteen years old, she was driving too fast in D.C. There was freezing drizzle that night. A homeless man stumbled into her path. She couldn't avoid hitting him, and he died. Because her father had diplomatic immunity, she was never charged. Instead, they sent her home to Austria. At the time, the media never covered the story. The next day was President Nixon's inauguration."

Kat slid the letter into her file. Dwight looked at her. "What becomes of that letter?"

"Nothing. Your wife was a juvenile, and I'm going to shred it. Juvenile records are sealed. The public has no right to know. Besides, you are the nominee, not Christine Pendergast. This letter is way below the belt. I'll let you know if I get more like it."

She stood. "If you don't mind, I have another story to finish before my deadline."

Dwight extended his hand to her. "Ms. Kowicki, when you first showed up at my garage, I was determined not to cooperate. Experience, mind you, nothing personal. Now, I don't know how to thank you. With your ethics and character, you're going to have a brilliant career, of that I am sure."

He saw her out. Gladys had on her coat, and said a goodnight. Dwight was left alone with a decision to make before he got home. What, if anything, should he tell Christine about this latest letter?

After Griff ran on the beach, he showered and slept. As he waited for Dawn in the lobby, he actually felt human. In cotton slacks and collared shirt, he hoped the restaurant was casual. He didn't want to leave either of his guns in the hotel room, so he wore both. One around his ankle, one at his waist under his shirt. Guess those guns meant this wasn't a date, but a chance to wrap up Skeeter's case.

A few minutes before six, Dawn arrived in a salsa-red Toyota, which Griff assumed must be her P-car. She stepped out and gave him the keys. "I don't mind if you drive. It's close."

Griff opened her door. "Better give me directions. You know, men never stop to ask."

Dawn laughed and he felt great. Behind the wheel, he glanced at her left hand. No ring. He followed her directions to a brightly tiled building. The sign read Antonio's.

"I thought you might be tired of seafood. This place has delicious northern Italian food. Brian and I always come here for our birthdays."

Griff turned off the car. "Is today your birthday?" He wished he had a present for her.

"Not even close. It's in March. A spring baby, my mother always said. I think that's why she named me Dawn."

Inside the restaurant, smells of garlic and spices filled the air. His stomach started to growl. At the hotel, he purposely ate nothing, except a candy bar, in anticipation of a wonderful meal. Seated in a booth, the lighting was just right. Fortunately for Griff, their server brought a plate of warm garlic bread and marinara sauce for dipping. Before he grabbed one, his mind rewound to Skeeter taking that chicken leg before Eleanor prayed.

He'd wait. "How is Brian?"

"Eating a mushroom and chicken pizza about now and loving every minute of it."

He kept a starving look from his face, but the smell of fresh bread was getting to him.

Dawn put a napkin on her lap. "Mind if I say a blessing for the food?"

He didn't, so she did with her eyes closed. Griff shut his and when she said "amen," he opened them to see her looking at him, her eyes shining. It was not hard to picture her walking alongside him on the beach, an orchid in her hair. With slim fingers, she took some bread. He followed her lead.

The conversation took off, figuratively, as they shared stories of learning to fly. Griff's first solo flight invigorated him. Hers was frightening. "It was easy getting my plane off the ground, and much harder to get it back on the ground."

They laughed, and the server took their order. Antipasto salad for the appetizer, eggplant and artichoke linguine for her and grilled sirloin for Griff. And coffee, plenty of it.

Over salad, Griff told her about Skeeter being held hostage by drug traffickers. Dawn covered her mouth with her hand. By the time he reached the part where Nick blasted them with his carbine, Dawn put down her fork and stared at him.

"You could have been killed."

Griff shrugged. "My job isn't always dangerous. Some days I whittle away behind my desk."

"I'm going to pray more often for you."

She prayed for him? Griff didn't ask why, just ate his steak. "That's what Eleanor said. It's funny, growing up, I never attended church, never prayed."

Dawn twirled linguine against a spoon. "What about your family?"

"Weren't interested. I thought religion was something parents did for their kids, just like they made 'em take music lessons, or anything else they needed to learn. And we just weren't the music lessons or church type. The other night in Eleanor's church, I saw things differently. It was as if another dimension opened. Like kids having a rhythm in them that helps them play an instrument." He didn't add, "But that was never nurtured in me."

Dawn held his gaze. Did his blithering make sense? Her black eyes reminded him of the night sky with glittering stars. His appetite suddenly disappeared.

"You astonish me, Griff. When we first met, I reacted to your being an FBI agent. Some agents I meet are tough and hardboiled. The constant crime they deal with wrings them out. You have shown me a side that I find, well, interesting."

He smiled. "It's your turn to tell me more."

"Did you know Pascal, the French physicist and philosopher, wrote that we try to fill the empty place within us with our surroundings? He said these are inadequate, because the infinite abyss can only be filled by God himself."

Griff was not sure he understood. "I read fiction, not philosophy. Is it something like that dimension I felt? It's hard to grasp when you've been going on logic all your life."

"That's what distinguishes faith from science. It's knowing in your heart something you can't see or prove. Have you ever read the Bible?"

Griff shook his head.

Dawn's eyes held his, as if she was finished talking. Then, she added, "The Bible describes faith as the substance of things hoped for, the evidence of things unseen." She looked at him for a long moment, "I had a search similar to yours, Griff, but I won't tell you about it tonight. A friend suggested I get a Bible and, this past year, I read the Bible through."

Griff thought Dawn seemed to understand things he didn't, even about himself. Was he on a search? "I guess I could order one over the internet."

She drew something the size of a deck of cards from her purse. "I hope you don't mind. After our earlier conversation, I brought this for you. It was given to me years ago by my Sunday School teacher."

Dawn flipped a few pages and showed him some words in red. "This is Revelation, the last book in the Bible." Her finger drew his eyes to the precise words. "Jesus Christ says he knocks at the door of our lives. If we open the door, he comes to live within us. I have seen some people invite Christ to fill that abyss and find God, but others never do."

She removed her hand, left the little book in his. Griff liked the feel of it. "I don't have a gift for you."

"No, no. It's not like that. Besides, you're treating for dinner, remember?"

Okay, he had said that. "I'll read it, Dawn."

"If you have questions, I would be happy to talk to you anytime. But, that's a conversation for another time. Right now, I would love some espresso."

Another mention of talking to each other in the future. Gone were the professional barriers and mistrust he felt in past conversations. He motioned for the waiter to take away their plates and placed new drink orders.

In a few minutes, Griff sipped coffee, this time decaf, and Dawn her espresso. "If Skeeter moves to Brighton and lives with Eleanor, what are the risks?"

Griff cradled the cup. "The casino down the road could be a problem, but he says he'll sign an agreement not to go in. As an enrolled member of the Seminole tribe, Skeeter will receive a monthly dividend, which might help him meet living expenses. Eleanor could tell him he has to work if he lives with her. She refuses to accept the dividend because it comes from gambling, which she feels deprives some people."

"I'm going to call her tomorrow and arrange to meet. She sounds like good people."

Their eyes dropped to their cups. They sipped their coffee, until Griff reached out from the silence. It was too much like being in an elevator. "Dawn, we did not meet by accident. We're both widowed, fly airplanes, and work in the justice system. Am I right?"

Her eyes did not meet his. He took that to mean she was unsure. Griff tried again, with what he hoped was a less threatening question.

"Does your work ever bring you to Washington, D.C.?"

"No."

Silence bloomed again like dandelions in a perfect lawn.

Dawn looked up at him now. "Will yours bring you back here?"

"Not any time soon. Maybe to Tampa when the drug case goes to trial if they need me to testify, but that's hours away from here."

Her eyes looked toward the door. Griff thought she might be anxious to leave, but he couldn't. Not yet. They had to grasp the moment, even if there were no words to describe it. He wanted the trip to the airport tomorrow to be fun.

Dawn tapped a finger against her cup. "There is a possibility I will be flying to Virginia."

"When?"

She pursed her lips. "I'm not sure, but sometime in the next few months."

"Is your family there?"

"No. Brian wants me to take him to see the Virginia Military Institute, for college."

That was in Lexington, a straight shot down I-81. Not far from his home. Griff swallowed. "That is an historic place."

Dawn shook her beautiful hair. "I promised Brian, if we went that far, we'd visit the Air and Space Museum and Arlington Cemetery, too."

Now, they were getting closer to the place he wanted to be, and he realized his feelings for her were strong. If he told her so tonight, it might frighten her away. Her putting on a wedding ring, taking it off again, troubled him. She was not ready for a relationship. Maybe he wasn't either, not really.

Griff touched the top of her hand. "I would consider it an honor to meet Brian, be your tour guide to FBI Headquarters and Quantico Marine Base. I have an in at the White House, you know."

"You mean the Secret Service."

"Think higher."

Dawn leaned back in the booth and laughed. "I told you before, Griff, you are a most interesting man."

Griff arrived home Saturday at four o'clock. He played several messages, one from his mother and dad, one from his grandmother in England. He called Gram first. Her words were coolly British, but her tone was warm. She missed him. Gram always called him Griffin, just like Eleanor had.

As they talked, Griff flipped through a stack of mail. "I've been away on a case. A funny thing, I missed you, too. When should I come for a visit?"

"Laddie, you get yourself on the first plane over here. I'm not any younger, you know."

"Nonsense, your legs are strong. You outwalked me to Land's End last time."

Gram's laugh was soft. "That was last year. Sadie has your room all aired."

Sadie was the housekeeper who had lived with Gram since Grandpa died. "I should be able to get there for your birthday. Would you like that?" He did not know her age, she never told it, but he guessed she was eighty-something.

She did like it. "You get a reservation, call me back today."

Today? That sounded urgent. "Gram, are you all right?"

"You go now, call me back."

They hung up and Griff felt a strange sensation. He thought about all the times she had come to mind recently. Now, Gram was calling him, practically urging him to get there by tomorrow. Not only had his Gram lived through bombings in World War II, she had been in the OSS, worked on signals and codes. And his grandfather, Admiral Topping, was considered a British war hero. He and Gram continued their work in the intelligence service until they retired.

They traveled the world, painting what they saw. Alone in Cornwall, Gram still painted, but now all her paintings were of the sea. On the internet, he booked an e-ticket for England. He called her and gave her the news. She sounded happy.

Griff was not one to call home, but perhaps his parents knew something about Gram. Mom and Dad didn't answer. Neither one had a cell phone yet. Next, he called Wally, the lost boy from Sudan who worked at Rob's Deli. "Mr. Topping, you are kind to make time for me."

Griff doodled on a pad. "Have you heard from the college?"

"That is why I called you, with good news."

"You got the scholarship?" He had meant to check, but forgot.

"Yes, Mr. Topping, and I have been accepted into your college."

He felt wonderful for Wally. "It will be your college, now."

Silence, then, "Mr. Topping." A hesitation.

Griff put a stop to that. "Wally, I asked you to call me Griff. Will you?"

Wally sighed into the phone. "It is a sign of respect to call our elders, mister."

Griff laughed. "Whatever makes you comfortable. Wally, I am proud and happy for you." He would have to find a way to show it to him. Before he could suggest a fitting celebration, Wally asked, "Since you feel that way, may I tell you something?"

"Sure, anything."

"The college has what they call orientation for new students and their parents. I was wondering—"

"How can I help?" Maybe Wally needed extra money or new clothes. Either one would be no problem. His checkbook was in the study he carved out of the smaller bedroom, but he had plenty to write a check today.

Wally cleared his throat. "Mr. Topping, if you cannot help, I will understand." The final words rushed out, like water poured from a pitcher. "Will you come with me to parents' day?"

Blood rose to Griff's face. "Yes." He added, completely sincere, "It would be my honor."

Griff recalled when he first met Wally. He'd been impressed with the young man and thought Wally had what it took to succeed. He needed a college degree to open doors. Griff felt great satisfaction. "Let me know what night you are available this week. We'll go out for pizza, to celebrate and plan for parents' day."

Wally relaxed. "Mr. Griff, I will check my work schedule. Thank you so much."

Griff placed the receiver onto the base of the phone. He had another call to make, to someone who had not called him. His heart urged him to call Dawn, let her know he was home. Instead, he used the land line to call Judge Pendergast.

"Mrs. Pendergast, this is FBI Agent Griff Topping. Can the judge take my call?"

She hesitated for a second. "I'll find him."

When Dwight came to the phone, he was out of breath. "Up to my elbows, replacing brake fluid on my GTO."

Griff laughed. "I thought you might say you were up to your eyebrows in alligators. The kind with sharp teeth who live and work in D.C."

Dwight breathed steadily now. "Them, too. Did you call about my nomination?"

"Sir, I have some news you must hear in person."

"How quickly can you get here?"

"As fast as my truck can fly."

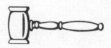

FORTY ONE

Dwight rushed to finish bleeding his brake lines and adjusting the brakes before Agent Topping came over. He wiped up spilled fluid, and put away his tools and his creeper on a shelf he built in the garage. In coveralls, he passed Christine in the kitchen, which smelled wonderful.

"That greasy jumpsuit goes in the laundry room."

"Not now. I'm in a hurry." He took the stairs two at a time, oblivious to her protests. After washing up, he changed into slacks and shirt. A thought burned in his mind. Griff's news might involve one of two things—his confirmation or the letter Kat brought yesterday to his office. Why else would a federal agent insist on driving right over?

Griff had the only other letter Christine received, but Dwight wondered how Griff could have heard about the one from yesterday. This morning he had casually mentioned to Christine that Kat had stopped by, but he was still looking for the right moment to tell her about the existence of *this* blue letter.

The doorbell rang. He rushed down the stairs to answer it before Christine could. On his front steps, in suit and tie stood Bernie, holding a silver gift bag. "For your anniversary."

Dwight swallowed. Was his wedding anniversary today? His mind did some quick math. No. It was next week. His hand hovered on the knob, then Christine's voice behind him said, "Bernie, what are you doing standing out there? Come on in."

That was Christine, always hospitable. Dwight let Bernie in, then closed the door.

Bernie handed Christine the gift. "I was on my way home from our annual Saturday partner's meeting. Saw the garage door open." He shuffled from side to side. "It's early, but tomorrow Rita and I are driving down to Smith Mountain Lake. I'm taking her away for a few days."

It sounded to Dwight like Bernie had to get his wife out of town, but he was not about to ask. He just wanted Bernie to leave before Griff Topping arrived. Bernie never just dropped by, so why today? He should have known that Christine's people sense, not to mention her doctorate in psychology, would prevent her from letting Bernie's hint go by.

She put her hands on her hips. "I'm making dinner, but I have a minute. Come on in, Bernie. How is Rita? I left a message a couple days ago and she never called."

Dwight intercepted Christine's hospitality and concern. "Christine, open Bernie's gift. Then he can get home to Rita and their packing."

Christine's blue eyes narrowed and she looked unhappy with him. Well, too bad. He moved to her side, put his hands in the bag, and lifted out a beautiful crystal clock. His wife placed it on the mantle, moving a photo to make room. "Bernie," she smiled, "it is lovely. Thank Rita for us."

Bernie ran fingers through sparse hair. "I will. Rita," he stopped. "She needs—"

Dwight realized the gift was a way for Bernie to come over and talk. Maybe he should call Griff, ask him to wait to stop over. He motioned to the sofa. "Christine, is there any coffee?"

"I'll get some. With sugar, right Bernie?"

He nodded, then took a seat. "Dwight, I don't know where to begin. Rita has been acting difficult ever since we got the place at the lake."

Dwight did not mention the call Rita had made to Christine, accusing her and Dwight of pressuring them to buy it. "Are you sure she wanted to buy it, Bernie?"

His friend looked worn. "I thought so. I've always wanted to live on the water and thought being close to our good friends would give her a boost. She sees the glass half-empty. Maybe I made a mistake purchasing it, but I love it there." When he looked at Dwight, his glass eye moved as well. "We both needed something different, with our daughter getting married."

Dwight looked toward the kitchen, where Christine was getting coffee. "I can relate to that." He started to tell Bernie about how he and Christine had begun volunteering at the church for just that reason, when Christine returned with the coffee.

She handed Bernie his coffee, then sat next to Dwight and gave him a cup. Dwight sipped his. "Maybe you should take Rita someplace besides the lake. Talk things out."

Bernie stared into his coffee. "You may be right."

The doorbell rang. Dwight literally jumped off the sofa. Bernie looked up, alarmed. "I hope it's not Rita. If she thinks I've been talking about her, she'll be angry."

Christine remained seated. "Nonsense. You came by to bring us a gift, nothing more."

Christine took Dwight's coffee, and he answered the door. It was Griff. "Agent Topping, please come in."

Griff must have seen Bernie because he asked, "Is this a good time?"

Before taking the agent into the study, Dwight introduced Griff to Bernie. Bernie asked Griff something Dwight found odd. "Agent Topping, were you just in Tampa, Florida?"

"I was. Your name is familiar, but I don't recognize you."

Bernie shook his head. "That's because you spoke with me on the phone."

Dwight wondered if Griff contacted Bernie as part of the FBI's background investigation for his Supreme Court nomination. If Griff was assigned to that, Dwight would not have confided in him.

Griff stepped back. "I remember. Your client, Tyler Cooper, owns the motor home we seized after it was used in a drug conspiracy case."

Dwight's mind tumbled. Before he could stop himself he blurted, "Tyler Cooper! Bernie, that's your client I let out on a bond because you argued he was an upstanding citizen with strong ties to the community." He turned to Griff. "I did not know you were involved in that case. Is that what you want to see me about?"

Bernie set down his coffee cup. "It is highly improper for an FBI agent to have ex-parte contact with a federal judge at his home. Dwight, I know nothing about Mr. Cooper's involvement in a Florida drug case. He told me he was not a part of that in any way."

Griff waved his hands in front of him. "Let me clear up a few things. First, the pending Virginia drug case Mr. Spitzer has before you, Judge, I have nothing to do with. Secondly, I am not here to talk about Mr. Spitzer or his client. Further, I don't want to know what Mr. Spitzer has to say about his client or what Mr. Cooper told him, because I am a witness in the Florida case." Griff leveled a look at Dwight. "I am here for other reasons, personal ones."

Bernie was not convinced. "I don't believe you. When I told you I knew Judge Pendergast personally, you never said you did."

Griff's eyebrows shot up his forehead. "You're calling me a liar?"

Christine tugged Bernie's sleeve. "This FBI agent is helping Dwight on something related to his confirmation. Bernie, an apology may be in order."

Dwight had let things spin out of control. He had never seen Bernie so emotional. His life with Rita must really be teetering on the brink. "Bernie, don't you trust me, after knowing me and working with me all these years, not to have ex-parte contact on a case?"

Bernie looked wounded, like he did when he came home from Vietnam, only these wounds weren't as easily treated. Still, he put out a hand to the agent. "I don't know what I was thinking. Sorry."

Griff shook his hand. "No problem."

"Bernie, Mr. Topping and I have an appointment. I thought he was at the door when you arrived."

Bernie shrugged, and Christine looked at Dwight. "Perhaps, if your meeting with Mr. Topping won't take too long, Bernie could go home and return with Rita. Join us for dinner."

Dwight decided that might just work to defuse the whole situation. "How about seven thirty?"

Bernie looked sheepish. "I am sure Rita would love to come to dinner. I promised to take her out."

Dwight took Griff to his study and shut the door, motioned to Griff to take a seat across on one of two armchairs. Griff settled himself and Dwight sat in the other. "Sorry about the grilling Bernie gave you. It's unlike him. Is your visit connected to Christine's letters?"

Griff looked puzzled. "No, why?"

"I have good reason to believe we've not heard the last of it, but let me get to that later. With my nomination hearing next week, the pressure is on. Did you see the TV ad yesterday that linked my father-in-law to the Nazi party? The special interest group ran it even though the allegation was proved to be a lie."

The agent twisted in his chair, stroked his moustache, and looked puzzled. Dwight sensed he had something sensitive on his mind. To help, Dwight said, "Whatever you wanted to see me about, I am ready to listen."

Griff drew in a breath. "Your Honor, I've been in Florida on a drug case. The last twenty-four hours I rode a shrimp boat through the Gulf of Mexico, then flew back to see you. I have no idea what is being said about you. Respectfully, I wouldn't put up with it, but then I'm not a judge, so I'll never be asked to."

From his desk, Dwight picked up a paperweight. It was one his father gave him when he became a federal judge. "This is a replica of a
Snark rocket that my father and I watched lift off at Cape Canaveral
when I was a boy. Dad helped design it, and inspired me to reach as
high as this rocket, no matter the difficulties. He never said no matter
the cost, because sometimes the costs are too great."

Griff took the paperweight, studied it. "Grandfather Topping used
to say something similar."

The agent handed back the rocket, and Dwight felt his steady look.
Was he finally going to tell him why he came?

"Judge, we are fortunate our families encouraged us to use our tal-
ents. Some folks have no parents to give them proper guidance."

"I sense you're not being philosophical. Does this involve my family?"
Dwight noticed a manila envelope on Griff's knee. "Is that for me?"

"Yes, but, because of your hearing next week, I will share what I
believe has the greatest bearing on your getting a kidney. Are you okay
with that?"

Dwight traced the rocket ship with his finger. If he knew anything
embarrassing to the President, he would have to reveal it. If he did not
know, but others did, there was a risk it could leak, and cause damage.
He decided to question Griff as he might a witness. In doing so, he
might violate the unwritten rule to which every lawyer subscribed:
Never ask a question you don't know the answer to.

"Have you found my brother, Arthur Bailey?"

Griff's hands curled the envelope. "I have no doubt, sir."

"Is he a possible donor for a kidney?"

"I am not sure. His lifestyle is such that it might be prudent to pass.
I have found someone who may be a better match."

That seemed impossible. "You're no medical doctor. How can that
be?"

Griff reached inside the envelope, drew out a photo and handed it
to Dwight. "This is your sister, Eleanor. She did not die in the car accident as you and your parents thought. She is alive in Florida. Did you
have any idea your mother was a full-blooded Seminole Indian?"

His sister was alive? All these years and he never knew it! Dwight
thought Arthur might be alive somewhere, but, until he needed a kidney, he'd never made a real effort to find him. He thought that his
parents wouldn't like it. They never talked of Dwight's adoption. He
was their son and that was the end of it.

Now, to learn he had a sister! Dwight looked at her photo. At the sight of her face, tears blurred his eyes. He blinked. Her eyes were his eyes. Dark hair, graying now, was pulled back, revealing her ears. There was no mistake—those diamond-shaped earlobes were just like his.

Griff leaned forward. "I have so much to tell you about her, all good. Want to hear it?"

Dwight couldn't tear his eyes from the photo. His sister! He nodded, but like dry peanuts, the words caught in his throat.

"I took Eleanor's picture with my digital camera and printed it out on my photo printer. She is a fine woman, lives on the Seminole Indian Reservation at Brighton, Florida. Runs a turtle and tilapia farm. Seems to be a thriving business. If you eat tilapia, it may be some your own sister raised."

Dwight wiped his eyes. "Does she know about me?"

"You asked me to keep it confidential and I have. Neither Arthur nor Eleanor knows who you are. I will tell you, Arthur and Eleanor have been reunited. On her own, she told me she had a baby brother whom she tried to find, but because he was adopted, she was unable to. I told Eleanor that I would help her find you. She was interested, gave me her phone number."

Griff reached into the envelope and handed Dwight a paper with her name, Eleanor Panther, Solid Rock Farm, and other vital information.

"Is Panther her married name?"

Griff shook his head. "She never married. It is your Indian clan name. Eleanor was raised by missionaries and, when they died, she took your mother's last name. Eleanor showed me a photo of your mother. She looks like her."

From his toes to his scalp, each one of Dwight's nerves pricked. In every way, finding a sister he thought was dead was more spectacular than being nominated to the Supreme Court. He had to talk with her.

But, after all these years, did she really want to know him? Dwight never knew he was Native American; he always thought he was half Italian. His parents never corrected that belief. Did they know the truth?

"Griff, could you grant me one more favor? Call Eleanor, tell her you found me and that I want to call her."

"I understand your hesitancy. Let me just say that Eleanor is the very meaning of the word grace, only magnified. She is more than kind;

she exudes a light. I think it's because of her faith in God. I'm not a churchgoing man, so this is all new to me."

Griff stopped, as if thinking and remembering. "In her home, I felt like family. After spending time with her, I want to learn more about what she believes. If you meet her, I have no doubt she will want to give you a kidney if there's any way that she can. You will feel like you have known her your whole life."

A soft knock disturbed them. Dwight got up, opened the door an inch. It was Christine. "I know you're busy." Her hands were behind her back. "I have to show you something."

"Both of us?"

Christine's blue eyes flashed, an icy contrast to pink spots on her cheeks. "Yes."

Dwight let her in. As she brought her hands around the front, Dwight spied a bit of light blue. He grabbed at it. "You got another threatening letter in the mail!"

She pulled it back from his grip. "Not exactly."

Griff stood and walked over to her. "Mrs. Pendergast, what is it then?"

She fluttered the half-folded note. "I found this, in Bernie's gift bag. Dwight, you were so quick to pull out the clock, you missed it. I am sure it's the same paper as the other two letters I received."

Griff held out his hand. "May I see it?"

She let him have it, then said, "It's Bernie's writing: 'Best wishes to our best friends.' He signed Rita's name. Dwight, what should we do? In a few minutes, they're coming for dinner."

Griff studied the note. "The last letter was typed. I doubt Bernie would leave one in his handwriting. It may be a terrible coincidence."

Christine straightened her hair with both hands, and sighed. "What if it's a cry for help? He wants to get caught, so he drops by. He never does that. Dwight," she grabbed his hand and held it. "You heard how upset he was to find the FBI agent was here. It all fits."

Dwight cleared his throat. "When I talked to Bernie, he claimed to know nothing about any letters. The reporter, Kat, received a letter on the same paper and showed it to me yesterday. I had not figured out a way to tell you, Christy. Besides, she decided to do nothing with it."

She gripped his hand so tightly, Dwight's fingers hurt. "More about Daddy?"

"No, worse. Whoever wrote it wanted the world to know about your accident."

Christine leaned against him, then straightened. "God has forgiven me for that." She quickly told Griff about the man who died as a result of her careless driving.

Griff seemed to tense. "There are too many letters. Could I see the one sent to Kat?"

Anger at his friend shook Dwight. His voice was hard. "Kat was going to shred it. It was on light blue paper, though. The same as the one in Bernie's gift bag. I can't believe he would stoop so low."

The doorbell rang. Christine pulled away. "Dwight, they're here."

Dwight turned to Griff for another favor. "Would you stay to dinner? It might ease the strain, and help us get to the bottom of this. I don't know what else to do."

Dwight heard himself talking, but inside he wanted to lash out at Bernie, ask him why he lied to him at breakfast, when it was him the whole time who was hurting them. The agent hadn't answered. Maybe Christine's cooking could tempt him.

"My wife is a gourmet cook." Then, turning to Christine, "Honey, what's on the menu tonight?"

She smiled bravely. "There's plenty for five. Garlic-crusted tilapia, roasted potatoes and romaine salad with raspberries and walnuts."

Griff smiled at Dwight. "I love tilapia, don't you, Judge?"

FORTY TWO

If Christine had seen the note on the blue stationery in Bernie's gift bag, she never would have invited them for dinner. It was too late to take back the invitation. Bernie and Rita sat talking with Dwight in the living room. Christine said a perfunctory hello, then retreated to her kitchen. Just now, the seaside blue she had painted the kitchen last year mocked her.

Say—was the color she painted her walls the same blue as Bernie's note? She wanted to run and ask the agent, who had stowed the paper in his pocket. Christine set the broiler for two minutes to toast her rolls and returned to the living room. "Griff, would you mind helping me?"

Even if he was searching for Dwight's brother, it was unfair to ask him to dinner with strangers. When he joined her in the kitchen, she whispered, "Hold that note against my wall."

"What?"

She gestured to his pocket. "Quick, before Bernie comes in. Put the note Bernie had in our gift," she pointed with her finger, "next to the refrigerator."

Griff did, yet she was sure he questioned her sanity. But, not for long. The pale color of the blue paper was identical to the paint on her kitchen wall.

Griff held it in place for another moment. "With so many shades of blue, I find this odd."

Christine put a finger to her lips. "That's what I thought. In fact, Rita—"

"What about Rita?"

Christine started at the sound of Bernie's voice. "Oh," she folded the blue note with her hand, "Griff was admiring the color of my walls. I was telling him Rita helped me pick it out."

Like the ace undercover agent she heard he was, Griff seized the moment. "That's right. As a pilot, to me it's the color of sky in early morning, after the pink has gone."

Bernie grunted. "FBI agent, flyboy, and poet to boot. Some guys just have it all, don't they? So, Christine, why do you need his help? Is he also a famous chef?"

Smells of burning bread caught her attention. "My rolls!" She grabbed a hot pad, opened the oven door and slid out the pan. "That was close. Bernie, you saved my dinner."

She ignored Bernie's sarcasm and redirected everyone's attention to the meal. "Griff, please put ice in the glasses and, Bernie, you can pour strawberry lemonade." Christine assembled the rest of her dinner and conscripted Griff and Bernie to set the table. She slipped his gift note into a drawer.

Her guests seated around the table, she said, "I'm going to say a blessing."

Bernie shot her a look, which she blocked by shutting her eyes. What to say? Her Grandmother prayed in German, and Christine's mind converted those words to English. It didn't sound right. She hoped the meaning was clear. "Father, bless the food and those who eat it. Amen."

Christine wanted the presence of God, but all she felt was nerves frayed to the breaking point and a desire to question Bernie. Was he so jealous about Dwight rising to the Supreme Court that he would stop at nothing to hurt them? Of course, he wrote the letters. He knew about her accident, he told her long ago that Dwight only married her to avoid Vietnam. He knew everything that was in the letters.

Instead, she asked him to pass the potatoes. Dwight tried to take the pressure off, by telling about a time he became a witness in a drug gang trial.

The agent seemed interested. "I hadn't heard that, Judge."

Dwight smiled. "The government's main witness was on the stand, a gang member who hoped for a light sentence. From the bench, I saw the witness keep looking to the rear of the courtroom. The prosecutor wasn't getting the answer he expected. At first, I thought someone was back there coaching him."

Griff asked a polite question to further the story. Dwight explained he saw a man in the last row of spectators. "He was not coaching. Both hands were around his throat, which he pretended to be choking."

Christine watched as Dwight's rendition of the choking man reddened his face. Was he trying to give Bernie a message? She could barely swallow her food, while her husband was on a roll. "After I whispered to my marshal to seal the courtroom, I dismissed the jury, and ordered the marshals to arrest the spectator. He was charged with obstructing justice, for intimidating a witness."

Griff asked for lemonade. "How did you like being cross-examined by a defense lawyer?"

Dwight took a bite of tilapia. "Christine, this is fabulous. I held my own. The spectator was a gang member, and it was satisfying to see him convicted."

Christine ignored Bernie's glum looks and examined Griff's face. She guessed he was in his thirties. He had the bearing of an honest man. She knew Griff was a widower and thought he was too young and good looking to spend his life alone. The whole night was surreal. Rita hadn't spoken one word since hello. Trying to take her mind off the letters, Christine took inventory of her daughter Veronica's single friends. Maybe she could make a match for Griff. By the time she ruled out every single woman she knew, Dwight's plate was empty. How long had he been sitting there, staring at her? She rose quickly. "I'll get the coffee."

Christine poured cream in a pitcher and put a silver spoon in the sugar bowl. Dark roast coffee went into Blue Willow cups. A sudden idea exploded in her mind. Yes, she would try it, come what may.

She set something else on the tray. In the dining room, she arranged cups before her guests, then the creamer and sugar by Bernie. The only item remaining on the tray was a thin blue paper—Bernie's note. Christine left it there, and left the tray on the table. No one seemed to see it.

Rita lazily stirred sugar into her coffee. "Have you found a dress for the wedding?"

Apparently, Rita had finally found something to talk about. "Yes to your daughter's wedding. No to Mandy's. How about you?"

Rita was describing her teal silk dress when Dwight interjected, "Rita, did Bernie convey our thanks for the anniversary gift? The clock is really nice. Christine put it on the mantle."

Rita appeared dazed. "What gift?"

Christine knew she had to push the issue, but she was unprepared for Rita's reaction. With two fingers, Christine lifted the blue note. "Bernie dropped it off, along with this note. It didn't look like your signature."

Rita reached over, snapped the note from Christine's fingers and quickly read the few words. When Rita looked up, Christine saw the beginning of the end to their close relationship.

Rita tore the note in two. Bernie reached for it, "What are you doing?"

His wife tore the two pieces into smaller ones. "Christine, I never sent this." She tore the paper until it was confetti. She scooped these into her purse. "Bernie, don't ever do that again."

Rita stood. "I wish you a happy anniversary. After so many years of marriage, it is a miracle you're still together." She snapped her fingers at Bernie. "Are you coming, or are you going to sit there looking like an idiot?"

Bernie's face was crimson. Griff poured himself a cup of coffee, and Christine imagined he wanted to disappear.

Rita edged toward the front door. "Well?"

Dwight tried to salvage the situation. "Rita, I am sure Bernie meant well."

"You know nothing about it. I want to go home. Bernie?"

Dwight stood. "You've been our friends for years."

Much like an actress about to leave the stage, Rita drew herself up. "With what my husband has been pulling lately, I fear that is about to change."

Bernie rose slowly, set his napkin next to his plate. His voice shaking, he nodded first to Christine, then to Dwight. "Linda's wedding has us both stressed. If you will excuse us. Good to finally meet you, Griff."

Dwight ushered Rita and Bernie to the front door. He talked to them in soothing words, saying what, Christine knew not. She slumped into a chair, looked at Griff. "I can't believe she did that."

Griff put down his coffee. "You ought to work for the FBI. When I saw that blue note come to the table, I knew something would erupt. I wouldn't have thought to use that move."

When the front door closed, Dwight joined them at the table, a stunned look on his face. Christine leaned over, took his hand. "Why did she tear up that note?"

The FBI agent rose. "I think you discovered who wrote the letters. Would you mind if I used the telephone in your study? I need to make a phone call on a matter we spoke of earlier."

Dwight nodded. "On Bernie's way out, I urged him to ask Rita if she wrote the other letters."

Griff dipped his head, "Excuse me," and left them.

Christine rushed into her husband's arms. "What did I do wrong?"

Dwight stroked her hair, hugged her to him. He lifted her chin, so she looked up into his eyes. "Nothing Christy. We'll find a way to get through this confirmation, I promise you. I just never thought we'd be facing opposition from someone who was supposed to be a good friend."

In Dwight's study, Griff dialed the phone. He was glad to escape and leave Dwight and Christine alone. After the roller coaster of emotions in Yankeetown, then with Eleanor, this madcap evening wore on his tired body and mind. He had little sleep since he returned from Tampa, and the two cups of coffee he drank at dinner raced through his system like rocket fuel.

Eleanor answered her phone with her usual chirpy voice, "Panther residence."

Griff was thankful she was home. It wouldn't be right to leave a recorded message telling her that the brother she had not seen in decades was found. "Miss Eleanor," why did Griff call her that? "It's Griffin Topping. How are you this evening?"

"I'm resting up from a busy day, Griffin. But it was a good one. Teaching kids to ride mustangs was nothing compared to the sharing we had around the campfire afterwards."

Griff didn't know what to say to that, so he remained silent.

Eleanor shifted gears, somewhat. "I have been thinking of you, Griffin, and my brother Artie."

"Your brother is why I am calling."

Eleanor drew a breath in sharply. "Is he all right?"

Griff told her that Skeeter had asked Dawn Ahern if he could live with his sister at the Solid Rock Farm. "He wants to sell his boat to the man who is now leasing it, and rent out his house to see if things work with you. Did Ms. Ahern call you?"

"Yes. Can you believe she is flying all the way from Panama City to see me?"

Yes, yes, Griff felt like saying, she is all that and more. "You and she share something—you both work hard."

Eleanor laughed. "Dawn will arrive in time to see the farm, and go to church with me. More than that, she wants my brother to have a meaningful life, and not just exist on the tribal dividend. I told Artie if he helps me with the turtles and lemons, if he works forty hours a week for three months without missing, I will buy him his own quad. He seemed really pleased. Oh, and Dawn said nice things about you."

She did? Griff wanted to know more, but "I see," was all he said.

"Dawn believes you are the reason Artie is willing to turn his life around—you give him the motivation."

Griff did not know if that meant because he insisted Skeeter cooperate with the DEA, or because Skeeter simply had been scared straight. "Miss Eleanor, you know your brother has to want to succeed. I believe he has an inner desire, and with you guiding him he has a chance."

"I pray that is so."

Griff cleared his throat. "You asked me to look for your brother, Dwight. I—"

She interrupted, "Last night I dreamed of him. We were back in Auntie Clara's chickee eating fry bread. In this dream, I saw him as a grown man. He told me he never ate fry bread before. I kept bringing it to him, and he kept eating it. Then I woke up. Is he alive?"

"Your dream is about to come true. I am at his house in Virginia. He is in another room, talking with his wife, but he knows I am calling you." He heard a sharp intake of breath. He thought he heard her whisper, something that sounded like, "Another miracle."

"Is his name still Dwight?"

"Miss Eleanor, your brother is Dwight Pendergast, the federal judge who has been nominated to become the next justice of the United States Supreme Court."

Silence, then weeping. If only she were not alone. Then, Griff realized, she wasn't. The God of her faith was right there beside her. Griff gave her time to collect herself.

"Does he want to know me?"

Griff assured her that he did. "He's lived all these years with the belief that you died in the car accident. He's pretty emotional, and he wants to fly there tomorrow. Dwight can tell you all that. I'm going to put him on the telephone, but I thought I'd pave the way to lessen the shock."

She sniffled, blew her nose. "How can I thank you?"

"You already have. One more thing. His confirmation hearing is next week, so I have not mentioned to Skeeter or Dwight that they are brothers. Can you keep it to yourself a little longer?"

"I understand—and I will try."

"Are you ready to talk to your brother now?"

"Yes, please."

Griff set the receiver down and found Dwight in the living room with Christine. The judge stood, "Did you reach Eleanor?"

Christine took his hand, her face beamed. "Griff, how can we show you how grateful we are?"

Dwight pumped his hand. "You deserve more than our thanks."

Griff pointed down the hall to the study. "She is waiting to talk with you."

Christine hugged her husband. "You go. I will say a goodnight to Griff."

First, Dwight motioned him to the study door. "You told her nothing about my kidney?"

"Right. I think Eleanor is awestruck that her brother is about to be confirmed to the Supreme Court."

Dwight gave a little salute. "I'll be in touch, Topping." He softly closed the door.

Christine hovered in the living room. He reached down to pick up his file from the coffee table, and she clasped his hand again. "You may have just prolonged my husband's life, which I thank God for."

Griff removed a blank piece of paper and wrote down Eleanor's information in case Dwight forgot to get her number. "Even I can see God's involvement."

In his study, Dwight gingerly picked up the receiver. His heart raced, his mouth was dry. What should he say to his sister, a grown woman of whom he had no memory? He had seen her picture. That was a place to start. "Eleanor, this is Dwight, your—" his voice collapsed. So did his mind. He managed a whisper, "Your baby brother."

He heard a sob, then a soft voice, like a lullaby, "Dwight, is it really you? I tried to find you, but couldn't. You were adopted and the records were sealed." She was really crying now.

So was he. Dwight tried to find the words to tell his sister how he felt. "I was told you died, Eleanor. How could they make such a mistake?" Dwight pulled a hankie from his back pocket, blew his nose.

Eleanor's voice shook. "I was banged up and the doctors thought I would not make it, so, after trying to take care of me and look after you and our brother, Auntie brought you both to the agency. Stayed at the hospital with me. There was no one else."

Dwight wished he could reach across the phone wires, hold her. "Eleanor, we want to see you, as soon as possible. My wife and I have two daughters, our oldest is married, expecting twins."

At this Eleanor stopped crying. "How wonderful, I'll be a great auntie. The Lord be praised."

"Agent Topping showed me your photo, and we look very much alike. He told me about your farm, your faith. Can you get away for a week or so? We would love it if you could stay with us." Dwight cleared his throat. "With my current obligations, I am unable to fly down to see you just now."

"A Supreme Court Justice will not have time for me."

Dwight assured her that he wanted her to come and asked if he could buy her plane ticket.

She was quiet, then thanked him. "I cannot let you do that."

He understood. They exchanged phone numbers and addresses. Then, a knock at the door. Still holding the receiver, Dwight walked over and opened it. Christine set a glass of tomato juice and plate of crackers and cheese on the table.

"My wife is here now. May I tell her you will come to visit?"

Christine gestured for the phone. He drank the juice while she talked. "Hello Eleanor. This is Christine. You are welcome to stay as long as you would like. After all, we have a lot to catch up on." Christine nodded. "Yes, I look forward to meeting you, too." She put her hand over the phone and whispered, "She'll call tomorrow with her flight."

Alone again, Dwight spoke to his sister for a while. Just talking with her over the telephone helped to fill in the blanks of years apart. Dwight couldn't wait to meet Eleanor, tell her how much he wanted to make up for the lost time. "Eleanor, Christine will pick you up at Reagan National. I would like to, but with all the media attention, if you were seen with me at the airport, we would be on national television in minutes. I'd like to get to know you before the world does."

FORTY THREE

D wight's heart beat strong and steady, even though more than a dozen television cameras beamed his confirmation hearing and every wrinkle of his face around the world. A trickle of sweat beaded by his lip. He felt it move and was tempted to wipe the moisture away. Within moments, to millions of TV viewers, it could seem like a pool of water, making him look guilty of some wrongdoing.

Memories of Nolan Cuttering withdrawing his nomination replayed in his mind like a bad movie and his hand stayed frozen by his side. Several Senators on the minority side had already hinted that because he fished, he hated animals, therefore he must have trampled the rights of the less fortunate somewhere in his judicial life. While no Senator yet accused him outright of bias or bigotry, there was one Senator left in this round. Then, if they wanted, they could each question him for five minutes.

Bang! bang! At the familiar sound, Dwight turned from a Senator at the far end of the majority to see Chairman Briggs bring the gavel down. A ten-minute break was timely. Dwight nodded to his folks, then hurried away. Christine caught his hand as they sought refuge from a crescendo of voices and lights in the hearing room.

The newest Senate building, the Hart's interior was wide open, all the offices were along the sides. On the way to Briggs's office, they passed a group of Native American activists leaning against the wall. Dwight pulled her into the conference room next to Briggs's private office, where he wiped his brow with his handkerchief. "They're going to testify against my nomination."

She leaned on the table. "All because of Owen Jones III. I'm glad he's not *my* son."

Dwight heaved a sigh. "No matter what the White House says, some of the tribes believe I dismissed the charges against Jones to protect the President."

Jasper Collins tried reasoning with them, pointing out that Owen Jones stole their money and had no influence over the Secretary. There was no changing their minds. The judge was prejudiced against them and would rule against their issues if approved for the Supreme Court.

Christine fell into Dwight's arms. He held her closely, grateful for how real she felt. A faint aroma of peppermint lingered in her hair from her shower. He kissed the top of her head. "Have any energy bars in your purse?"

Christine pulled out two, gave him one. "Dried cranberry and roasted almonds. That should tide you over for another hour. How are you holding up?"

Dwight ripped off the wrapper. "After sixteen hours of questioning, I'm sagging like the old seat cushion I bring along fishing."

She patted his cheek. "At least they did not ask you about—" she stopped.

"You're right not to mention it in here." He tapped his ears. "You know what our mothers say about walls."

She looked puzzled. Dwight explained, "You know, walls have ears," then took a large bite.

"Thankfully, no Senator has alleged that Daddy is a Nazi-lover." Tears sprang again, and she balled her fists, dabbed them to her eyes. "He fought in the Austrian army, but he wasn't a Nazi. He detested Hitler."

Dwight reassured her. "Don't let them get to you. The Austrian government issued a statement that your father was an honorable man who served his country well as Ambassador."

With a small compact, Christine applied fresh lipstick. "I'm sure that's why no Senators attacked you with it. Lars Zorn is next, right?"

Dwight touched her shoulder. "Are there crumbs in my teeth?"

"You look fine. I hope they don't spring any surprises about me. Can we say a prayer?"

Dwight was unsure of the words, but he asked Almighty God to help them through what stretched before them. "Give us courage. Amen."

Christine squeezed his hand. "Okay, I feel stronger now. Go get 'em Judge."

Senator Lars Zorn believed extra preparation made up for junior status, and his last seat at the semicircular dais. He knew the camera would show the empty seats of the more senior Senators who had vacated them, ostensibly to get on with other Senate business, but he was here and armed to the teeth.

Armed to the teeth. He spoke a similar line in a movie once, and he liked how it sounded. Here came the nominee. Lars watched Pendergast stride into the hearing room. His demeanor smacked of arrogance. Well, that smug look would soon end, if Lars had his way. Next came his wife. Now, she was an attractive woman. Lars left his seat, walked to the witness table.

With national television coverage, he'd not miss an opportunity to be seen smiling with the judge, even if he did not vote for him in the committee. He shook Dwight's hand, thanked him for his patience, while searching for weakness. He didn't find any. Lars stepped to the row reserved for family and told Christine how happy he was to meet her, the whole time smiling and hoping he looked presidential to the viewers.

Back in his seat, Lars looked at the questions Arnie prepared. According to the time clock, the hearing would begin in one minute. He leaned back to Arnie. "You are *sure* your information is correct?"

"Positive."

"There is no chance I will end with egg on my face before millions of voters who are glued to their televisions?"

Arnie leaned so close to the Senator, he whispered in his ear. "I have a source in the White House who showed me part of the judge's file."

Lars snapped, "Say no more. I don't want to know." He glanced back at the witness table, where Dwight sat alone, a glass of water by his folded hands. The man looked serene. From his film experience, Lars knew the judge's chiseled face and tan skin carried well on camera. And his wife, whom Lars knew was Austrian, was a beauty.

Americans liked to watch good-looking, nice people. So far, Judge Pendergast conducted himself superbly. He answered tough legal questions by referring to the Constitution and case law. He had defended his state appellate court opinions with flair. Lars had a law degree, but never became a licensed lawyer. No way could he trick the judge into making a mistake on the law. Pendergast was too smart for that.

During the hearings, Lars watched and waited. Now, was the time to spring a trap, when the nominee was tired. The clock read thirty seconds. Lars noticed a woman take a seat next to Mrs. Pendergast. In her yellow woven blouse, red skirt, and silver belt, the woman looked like she had stepped out of a native American tourism brochure. On her head, she wore a colorful round hat. The smile she gave Christine told Lars the women knew each other.

Lars turned to Arnie, but he didn't point. "Who is she? The Indians are testifying tomorrow for our panel, against the nominee. Why is she sitting with his wife?"

Arnie took a verbal jab. "Maybe they went to the actor's guild and rented her for the day. Makes it look like he has support from Native Americans. But, we're ready for them."

With his gavel, the Chairman banged quiet any reply by Lars. "Senator Zorn, your turn to question. Set the clock for fifteen minutes."

Lars smiled at Dwight and, for the benefit of the television audience, he promised to question just long enough to clear up a few things. "For instance, you bought your chalet at Smith Mountain Lake from Max Jenkins, a defense contractor who worked with your father. You paid a low price. Later, you wrote an opinion dismissing a case against that contractor for breach of contract. Can you explain that?"

Dwight's father sat behind the judge, but Lars saw that Dwight did not turn to look at him nor did he flinch. The cameras would help Lars. No doubt as he waited, one of the photographers was zooming in, to show anger or other raw emotion.

"Senator Zorn, the value of lake property has skyrocketed. When I bought our cottage, it was a fair price. I have, for the record, a letter from the Commissioner of Revenue, who has worked in Bedford County for twenty years. He writes that I paid the full asking price, which was consistent with values at the time. As for my ruling, my entire panel agreed with the trial court, which granted a summary judgment for Jenkins and Richter Space Industries. Contrary to your suggestion, there was no connection."

Dwight nodded to the Senator, a polite smile on his face, as if demanding the next question. Zorn shook his head. "That answer won't satisfy Americans that you are honest."

Lars saw his group of Native American supporters fidgeting, as if they were waiting for him to take their side. This question should nail him. "Native tribes were victimized by Owen Jones III, when they legitimately hired him to help them get a federal designation. Can you explain, when justice was in your hands, why you would dismiss the case and victimize them all over again?"

Lars leaned back, ready to watch Dwight's star fall with his answer. The witness sipped water, but spoke clearly. "When the government's key witness went missing, the defense filed a motion to dismiss. I gave the government time to produce their witness, which they did not. Because the government failed to show a conspiracy to commit bribery, justice was served."

"Some say your true motive was to help the President. Can you defend that charge?"

Dwight moved close to the microphone. "For bribery, there has to be evidence that Jones could obtain a favorable ruling from his father in exchange for some benefit. There was no evidence that there had been any attempt by the tribe, or Owen Jones III, to bribe the Secretary. I simply followed the rule of law—"

Lars really couldn't care less what Pendergast said. His main concern was how he came across on television. The word "brilliant" leapt to mind. Lars had to corner him. He interrupted. "Isn't that because you cut the government's case out from under the prosecutor?"

Judge Pendergast was not rattled. "The law says an undercover agent, working for the government, cannot be part of a conspiracy. The other co-conspirator was promised immunity and told that he would not have to testify. I did not make up these rules, nor give the original informant that promise. I followed the law."

Dwight finished by smiling at Zorn. "Owen Jones III may have defrauded the tribe, but he wasn't charged with that. Mr. Jones has yet to be tried for kidnapping the agent."

Lars realized he lacked the legal expertise to match wits with the judge. Time was ticking, and he had not landed even a glancing blow. He checked the sheet in front of him. That left the one area which only he and Arnie knew about. "Judge, you are young for the Court. If confirmed, you could serve many years, provided you are in good health. The information the White House gave us claims you are in good health. Is that true?"

"I feel that I am."

"Is it true that the only way you can continue performing your current duties as a District Court judge is by receiving kidney dialysis several times a week?"

Dwight looked floored by the question, and Lars felt a measure of success. Hooray for me, he wanted to shout, but instead smiled for the gaggle of photographers seated on the floor in front of the dais, clicking photo after photo of him, then the nominee, some moving in for better shots.

Dwight wiggled in his seat, leaned into the microphone. "Senator, while fishing I fell into the lake and cut myself on the dock. In brief, I ingested contaminated water and the bacteria in that water damaged my kidneys, which led to renal failure. I am on dialysis. Recently, a potential donor and I were tested for compatibility. Soon, I will receive a kidney transplant."

With a building sense of satisfaction, Lars grabbed his microphone with both hands, and went for the jugular. "Judge, did you withhold this major health problem from the President or did he withhold it from the Senate?"

Before the witness could answer, Lars saw a blur of color. The woman next to Christine moved to sit in an empty seat next to the judge. She leaned over, whispered in the nominee's ear. Pendergast covered the microphone with his hand, and looked at Senator Briggs. "Excuse me, Mr. Chairman." The whispering continued, as Dwight shook his head.

Lars interrupted as the hearing room exploded with whispers. "Mr. Chairman, will you please add more time for me. The witness is being distracted and not answering my question."

Briggs pounded his gavel. "Quiet. Judge Pendergast, would you like a brief recess?"

Dwight composed himself. "Mr. Chairman, I'm sorry for the interruption. As the Senate knows, I was adopted by my parents. For years, we believed my sister had died. Thankfully, that wasn't the case. The lady sitting next to me is my sister, whom I have just met. I'm learning she is a strong lady, and now she wants to address the Committee. This is one time when my judicial authority is meaningless. Mr. Chairman would you mind hearing from my sister, Eleanor Panther?"

Over Zorn's objection, the Chairman simply waded into uncharted waters with a goofy grin on his usually stern face. "Ms. Panther, we welcome you here today. I grant you five minutes from my time."

Lars watched in disbelief as Eleanor removed her decorative hat and placed it on the table in front of her so-called brother. He could not believe the circus Briggs was letting this hearing become, just when he had Pendergast on the ropes. Cameramen crawled across the floor to get her photo for the front page. Lars had to admit, she had a regal bearing.

"Mr. Chairman and Senators, this past week, I have had a renewed interest in this hearing." The Panther woman moved closer to the judge, put her arm around his shoulder. The clicking cameras sounded like thunder.

"This is my baby brother. I want you to know something important about him. Senator Zorn suggested that Native Americans cannot trust my brother, but they should know that our mother was a full-blooded Seminole Indian. When we were small, our Aunt Clara enrolled us both as members of the Seminole tribe."

"This red-plaid Seminole hat," she caressed the fabric, "belonged to my mother's father. These protesters have nothing to be concerned about. Because, he is one of us."

Eleanor began to weep. The judge's wife leaned forward, handed her a tissue. Amazed by such superb orchestration, Lars knew that no professional screenwriter could not have written a more powerful script. Eleanor must be an actress, and she deserved an Oscar. He began to realize that, this time, he was beaten.

She wiped her eyes, the cameras snapping away. "Senators, please do not be concerned about his health. He and I have completed all the tests. I am a perfect match to donate one of my kidneys, and it is my honor to do so just as soon as possible."

When she reached over and patted her brother's hand, Lars wanted to clap. Bravo.

Eleanor, or whoever she was, continued. "Soon, Dwight will have a new kidney and it will be mine. He will be the first Native American confirmed to The United States Supreme Court. I think you should all be as proud as I am. Thank you for giving me a chance to share."

As quickly as she had interrupted the hearing, Eleanor was done. The Chairman seized control of the microphone, but the room was alive with sound. Briggs brought down the gavel. "Ms. Panther, thank you for providing us with this vital information. Reset the clock and give Senator Zorn another five minutes."

Upstaged, Lars looked at the sheet in front of him. Ah, one more thing to ask. "Judge, after you dismissed the case against Owen Jones III, the Secretary of Interior's son, a Russian named Lev Federov was arrested for allegedly kidnapping and holding hostage the FBI agent, which permitted you to dismiss the case. Are you behind the move to now dismiss all charges against Federov?"

That question got the cameras clicking on Pendergast's stoic face. Lars saw the judge's eyes flicker—he had him now. He even took a sip of water. What would he say?

"Another federal judge is assigned to that case. I have no influence over it."

Zorn pressed on. Let the nation think the President was behind it even if he had no proof. "Still, another judge appointed by our President could dismiss the case before it goes to trial."

The witness looked confident. "Senator, I realize you are not an attorney. A defendant can be released from charges if the U.S. Attorney's office requests a dismissal, no matter the judge."

Outmaneuvered, Lars yielded back his time, but not before firing a final shot. "Yes, and Americans know that every U.S. Attorney is put in office by the President. Mr. Chairman, I am through with Judge Pendergast."

Even to Senator Zorn, that sounded weak. He had failed to demolish the judge, as Arnie had promised. One thing remained for Lars to do. To walk away from this now would be like retreating under fire. His mind seething, he wrote on a pad. *Arnie, a good warrior knows when to fall on his sword. Clean out your desk.* He signed his fluid "LZ," and passed the note to Arnie, who sat behind him.

As Dwight was making his way out of the Senate hearing room, smiling for the cameras, his wife and sister flanking him, Griff was in his office, about to finish one matter that was set in motion before he left Florida: He and Sal were going to get Tyler Cooper, put him in handcuffs. No doubt Bernie Spitzer would go wild, but Bernie was on his own. He wasn't even sharp enough to surrender his client before now and keep him from spending the weekend in jail. In Griff's mind, Cooper spending any time behind bars was a positive result to Bernie's incompetence.

Once he nabbed Cooper, Griff had other plans. Dawn and Brian were flying in, and he'd pick them up at the airport, drop them at their hotel. Tomorrow, they would all drive to the Virginia Military Institute.

Griff went to Sal's cubicle to light a fire under him and Frank Williams, who was back in town from Phoenix. Yesterday, Frank testified against Owen Jones III at a pretrial hearing. Griff had, too, and the result was that Jones would not only stay in jail until his trial, but he would have a new court-appointed attorney. Constance Ingles refused to represent him, but Griff did not know why she was off the case. He had other things to worry about, like getting Cooper before he fled the state.

Five minutes later, Griff was in his bucar, with the dynamic duo of Sal and Frank right behind. They would follow Tyler Cooper from his financial office, and arrest him as soon as he pulled in his driveway. Griff watched Cooper lock the building door. His eyeglasses turned dark as he walked to a blue Ford T-Bird, carrying a heavy-looking briefcase.

Griff was the first out of the lot. He and Sal talked to each other on radios as they tailed Cooper to his home in Columbia City. There was a scary moment when Griff lost sight of Cooper on I-495, but Sal picked up the trail and stayed on him all the way to the subdivision.

Before Cooper even put his car in park in the driveway, Griff and Sal angled their bucars across the entrance. Griff hopped out and ordered Cooper, "Keep your hands on the wheel, Bud. You're under arrest."

Griff quickly read Cooper his Miranda rights, then Sal swung open the other door and searched everything within Cooper's reach. Sal gathered up the man's briefcase and handheld computer, which was also his cell phone. The warrantless, but lawful, search completed, Griff ordered Cooper out of the car and cuffed his hands behind his back, for his neighbors to see. A few came outdoors and stared from their driveways. Frank Williams put Cooper in Sal's backseat and kept an eye on him.

As he and Sal secured Cooper's cell phone and briefcase, Griff had to laugh. "Hey Sal, Cooper was kind enough to be carrying his PDA and a briefcase full of records. I am glad we didn't let him turn himself in. We would never have gotten this evidence without a warrant."

Sal grinned. "Yeah, his car is a real treasure trove."

Sierra Cooper had come out of the house and she looked terrified. She gave Griff the keys to the red Suzuki 4x4, the vehicle her husband had driven from Florida. While Sal seized it from the garage, for being involved in a drug conspiracy, Sierra pushed a cordless phone in Griff's face. "Our attorney wants to talk to you."

Griff took the phone from Sierra, who was crying now. "Agent Topping."

"This is Bernie Spitzer. You know I represent Mr. Cooper. As a friend, you might have had the courtesy to tell me there was a warrant so that I could bring him to your office."

This time, Griff tried not to offend Bernie. "I'm sorry. When you called me in Florida, you said you were no longer representing him, and I assumed he would get a court-appointed attorney, claiming he was indigent. He'll be detained at the Alexandria City jail for the weekend."

Bernie sputtered, "How much bail? I'll have his wife go down and pay it."

Griff shook his head. For a senior partner in a top Washington firm, Bernie was awfully green. He couldn't believe he had to walk Bernie through it. "Tyler can't be bailed out until he appears before a federal magistrate. There will be one in court Monday morning. Your client left Virginia while on bond, and now he's charged with a new crime. Don't expect him to be released again."

"Maybe if I call Dwight Pendergast, I could get a bond hearing today."

Griff held the phone away from his ear. "Bernie, Judge Pendergast already went out on a limb for you with this loser once. Do you want to burn your friend again? I'd let this go."

He hung up on Bernie, still shaking his head. He had to get going. Before Sal and Frank drove Tyler Cooper to jail, Sal pulled Griff aside. "I didn't get a chance to tell you what happened with Lev's father. Mr. Federov met me at a hotel near Dulles Airport while you were down in Florida. Remember?"

Griff stood by his car, one foot in, one foot on the driveway. "He came all the way from Russia to see you?"

Sal grinned. "Yeah, I'm so important. We thought Lev's story was strange. It gets more weird. Turns out his father was a double agent, telling the Russians everything the FBI was asking him. Dmitri Federov was their spy, not ours."

Griff was incredulous. "Why tell you all that? It doesn't make sense." He smoothed his moustache, which always helped him think. "Unless—"

Sal interjected. "He wants to help his son. You got it. Federov is upset by Lev's arrest. Says if his son is not released, he's going public with what he learned about the Kennedy assassination when he was in the Soviet intelligence service." Sal lowered his voice. "He hinted it won't be well received."

Griff wasn't too worried. "It's bogus. No chance that story will go anywhere."

While Sal leaned on Griff's bucar, he waved at Cooper in the back seat of the other car. "Topping, it already has. Yesterday, I was told to take my file, all my notes, and head down to see Director Kirkwood. I did, and guess what?"

"You're being transferred to the work with the Russians?"

Griff's friend looked stricken for a moment, like that was a grue-some thought. Then, Sal shook his head. "Nah. I waited an eternity in the reception area. Kirkwood stalked out of his office. A bunch of suits were sitting there with visitor badges. Course, they didn't talk to me. The Director took my file, they all went in. Left me sitting there, staring at my wingtips. Fifty minutes go by. Some agent I don't know comes out, tells me to leave. Bottom line, the Director kept my file and my notes."

Griff tapped his one foot, then the other on the doorframe. He didn't want dirt on his shoes when he picked up Dawn. "Now what?"

Sal talked on. "When I got downstairs, I pretended to sign out, so I could see who signed in. It was three guys from the Institute for Intel-lectual Pursuit."

Griff stuffed his hands in his pockets. "Most agents know that's a CIA cover."

Sal stared at Griff. "Which is where Kirkwood came from. CIA."

"What will you do?"

"I have no file, no notes, no nothing. Topping, my meeting with Dmitri Federov never happened."

Griff could only shake his head. "Sal, I wish I had been at the meet-ing with you and Federov. Then, you'd have a witness."

Sal kicked a tire. "Topping, no you don't. I have a feeling this thing is not over."

FORTY FOUR

This Saturday had not come soon enough for Dwight. He held Christine's hand in his larger one, but not for a stroll in the park. They joined hands in the very place their lives began to change, and grow into something more beautiful. In the Episcopal Church where they helped the homeless, Reverend Jonathan Pearce read verses from a Bible, which Christine had selected for this ceremony to renew their wedding vows.

Above their heads, rays of sun beamed red and gold through a stained glass rendering of Jesus holding a lamb. Dwight saw pure delight on Christine's features as the words flowed around them. "Love always trusts, always hopes, always perseveres. Love never fails."

Reverend Pearce's voice carried to the guests in the pews. Veronica and Stuart sat next to Mandy, who was beside Eleanor. Mandy's boyfriend, Chad, elected to go to a baseball game instead of joining her. Louis and Naomi were in the second row, as were Wendell and Hazel Cochran. Other friends and colleagues filled two of the other rows. Bernie and Rita were missing.

After Rita admitted she wrote the letters, Bernie took her to Hawaii, but not before he had apologized to Dwight. Rita had grown jealous that Bernie once loved Christine. No matter that it was a brief college romance that happened more than thirty years before. Apparently, her envy of Christine raged out of control. Dwight told Bernie they needed more than a vacation, more like some marital counseling.

But today, not even thoughts of his friend's troubles could wreck Dwight's happiness. He lightly squeezed Christine's hands. How great it was to hear the Reverend introduce them to the congregation as Mr. and Mrs. Pendergast. He and Christine had faced the pain of the past together. Now they found hope in the name above all names and were making a new beginning in his strength. A round of applause. He didn't hear the words telling him to, but Dwight kissed his bride.

Christine plucked three roses from her bouquet, handed a stem to each of her daughters, then one to Eleanor. To the strains of Bach on the organ, the same piece they each heard many weeks before, Dwight walked Christine up the aisle, which they never got to do when they were married by a justice of the peace. His heart was filled with such tenderness for her.

At the back of the church, Dwight hugged her, whispered in her ear, "You were a beautiful bride when we first married and you're more beautiful today."

Her smile was radiant. "Thank you, Dwight, for agreeing to this before your surgery next week. Most men would be reluctant. I am so proud of you, Justice Pendergast."

Dwight held her hands in his. Next week, he would receive one of Eleanor's kidneys. "Christy, don't be afraid. Eleanor and I will be fine. I sense God's purpose, even if we cannot know what it is until it unfolds."

Guests streamed up the aisle. The first, Mandy, fell into her mother's arms. Christine held her until she pulled back. "Mom, Dad, when you tried to tell me your lives had new meaning, I did not care to hear it. But, after seeing you standing up there, pledging to love and honor each other all over again, to follow Jesus together, I can see I'm not ready to marry Chad, and I'm calling off our wedding."

She dashed down the steps. Christine was about to follow, when Dwight stopped her. "Our daughter is growing up. Give her a few minutes, and we'll go down together."

Under a white tent on Louis and Naomi's sprawling acreage near Mount Vernon, Christine sipped a glass of sparkling cider. Veronica was sharing possible baby names. Christine touched her hand. "Honey, whatever you and Stuart decide is all right with us. We are both proud of you."

Her daughter looked so grown up, with her hair pulled behind her head. "Ronnie—" Christine used the pet name she had called her when she was a child, "I hope you know how much I love you."

Veronica's black eyes looked troubled. "I am beginning to feel you do, Mom. Somehow, I always thought you approved of Mandy more than—" Her voice broke.

Christine reached over, hugged Veronica tightly, then released her. "I am sorry we have not had a better relationship. It is *my* fault. You never did anything to cause it, Veronica. You've always been a wonderful daughter. Can you forgive me?"

Veronica embraced her mother. They both shed tears, tears of healing. Christine had so much to make up for. Veronica dabbed her cheeks. "I'd like to think today is a fresh beginning for us, too."

Christine wanted that, too, and told Veronica so. Her daughter's smile lasted only an instant. "Mom, this is terrible timing, but Stuart's over by Daddy, glaring at me. I'm supposed to rest on the weekends. Doctor's orders."

Christine patted her hand. "I'll walk you over."

Both women rose, and Christine linked Veronica's arms in hers. "Sometime, I'd like the two of us to have lunch, and I'll tell you about my new plan for what I am calling the Austria House. Even your Dad doesn't know about this yet, but I dream of turning our lake home into a retreat for people who need to find peace in their lives. Just like I did."

Veronica stopped. "How fabulous. I want to hear everything."

Christine guided Veronica to her husband, placed her hand in his. "Stuart, I want you to take my daughter home and put her to bed. We've got to take good care of her and those grandbabies."

They all laughed, and Christine waved as Veronica walked away, then turned to smile at her mother. Before Christine could find Dwight, she felt a tap on her arm. It was his sister, Eleanor, who wore a perplexed look. "Christine, I hope you don't mind but I heard you mention you found peace, and I need your help finding that myself. I wonder, would you talk with me about it?"

"Of course." Christine looked around and spotted lawn chairs on the patio, far from the guests. "Let's sit over there."

They did, and it took Eleanor sometime to begin. "You have a great love for children, I see. Well, I know of a sad little boy who had none of the advantages of Dwight. He lived in foster care, was never adopted, and ended up in the criminal justice system."

Christine's kind heart went out to the man whose story she had just heard. "That's terrible. What can I do to help?"

Eleanor played with her beads. "After I tell you his story, I would like you to tell me how he can meet the brother he has never known. I feel strongly this must be done before the brother has his surgery."

In another part of Virginia, the afternoon was perfect for a different

celebration. On the way to Eva's task force reunion, Dawn was telling
Griff what a great time she and Brian had had at the White House,
when her son tapped her shoulder. "Mom, tell Griff what we decided."

Dawn's smile was wistful and happy at the same time. "My son's
heart is set on VMI."

Brian added, "If they'll have me."

Griff turned the corner to Eva's street. "You have what they want."
The news came on and Griff heard Pendergast's name. "Wait, let's listen." He turned up the radio so that Brian could hear the commentator
from NPR talking about Dwight's nomination to the Supreme Court:
"Last night, the U.S. Senate made history when they voted unanimously
to put the first Native American justice on the Supreme Court."

Griff let out a whoop, then shut off the radio. Dawn laughed. "I've
learned your secret."

She looked especially nice, with her black hair woven into a giant
braid draped over her shoulder. Colorful beads around her neck con-
trasted with her blue Hawaiian-print sundress. Griff parked his truck
in front of a low ranch house. He turned to see both Dawn and her
fourteen-year-old son.

"Which secret is that?"

Dawn picked up her purse. "I know who you were trying to get a
kidney for and why you met Eleanor. Well done, Agent Topping. I am
impressed."

She was? Dawn opened her door. She slid out and moved the seat
back for Brian to jump down. Griff hurried to her side. "It's terrific that
Dwight will get his new kidney as a Justice on the Supreme Court."

Sounds of laughter in the backyard drew Brian ahead of them. Dawn
tapped Griff's arm. "So, that makes Skeeter his brother."

Dwight lifted a finger to his lips. "Skeeter doesn't know, yet. As I
heard you say once, that is a conversation for another time. Come, meet
Eva and Scott. I think they're going to like you."

For the next hour, Griff relived memories of cases past with the
federal agents and police officers who made them, and prosecuting attorneys who tried them. Dawn meandered in and out of the kitchen,
at ease with his friends and colleagues. She was never far from Griff's
sight.

Proudly wearing an Air Force cap given to him by Scott, Brian en-
tertained Eva's kids, Kaley and Andy, by throwing footballs and frisbees.
Griff listened to Eva's white-haired grandfather, Marty VanderGoes, as

he told real-life stories of living in the Netherlands as a young man, and hiding Jewish people from the Nazis. Marty was handing out Dutch peppermints, when Griff saw Dawn walking around the yard holding Eva's youngest, one-year-old Martin. She looked even prettier with a child in her arms.

Behind him a soft voice: "Griff, we need to talk." He knew, without turning, it was Eva. She pulled him by the elbow away from the others. "You've been holding out on me. Dawn says you and she have known each other awhile. That she went flying with you."

Eva's blue eyes danced. "Did you bring her here for my approval?"

Griff felt his shaggy brows rise. "I, uh, she and I—"

"Oh, never mind. You have it. She is perfect for you."

Glad to hear Eva say so, still he didn't know how to respond. Respect for her judgment, helped him find the words. "I haven't enjoyed being with any other woman as much since we both lost Jillie."

He wished he hadn't brought up Eva's twin sister's death. He hoped Eva would understand and not be hurt. She did. "It's okay, Griff. I approve." Her eyes traveled to Scott, who at that moment was putting fire to the coals. "Guess who just called?"

Griff followed her gaze. "A new terror attack and Scott's going to the Pentagon."

Eva laughed. "And I thought I had work on *my* mind. No, Trenton Nash is coming with his fiancée, Hannah Strobel. He graduated from George Mason and right now is being interviewed for the job of youth pastor at a Bible Church in Springfield."

Memories flooded into Griff's mind, memories of trying to mentor the headstrong deputy sheriff while they worked together in the task force. "Youth Pastor, huh? Well, I look forward to seeing him. That would be quite a transformation."

Dawn started their way. Eva waved to little Martin, who was squirming with delight at the sight of his mother. "Griff, having you here with Dawn and knowing Trenton is coming with Hannah makes this reunion worthwhile, even if the whole crew couldn't make it."

Griff flashed Dawn a smile as she passed the baby to his mother. Eva nuzzled Martin's neck. "Time for this little guy's nap."

Martin squealed, which made Griff and Dawn laugh. Eva left them together, near the waterfall and lily pond. Griff steered her to a wooden bench. "How do you like it here? Virginia is a lot different from Florida. You're some ways from home."

Her dark eyes flickered to her son, who tossed a ball to Andy. "We've enjoyed our trip here so much. Brian especially liked Andrews Air Force base. How did you pull that off?"

Griff nodded to Scott, who stood by the grill, barbecue tongs in hand. "Eva's husband is great."

Scott called over to them. "Beef or turkey burgers?"

Griff yelled back, "Beef for me. Two if you have enough."

Scott replied, "And for Dawn?"

She shot back, "Neither, I'm a vegetarian."

Griff swallowed. Where did that come from? He thought a vegetarian was akin to being a communist. Or, he had until this moment. Of the recent changes in his life, Dawn was the best part.

Scott was not perturbed. "Eva marinated portabella mushrooms. What about Brian?"

Dawn laughed. "He'll have the same as Griff."

Well, that was something. Griff stared at her, "You don't eat any meat?"

Dawn's eyes twinkled. "Chicken and fish, and only now and then. It's a health thing. Don't worry about it." She changed the subject. "I thought Brian would miss Panama City and all his friends. But, he tells me he can't wait until we come back for another visit."

Griff took one of her hands in his. When she left it there, and did not pull it back, he simply looked into her eyes and forgot all about her strange eating habits. "Neither can I."

EPILOGUE

Senator Zorn rejected defeat. It was too much like playing a bad part on screen. In his Hollywood years, he had a knack of choosing roles that made him millions of dollars. With Pendergast confirmed, Arnie Berglund was one sacrifice Lars had to make. The reason for Arnie's leaving—that Arnie used a source inside the White House to feed him restricted information—was made public when the President fired Barbara Jo Houston.

Because Lars fired Arnie *before* it all came out, not only did he appear ethical, he distanced himself from the political fallout. The President was on the defensive and, to Lars, that was a good thing. A week after the confirmation, Lars had a new plan in place to boost his political fortunes.

He was about to be briefed by a trusted source on a matter critical to the nation's security. Even before Lars made a name for himself in films, he'd known the CIA's Deputy Director of Intelligence, Wilt Kangas. Lars was an agent at FBI headquarters when he met Kangas, then his counterpart at the Agency. Wilt followed Lars's suggestion and arrived before the Senator's staff appeared for work that morning. Lars did not want it known they were meeting.

He grabbed Wilt's beefy hand. "Let's dispense with the hoopla. This briefing is classified. You are here because I'm on the Senate Intelligence Committee and have clearance. Under no circumstances will I tell my staff. That said, what do you know about Jones, the Secretary of Interior? I was not on the Energy Committee that approved his nomination. I smell a rat. Is he one?"

Wilt Kangas was an imposing figure, even while sitting in a chair. Lars learned early on that Wilt had integrity and would never be a party to shenanigans. With a voice deep like Gregory Peck's, Wilt began his briefing. "I need to start with Owen Jones III and his kidnapping charge. The U.S. Attorney and the Agency have agreed. Lev Federov and his girlfriend will testify against Jones and their cases will be dismissed."

Lars resisted the urge to take notes, which wasn't permitted. He made a tent with his hands. "And?"

As Wilt crossed one leg over the other, he shifted his entire body. "The thrust is this. Years ago when Lev's father, Dmitri Federov, was a Soviet military attaché in DC, he approached the FBI and offered to provide Soviet intelligence. In fact, he was working for the Soviets. We now know his ploy was directed by the KGB, so Federov furnished mostly low-level and easily corroborated intel to the Bureau, all the while he was learning sensitive information for the KGB about the FBI's methods."

Lars struggled to understand. "Jones Junior hires Federov's son, Lev, to kidnap a federal agent. Was Secretary Jones involved? Does this scandal reach to the White House, this President?"

A career spook, not inclined to political persuasions, Wilt raised a large finger. "Lars, I am giving you the facts because you asked. Do not insert politics in my presence. It won't wash."

"All right. Go on."

"Federov was a double agent. That the Soviets permitted him to bring his family to the U.S. convinced me back then he shouldn't be trusted—but never mind that now. The Bureau gave, and Dmitri took, a stipend, all to convince us that he was not a double. Just before the Iron Curtain fell, the Soviets summoned Dmitri home, but Lev refused to go. He liked it here, considered himself an American."

"Can't blame him. In the 1990s, Russia was a rough place."

Wilt shook his prominent head. "Dmitri was livid, said he felt betrayed by his own son. Can you imagine that, after the false life he lived? Refused to help the son financially or in any way. The kid scratched out a living, became a gardener in the better neighborhoods in Virginia."

Lars cut to the heart of his inquiry. "When he was in private practice, Secretary Jones assisted the Russians with oil leases. He must be connected to Federov."

Wilt's lips parted, which was as close to a smile as he ever got. "You always did jump ahead. Stay with me a minute longer. Dmitri Federov cashed in on his American business contacts and is now a senior partner, if you can call it that, in one of Russia's largest oil and gas companies. Before Jones became Interior Secretary, he practiced oil and gas law in the District. His firm was hired to represent Federov's company on trade and speculative lease agreements with the U.S. What I say next, Senator Zorn, is top secret. It goes no further."

Lars nodded fiercely. "Of course, of course." And, just as certainly, he prepared his mind to memorize Wilt's exact words.

"The Agency now knows that when Owen Jones III was arrested the first time, for conspiracy to bribe his father, Secretary Jones called Dmitri Federov."

"Whom he worked with when he was at the law firm."

Wilt nodded. "It was Dmitri who suggested they use an old intelligence technique of leaving money and a cell phone on Lev's seat. We know this because, when Lev was arrested by the FBI, Dmitri himself reached out to old contacts at the FBI to help get his son out of trouble. Mr. Federov is providing us other intel, but that isn't part of our meeting, nor will it be."

Lars studied Wilt. Whatever he knew, he would not tell Lars. The Senator moved on. "So you're saying Secretary Jones was involved in trying to eliminate the FBI agent, Frank Williams, as a witness against his son? Does that mean Jones takes bribes to give Indian Tribes federal designations?"

His lower lip extended, Wilt finally replied, "Jones may not be Secretary much longer."

Zorn could hardly contain his excitement. He leaned forward. "What do you know?"

Wilt Kangas crossed his arms, stared back at Lars. "I have my sources inside the U.S. Attorney's office. You had better act fast, whatever it is you mean to do, because the informant who started the case against the son has produced some pretty interesting bank records that can be traced to the father."

Wilt simply gazed back at Lars, as if he should draw his own conclusions, and despite Lars's prodding, he refused to say more.

Lars held up his hand. "Okay. If I hold hearings about Secretary Jones, his links to these crimes and the Russians, how much can I reveal?"

Wilt shifted. Clearly, he did not relish this briefing. Lars knew he lived in the secret world, and liked it when national secrets stayed there. The DDI was cleaning out the Agency, giving polygraphs to the staff, trying to plug the leaks. Lars found that amusing. So long as information was power, leaks would never stop, not ever. He waited for his friend to tell him what he could tell.

Wilt took his time getting out of the chair. "Don't use anything I told you. Don't quote me. Some of what I said about Secretary Jones's law firm and its connections are available through commercial records, kept in the ordinary course of business. Your staff will find them if they look long enough. I will help in directing your subpoenas to proper targets, but that is all. Now, I have an appointment with my Director."

They shook hands, and Lars showed Wilt Kangas out the side door. He quickly called Ingrid Lundstrom, his new Chief of Staff, hoping she was at her desk early. She was, and hurried right in. Another tall Swede, Ingrid was recommended to him by the senior Senator from Minnesota, where she attended college. A standout basketball player, Ingrid dribbled her team to the national championship, and starred in cereal commercials before she went to law school. Lars liked it that she had served in the White House Counsel's Office under the former President, who was in the same party as Lars.

He wasted no time. "Ingrid, by five o'clock, I want everything, and I mean *everything* you can dig up on Secretary Jones. My source, who will remain unidentified, will help us from there. Americans have a right to know his misdeeds, and I mean to expose them." He paused. Her eager smile encouraged him to boast, "And, I feel certain, today is the beginning of the last days of this President being in the White House."

ABOUT THE AUTHORS

Diane Munson has been an attorney for more than twenty years. She served the U.S. Department of Justice as an Assistant U.S. Attorney in Washington, D.C., where as a Federal Prosecutor she brought indictments, tried criminal cases, and argued appeals. Earlier, she served the Reagan Administration, appointed by Attorney General Edwin Meese, as Deputy Administrator of the Office of Juvenile Justice and Delinquency Prevention. She worked with the Justice Department, the U.S. Congress, and the White House on major policy and legal issues.

More recently she has been in a solo general practice specializing in helping families and representing children and parents in cases of neglect and abuse.

David Munson served as a Special Agent with the Naval Investigative Service, U.S. Customs, and U.S. Drug Enforcement Administration over a 27-year career. During his career he conducted many investigations and often assumed undercover roles. He infiltrated international drug smuggling organizations. In this role he traveled with drug dealers, met their suppliers in foreign countries, helped fly their drugs to the U.S., then feigned surprise when shipments were seized by law enforcement. Later his true identity was revealed when he testified against the group members in court.

While assigned to DEA headquarters in Washington, D.C., David served two years as a Congressional Fellow on the Senate Permanent Subcommittee on Investigations chaired by Sen. Sam Nunn, D-GA.

Prior to writing this novel, Diane and David were trained as Christian mediators and created a mediation firm where they helped many people seek forgiveness and restoration in their relationships by applying Scripture to their lives. They have seen that justice and forgiveness are possible, no matter the circumstances.

As they travel to research and cloister to write, they thank the Lord for the blessings of faith and family. David and Diane Munson are collaborating on their next novel.

www.DianeAndDavidMunson.com